The
Last Kiss
Goodbye

By Tasmina Perry

Daddy's Girls
Gold Diggers
Guilty Pleasures
Original Sin
Kiss Heaven Goodbye
Private Lives
Perfect Strangers
Deep Blue Sea
The Proposal
The Last Kiss Goodbye

The
Last Kiss
Goodbye

TASMINA
PERRY

headline
review

First published in 2015 by HEADLINE REVIEW
An imprint of HEADLINE PUBLISHING GROUP

1

Cataloguing in Publication Data is available from the British Library

ISBN 978 1 4722 0840 8 (Hardback)
ISBN 978 1 4722 0841 5 (Trade paperback)

Typeset in Caslon by Avon DataSet Ltd, Bidford-on-Avon, Warwickshire

Printed and bound in Great Britain by Clays Ltd, St Ives plc

HEADLINE PUBLISHING GROUP
An Hachette UK Company
Carmelite House
50 Victoria Embankment
London EC4Y 0DZ

www.headline.co.uk
www.hachette.co.uk

For my mum

Prologue

Buckinghamshire, early 1961

He was late, of course he was. Dominic Blake was always late, he was famous for it. If there was a party, a card game, even a wedding, you could be sure that Dominic would be the last to arrive, pushing back his hair, grinning sheepishly to charm his way out of trouble. It was all part of the act, but still. Dominic hated letting Vee down, but tonight it couldn't be avoided.

'Dammit,' he muttered as he took the corner too fast and bumped up on to the kerb. 'That'll have to do,' he said, jumping out of the AC Stag and dashing up the stone steps of Batcombe House.

'Evening, Connors,' he said to the elderly man who answered the door. 'They still eating?'

'Lady Victoria is in the dining room, sir,' said the butler. 'Although I believe pudding is just being cleared.'

'Splendid,' said Dominic, straightening his bow tie and pushing through the double doors.

He was greeted by wolf whistles and an ironic round of applause.

'All right, all right,' he said, holding his hands in the air. 'I know, I'm a bloody let-down as usual.'

He crossed the room to the woman sitting just to the left of the head of the table and bent to give her a brief kiss on the cheek. 'Sorry, Vee,' he said. 'I don't know what you must think of me.'

'You know damn well what I think of you, Dominic Blake,' she said, but her words were undercut by the hint of a smile on her red lips. 'It seems you have broken up my civilised dinner party, so I expect you to make it up to me with some scandalous gossip.'

'I'll do my best.'

'Coffee will be served in the drawing room,' she said, getting to her feet and addressing her guests. 'Mr Blake will be dancing the fandango as penance.'

Dominic gave a showy bow to more whistles as the group rose from the table. The cream of high society, he thought as he watched. The men, faces flushed from claret, in suits cut by tailors inherited from their fathers; the women in silk and pearls, their eyes always moving. Money oozed from each of them: the way they walked, their laughs, the feeling that nothing could touch them.

'Let's have it then,' whispered Victoria, moving close.

'Have what?'

'Your excuse, of course. I know you have one. What was it? Pressing meeting at the Admiralty? On the run from Maltese gangsters? A sick grandmother?'

Dominic laughed.

'Not this time, Vee. I overslept, it's that simple.'

'*Overslept*?' she laughed, glancing across at the elaborate gold clock on the mantelpiece. 'Dominic, it's nine forty-five in the evening. What are you, a vampire?'

He leant in to whisper. 'Well, there was a young lady I met in the bar at Claridge's, and she was very insistent that I—'

Victoria put a hand on his shoulder. 'No, no, on second thoughts, I don't want to know. I'll just content myself that you're here now. Besides, I hope it's nothing serious, this young lady at Claridge's. I have invited a couple of extremely lovely women along this evening. Beautiful, connected . . .' she whispered theatrically.

'Any woman is a disappointment after you, Vee, you know that,' he laughed, giving her shoulders an affectionate squeeze.

Vee gave an ironic 'Ha!', but Dominic could see that she was pleased with the compliment. The funny thing was, it wasn't empty flattery: Lady Victoria Harbord was pretty much every-thing he'd ever wanted in a woman. She was beautiful, elegant and fiercely intelligent, yet she was generous and had a taste for the unconventional, which explained both the modern decor of the room and the fact that Dominic Blake – editor-stroke-adventurer – was invited to her soirées.

Perhaps if things were different, he thought, as a short, rotund man in a dinner suit came and snaked his arm around her waist.

'Dominic. You made it,' boomed Tony Harbord in his thick American accent. 'Now what are you gossiping with my wife about this time?'

'She's trying to set me up,' he grinned, winking at Victoria. As she smiled back, he wondered, not for the first time, whether his friend really was in love with the wealthy New Yorker. It would not have been the first time that a woman of impeccable breeding and title had married for money, but although Victoria and the much older Tony seemed like an odd couple superficially, Dominic was often touched, enviously so, to see the real affection between them.

'Good,' laughed Tony, snipping the end off the cigar he was

holding with a gold cutter. 'The sooner you find someone, Blake, the better. You need to settle down, if only to stop you and my wife becoming the subject of gossip yourselves.'

Dominic had to admit it was a pretty good party. Sometimes, even with Lady Victoria's uncanny knack of picking interesting people, society shindigs could be deadly dull, with everyone reverting to type: the men banging on about politics and the likelihood of a good shoot at the weekend, the women sticking to anecdotes about their children, every one of them a budding Rachmaninov, Picasso or Cicero.

Tonight, however, he had talked to a poet who believed plants could converse with each other, and a prominent Tory who hinted at a secret passion for naturism – 'Don't you find all these starched shirts so constricting?' he'd asked.

He had sipped brandy with Jim French, a Texan industrialist friend of Tony's, whom he had known previously only by his ruthless arms-dealing reputation. He had disliked French on sight, but had still recognised that he would make a fascinating profile for *Capital*, the magazine he edited. He had mentioned this fact to Victoria, hoping that she could engineer another meeting between the two of them, before she warned him it was not wise to make enemies of the rich.

The most rewarding conversation had been with a librarian from Oxford, who, with the minimum of prodding, had been glad – relieved, in fact, Dominic thought – to reveal that he had spent the war developing chemical weapons in a stable in Wiltshire.

'Do you know,' said the old man, 'it was the best five years of my life. Yes, people were dying – my own brother was blown up at Arnhem, you know – but one had this great sense of *doing* something, of being part of something bigger than oneself, if that makes any sense. I'll be frank, young man, everything since has been something of a let-down.'

Dominic eventually excused himself to go and get some fresh air. As he looked back towards the party, he smiled, hiding it by raising his brandy glass to his lips. It was funny: he knew something about everyone here. Not all of it scandalous, some of it just revealing. But why did they tell *him*? In theory they should have avoided him like the plague. People knew he was the editor of *Capital*, one of the more playful but still heavy-hitting magazines on the news stand. He was also known as one of the biggest gossips and playboys in town, an image he was happy to cultivate. And yet he had always found that people opened up to him. Maybe it's my honest face, he thought with another smile.

The truth was actually much more straightforward: he got answers simply because he asked. The English were far too polite to enquire into other people's business, and consequently, when someone *did* ask, they were usually so relieved, everything poured out.

Dominic had noticed this at a very young age, when his parents' friends had come to visit at their modest home in the country. The rich loved to talk. Gossip, not money, was what made their world turn. And the one thing the wealthy liked to talk about more than anything else was themselves. No use making a killing on krugerrands or bedding your best friend's wife if you couldn't boast about it, right?

He found himself in the library, a room he knew had a set of French doors that led out on to the fragrant garden. He paused, running his finger over Victoria's fine collection of leather-bound books, then turned as he heard a noise behind him. A beautiful blonde was standing in the door frame, hand on hip, looking every inch a film noir femme fatale.

'Hiding from me again, Dommy?' purred Isabella Hamilton, wife to Gerald Hamilton, the cabinet minister. 'You arrived so late, I thought you were avoiding me.'

She walked slowly, deliberately towards him, her heels clicking on the library's wooden floor.

'I'd never hide from you, Izzy,' he said, his mouth curling seductively. 'But we don't want any awkward situations. Not in front of everyone.'

'You can put me in any awkward position you like, Dominic Blake,' she smiled, drawing a finger up to his cheek and stroking it. 'You know I'll do anything you want. You only have to ask.'

'Izzy, we can't . . .' he said, taking a small step back.

'Why not?' she whispered. 'It's not as if we haven't done it before.'

A montage of delicious images sprang to the forefront of his mind.

'I want you,' she whispered into his ear.

'Izzy, please.' He was finding it increasingly hard to control himself.

'I want you now,' she breathed, brushing her lips softly against his.

He felt a stab of guilt, a shot of regret, and reached for her hand as he shook his head slowly.

'We shouldn't,' he said more forcefully.

'Why not?' she pouted, pulling back.

'Because we shouldn't.'

Isabella took a moment to compose herself, knowing that she was not going to get her own way. Not this time.

'You're sure about that?'

'I'm sure,' he nodded.

'Then I'd better get back,' she said, her beautiful mouth pursing. 'You know how Gerald misses me.'

'I'm not surprised,' he replied with genuine affection.

Her expression softened and she kissed her finger and pressed it against his lips.

'Goodbye, Dominic,' she said, and he closed his eyes, enjoying the warm, suggestive touch, knowing that this was the last time he would feel it.

He watched her leave, her slim silhouette retreating into the light and noise of the party, and then lit a cigarette.

Pushing back a heavy green velvet curtain, he opened the French doors, enjoying the cold air slapping against his face, and blew a long, twisting grey smoke ring.

Here he was, at one of the most fashionable parties of the year, surrounded by society's beau monde, and yet he felt hollow and unsettled.

Maybe Tony was right. Maybe he needed to settle down. He'd had enough of using beautiful young women like Isabella, and all the other interchangeable blondes, brunettes and red-heads. Maybe he needed to change his life, although it was never as easy as that, he thought, frowning as he watched the smoke float up into the dark night air.

'Dominic.'

The voice was not at first familiar. For one anxious minute he thought that Gerald Hamilton had come to pay him a visit, before he registered an accent and recognised it.

'Eugene.' He smiled with relief, stubbing his cigarette out under the sole of his shoe.

He had known the Russian naval attaché, stationed at his country's embassy in Kensington since Christmas, and liked him a lot. At first he had been surprised that Eugene was invited to society parties and dinners such as the one they were at tonight – people were suspicious of the Soviets, and rightly so, with the Cold War raging. But the truth was that someone considered mysterious and forbidden – someone like a handsome Soviet naval attaché – was as welcome in the salons of the upper classes as Dominic was.

'How are you, my friend?' he asked, extending his hand and resting it on the Russian's shoulder.

Eugene simply nodded.

'Can we talk?' he asked.

Dominic was always ready to listen. He took his cigarette case from his pocket, opened it and offered his friend a tobacco-brown Sobranie.

'Of course,' he replied as they stepped out into the garden.

The air was fragrant, the smell of daffodils and damp grass potent and luscious, and the full moon spilt lazy, creamy light around the garden.

They sat down on a stone bench, and as Eugene began to talk, Dominic crossed his legs and blew another smoke ring, preparing to listen, not knowing that the conversation he was about to have was one that would change the entire course of his life.

Chapter One

London, present day

Abby Gordon looked down at the curled sepia map spread out on the oak table in front of her and sighed. I mean, who cares where Samarkand is anyway? she thought rebelliously. She had a sudden urge to scrunch the map up into a ball and toss it into the incinerator. She imagined the fire catching, watching as it glowed and burnt. Shaking her head she looked around the room, wondering if anyone had noticed that she was blushing. No, only nice Mr Bramley, an elderly academic bent over his research on the other side of the glass door.

Mr Bramley certainly cared very deeply for this map. Mr Bramley would probably jump into the incinerator to save it.

Get a grip, Abby, she told herself, imagining poor Mr Bramley on fire.

There had been a time, not so long ago, when she had loved her job as an archivist at the Royal Cartography Institute. Okay, so it wasn't the Tate or the Courtauld Institute. She didn't spend her days cataloguing priceless paintings like some of her friends from her art history degree course were doing. She wasn't working for a hip gallery or a prestigious auction house, or acting as assistant to some famous photographer. But the RCI's archive was spoken of in hushed tones by map nerds and geography enthusiasts around the world. Abby wasn't one of them herself, but she couldn't help delighting at the treasures she found among the clutter. There were the maps, of course, thousands of them, all kept in climate-controlled (which meant chilly if you hadn't worn tights) walk-in cupboards. There were atlases, some common, some very rare and valuable, including one once owned by Marie Antoinette, a heavy leather-bound tome that no one – not even her boss Stephen – was allowed to touch. And there were the artefacts: an old boot, an oxygen tank, a tarnished brass compass, most of which were stuffed randomly into the cardboard boxes next to Abby's desk. On the face of it they were just bits and bobs from long-forgotten expeditions. But every one of them had a story behind it – Captain Scott's compass, Stanley's pith helmet, an ice pick that had gone on the first ascent attempt of Everest.

But most surprisingly, for an organisation dedicated to maps, the bulk of the collection was photographs. Hundreds of thousands of negatives and slides, collected from every expedition since the invention of the camera. The trouble was, most of them had never left their boxes, and that was the reason Abby had been recruited eighteen months earlier: to catalogue them and, hopefully, bring them out into the light. It seemed like a never-ending task.

Taking a deep breath, she rolled up the map and slid it carefully into its tube, pleased that she had struck off at least one thing on that day's to-do list.

Russian Steppes, printed and hand-coloured c. 1789, Morgan Johnson. Abby knew it was worth thousands of pounds, if it ever made it to auction. Not that it would. It was stuck here in the dusty basement of the Royal Cartography Institute, shoved on a shelf, waiting patiently for someone to look at it, to care about it.

Well, she knew how that felt.

The phone rang.

'Hello, Archive,' said Abby in her best telephone voice. 'Hello?'

There was heavy breathing, muffled sounds of chatter and laughter in the background. She knew instinctively it was her boss reporting in from a long lunch.

'Abigail, it's Stephen. Can you hear me?'

Abby managed a smile. Stephen Carter, director of the archives at the RCI, was hopeless on the phone. He always behaved as if he were a Victorian gentleman and this was his first time using one of the new-fangled machines.

'Everything all right back there?'

Abby looked up at the teetering pile of boxes.

'Nothing I can't handle.'

'Good, good,' he gushed. 'Now I just wanted to let you know I'm not sure I'll be back this afternoon; you know how these meetings go.'

She did indeed. Stephen was slurring his words a little.

'Good news, though,' he continued. 'Christine has some exciting information about the exhibition. I can't wait to tell you.'

Today was Stephen's monthly lunch date with Christine Vey, director of the collections, a pompous woman who had zero interest in the RCI but a lot of interest in furthering her career. Christine's plans always made Abby uncomfortable; they were never good news for the people who worked at the Institute.

'Anything I should know about?' she asked.

'We'll talk about it tomorrow,' said Stephen. 'In fact we should have a debrief on where we are up to. Christine wants a full

11

written update. She's really gone out on a limb for us agreeing to this exhibition, so there's no letting her down. Are we understood?'

'Of course,' Abby muttered, quickly typing out an email, a group message to Anna, Ginny and Suze, her three best friends, checking that they were still on for drinks that night.

'First thing tomorrow we'll run through the final image selection, and then you can walk the slides and negatives over to the lab,' continued Stephen, his words tumbling out of his mouth as he hurried to finish the call.

'Now, I must fly. Oh, and could you prepare the 1789 Johnson for Mr Bramley? You know how particular he is.'

'Already done,' she said as Suze pinged an email straight back.

See you at the bar. So glad you are feeling up to this.

'Excellent, you are a treasure.'

And then he was gone.

Abby put the phone back in its cradle and glanced at her watch. It was not even 4.30. Ages until she could justify leaving, even if Stephen wasn't due back in the office.

Besides, there was the debrief to prepare for. Stephen Carter was not a bad boss, but he was a stickler for detail, a sucker for pleasing the powers-that-be, and as she was technically only a temporary member of staff – thanks to her rolling contract – she knew she would be the scapegoat for any archive mishaps, failures or inconsistencies.

Now that she was on her own, now she was supporting herself, with no safety net of family or lover, she didn't like to think of the consequences if anything happened to her job.

She felt herself getting teary, but blinked back the emotion as she made her way into the photography room: long rows of battleship-grey metal shelves, each one holding dozens of filing boxes filled with negatives, slides and prints.

She moved down the rows, running her fingers over the boxes. This was actually the part of her job Abby loved the most. Maps she couldn't get too passionate about; how could anyone get worked up about a badly drawn picture of Lancashire? But with the photographs, it was different. There was something magical about them. They were intimate records of a special time before the world was really known, taken by the few people who dared to go out there into the wilds. She sat down on an office chair and pulled down a box. Broadly, her job was to catalogue the collection, writing up what was in each box: expedition, year, part of the world, names and achievements, that sort of thing, so they could all be logged on to her computer and cross-referenced.

But she also had another task: she had to make these ghosts pay. That, really, was the reason why she had been hired: she had been brought on board to curate exhibitions, to bring these long-neglected slides to the attention of the public.

Their first exhibition, to celebrate the Institute's bicentenary, was to be held in three weeks' time, and Abby wasn't entirely sure they were ready. Selecting the images to display had been easy. The title of the show was 'Great British Explorers', and there had been plenty of spectacular expeditions to choose from: ascents of Everest and K2, trips to the Poles, even Livingstone going up the Nile. But there was still something missing, something that left a hole at the centre of the exhibition, something she couldn't quite put her finger on, and she was hoping that she would know it when she saw it.

Taking a deep breath, she pulled out a narrow box and opened it. Inside was a selection of slides. She took the first one and held it up to the light. A group of small figures, dwarfed by the snowy peaks behind them. She held up the next: a mid-shot of a team of porters, grinning at the unseen cameraman. She looked at the side of the box; it was labelled *Mortimer Expedition, Nepal, 1948*.

She rolled her chair over to the light box, flicking it on and using a loupe – a sort of glorified magnifying glass that allowed you to see the image as if it had been printed full size.

The stark monochrome image of the jagged Himalayan peaks was striking, but it just wasn't different enough to the dozens of other stunning images she had of snowy hinterlands. And that was the problem – the exhibition was looking very snowy, very hilly, very white. Very one-note.

She puffed out her cheeks, wishing she was allowed to bring a cup of tea into the photograph room. But that was forbidden in the confined, claustrophobic space that reminded Abby of one of those old submarine movies.

Minus the well-toned sailors, she thought grimly.

For a moment she regretted working in such a dark and isolated environment. Her friends had certainly thought she was mad when she had given up a full-time job at the V&A. But they hadn't known her true reasons for leaving. Hadn't known why she had swapped it for a freelance position at the RCI.

Abby and Nick Gordon had kept their struggle to have a baby very private. Even though they had been the first couple in their friendship circle to get married, no one asked them when they were going to hear the patter of tiny feet. They were a thirty-something couple living in London, having fun and throwing themselves into their careers. Besides, it was something of a taboo subject. An intimate issue. If you suspected a friend of having fertility problems, you certainly didn't ask. Not unless they wanted to share it with you.

Abby and Nick had been warned how difficult IVF was going to be. But she hadn't expected it to be so physically and emotionally demanding. She'd given up her job and taken a flexible position at the Institute. But still there was no baby. And then there was no husband.

She pulled down another box, black-and-white prints this time. *Peru, Amazon*, said the label, *1961*.

She focused hard, trying to forget about the images of Nick that popped into her head at random.

Sitting down, she took the photographs out of the box, balancing them on her thighs as she leafed carefully through them.

The first was of a man tending to some mules, a wide-angle of a long valley, lush with rainforest. The second was a beautiful close-up of a hummingbird, the third a gaggle of porters carrying huge baskets, their faces worn and weathered by the sun.

At least it's not snow, she thought, sensing that she might find something of use in here.

She carried on flicking through the images until one photograph forced her to stop in her tracks. A picture of a man and a woman inches apart. His hand was on her cheek, her palm over his, in what looked like a tender goodbye. Abby put her own hand to her mouth, her breath frozen in her throat. It was beautiful, moving, and yet she couldn't really say why. It wasn't such an unusual scene, the sort of thing you saw every day at stations and airports.

But this was different; there was tension, heartache here. The woman looked distraught. But why? Who was this man? And who was his lover?

She flipped the picture over. The label on the back read: *Blake Expedition, Peru, August 1961.*

She could tell from the other photographs that he was going into the jungle. Was she begging him not to? And had he still gone anyway? She wondered how old these two lovers would be today, whether they were still alive and if they were still together.

She looked back at the picture. God, it was good. And she just knew it would be perfect for the exhibition. She had already collected enough of those jaw-dropping high-impact shots – tiny figures hacking their way up a rock face or icicle-festooned ships stuck in ice floes – but this? This was different. This image had emotion, a sense that there was more to exploration than simply getting up and going. It rooted the heroic act in the real world, made you think: What if I was going? How would I feel? And how would I feel if I was being left behind? It was a photograph that spoke quite clearly of the power of love and the fear of loss.

She didn't realise she was crying until a fat tear splatted on to the light box.

You can't go dripping all over the priceless artefacts, she scolded herself, running out of the photograph room to find a tissue.

'Abigail? Are you quite all right?'

She turned to see Mr Bramley staring up at her. Christopher Bramley was one of their regular members; he often came down to the archive for support material for his research. White-haired and bent, he rarely spoke except to request some document or map.

'Yes, fine, thanks,' said Abby quickly, rubbing her damp eyes.

The old man raised his eyebrows. 'I do hope so,' he said kindly.

She wondered how much he knew about her life. Whether he had heard.

'Here you go. The maps you were after,' she said more brightly.

'I think I'm your last customer of the day. The Institute is rather empty out there,' he smiled, rummaging around in his pocket, pulling out a tissue and handing it to her. 'I'm sure Mr Carter won't mind if you lock up early and go home.'

She nodded, deciding that was just what she would do, and returned to the photograph room to finish up.

She slipped the Blake print into a cardboard envelope, resolving to ask Stephen about it tomorrow. After all, he had worked in the collection for over ten years and had an encyclopedic knowledge of every explorer and map-maker in the last three hundred.

She flipped off the lights, checked that everything was locked and pulled on her jacket.

'See you tomorrow, Mr Bramley?' she said, swinging her bag over her shoulder as she walked through the research room.

'Oh, I shouldn't wonder,' replied the old man. 'Off out?'

'Yes, actually. Just drinks with a few friends.'

He smiled. 'You enjoy yourself, Abigail. You deserve it.'

She grinned in reply. She hadn't been looking forward to her night out with the girls, but now she decided it was just what she needed. She ran up the basement stairs to the ground floor, where light flooded the Institute's atrium. Back to civilisation, she thought, glancing at her mobile phone and seeing that she had missed a call in the signal-less basement.

She dialled to retrieve the message, and felt sick to the pit of her stomach when she heard it.

'Abs, it's me. Nick. Call me back. We need to talk.'

Chapter Two

'Can you believe he wants to *talk*?' said Abby from her bar stool in Hemingway's cocktail lounge in Wimbledon Village. She felt sure she was slurring her words, and she had only been here twenty minutes.

'What do you think he's got to say for himself?' said Suze spearing a bright green olive with a tooth pick.

'Nothing I want to hear,' said Abby, feeling more and more provoked by the phone call from her husband.

'Look. The manager has found us a booth,' said Anna, jumping up and grabbing the pitcher of Pimm's. 'Come on, before a gaggle of sexy tennis players beats us to it.'

'Chance would be a fine thing,' smiled Abby, although her heart certainly wasn't in laughing.

It was Wimbledon fortnight, and there were always celebrities or famous sports stars to be seen around the smart SW19 postcode after the day's play at the All England Club had drawn to a close.

Anna, Suze and Ginny, Abby's three closest friends, had decided that she had been hibernating far too long, and that a night out in Wimbledon's buzziest fortnight was just the ticket to resuscitate her social life.

Normally she would have agreed. Normally this was her favourite time of the whole year, a time to sit out at pavement cafés, joking with her friends and watching the world go by. But tonight it had been tempting to head straight for home when she got off the tube – her little terraced house was just off the foot of the hill on the walk up to the Village – just as she had done every night for the past six weeks.

Leaving work, Abby had felt some enthusiasm for her night out, but now she was here, she knew she wasn't in the mood for laughing, drinking cocktails or pretending that she was carefree. She didn't want to see anyone, talk to anyone. Deep down, she knew that she couldn't stay a recluse for ever. She knew she had to get back out into the world and make some decisions. She knew that she had to man up and finally talk to her husband, because she couldn't carry on ignoring his messages. But if the time had now come to confront Nick Gordon, she still didn't know what to say, and she was hoping that a conversation with the girls might provide her with some answers.

'Ginny's here,' said Suze, as they all slid into the cream leather booth. Abby groaned silently at the sight of the tall brunette walking into the bar. Any other time she would have been delighted to see her old friend; along with Anna, a high-flying lawyer, Ginny was her most capable mate, a kick-ass, no-nonsense financier, the sort of person you wanted on your side in a crisis. But she was also Nick's sister, and even though she had made all the right noises about her 'idiot brother', calling Abby every few days, sending details of counsellors and therapists and little parcels of macaroons and biscuits, Abby never felt as if she was entirely on her side.

'What have I missed?' asked Ginny, sliding in next to Anna.

'Nick's rung,' said Suze, looking up from her cocktail.

'And did you speak to him?' asked Ginny, as if she were addressing a boardroom.

Abby shrank into her chair and shook her head.

'He's called six times already this week. I haven't spoken to him but he won't leave me alone. At this rate I won't be needing a divorce. I'll need a restraining order.'

Her friends laughed politely, but she could tell that the D word was like a grenade thrown into the conversation.

'Have you at least spoken to any of the counsellors I told you about? Melanie Naylor is particularly excellent,' pressed Ginny in her no-nonsense style. 'Very high-profile client list.'

'But counselling would mean I want to save my marriage.'

'You've got to give it a try,' replied Ginny bluntly.

'I'm not saying you're being too harsh, Abby . . .' began Suze, topping up her glass until the Pimm's hovered less than a millimetre beneath the rim.

'But you're saying I'm being too harsh,' said Abby, feeling cornered.

'You can't avoid him for ever,' said Anna more kindly. 'Deleting his messages doesn't mean you can wipe out everything that's happened.'

'How could I ever forget that?' said Abby, reminded once more of the moment her life had been blown apart.

A text. That was how she'd found out that her husband had been unfaithful. They had been driving to a friend's house for Sunday lunch, and had stopped at a petrol station for some fuel. Nick had run out to pay and had left his phone on the seat, the same phone Abby had used ten minutes earlier to tell the friend that they were running late, because her own phone was out of juice.

She had expected to see a few platitudes from their host. *Don't worry! The chicken is still roasting! Take your time* ☺

Instead she had read a message from some woman whose name she still didn't know. A handful of words that had been like a nuclear explosion in her marriage.

Please. Let's just see each other again. I know it's scary but I think we are good together. X

The smell of the petrol fumes and the treachery of the words had almost made her vomit. She had looked up and seen Nick running across the forecourt, two bars of her favourite chocolate clutched in his fist, smiling despite the lashing of spring rain, and for a second she had wondered whether she should pretend not to have seen the message. Wondered whether she should just let her life carry on, unaffected by what she had read.

With a matter of seconds to make that choice, she had handed him his mobile as soon as he got into the car.

'You've had a text,' she had said simply, and immediately caught the flicker of panic across his face, knowing before he had even read the message that things would never be the same again.

When he did read it, he didn't try to deny anything.

By the time he had croaked 'I'm sorry, Abs,' she had stumbled out of the car, her sight clouded with tears, the sound of car horns ringing in her ears. Nick had followed her, his long strides quickly catching up with hers. He'd grabbed her shoulders, and perhaps to an onlooker, thought Abby some time later, they might have looked like a couple in a Nicholas Sparks movie poster about to have a passionate embrace in the rain.

Instead he had explained that *she* was a client and that he had got drunk on one of his many business overnighters and ended up in bed with her. It was a one-off, he had pleaded. She had meant nothing, he'd had too much to drink and was depressed.

21

But Abby couldn't bear to be near him after that. Couldn't bear for him to touch her. She'd hailed the nearest taxi, and by the time he returned home, she had cleared out his things, stuffed it all – even a beautiful pink cashmere scarf he had bought for her birthday, and some tickets for an outdoor cinema event – into bin bags and left them in the hall, screaming at him to leave, hurling every obscenity she could think of at him.

Abby played with the stem of her cocktail glass.

'Thanks for coming out tonight.'

The girls nodded in encouragement.

'Can't pass up the chance to spot Federer,' smiled Anna, trying to lighten the mood.

'So, what's everyone's news?' said Abby more brightly. The last thing she wanted was to dwell on her own problems.

'Work, work, work,' groaned Ginny. 'I've got a deal on that is taking for ever.'

'And I think I have become the anti-Bridezilla,' said Anna.

'Anna, you are getting married in six weeks. You're supposed to be getting teary with the florist by now. Having hissy fits with the cupcake supplier, that sort of thing,' quipped Ginny.

'There are going to be no cupcakes at my wedding,' laughed Anna.

Ginny grinned. 'Killjoy.'

'Well I went to see a clairvoyant this week, and she said I'm about to get swept off my feet,' announced Suze, who had been single ever since she finally left her cheating sports-agent boyfriend Terry.

'I'd love to be swept off my feet,' said Ginny with feeling. 'Not just because I'm so bloody busy I haven't got time for go-slow romance. I adore the idea of the grand gesture, like getting whisked off to Paris or Rome.'

'Like Mikhail Baryshnikov did with Carrie in the last season of *Sex in the City*,' noted Abby.

'But look how that turned out,' replied Anna cynically.

'What happened?' Popular culture always seemed to have passed Ginny by.

'He hit her,' replied Suze. 'Petrovsky slapped Carrie.'

'Yes, but she was in love with Big anyway. It would never have worked,' pointed out Abby, remembering every moment of her favourite show. 'And then Big came to Paris to rescue her.'

'Now that was a grand gesture,' nodded Suze sagely.

The waitress brought over some bar snacks, and Abby nibbled at a chicken wing.

'I don't know about grand gestures,' said Anna, directing her attention at Suze. 'I think they can be hollow. It's easy to spend money, or shout loud. I think it's the little things that mean a lot. I love it when Matt goes out of his way to help me without me even asking. Or buys me a book I mentioned in passing ages ago.'

Ginny pulled a buzzing mobile from her handbag.

'Bloody hell. New York,' she muttered before excusing herself and exiting the bar to take the call. Abby felt her shoulders slump in relief.

'She's Nick's sister, but she wants the best for you,' said Anna intuitively.

Abby looked at her friend. 'Which is what?'

There was an awkward silence.

'What are you going to do, Abs?' said Anna finally.

'Get a solicitor. Fill out a few forms. Boom. File for divorce. I think that's how it goes, isn't it?' Her voice cracked, and she tried to steady herself with a long swig of Pimm's.

'Are you sure that's what you want?'

'What's the alternative? That I *forgive* him? I can't. I've gone over and over it in my mind, but he slept with someone else, and I can't get past that. The betrayal, the lies . . . the trust has gone. And once it's gone, you can't get it back. Things could never be the same between us again.'

'But it doesn't mean he doesn't love you,' said Anna thoughtfully. 'Men are weak. If it's put in front of them, they'll take it. Look at Tiger Woods.'

'Let's not,' said Suze, rolling her eyes. 'He had more than one mistress come out of the woodwork.'

· 'She wasn't Nick's mistress,' replied Abby sharply. Suze gave her a cynical look.

'Don't go getting all protective over him.'

'I'm not protecting him. I'm protecting myself,' said Abby.

'You never know what you can forgive until it happens. I see it all the time at work,' said Anna. She was a media lawyer, and the bulk of her time was spent securing press injunctions to protect her clients' indiscretions. 'All these people doing stupid, selfish things – making sex tapes, having affairs with co-stars – and time and again the wives or husbands forgive them.'

'Maybe it's different with celebrities,' replied Abby.

'It's just easier to forgive, easier to put up with it,' said Suze, shrugging her shoulders. 'Terry was an absolute dog. The amount of times I turned a blind eye to lipstick on his collar because the alternative meant moving out, looking for a new flat, being on my own and going through the whole rigmarole of finding someone else. Sometimes it's easier to just keep quiet, even though each time I forgave him, I lost another piece of self-respect.'

'Don't look now,' said Anna, dropping her voice to a whisper, 'but I think that blond guy at the bar is checking you out, Abs.'

Abby hadn't felt sexy or attractive for a very long time, and the thought of someone eyeing her up made her jumpy. She shot a discreet glance in the direction of where her friend was looking. A handsome twenty-something man was indeed looking her way, an amused half-smile on his lips.

'Damn, Abs, he's gorgeous,' hissed Suze.

Abby grabbed her drink, wondering if everyone in the bar could see her blushing. Hell, you could probably see it from space.

'Not interested,' she said firmly. 'I'm no longer interested in men. It's all about cats and cupcakes from now on.'

Suze grabbed the jug of Pimm's and upended it into her glass.

'Are you sure you don't want a crack at him?'

Abby smiled and shook her head.

'In that case, I'm going to get pissed and have a go myself. You never know, Anna, I might end up bringing a plus-one to your wedding after all.'

As they watched Suze approach the handsome stranger, Abby couldn't help but feel a spark of admiration for her friend, so hopeful in her quest for true love.

Anna folded her arms on the edge of the table.

'People make mistakes, Abby. I don't think it's so bad to forgive,' she said quietly.

'Whose side are you on here?' Abby said briskly, then stopped herself, not wanting to be unkind to Anna, who these days she considered her closest friend, the one she felt she had most in common with, the one she knew she could turn to in a crisis. *Had* turned to, in the days after her separation, when Anna had spent hours on the phone with her, not judging, just listening.

'I'm on your side, Abs,' said Anna, putting her hand on her forearm. 'I just know how much you love Nick. How much he loves you and how good you were together.'

'Before he broke my heart,' said Abby softly.

Anna rooted around in her bag and pulled something out. 'Here's Matt's business card,' she said, pushing a sliver of embossed white card her way. Anna's fiancé was one of London's top divorce lawyers. Abby knew of a dozen other ways to contact him, through Facebook, email, LinkedIn, which she had felt very grown-up joining in recent weeks. Matt was her mate; she could just phone him up if she wanted to speak to him. But there was a gravity in Anna's gesture that made Abby appreciate that this was the rest of her life they were dealing with.

'You know how good he is,' added Anna. 'But if it's all a bit embarrassing, he's got a couple of amazing associates who could act for you . . . if you're sure that's what you want.'

The thought of it made Abby sick. Selling the house, splitting the assets, never seeing Nick again.

She closed her eyes, imagining how much she would miss his presence in her life, even those terrible recent text messages begging for forgiveness. Nick Gordon might have broken her heart, but he had been the love of her life, and the idea of never seeing him again, never hearing his voice was almost too much to bear.

'So what are you going to do?' asked Anna, draining her glass.

'I've got a lot of thinking to do,' replied Abby quietly.

It was the understatement of her life.

Chapter Three

Abby wasn't in the mood for work. To be honest, she hadn't been in the mood for work for quite a while now, but this morning as she walked up Exhibition Road from the tube, she was dreading it more than usual. She took a sip of her latte, hoping it would go some way to clearing her head, but it didn't seem to be working. The sunshine kept glinting off the windscreens of cars, and despite her oversized sunglasses, the light and the noise and the after-effects of the night before were making her head pound like a drum. What had possessed her to go out for drinks in the middle of the working week? She wasn't nineteen any more; she couldn't bounce back from a hangover the way she had done at university.

She crossed the road, narrowly missing being hit by a white van. The driver blared his horn at her and yelled something out of the window.

'Big night?'

She almost dropped her coffee as she turned to see a beaming face.

'Lauren! You nearly gave me a heart attack,' she gasped.

'Sorry, but you were miles away. Thinking about all those

cocktails you drank last night, were you?'

Abby was momentarily thrown by the accuracy of her friend's assessment. There had always been an air of the mystical about Lauren Stone, the Institute's librarian, although much of it was by design. The boho smocks and purple tights, the geeky glasses and the obsession with horology – it was all carefully stage-managed to distract from the fact that Lauren was both beautiful and super-bright.

'Sun's gone in,' she said, nodding towards Abby's sunglasses.

'I'm feeling a bit fragile.'

'So what was last night's occasion?'

'Just a girls' night out. A lot of bitching about how crappy men are, and more Pimm's than is healthy or sensible.'

'Good for you,' said Lauren, putting her hand in her bag and pulling out a banana. 'There you go. Potassium.'

'Are you sure?'

'Don't worry, I have an entire bunch of them in here.' Lauren grinned. 'I have a monster hangover too.'

'Oh yes?'

'I had a date.'

'Tell me more. Anyone I might know? Anyone interesting?'

'Very interesting. Alex Scott from the V and A.'

'Result!' laughed Abby, aware of the museum's resident heart-throb. 'Tell me more.'

'I'll tell you later,' said Lauren with a wave of the hand. 'Let's see if he calls back first.'

They turned in through the gates of the RCI building and waved their passes at Mr Smith, the geriatric security guard, who was sitting more or less upright next to the reception desk. Abby often wondered why they bothered, considering he only had to remember a few female faces and was hardly likely to jump up and accost them, but it had become something of a habit.

'So how's the exhibition shaping up?' asked Lauren as they prepared to go their separate ways.

'Getting there, I suppose, but Stephen's vision of what constitutes an iconic image and mine rarely seem to meet.'

Lauren snorted.

'Not surprised; I've seen how the man dresses. Taste is clearly not one of his gifts. Well, if you need any help, just give me a shout. I'm not exactly being run off my feet at the moment.'

'You can send me a long, juicy email about your date with Alex Scott then,' grinned Abby.

She reluctantly left Lauren and descended the old stone steps into the basement, taking a deep breath before she stepped through into the archive.

'Morning, Abigail,' said Stephen, raising his eyebrows at the clock above the door. 'Two minutes past.'

It was another of the little rituals they lived by. Abby worked late almost every evening, often coming in at weekends if a member required something specific from the archive at short notice, and yet Stephen insisted on pointing out every time she was even a second late.

'So. It was a very enlightening meeting with Christine yesterday,' he said when Abby had sat down at her desk. A smug smile spread across his face. Abby tried not to think about her boss's sexuality – until recently, she hadn't even been sure if he was interested in women or men. That was until Christine Vey's arrival at the RCI. Now, just the mention of her name seemed to send Stephen into raptures.

'So,' he repeated, putting on his glasses. 'The good news is that Christine has invited several members of the press to the launch night of the exhibition, and quite a few of them have accepted.'

'Fantastic,' said Abby, thrilled that her efforts might get some recognition in a national newspaper.

'It gets better,' he said, raising a hand. 'The *Chronicle* are sending along one of their top journalists to do a review. And if they think the images are strong enough, they'll run a four-page feature in the Saturday edition.'

'It had better be good then,' said Abby, feeling excited and nervous.

'Indeed. In fact I'd better have a look at your shortlist later today so we can make a final selection of images. If the press are coming, the exhibition has to be electric. It has to sing, my dear Abigail.'

His words reminded her of something.

'On that subject,' she said, hunting around her desk, 'I wanted to pick your brains about an image.'

'Pick away,' said Stephen sagely.

She pulled out an envelope and passed the photograph inside to her boss.

'I found this in the collection last night,' she said, leaning forward. 'Peru, 1961. The Blake Expedition . . . Does that mean anything to you?'

'Dominic Blake,' said Stephen, nodding. 'He was mapping a remote section of the Amazon rainforest, or at least that was the stated aim of the expedition. There were rumours, of course . . .'

'Rumours?'

'Oh, that he was really looking for Paititi, the lost city supposedly stuffed with jewels.' He gave the photograph a cursory glance, then flipped it back to Abby. 'Pure nonsense, of course, just like El Dorado, one of those old wives' tales that quickly become legends because people want to believe them.'

'So he never found it?'

'Never found anything,' said Stephen. 'In fact, he never came back.'

Abby almost gasped.

'He died?'

'One assumes,' shrugged Stephen. 'I believe this was the last official photograph from the expedition. He went deep into the jungle and was never seen again.'

Abby felt her hands begin to tremble. She didn't know why she felt so shocked, so sad.

'What's the matter?' Stephen asked.

'Nothing,' she said quietly. 'I suppose it makes the picture even more powerful. More perfect.'

'Perfect for what?' said Stephen crossly.

'For the exhibition.'

'Don't be ridiculous,' he scoffed. 'We can't use this. It looks like a photo story for *Jackie* magazine.'

Abby was determined to stand her ground.

'By our own admission we have to make the show as powerful as possible, and this is exactly the sort of image that should be at the heart of it.'

'Abby, Blake was a very minor adventurer, a playboy by all accounts. I don't need to remind you that the show is called "Great British Explorers". We are here to celebrate the best. The very best.'

It was easy to be swayed by Stephen's self-confidence, but Abby felt suddenly passionate about the Blake photograph.

'We have plenty of shots that put across the triumphs of exploration: Everest, the Poles, Burton at Lake Tanganyika, the Northwest Passage. But I think the man in the street finds it hard to understand the courage and grit required to do such things. Conquering Everest just doesn't have the same resonance it had fifty years ago, not when everyone knows someone who has run a marathon, or walked up Kilimanjaro for charity. This is the GPS generation, Stephen. People aren't impressed by explorers any more. They don't understand them. Not like you do.'

GPS generation. Abby was pleased with that one, and she could see that it had struck a nerve. Stephen was looking sombre.

'That's a depressing way of looking at it. But I suppose you have a point,' he said, rubbing his chin.

Abby nodded.

'This show shouldn't just be about summits and triumphs and firsts. It should be about loss and courage and heart.' She thumped her hand against her chest, surprised at how strongly she felt about this.

Stephen fell silent in thought, then nodded.

'Hmm,' he said, tilting his head to look at the photograph. 'I suppose we could pitch it as a companion piece to the letter written by Captain Scott's wife.'

'Yes, I really think you've got something there,' said Abby, holding her breath. Experience had taught her that Stephen's fragile ego needed to believe that every idea was his own.

'All right. Add the Blake images to the Southern Hemisphere section and find out a bit more about the woman in the picture.'

Smiling, Abby picked up the phone and dialled an internal number.

'Hello?' said a husky voice.

'Get you, sexy lady,' laughed Abby.

'Oh, it's you,' said Lauren morosely.

'Hoping it was George Clooney looking for a map of Darfur or something?'

'I was just hoping Alex might ring.'

'Sorry to disappoint. Just wondering if you could help me find out about Dominic Blake. Sixties explorer type. I particularly need to know if he was married.'

'I was just about to sit down and have a sneaky read of *Grazia*,' said Lauren, more light-heartedly.

'Stephen wants it asap.'

'Okay, okay. Pop up later and I'll see what I can dig out for you.'

'Check him out,' said Lauren, opening a copy of *Three Centuries of Exploration* by Peter May, the bible of expedition document-ation. She thunked the volume on to her desk and pointed at a handsome man in a parka. 'Is it wrong to fancy a dead person?'

'He was very good-looking,' said Abby, scanning the text.

'If he was around today, he'd have his own show and a range of sleeping bags,' said Lauren. 'How much do you know about him? It's a really sad story.'

Dominic Blake was standing in a formal shot on a mountain-side, piles of equipment in the background, rope looped around his shoulders. It was stiff, posed, but he certainly stood out, his gaze coming straight down the lens as if to say 'Yes? And you are?' There was just the hint of a smile, too.

'Where's he off to in this one?' asked Abby.

'The Karakoram Pass,' said Lauren, reading the caption.

'He got around.'

'You have no idea. I called my mother. You know she was a bit of a mover and shaker in the sixties. According to her, he shagged half of high society. Why the sudden interest?'

'I'm thinking of using a picture of him in the exhibition.'

'I'd better tell my mum. Might get you one more punter through the door.'

'What about the wife? We'll have to do some notes to accompany the images.'

'I haven't been able to find out about that. Dominic's got a Wiki page, but it doesn't say much. Went to Cambridge, edited a long-defunct magazine called *Capital*, wrote a few books, travelled the world. Seems he wasn't married.'

'Well he looks pretty much in love here,' said Abby, showing Lauren the photo she had brought with her.

Lauren sighed as she looked at it.

'Wow. What wouldn't you give to have a man look at you like that? Lucky lady.'

Abby silently agreed with her.

'There were a few more photos in the set,' she said. 'You can see the woman's face better in this one.'

'Well let's see if we can track her down that way,' said Lauren, clicking on Google Images and tapping in the words 'Dominic Blake', '*Capital* magazine' and 'girlfriend'.

Some random images appeared on the screen. A few of them were even of the right Dominic Blake.

'We've got a stash of old society magazines over there. Have a look through while I try the online *Spectator* archives.'

Abby wandered through the shelves of the library. It was an impressive place, stacked floor to ceiling with books about everything that might interest the Institute's members, from geology to the birds of the northern tundra.

She heaved one of the leather tomes on to a reading table: *Bystander* magazine, 1958–62, all carefully bound together. She smiled: to many of the well-born RCI members, the people featured inside this society journal were probably friends and relatives. She flipped to January 1961 and found the party pages: lots of photographs of toffs having fun. Apart from the fashions and the grainy photography, they could have come from the social pages of *Tatler* today. The same bright faces, the same cocktails, the same swish houses just glimpsed in the background. She turned to the February issue, then March, April, May, June and July. And there, nestled among the coverage of the 1961 Monaco Grand Prix, was the handsome face she was looking for. It was unmistakably Dominic Blake, sitting holding a cigarette, his arm draped along the back of a sofa. Next to him was a woman, laughing. Abby stopped. It was her. She glanced down at the caption: *Adventurer Dominic Blake and Rosamund Bailey. May 14th, 1961.*

She took the book over to Lauren.

'She's called Rosamund Bailey.'

'I've heard of that name,' said her friend, typing it into a search engine.

Abby's eyes opened in surprise as thousands of entries came up.

'She's more famous than Dominic,' muttered Lauren as they read her Wiki page.

Rosamund Bailey is a British journalist and political activist. She wrote the controversial 'View from the Gallery' column in the Observer *newspaper and was involved in setting up Greenscreen, the eco-pressure group, and FemCo, the charity credited with changing international law on the exploitation of women in the Third World.*

Wow. Abby had been expecting some Home Counties housewife. Rosamund sounded like Superwoman.

She scrolled through the many archived articles the woman had written: 'What Price a Life?' 'The Conservative Approach to Poverty', 'Must We Rattle America's Sabres for Them?' She only had to dip into them to see they were left-leaning polemics. The biography went on: ban the bomb and CND marches, demonstrations at Downing Street, actions to stop the Vietnam War. Throughout the following decades, Rosamund had been involved in a variety of government think tanks and appeared on heavyweight TV and radio programmes. Abby was surprised she hadn't heard of her before now.

'Blimey. Bit of an odd match. The playboy adventurer and the firebrand feminist,' she said thoughtfully.

'Do you think she's still alive?'

'She's probably not that old,' said Abby, doing the mental maths. 'Mid-seventies?'

'You should track her down. Invite her to the exhibition.'

As Abby returned to the basement, she was stopped by Mr Smith, who was holding an enormous bunch of flowers.

'These were just delivered for you, Ms Gordon,' he said with a hint of embarrassment. He held them out to her; when she didn't immediately clasp them to her bosom, he added uncertainly, 'There is a card.'

She felt a sinking feeling in her stomach. She opened the envelope and read the message.

I will always love you.

She stared at the flowers sadly. They were beautiful: a delicious arrangement of peonies and lilies from her favourite – and usually too expensive – florist in South Kensington.

She closed her eyes and steadied her resolve. It was a trick, a bribe, an empty gesture of flattery . . . She wasn't going to fall for this. Not today.

She removed the card and handed the flowers back to Mr Smith.

'I think there's been a mistake. They are for Lauren Stone in the library.'

'That's not what the man said . . .' said the security guard, looking confused.

'Please,' she said softly, and Mr Smith nodded as if he understood.

By the time she got back to the archive, Lauren had already called her extension.

'I got flowers,' she said sounding as if she was hyperventilating. 'Alex sent me flowers.'

Abby cursed herself for not thinking that one through, panicking at the idea of her friend calling Alex Scott to thank him for flowers he had not even sent.

The truth was on the tip of her tongue, before she heard the joy and excitement in her friend's voice.

If Lauren called Alex Scott and he was interested in her, it would sort itself out. If he had no romantic intentions, then at least the flowers would make Lauren look popular. It was a win-win situation, thought Abby, deciding to keep quiet and let the flowers make somebody happy.

Glancing at her watch, she saw that it was lunchtime. The basement was feeling stuffy and lifeless again. She had to get out; she needed to breathe fresh air, see trees and people and . . .

She recognised him instantly, even before she was through the revolving doors of the Institute. She almost spun herself back into the building again, but this was it. Time for confrontation.

'Hello, Nick,' she said brusquely.

'Happy anniversary, Abby.'

Chapter Four

He was still as handsome as ever.

Part of Abby was hoping that in the past six weeks he'd have aged a decade. That his thick dark hair would have turned thin and grey and those deep green eyes lost their sparkle. But no. He still looked bloody gorgeous. A little slimmer in the face, perhaps, but he even had the cheek to have a tan.

'Please, Abby, talk to me,' said Nick, trotting to catch up with her. 'We owe each other that.'

'I owe you nothing,' she replied, not even looking at him, surprised at the venom in her voice, a venom she hadn't thought she was capable of possessing.

She willed herself to stay calm. She had to do this. She had to remain mature and composed; businesslike, she decided quickly. Yes, she should see this as a professional conversation. As if she were phoning the photo lab to order a set of silver gelatin prints or arranging a venue for the exhibition.

'Did you get the flowers?'

'Thank you,' she said, finally stopping in the middle of the pavement.

'Six years. Twelve years really. Twelve years of being together.'

She nodded tightly, thinking back to that hot, lazy summer after their first year at Glasgow University. Exams were finished and a group of her friends had arranged to go to Glastonbury. Glastonbury! She still couldn't quite believe she had agreed to go. Quiet, sensible Abby Bradley, whose CD collection consisted of rom-com soundtracks and whose sole drug consumption over her first third of university life was a quarter of an e during Freshers' Week.

But after months of studying hard and working almost every holiday and weekend, Abby was determined to have some fun, and being the organised sort had prepared accordingly. A pink and white floral tent had been purchased from Millets, water-proofs borrowed from more outdoorsy friends. She'd bought a flask, spare socks, and a camping stove, only becoming mildly anxious when her flatmates had stuffed a packet of Rizlas and a box of condoms in her rucksack. She knew they were right. She had to prepare for all eventualities.

She'd met Nick Gordon within an hour of getting to Worthy Farm. He was another Glasgow University student, from Leeds, a friend of a friend of her housemate's, and had turned up to Glastonbury without a tent. It had been stolen at Central station, he'd explained to his adoring audience of new female friends, most of whom immediately offered their sexy, witty new acquaintance a place in their own tent for the weekend.

Later Abby found herself alone with him. Her friends and his had disappeared to see some band she had never even heard of, and she lost track of time as she drank cider, talked and laughed with him, surprised at how much they had in common, thrilled that such a good-looking guy with that dry, northern sense of humour, was paying her so much attention.

'Why did you come to Glastonbury without a tent?' she asked him, as they walked away from the people and the noise.

'Couldn't waste my ticket,' he replied. They found a spot on the outskirts of the farm overlooking the Somerset Hills and the Pyramid Stage in the far distance.

'I'd have thought it was fate telling me not to go.' She smiled, taking slow sips of warm cider, thinking how content she was just sitting there with him.

'I don't know. I think fate did bring me to Glastonbury this year,' he said before he kissed her.

She couldn't really remember being apart from him after that. Nick made her a better version of herself. A happier, more spontaneous Abby than the girl who had left her home town of Portree on the Isle of Skye.

They travelled back to Glasgow together, found a flat, moved in with each other for their second year, and if Abby thought it had been a rushed and rash decision, she needn't have worried. They understood one another. Their relationship was easy, the sex was great and they never ran out of conversation. They decamped to London after graduation, bought a flat, not even contemplating the idea of living apart, and got engaged at twenty-five, the first of their friends to do so. Nick didn't have to ask anyone for Abby's hand in marriage. Abby had no family. No one close, no one who really cared. So there at the altar of the remote St Agatha's Church in Yorkshire, six years after the Glastonbury weekend when they had met, Nick Gordon became her husband, her family, her everything.

'Should we walk to the Serpentine?'

'Fine,' she said as she watched the muscles in his face relax.

They threaded their way through the people and traffic of South Kensington to the open green space of Hyde Park.

'How are you?' he asked, rubbing the sweep of stubble on his chin.

'You mean how has the fallout from my husband's infidelity been?'

'I don't know how many times I have to say I'm sorry, Abs,' he said, pushing the dark tufts of hair anxiously from his forehead.

'Say it again,' she said sharply.

There was an awkward silence.

'I love you so much, Abby.'

'I think you've shown me exactly how much you love me.'

'And I miss you.'

She didn't want to tell him how much she missed him too. How she had never felt more lonely than that first night she had slept in an empty bed. And the six weeks since had seemed like an eternity, days bleeding into one, endless hours of feeling hollow and broken. It was as if she was locked into a suffocating twilight, like some Arctic winter's day when the sun never rose and the thought of ever feeling warmth on her face felt impossibly distant. She missed him too. More than anything. But she wasn't prepared to admit that now.

'I was thinking, maybe we could go away for a couple of days. I rang Babington House, and they have a room next weekend. I thought we could go and talk.'

'Is that where you think this is going, Nick? A mini-break in some boutique hotel where we have kiss-and-make-up sex in a four-poster bed. Is that how the script goes next?'

'You said you always wanted to go to Babington.'

'Not under these bloody circumstances.'

She sat down on a bench. She could feel her anger being slowly replaced by a sad, weary resignation.

'How did we get here, Nick?' she said finally. She looked at him closely and noticed pale lilac semicircles under his eyes.

'I was an idiot.'

'Yes, you were.'

It was another few seconds before he spoke.

'We let it die, though, didn't we?'

She turned round and looked at him in shock.

'All this time, since the second I found out about you and that woman, I've been torturing myself. Was I not beautiful enough for you, funny enough, smart enough? Anna, Ginny, Suze, they all told me I was being stupid, they all told me it wasn't true. *You* had the problem, the wandering eye, the overactive libido, not me. But now you're telling me this somehow *is* my fault. *We* let it die.'

'Abby, I have never met anyone as lovely as you. I never will.'

His natural confidence, the easy-going intelligence and charm, had evaporated.

'I was wrong to be unfaithful and I will never, ever forgive myself. But the last two years . . . the ovulation kits, the time-tabled sex, clinics, doctors, acupuncturists . . . Everyone just treating me like a sperm donor. It got so mechanical, Abby. So joyless. We were trying so hard to have a baby that we lost sight of us. *You* lost sight of us.'

'So you jumped into bed with the first slapper that batted her eyelashes at you in a hotel bar.'

She closed her eyes, the breeze brushed against her face, and instead of visualising her husband in bed with another woman, she could only think about the night that he had proposed. Christmas Eve in New York City. The first time she had ever been to the Big Apple. She had always wanted to go there at Christmas, and when Nick's fledgling IT business had won a big client, he had decided to treat them to a mini-break. They'd had a room with a view of Manhattan and the park, and it had begun to snow. He'd stood behind her, arms wrapped round her waist, chin resting on top of her head, and they'd watched the snowflakes flutter past the picture window of their hotel room.

'My forever girl,' he'd whispered into her hair. And she had never had a reason to doubt him. Nick and Abs. Abby and Nick. Everyone said they made the perfect couple, and she had wanted to believe it. Until now. *My forever girl* had been a lie.

'I should go. I need to get some lunch.'

'I bought you a sandwich,' he said, thrusting a Pret A Manger bag at her.

'The grand gesture,' she muttered, remembering her conversation with the girls yesterday.

'Abby, please. Give me a chance.'

'A chance? To do what?'

'To make it better, to make it right, to show you how much I love you.'

'My forever girl,' she said softly.

'What?'

'You don't even remember,' she said, shaking her head.

Tears were collecting in her eyes and she didn't want him to see her cry.

'You should know I have instructed a solicitor,' she said, trying to save some face.

It wasn't strictly true, but Matt Donovan's business card was sitting there in her purse.

'And that's what you want?' he asked slowly.

Fight for me, she said silently, willing him to do something, anything, knowing that this was the moment, crunch time, the fork in the road for their future. It couldn't end like this. In Hyde Park, holding a sandwich.

Time seemed to stand still. She looked at him, beautiful and unbearably forlorn, and finally she nodded.

Chapter Five

A smile. It wasn't an expression that Abby was used to seeing on Stephen's face. Disinterest, frowning distaste or a smug, airy sort of arrogance were his default states, depending on whether he was being asked to deal with the modern world – the media, the general public, lunch orders – or the world contained within the archive.

'It is rather splendid, isn't it?' he said, a nervous hand sneaking up to tug at his collar. Stephen had dressed up for the exhibition's opening night, and Abby suspected it had sent him into something of a panic. She had never seen him in anything but his comfortable cords-and-cardigan combo, but tonight, he looked like Oscar Wilde. A bottle-green velvet jacket and a purple knitted tie over bright red cords and suede brogues: he clearly fancied himself as a romantic poet or classicist painter. Abby was just happy to see him in a good mood.

'Yes, I think you've done a wonderful job, Stephen,' she smiled.

'Oh don't be so modest, Abigail, it was a team effort,' said Stephen. Magnanimous, too? thought Abby. What next? Group hugs?

Still, Abby was proud of what she had achieved here. The MINA gallery on the ground floor of the Redstone Tower on London's buzzing South Bank wasn't a huge space, but it was modern and glamorous, with glass walls at either end of a whitewashed and stripped-oak room. She knew that Stephen would have preferred a more traditional gallery, with wood panelling and creaky floors, but she had stood her ground; the whole point of the exhibition was to bring these long-forgotten photographs to a wider public. If they'd been hidden away in some fusty establishment in Mayfair, they would have stayed forgotten.

She had quietly persuaded Stephen by bringing him down to the MINA and pointing out that the tower stood on the site of Spanish Wharf, a quay from which clippers and square-riggers used to sail, returning with loads of tea and spices, along with new maps, drawings, artefacts and stories of the outside world. 'There's no other location in London – in England, in fact – that better represents the notion of heading into the unknown and bringing back knowledge.'

She had heard him repeat her words dozens of times over the past few months as they had hit the phones to drum up interest among collectors, academics and – she could almost picture Stephen shivering – the press. But it had paid off.

The gallery was filling up already, and it was only 7.30. Men in suits and open-necked shirts, women in short dresses and high-heeled shoes, all laughing, sipping the free wine and gazing at the beautifully framed photographs and artefacts.

'Is that the man from the *Chronicle*?' said Stephen from the corner of his mouth.

'Not sure,' said Abby honestly. 'Lauren's on the door and I told her to tell me as soon as he got here. But the woman from the *Times* has arrived, and I got a call twenty minutes ago to say that *Vogue* is sending a photographer.'

'*Vogue*? Really?' said Stephen, pulling himself a little more upright.

'I should go and check the guest list,' said Abby, wanting something to do. She was not particularly comfortable at showy social occasions, or skilled at making chit-chat as Stephen had been encouraging her to do.

'Go get 'em,' he kept whispering if they saw anyone lingering more than thirty seconds in front of a photograph.

But while the thought of giving the hard sell to any of these sophisticated-looking guests made Abby feel a bit sick, it hadn't been necessary. They had sold a dozen prints already, keeping her busy with the orange dot stickers she was using to indicate a sale.

She smiled with satisfaction as she looked around the room. In recent weeks, throwing herself into the organising of the exhibition had been a way of dealing with her sadness. But now the success of Great British Explorers was a genuine source of pleasure.

She had known that the photos had the potential to capture the imagination, but people were really staring at them, leaning in to look at a face or a detail. Usually at these affairs people came for the free bubbly, but today they were actually looking at the pictures, actually enjoying themselves.

'Abby, Abby,' said Lauren, running over. 'He's here. The guy from the *Chronicle*. Him over there,' she said, pointing to the back of a man.

Abby looked around for Stephen, but he had gone to talk to the director of the gallery.

'Go and introduce yourself,' encouraged Lauren, giving her friend a gentle nudge.

'Do I have to?' whispered Abby, feeling panicky.

'You'll thank me for it,' grinned Lauren, rushing back to her station at the door.

The man was bent over a cabinet reading the letters sent between Captain Scott and his wife, but Abby could see that he was tall, with dark blond hair cut short, and elegantly dressed in dark trousers and a pale blue open-necked shirt. She took a deep breath.

'Mr Hall?' she said. He looked up, and she was momentarily taken aback by his good looks.

'Yes, sorry,' he replied. 'I was miles away – the Antarctic, actually.' He grinned, and his eyes, almost the same blue as his shirt, twinkled mischievously.

'Abby Gordon,' she said, offering her hand. 'We spoke on the phone?'

'Abby, of course,' he said, shifting his wine glass to his other hand. 'Elliot Hall, from the *Chronicle*, but then you know that, don't you? Sorry, I seem to be making a terrible first impression.'

I wouldn't say that, thought Abby, immediately dismissing the thought. He was handsome, in a slick, public-school sort of way, if you liked that sort of thing – and I most definitely do not, she scolded herself.

'Looks like the exhibition is a success.'

'Early days, but yes, people do seem to be engaging with the images.' She winced at herself. Her words had the charisma of an automated phone message.

'Well, I'm not surprised,' said Hall, nodding towards the photo of Dominic Blake and Rosamund Bailey. 'That's an amazing shot. Usually these collections are as dry as the Gobi, but that really brings the thing to life, especially as you've placed it next to Scott's letters. I felt a tear come to my eye.'

Abby looked at him, trying to work out if he was mocking her. Typical posh-boy journo, she thought, taking the mickey out of everything. Well, as long as he gives us a good write-up . . .

'I found that photo buried in the archives. I just thought it was too moving not to be included.' They moved across to the photograph and Elliot put his finger against the six orange dots.

'Selling well. Your instincts were right.'

'There's an amazing story behind it, too,' said Abby babbling nervously. She took a glass of orange juice from a passing waiter and sipped at it. 'That was the last time they ever saw each other. He disappeared on the expedition, presumed dead. No one ever found out what happened to him.'

'The last goodbye,' said Elliot quietly.

'That's exactly what it was,' said Abby, feeling a swell of admiration for the way he had described it.

There was a moment's silence, and Abby felt compelled to fill it.

'Actually, I tracked down the woman in the shot. We didn't mention it in the notes, as my boss thought we should just concentrate on the explorers, but she is quite interesting too. She was a famous journalist in the seventies and eighties. Rosamund Bailey. Appears to have dropped off the radar lately, though.'

'Rosamund Bailey?' repeated Elliot with surprise.

'Yes, do you know her?'

Hall shrugged. 'Not really, a little before my time, but her name was mud at home. My dad didn't get along with her, not surprisingly. She was the star columnist on one of the rival papers, and she seemed to delight in attacking him.'

'Your dad?'

'Andrew Shah.'

'Lord Shah? The press baron? I mean, the media mogul, uh . . .'

Elliot laughed. 'Don't worry, I've heard much worse. I believe his nickname at the time was "The Butcher of Fleet Street". Wasn't exactly a model father, either, but that's another story.'

'I'm sorry,' said Abby. 'I didn't mean to . . . I should have known.'

'Seriously, it's fine,' said Elliot. He held her gaze for a fraction longer than was necessary, and Abby could feel her cheeks flushing with colour.

'I took my mother's name for a nom de plume for that exact reason. Dad tends to polarise opinion, which can be both a blessing and a curse in my business, as you can imagine.'

'Does that make you a lord too?' she asked. 'Or will you be when . . . ?'

What kind of question was that?

Elliot shook his head.

'Afraid not. It was one of Thatcher's political peerages, lifetime only. Besides, I have an older brother, so he's the one who will inherit the estate, the vast debt and the two hidden mistresses.'

'Really?'

Elliot started to laugh. 'No, Abby, not really. Not the mistresses, anyway. Dad's far too busy playing with his Monopoly set to waste time on anything as real as passion.'

'I invited Rosamund Bailey along tonight,' said Abby, feeling a spark of conspiracy between them.

'Is she coming?' he asked with interest.

Abby shrugged. 'She didn't reply, so I suppose not.'

'Or maybe she's just not very good at RSVPing. Come on. Let's go and look for her.' He touched the small of her back, and she flinched nervously.

'I should go and mingle,' she said, stepping back as politely as she could.

'Come and mingle with me,' said Elliot with a half-smile. 'If Rosamund Bailey is here, then it's a brilliant human interest story.'

Abby paused, then nodded. Stephen had stressed the importance of getting as much press coverage as possible. 'Press coverage means awareness. Awareness means sales. Sales mean a future for the Institute,' he had impressed in a team pep talk before the start of the show.

She was about to suggest asking Lauren if Rosamund Bailey had been ticked off on the guest list when she looked towards the gallery door and saw an elegant and well-preserved woman arriving. She was smartly dressed in a grey dress and a beige mac. There was a string of chunky beads around her neck and low-heeled court shoes on her feet. Her brown highlighted hair was tucked neatly behind her ears. Shaking her umbrella, she left it in the corner of the room and handed her invitation to Lauren.

'That's her,' Abby hissed. 'I found a clip of her appearing on *Newsnight*.'

'Then what are we waiting for?' Elliot replied, making a move to go over.

'No, just wait a minute,' she said, touching his arm.

They watched Rosamund start to circle the room. She moved slowly but gracefully, pausing to take out a pair of glasses, which she put on before she began to inspect the photographs. Abby and Elliot watched her without speaking. Rosamund took great interest in each and every picture, but she looked increasingly anxious as she came closer and closer to where they were standing.

At last she stopped in front of the picture of herself and Dominic, and Abby felt her own breath freeze. She thought she heard Rosamund sigh. It was the tiniest sound, barely audible against a backdrop of laughter and clinking glasses. Then she bowed her head and Abby watched her eyes momentarily close.

'The Dominic Blake expedition,' said Elliot smoothly, taking a step forward.

Abby watched him, not sure how it was possible for one person to possess such natural confidence. She knew it would have taken her five minutes to pluck up the courage to speak to Rosamund.

'One of the great sixties explorers,' he added knowledgeably.

'Really,' said Rosamund, unable to tear her eyes away from the photo.

'I think this single image says everything you need to know about this exhibition. Adventure, heroism, love.'

She turned to him, and Abby saw that her eyes were glistening.

'Are you all right?' asked Elliot with concern.

Rosamund blinked away her emotion and her mouth creased into a small smile.

'I'm fine. It's just that I'm the woman in the photograph.'

Abby knew that she couldn't just stand there like a lemon.

'Miss Bailey? I'm Abby Gordon from the RCI. I sent you the invitation.'

Rosamund extended her hand.

'Thank you for thinking of me. How on earth did you track me down?'

Abby smiled, not wanting to admit to the subterfuge. The *Bystander* magazine, the internet trawl, the electoral roll search.

'Champagne?' she asked, deflecting Rosamund's question by taking a glass from a passing waiter and handing it to her.

'It's an excellent show,' said Rosamund, gesturing around the room. 'You've included the Clayton expedition. Such a tragedy,' she said pointing to a group of men at the bottom of a picture. 'Three people died on that one. And they barely got a look at the summit.'

Abby was surprised. She had chosen the image because it was

a little-known expedition, a failure by most standards but one that held an interesting story: Captain Archie Clayton, the climb's leader, had sacrificed a clear run at the summit when one of his Sherpas had become sick. He had immediately taken the decision to carry the ailing man down, making him a laughing stock on his return to England. Few people knew enough about mountaineering to be able to identify the expedition from one shot.

'You know your stuff.'

'I loved a man who loved exploration,' Rosamund said simply.

'Elliot Hall from the *Chronicle*,' said Abby's new friend, introducing himself.

The old woman smiled knowingly at him.

'The youngest Shah, I presume? You have your father's cheekbones.'

'My . . . cheekbones?' said Elliot, clearly taken aback.

'Oh, Andrew is an unmitigated shit, I'm sure you know that as well as anyone. But he was a handsome shit. I hope you have only inherited the former quality,' she said mischievously.

'I fear I fail on both counts, Ms Bailey,' said Elliot, recovering his poise.

'A charmer, you certainly have that going for you.'

'Ms Bailey . . . Rosamund,' stuttered Abby. 'I wasn't sure if you'd come.'

'I wasn't at all sure myself,' said the woman, the smile draining from her face. 'But I was intrigued about the photograph you mentioned in your note. You know, I've never seen it. Not this exact one. Willem, the chap who took it, sent me a lovely print when Dom disappeared, but this picture . . .' Her voice trailed off with emotion.

'Where was it taken, Rosamund? If you don't mind me asking,' said Elliot.

She took a moment before she spoke, as if it was painful to resurrect her memories.

'Dom was going into the heart of the Amazon,' she said finally. 'It was a solo trip, but he needed a team to launch him out. This was in the village of Kutuba. The last town before he set off.'

'I didn't realise it was a solo trip.'

Rosamund gave a sad nod. 'Perhaps if someone had been with him, we would have more idea about what happened to him.'

'And how do you feel, seeing the photo?'

With a speed that surprised Abby, the older woman turned to face Elliot. 'Don't think for a single moment that you'll be getting an exclusive interview from the weeping fiancée, Mr Hall.'

'I didn't mean it like that,' he said quickly.

'I worked in Fleet Street for over fifty years. I know why you are here and what you want, and I don't mean a free glass of wine and the company of attractive ladies.'

She glanced at Abby, her scold executed with the good nature of someone older and wiser.

'I know how easy it is to see something as just a story, but don't forget that there are real lives going on behind a headline or a picture.'

'I didn't know he was your fiancé.'

Rosamund nodded. 'Yes, he was. It was all such a very long time ago, but standing here tonight it feels as if it was yesterday.'

She peered at the price tag on the photo.

'Golly,' she said quietly, as if she were baulking at the cost. 'I assume these are limited-edition prints.'

'Yes.'

'I'd better get a move on and order one, then.'

'No need. I'll arrange for one to be sent to you,' said Abby, knowing that she should probably keep this gesture from Stephen.

'How kind,' smiled Rosamund, visibly softening.

'One quote?' asked Elliot, sensing his opportunity.

'I think the photo speaks for me,' she said, taking off her glasses and putting them in her pocket ready to leave. 'It tells you about the power and the powerlessness of love.'

Chapter Six

'This is outrageous!' said Rosamund, throwing the magazine down on the cluttered desk. Across the room, a pretty girl pushed the horn-rimmed glasses up her long nose and peered at the cover.

'*Capital*? I don't know why you bother reading that rag. It's the mouthpiece of the establishment.'

'Exactly,' said Rosamund. 'That's why we have to read it, Sam – every week, religiously. How else are we going to understand what the enemy is thinking?'

There was a snort from behind her. Brian was tall and thin and dressed in the beatnik uniform of drainpipe denims and a baggy, slightly careworn oatmeal jumper.

'The enemy?' he sneered, pushing his long fringe from his narrow face and casting a cynical eye around the office. 'If this is a war, then I'd have to say we're losing.'

Rosamund was about to object, but frankly, it was true. The Direct Action Group occupied a small room at the top of two flights of stairs behind a peeling door on Brewer Street in

London's Soho. The room itself hovered between intimate and dispiriting, depending on your mood, the four overflowing desks illuminated by one yellow-filmed window and a single naked light bulb hanging from a partially stripped wire. The filing cabinet could not be opened because every foot of floor space was taken up with piles of books, newspapers, and boxes of posters and handbills for protests, benefits and gatherings of support for various causes. Even more depressingly, whatever pretensions the DAG had towards respectability or professionalism were somewhat undermined by the fact that they had to share the front door with the 'models' who worked on the floor below.

Brian had put up a poster in the stairwell declaring the DAG's support for 'workers in the erotic arts', and had taken the girls' silence on the matter as ironic confirmation of his theory that 'we're all getting fucked, one way or another'.

'What's got your blood boiling this time, Ros?' asked Sam, reaching for the magazine. Her plummy voice betrayed her time at Cheltenham Ladies' College, but she was earnestly committed to each and every cause the group held to be worth fighting for – so much so that she was paying the rent on the office with a twenty-first birthday inheritance.

'That opinion piece on page fifteen,' said Rosamund. 'The one entitled "An End of Sense".'

'What's it say?' asked Brian.

'Oh, nothing new. Just more patronising twaddle about how the race question can be answered by sending immigrants back to their homelands.'

Brian clucked his tongue. 'Typical right-wing rubbish. Why can't they see that the Empire died with Victoria?'

'Exactly,' said Ros, warming to her subject. 'He has the temerity to say that Indians are happier where they are. I mean, why shouldn't they be allowed to make their own choices? If they want to come to the UK to seek a better life, who are we to deny them a decent standard of living?'

'Hear, hear,' said Sam.

'Who wrote the piece?' asked Brian.

Sam lifted her glasses. 'Dominic Blake,' she confirmed, scanning the text.

'Never heard of him.'

'The editor, apparently.'

'Fashioning a magazine out of his privileged bourgeois views,' said Brian sourly.

'Well, whoever he is, we shouldn't let him get away with it,' said Sam fiercely. 'We should write to the letters page immediately.'

'Like they'd print it.'

'You're right,' said Ros, snatching the magazine back from Sam. 'We're the Direct Action Group. Let's take direct action.'

'Such as?'

'Such as going down to the *Capital* offices in . . .' she flicked through the pages quickly, 'in Holborn and shaming them into a retraction.'

Brian gave one of his bitter laughs.

'You really think they'll change their minds because we turn up?'

Rosamund turned to him, exasperated. Sometimes she wondered why she paid Brian, and then she remembered she didn't. The DAG funds couldn't stretch as far as their own telephone, and salaries were a distant fantasy. The staff were therefore made up of people like Sam who brought money for the office and contacts to the table, and people like Brian, who was so rabid with commitment, the lack of funds was considered part of the struggle.

'You could well be right, Brian,' she said as evenly as she

could. 'We all know how much prejudice is bred into people like this, but if we don't challenge them, how can we ever hope to change their minds about anything?'

Brian didn't look convinced.

'All right,' he sighed, looking up at the clock above the office door. 'But who are you going to get to come on a protest at lunchtime on a Friday?'

Rosamund thought about it for a moment. He was irritating, but he had a point.

'We'll find someone,' she muttered as she headed down to the street to think.

They gathered in a loose knot at the revolving front door of the building. Rosamund could see herself reflected in the polished brass plaque reading 'Brook Publishing: London, New York' and tried to ignore the fact that there were only five of them.

'At least we have placards,' said Sam, seeming to read her thoughts.

Ros nodded. With just a couple of hours' notice, finding people to lend weight to the protest had not been easy. On the way to the *Capital* office she had managed to convince two friends, Alex and George, to come along on the proviso that she meet George for a drink after work at some unspecified point. They were both tall and imposing, especially George, who had the build of a wrestler, but more importantly, they both worked at Jenning's, the printers hidden on a back street behind Piccadilly, and consequently had easy access to both stiff card and paints. The placards reading 'Down with Capital' and 'Listen to the People' weren't particularly inspired, but Brian had come up with 'Blacks In', generously daubed in red, and the possibly offensive 'Go Back to Eton'.

They had also managed to mimeograph a one-sheet polemic

Ros had dashed off on the office typewriter entitled 'Capital: Bold-Faced Lies', which, along with a DAG information leaflet, they were forcing into the unwilling hands of passers-by.

The choice of a lunchtime protest had been unexpectedly fortuitous, as it meant the entire *Capital* building had to run the gauntlet of their slogans as they headed out for sandwiches.

'Withdraw the article!' shouted Alex.

'Fire Dominic Blake!' yelled Ros to bemused glances from the secretaries and post boys hurrying in and out of the polished brass and glass front doors.

'I'm not sure the message is getting through,' said Sam from the side of her mouth.

'That's not the point,' said Rosamund. 'The point is we air our views, exercise our democratic right to protest. Whether it changes anything is neither here nor there; the fact that we're doing it is all that matters.'

She caught Sam's raised eyebrows. She wasn't at all sure she was convinced by her own argument either. The Direct Action Group was coming up to its two-year anniversary, and in her darker moments Ros wondered what her beloved pressure group had actually achieved, beyond a police caution six months ago when she had chained herself to the railings outside the Houses of Parliament.

'Miss?'

She jumped as someone tapped her on the shoulder. A young man, no more than sixteen, was standing there wearing an ill-fitting suit – probably a hand-me-down from his father, she thought, immediately regretting being so glib. Either way, he looked terrified.

'Yes?' she said as gently as she could.

'Would – would you mind coming this way?' stuttered the boy.

'What? Where?'

'Upstairs,' he said, motioning into the building. 'My boss wants a word with you.'

She felt a little jolt of alarm, but Brian and Sam nodded in encouragement.

Handing her placard to Sam, she walked into the building, glancing at herself in the mirrored wall of the reception. She looked pale from the cold and wished she had some colour to her face to balance the darkness of her hair. Ros had a difficult relationship with make-up. She disliked the tyranny that a 'full face' suggested, but secretly admitted that a slash of red lipstick could give a girl an instant lift of confidence.

Reminding herself that she had a masters degree from the LSE, she followed the boy up a flight of stairs, into a smoky open-plan office full of desks and typewriters. There was a room at one end with large glass windows. She could see inside and noticed a man standing up behind his desk on the phone.

The boy knocked on the door and the man put down the phone and gestured for Rosamund to come inside.

Now *his* suit certainly fits, thought Ros, taking a minute to observe him. In fact you could tell at a glance that the man in question had spent a lot of time at the tailor's. His jacket was quite short, the lapels narrow, and the colour, dove grey, matched his eyes. He held up the mimeographed sheet and raised his eyebrows as if to say 'Well?' Rosamund felt her heart jump; if there was an enemy, he was putting himself in her sights.

'You've read our views?' she said as calmly as she could.

'I'm Dominic. Dominic Blake, editor of *Capital*,' he said by way of brusque introduction. 'And yes, I have read your . . . piece, Miss . . .'

'Bailey. Rosamund Bailey. Chairwoman of the Direct Action Group.'

She glanced at him and found the way he looked disconcerting. When she had pictured the author of the controversial article, she had imagined a stuffy gentleman in a waistcoat and perhaps a monocle, some stodgy old-timer stuck in the Empire, with narrow-minded colonial views to match. But the man before her was about thirty, slim yet muscular, with rich brown hair swept back from his forehead in a fashionable rakish style.

'Please, take a seat,' he offered.

'I'd prefer to stand,' she said stubbornly, smoothing down the lines of her coat as if she were about to be inspected.

'Fine,' said Blake, sitting down and lighting a cigarette with a gold lighter, tossing the packet on to the desk in front of him.

'So. You've taken offence at *Capital* magazine.'

Ros bristled. There was something very superior in the way he spoke. She reached into her bag and pulled out her copy of *Capital*, folded open at the offending article.

'This,' she said, holding it up and feeling her cheeks go hot. 'This piece is a disgrace.'

'That?' said Blake, clearly bemused. 'What on earth have you found to take offence at in my column?'

'What have I found?' laughed Ros, incredulous. 'Everything about it, you racist, capitalist pig! How can you stand there defending it? Aren't you ashamed?'

Blake frowned and took the magazine from her. 'Have you actually read it?'

'Of course!' she spat. 'I've never read anything so patronising, so insulting to another race of people in my life.'

'What was so offensive?' he asked, looking increasingly puzzled.

Ros started to shake her head. She had guessed that Dominic Blake would be thick-skinned and self-righteous, but his reaction now beggared belief.

'Your attitude towards the race question,' she said. 'At a time when there is literally rioting on the streets over the notion of repatriation, do you really think it wise to be blithely fanning the flames?'

She stopped, suddenly aware that Blake was smiling. She was also aware, despite herself, that when he smiled, his grey eyes crinkled at the sides in a most attractive way.

'You haven't read it at all, have you?' he said, snapping her from her drifting thoughts.

'How dare you?' she replied. 'I read it this morning. You argue that Indians should be sent home, and that they're better off starving back in India.'

'I say nothing of the sort,' said Blake, the smile fading. 'If you had taken the time to actually read my argument instead of flying off the handle at the first difficult word, you'd have seen that I'm not talking about India at all.'

'Excuse me?' said Ros.

Blake took a deep breath and let it out, his irritation plain.

'I have recently been travelling in the Amazon basin – South *America*, Miss Bailey.' He waved the magazine in the air. 'In this article, I actually argue that we should leave the Indians – *Amazonian* Indians, that is – alone. I write that my observations in the jungle were that they were perfectly capable of getting by in their own environment.'

'Yes, but—' began Ros, trying to regain the upper hand, but Blake simply waved her objections away with a waft of the magazine.

'Moreover, I argue that when we stick our oar in via missionaries or raw commerce, we make these Indians reliant on us and turn them from proud, self-sufficient people to itinerant casual labourers by robbing them of their self-belief.'

He fixed Rosamund with a withering look.

'If you had noticed, that is a notion that could be extended to the wider race question, as you put it, regarding the recent immigrants from India – that's the India in *Asia*, by the way.'

'Why do you care about the Indians?' she muttered, feeling cornered.

'Compassion is not the exclusive right of socialists, Rosamund,' he said with a hint of irritation. 'In fact, in many cases they're completely devoid of that one quality.'

'That might be so, Mr Blake, but I still know the sort of magazine this is. The sort of man you are.'

'And what would that be?' he asked with the hint of a smile, blowing a thin line of grey smoke at the ceiling.

'Public school, landed gentry. A right-wing dilettante who decides to edit his own magazine with the sole intention of peddling his establishment views. Just because you've been on holiday to the Amazon rainforest doesn't change the ideas that have been ingrained into your type for generations.'

Dominic took a long drag on his cigarette.

'Until he died six years ago, my father was the manager of a grocery shop in Oxford. I was lucky enough to go to a decent boarding school in Kent, but that's a world away from Eton, believe me. My political views are fluid, but in most people's eyes quite central, and I launched *Capital* because I recognised that we are living in changing times and I wanted a talking shop to represent the excitement and change that is going on in London.'

The tinny chants of the Direct Action Group, huddled outside, floated through an open window, and Ros knew she could not stay here another moment.

'Hmm,' she said, trying to retain some dignity.

'Can I ask you a question?'

She didn't reply.

'You don't care for *Capital* magazine, but what is it you do care about, Rosamund Bailey?'

He looked at her directly, and for a moment he caught her off guard. Cursing herself for getting distracted by his eyelashes, she regained her poise.

'I care about equality, fairness. I believe that everyone should have a chance regardless of who they are or where they were born.'

'I think most people, on either side of the political fence, want that. Conservatism is rooted in meritocracy, liberalism in equality, but aren't they just different ways of saying fairness?'

Ros snorted. She didn't like feeling caught out. She liked being able to run people around in argumentative circles, but something was stopping her from taking Dominic Blake on.

'Come on. Be more specific,' challenged Blake. 'What issues do you really care about? When you read the paper, what makes you boil with anger?'

'I care that nuclear arms development is carrying on unchecked. I care that women's rights are still not even nearly equal to men's . . .'

'So write about it. For me. For *Capital*. Tell me what's wrong, and why.'

'Write for you? For *Capital*? You must be joking.'

'I don't joke about who I want to contribute to my magazine.'

'I don't want to write for *Capital*,' she spluttered, not believing he had just suggested it.

'Why not?' he challenged.

'You might not think it's a right-wing mouthpiece but I certainly do.'

'Miss Bailey, rallies in the street, even in Hyde Park, are all well and good, but more and more I think that politics is going to be fought in the papers, in radio debates and on the television news. I don't doubt that you want your views to be heard, but what better way to do that than to have them printed in a serious magazine with clout that reaches people who can effect change?'

'As if your readers are going to like my views,' she scoffed.

'Precisely,' said Dominic bluntly. 'Half of them probably don't ever hear opinions like yours. They have friends just like them, who think just like them. How can you change how people think if you don't give them something to think about? To make waves, Miss Bailey, you have to throw the pebble in the pond.'

Rosamund looked at him with resentful new eyes. A voice in her head told her that what he was saying made sense, but there was no way she was going to admit that to herself, let alone to him.

'I should go,' she said, glancing away.

'That's a shame.' He picked up her hastily copied handbill again and shrugged. 'Someone gave me one of these before you came in. I read it and thought it was good. For an overheated, one-sided argument, anyway. You have talent. Cut out the hectoring tone, and I do believe that people would enjoy reading your stuff.'

He stubbed out his cigarette in a glass ashtray and opened his desk drawer.

'The offer's there, anyway,' he said, pushing a business card across to her. 'Perhaps you can ring me next time, instead of shouting outside my window.'

Chapter Seven

It was an ordinary street. So ordinary, in fact, that to Ros it almost felt like a parody. The trees, the neatly parked family cars, the low red-brick walls marking the edge of well-tended gardens trimmed with hedges and flower beds; it was as if someone had painted a picture entitled *English Suburban Idyll* and blown it up to full size. The strange thing was how distant, how detached from it Ros felt. Acacia Avenue, Teddington, had been the street she had played in as a child, running in and out of other families' little gardens, riding her scooter then her bicycle along the pavement, chalking hopscotch squares on the flagstones. But now it was as if she was watching a movie of someone else's life. It was familiar, yes, but at the same time somehow nothing to do with her, even though it was her home.

She stopped at the gate to number 22. White, wooden, the struts fanned in the shape of a rising sun; she knew exactly how it would creak the second she pushed it.

'Is that you?' shouted a voice before she was even through the doorway.

It had been cold, dark and raining when Ros had got off the train, but the kitchen was flooded with warmth from the oven, mixed with the smells of cooking and early daffodils in a jug on the table.

Clearly her mother had been baking: there were a variety of mixing bowls, jars and packets on the counter top, next to a set of scales and an open recipe book, everything covered in a thin layer of flour.

'Excuse the mess,' said her mother, moving a pile of books from the wooden table and pulling out a chair.

'Your father's in the greenhouse, planting tomatoes. God knows why we don't just buy them from the greengrocer like everyone else, but he swears they taste better.'

Rosamund looked out of the window and smiled.

Samuel Bailey had spent his days working in a high street bank, opening accounts and setting up mortgages and modest loans, a job that Ros had always got the sense he never much cared for. But in the evenings and at weekends, he would throw himself into a dazzling array of hobbies. The house was stuffed with the results of his enthusiasms: a wonky toast rack from his dalliance with woodwork, an abandoned clarinet from when he was going to be the new Benny Goodman, the many shards of glass and broken pipe stems in a cabinet in the entrance hall testament to the time he had read a book on archaeology.

'Dad, come in,' she called, suddenly feeling the urge to speak to him.

Her mother poured her a cup of tea and sat down opposite her.

'How was your day?' Ros asked.

Valerie barely glanced in her direction. 'We'd better wait until your father comes in to discuss that one. Get the cutlery and glasses and put them on the table, would you? The dumplings just need another couple of minutes, but then we're ready to eat.'

Samuel Bailey came into the house and kissed his daughter on the top of her head.

'All done,' he smiled, washing his hands with the bar of coal tar soap by the kitchen sink. 'We should have tomatoes, runner beans and onions by June.'

'I can make chutney,' said Valerie vaguely.

Ros found herself smiling. Sometimes she felt a bit of a loser for still living at home at the age of twenty-four; everyone else she knew – school and college friends – was either married or had little bachelor flats or house shares around the city. She was aware that the arrangement saved her a great deal of money; she would never be able to afford to work at DAG if she had to pay rent. But it was more than that. Passion and emotion was the office oxygen at the Direct Action Group, but that made it stressful, and so she enjoyed returning to Teddington every night, away from the bright lights of Soho and the struggles of the world, to her parents' homely chit-chat.

Wearing two oven gloves, Valerie lifted a casserole dish on to the kitchen table and asked her husband to pour them all a glass of water.

'Marion next door gave me the recipe,' she said, waiting for her family to taste the food and compliment her.

'Delicious,' said Samuel, noting his cue.

'So? Your news?' asked Rosamund.

'It looks like Grandma and Grandad are moving in,' said Samuel bluntly.

'Why?' asked Rosamund with surprise.

'Grandad is suffering with his leg, and Grandma's wrist hasn't been the same since she fell outside the post office,' explained her mother. 'The truth is, they're struggling, so I suggested they'd be better off here.'

'*They* suggested,' muttered Samuel from his seat.

Ros felt a flutter of panic, quickly seeing the implications of this move.

'Where are they going to sleep?'

She didn't miss the look between her mother and father.

'There's only one option really. They'll have your room and you'll move into the box room.'

'The box room?'

'I know it's not ideal, darling, but we don't have much choice. They're my parents, your grandparents, and they need us. They need help.'

'I can't sleep in the box room. I'm not even sure it's long enough for a bed.'

'I agree,' said Samuel.

An awkward silence settled around the room.

'I'm going to have to move out,' said Ros slowly. It was less a question, more a statement of fact.

'It might be the push you need,' replied her mother encouragingly.

Ros looked at her cautiously.

'What do you mean? The push I need?'

'Darling, you know how much we love you, but your father and I have been talking, and we think that living here is holding you back in your career.'

'How is it holding me back?'

Another look of complicity.

'Rosamund, you have a masters degree from the London School of Economics. You are as smart as a whip and the world is your oyster. We know you love what you're doing . . .' Ros could tell her mother was treading carefully here, but she could predict what was coming next. 'But when are you going to get a proper job?'

There. There it was. She almost felt a sense of triumph when she heard it.

'I run a political pressure group, Mother. We have an office and I employ—'

'A *real* job, Ros,' she interrupted. 'With a salary and a pension. Something with prospects. This isn't the Student Union any more, darling.'

Ban the bomb, troops out, crush apartheid; Rosamund had drunk it all in, and it had filled her up like oxygen. Within weeks of arriving at the LSE, she had organised a sit-in at the university refectory in protest at the sacking of a porter, revelling in the fuss and, yes, she had to admit, the power. It had fizzled out after two days when her fellow protesters began drifting off to lectures, but it had been a revelation to Rosamund, and she had carried on fighting against perceived injustice. She couldn't believe her mother was dismissing it as some sort of ill-conceived hobby.

'Of course things might be different if you were married. If you were supported. Janet down the road does wonderful work for charity, but her husband is an accountant, brings home good money.'

Ros was now feeling hot with anger. 'What I do isn't about making money. It's about making a difference.'

'How about making a living?' said her mother more tartly. 'You can't even afford a roof over your head. Now, I have to go and make a phone call.'

'Who are you calling? Grandma?' Ros said childishly.

'I'll leave you two to talk.' Valerie didn't even glance in her daughter's direction as she left the room.

When she'd gone, the tension subsided a little. Her mother had always been the more fiery of her parents, a woman never afraid of speaking her mind, and the two women regularly locked horns. At least Ros knew where she got her feistiness from.

'If it's any consolation, I'm not looking forward to them moving in either,' said Samuel, finishing the last of his stew.

Rosamund managed a thin smile.

'I remember when we went on holiday with them to Worthing. You thought the bomb had dropped – it was Grandad's snoring through the caravan walls.'

Neither of them spoke for a moment.

'So what is this, Dad?' Ros said finally. 'Tough love?'

'You know this will always be your home. There will always be a bed for you even if I have to sleep in the greenhouse. But your mother has a point about getting out there.'

'You don't approve of my work at the Direct Action Group? You of all people?'

'Of course I do,' he said, as father and daughter looked sadly at one another.

The Baileys – the Bazelskis as they had been then – had come to England just before the war as refugees from Hungary, where they had seen politics swing back and forth with deadly force until it had become life or death for anyone with a Jewish background.

Ros remembered listening to Samuel's stories as a teenager. His recollections of her birthplace, Budapest. How settled and happy he and Valerie had been, until the growing power and sinister ambitions of neighbouring Nazi Germany became impossible to ignore. His crucial decision to leave Hungary with his wife and young child when the government starting passing anti-Jewish legislation.

'Why did no one stop them?' Rosamund had asked time and time again when she had learned how their relatives had been sent to Auschwitz and Treblinka, and the only way Samuel could respond was to say that perhaps nobody had realised what was happening until it was too late.

Rosamund lived in a state of perpetual concern that the same thing could happen again, and had made a vow to herself to always make her voice heard, to do whatever she could, in whatever small way, to help stop similar atrocities.

Samuel shifted in his seat uncomfortably.

'I know how important politics is to you, darling. Your mother isn't saying don't do it. She is saying that spending almost two years working for nothing, with no prospect of ever getting paid, might not be the best use of your talents and qualifications, and I agree with her.'

'Well what do you suggest?' she asked, meeting his gaze with a direct challenge.

'Become an MP. You'll get a salary, a pension, the chance to make a difference.'

Ros snorted. 'I don't want to spend my whole life declaring the local gymnasium or post office open.'

'What happened to "I want to be the first female prime minister"?' said her father more softly.

'I was ten years old.'

'You were still serious.'

'No major country in the world will have a female head of state. Not in my lifetime.'

'Indira Gandhi is Congress President in India. I think you underestimate the potential of womankind.'

'More like I understand the prejudices that exist in this country.'

'How about journalism? That's how many politicians got started.'

'Like who?'

'Like Churchill. Even if you never join a party, never try for selection as an MP, it's a rewarding career. You were always such a nosy child,' he smiled.

Ros couldn't be cross with him any longer.

'You know, you're the second person this week to suggest I go into journalism.'

'Who was the first?'

'Just someone I met.'

'Oh yes?' smiled her father knowingly as she felt the base of her neck flush pink.

Dominic Blake. Since their protest outside the *Capital* offices three days earlier, the man had kept popping into her head unbidden. The good looks he was quite clearly aware of, his regular features, full lips and soft grey eyes, both irritated and fascinated her to the point that she wasn't sure whether she wanted to exorcise all thoughts of him immediately or close her eyes and think of him again.

But it was more than the way he looked. Dominic Blake had surprised her, intrigued her, and his words had lifted her spirits, quite an achievement considering she had expected him to be a complete pig.

Write for me. You have talent. Change the way people think. I think you'd be good at this.

Although she was a confident woman, Rosamund wasn't exactly sure what she was good at any more. At school and university, her talents and efforts, and their rewards, had been clear to see. Her clean sweep of A's at A level, her first-class degree. The Direct Action Group tried hard, they gave it their all, but they hadn't really changed anything except the odd light bulb in their office.

So it was nice to be told that she was good, that she was talented. To hear the words out loud and to know that Dominic Blake believed in her, regardless of his political views, made her smile at night.

'Nothing like that,' she said quickly, aware that her father was waiting for a response. 'He's an editor. He saw something I'd written and thought I had potential.'

'Then listen to the man. He knows what he's talking about.'

Rosamund scoffed at how ridiculous she would have found those words just a few days earlier.

'So what do you think?' asked her father softly.

Rosamund did not like to admit she was wrong, but a voice in the back of her head was telling her how selfish she was being, and that Grandma and Grandad's arrival might even be fortuitous.

She puffed out her cheeks, aware that the deal had been done. Aware that it was possibly the best thing for her, but still racked with a sense of uncertainty about the future.

'When are they moving in?'

'Your mother mentioned next week.'

'Next week!' Her immediate reaction was to laugh.

'I can give you the money for a deposit and a couple of months' rent.'

'Dad, I'm twenty-five next month. I'm not taking any more handouts from you.'

'Are you sure?'

'I've taken enough. I'm sure I can up my shifts at the café.' She waitressed at weekends to earn herself some pin money.

'Come here. Come round to me.'

She laughed and stayed in her seat.

'I'm comfy, and my feet are tired.'

'Get round here, Rosamund Bailey. You're twenty-four. You're not old enough to have tired feet and still young enough to give your old dad a hug.'

She went round to his side of the table and Samuel put a paternal arm around her waist.

'Do you know what the secret to being happy is?'

She gave a shrug.

'Acceptance.'

'You mean I have to expect less?' she said sharply.

'I think you're happy at the DAG, Ros, but I don't think you are content. You won't be content until you accept that in life there will be some things, some people, some situations that you just can't change.'

She nodded politely, although privately she didn't agree with him.

Her father might be content with his clarinet and his tomato plants, but Rosamund Bailey still wanted to change the world.

Chapter Eight

'You're just in here,' said Sam as they reached the top floor of her house in Primrose Hill.

Lugging her two suitcases and her big leather satchel, Ros followed her up the stairs and into the room that was to be her temporary home.

'Sam, this place is amazing,' she said dropping her cases in disbelief, not quite believing that her friend had described this as the box room. It was a magnificent space, thought Rosamund, calculating how many times bigger than the DAG office it was. Occupying the entire width of the house, it was flooded with lazy early-evening light, and when she got closer to the window, she could even see Regent's Park in the distance.

'Well, you get more for your money in Primrose Hill,' said Sam, throwing a clean towel on the bed. 'It was either a shoebox in Knightsbridge or a whole house in a spot that sounds like a beautiful country village. Besides, there's lots of interesting people around here. Musicians, artists, writers . . . I should introduce you to Sylvia Plath who lives round the corner. American, frightfully bright. Almost as clever as you.'

'Sam, this is so kind of you,' said Ros, still thrilled that her friend had made the generous offer of lodgings when she had heard about Ros's expulsion from home. 'I've managed to get more shifts at the café, so I can pay you in a fortnight. In the meantime, grab a couple of glasses and help me unpack. I have wine,' she grinned pulling a bottle of red out of her satchel and handing it over.

Sam hesitated and put the bottle on the bedside table.

'What's wrong? Don't tell me you've gone teetotal on the quiet.'

'Nothing like that,' said Sam, waving a hand. 'I'd love to stay and help out, but I've got to scoot off in a couple of minutes.'

'No problem,' smiled Ros, trying to hide her disappointment. 'Let's save the wine until tomorrow. Where are you going? Somewhere fun?'

'Out with Brian,' she said more quietly.

'Is that all?' said Ros, laughing. 'I thought you had a hot date or something. I'll just put my stuff away and change my dress, then I'll come with you. Maybe we can sneak the claret into the pub. It's good stuff.'

Sam looked awkward, nervous, then her broad mouth uncurled into a small smile, like a flower welcoming the spring.

'For the smartest person I know, you can be incredibly daft, Rosamund Bailey.'

'What have I done now?' grinned Ros, perching on the edge of the bed.

'I mean I'm *going out* with Brian. Have been for a couple of months now.'

Ros's heart started to beat harder in disbelief and panic.

'You're going out with Brian?' she said finally, still not able to process it properly.

'It just happened one night in the office. We never planned it,' replied Sam nervously.

One night in the office, thought Ros, trawling desperately through her memory bank. She was almost always the last person to leave, hardly ever had the day off work. She just couldn't believe this had been going on for two whole months and she hadn't noticed anything.

'Wow,' she said finally. She was rarely lost for words, but right now she didn't know what to say.

The impossibility of the situation she now faced was immediate and obvious. As Sam's friend, she was not sure she approved of Brian as a romantic choice. She had only recently admitted to herself that she didn't even like her DAG colleague. That the anarchist streak she had so admired at university was actually driven by ego, and that his passion was thinly veiled belligerence. And as the founder and unofficial chief of the Direct Action Group, she was quite horrified that two out of the three members of the team were now in a sexual relationship.

But as Samantha's new tenant, one who was currently reliant on her friend's good will, Ros knew she had to tread carefully, otherwise she would be back in Teddington, listening to her grandfather's snoring.

'I should have told you earlier,' said Sam quietly.

'I'm sure you had your reasons.'

'I didn't want to say anything until we were sure about our relationship.'

Ros kept quiet until she had collected her thoughts.

'I want you to be happy, Sam. I'm just worried about conflict in the office.'

'Conflict?' smiled Sam. 'As you said, I'm happy. We're very happy.'

'But what if you break up?'

'Come on, Ros. I've only just started seeing him and already you're talking about it being over.'

'I'm just being practical.'

Sam folded her arms in front of her. 'Ros, we work for the DAG for free. I love my job. I enjoy working with you, and the idea that we can change things makes me excited whenever I go into the office. But it's not everything, and if it comes to a choice, then I choose having a personal life,' she said, the threat subtle but unmistakable.

Ros felt cold at the prospect of Sam, or even Brian, leaving the DAG. How could she have a pressure group that comprised a single person?

She looked at her friend – the carefully applied make-up, the smart dress – and felt a crushing disappointment that she could sell out for a man.

'I'm just watching out for everyone,' she replied, deciding that tonight was not the time to discuss it.

'Don't worry. I'm a big girl,' said Sam more good-naturedly.

'Have fun tonight. Say hi to Brian.'

'I will. Make yourself at home.'

'Thank you. Thanks again for everything,' said Ros as the door closed behind Sam.

When the front door slammed shut fifteen minutes later, Ros peered out of the window and watched the tail lights of Brian's Hillman Minx disappearing into the encroaching night.

She frowned, still not able to understand how she had been blindsided by Sam's revelation, but decided to unpack before she gave it any more thought.

She squatted down on her haunches and popped open her suitcase, pulling out the contents and arranging her clothes into piles on the bed. She was not a naturally organised person, but sometimes she liked bringing strict order into her life to make her feel more in control.

She hung up her skirts and blouses and her one good coat in the small wardrobe, put everything else in the oak armoire, then sat on the bed feeling restless.

Sam's Primrose Hill house suddenly felt very large and quiet. She picked up the bottle of wine and went to go and find the kitchen, pausing at the bookcase in the hall to pick something to read; her own box of books was due to arrive on Sunday, when her father had promised to deliver the rest of her possessions.

A short rummage around the kitchen drawer yielded a corkscrew and a goblet. She opened the bottle, poured herself a glass and took a sip, feeling her shoulders slump.

She had been excited about moving into Sam's, not just because it resolved a problem, but because she secretly liked the idea of more freedom. Even at university, she had lived at home, aware that money was tight, aware that a student flat share was profligate and that staying with her parents was the more practical solution. She had thrown herself into student life as much as she could, but having to get the last train home to Teddington had certainly limited her opportunities.

Now that she had moved to Primrose Hill, she didn't exactly want to make up for lost time – how could she possibly lead the Direct Action Group if she had a midweek hangover? Even so, she'd had visions of spending weekends with Sam discussing books and jazz and art and visiting clubs, museums and galleries to make those conversations come alive.

Now that Brian was on the scene, that particular fantasy was unlikely.

A distant ringing of the phone shook her from her thoughts. Locating the sound in the hall, she ran to answer it, picking up a pen in preparation for taking a message.

'Hello, Campbell residence,' she said as politely as she could.

'Is it possible to speak to Rosamund Bailey?' came the reply.

She put the pen down in surprise.

'This is she.'

'It's Dominic Blake. From *Capital* magazine.'

'Dominic Blake?' she said in confusion. 'How on earth did you find me here?'

'You gave me this number.'

'I did,' she responded quickly, remembering the copy she had filed and the accompanying note with her new contact details.

There was a moment's silence.

'Thank you for the piece.'

'How was it?' she replied anxiously.

'You didn't let me down.'

'You liked it?' she said, her voice rising in excitement.

'It needs a bit of editing. Perhaps a couple of paragraphs need expanding to extend the points you make, but I enjoyed it very much. We should probably arrange a time to knock heads to discuss it. Are you in a rush? Are you still at work?'

'No. Our office doesn't have its own phone. This is my home number.'

'Then I'm sorry for intruding. On a Friday night as well. I lost track of the time. Sometimes we work ridiculously long hours here because of the small team.'

Ros laughed. 'Don't worry about it. I was only unpacking.'

'Unpacking?'

'I've just moved to London.'

'Where were you before?'

'Teddington,' she replied.

'Exotic Middlesex.'

'You're laughing at me.'

'I know it's more than my life's worth. So it's your first evening in London,' he added after a moment.

'You make that sound like something to celebrate.'

'It is. I remember the night I arrived in London. I changed my shirt and went out until dawn. I don't think I've ever felt more excited about life and the promise it held than when I walked over Waterloo Bridge at midnight.'

'Well my housemate's gone out, so it's just me and a bottle of claret. Unless you wanted to discuss my article,' she quipped before she had even realised what she'd said.

'You want to talk through your article over a bottle of claret?'

There was a hint of amusement in his voice and it embarrassed her.

'No, it's Friday night. Of course you've got plans,' she backtracked.

'That depends.'

'Depends on what?' she asked, her heart beating hard from excitement and awkwardness.

'Is it good claret?'

'It almost bankrupted me.'

'Then you should probably keep hold of it.'

'Of course,' she said softly, aware that he was letting her down gently.

'We'll just have to go to the pub then,' he added.

'To discuss the piece?'

'Of course.'

She glanced at her watch: 6.30.

'Where are you?' he asked.

'Primrose Hill. I could get to Soho for eight o'clock.'

'Or I could come to you. I'd hate to be responsible for a young lady walking around Soho on her own at night.'

'I can look after myself.'

'I'm sure. But I have wheels. How about I pick you up in an hour?'

Chapter Nine

Principles? Rosamund wasn't sure she had any. Not real convictions anyway, she mused as she allowed Dominic Blake to hold the passenger door open for her.

She certainly hadn't been robust enough with Sam about her relationship with Brian, and here she was, on a Friday night, about to go out with a practical stranger because it had seemed easier to just say yes.

Dominic walked round to the driver's side and hopped in to the tiny interior of the racing-green Stag. The chassis of the car was so low-slung that Ros thought her bottom might drag along the road, and her arm brushed against Dominic's as soon as he sat down.

'Well this is a change from the last time we met,' she said as he fired the engine.

'I was hoping you'd be a little less angry with me by now,' he replied with a sidewards glance and a grin.

'So that's why I'm getting a one-on-one with the editor on a Friday night?'

'You make my motives sound suspect.'

Ros looked at him – his smooth profile, his easy confidence at the wheel – and decided she was not going to let him think she was the sort of girl who would fall so easily for his charms.

'I think you're someone who probably needs to be liked,' she observed, noticing that he'd had his hair cut since the last time they had met.

'Or perhaps I think we got off on the wrong foot. And that I see *Capital* writers as friends. Besides, it was you who suggested meeting up, if I remember rightly . . .'

'To discuss the article.'

'Of course,' he replied.

She sank back in her seat feeling embarrassed, wishing that the cabin of the car wasn't quite so small, wishing she wasn't breathing in his clean, fresh smell, a soft scent of soap and cologne.

'So where are we going?'

'I don't know,' he said honestly. 'I don't really know this part of town.'

'Why, where do you live?'

'Tavistock Square. Do you know it?'

'Charles Dickens used to live there.'

'You do know it,' he smiled.

'I like walking around London reading the blue plaques.'

'How about here?' he asked screeching the car to a halt outside a traditional-looking pub with hanging flower baskets.

Ros looked behind her and laughed.

'We haven't even come a hundred yards.'

'Yes, but it's cold and I need a drink.'

'And you wouldn't want to miss the opportunity to show off your car.'

Ros paused for a moment at the doorway of the pub and looked inside. She had no idea what to expect of her local drinking den.

After all, she had only lived in Primrose Hill for an hour and didn't know whether this was a reputable place to drink or the local gangsters' pub. But the scene inside was soft and warm, with tables of old men, beatniks and bearded intellectuals sitting alongside one another in a good-natured Friday night fug. In his navy Crombie coat, Dominic looked right at home.

As he went to the bar, Ros scolded herself for being so chippy with him. It had taken her a week to pluck up the courage to call him, but when she had done so yesterday, and pitched him an idea about the contraceptive pill transforming the economy, he had commissioned it on the spot. Her copy deadline had been two weeks hence, but she had gone back to Teddington and fired off one thousand words that evening, her thoughts and arguments pouring out of her and slotting together like the simplest of jigsaw puzzles, even though it was her last night at home. She had arrived at the DAG office at seven o'clock that morning to type it up, and when she had hand-delivered it to the *Capital* offices at lunchtime, she had felt pure exhilaration and the desire to do it all over again.

She looked up and saw Dominic chatting to the barmaid. He was only buying two pints of cider, but from the conversation he appeared to be having with her, it was as if they were old friends. As he returned to the table, Ros watched the barmaid's eyes follow her most handsome customer.

'So you liked the piece?' she said, taking a sip of her pint.

'I called you as soon as I'd read it. You have a natural talent, Ros.'

'I'm just glad you don't think I'm a promiscuous bohemian,' she said with a sigh of relief.

'Pardon?' he said, almost spluttering out his drink.

'Maintaining that the pill will be a good thing for society,' she replied quickly, not quite believing that she had referred to herself as promiscuous in her first five minutes of conversation.

'No, I don't think you're a promiscuous bohemian,' he laughed, looking at her from under those dark, disconcerting eyelashes. 'Although I do believe you've got the potential to be a very astute economist. What was it you said about the pill getting a generation of women to work, putting women in government, on to boards, in power . . . Macmillan will bring its release on to the NHS forward by six months once he reads this. Or maybe not,' he added with a cynical smile.

He pulled the article from the inside pocket of his jacket and reread it.

'You didn't submit a title. Got any ideas?'

'How about "Women on Top"?' she suggested, before realising the double entrendre. 'Or maybe not.'

'No. That's brilliant,' he said, scribbling the words on the top of the feature and handing it back to her. 'It's going to get the *Capital* readers a bit hot under the collar already, so in for a penny, in for a pound and all that.'

Still flushing with embarrassment, Ros skim-read the notes and suggestions that had been written all over the page in red pen. There were so many of them, she thought her piece must have been absolutely hopeless, and it took another minute of reassurance from Dominic before she understood that these were simple editing points.

He took off his coat and sat back in his chair, his arm resting along the top the banquette.

'So when are you going to write something else for us?'

'Is that what this is? A job interview?'

'Something like that,' he said, not taking his eyes off her.

'As long as you don't slot my column next to some dreadful right-wing piece about capital punishment or fox-hunting.'

Comhairle Contae County Council

Dun Laoghaire Rathdown Libraries
Dalkey

Customer name: Allen, Helena
Customer ID: **********9664

Items that you have borrowed

Title: A good enough mother / Bev Thomas.
ID: DLR26000008049
Due: Wednesday 8 September 2021

Title: After the fire / Jo Spain.
ID: DLR26000015747
Due: Wednesday 8 September 2021

Title: The last kiss goodbye / Tasmina Perry.
ID: DLR20000249409
Due: Wednesday 8 September 2021

Title: You were gone / Tim Weaver.
ID: DLR25000012006
Due: Wednesday 8 September 2021

Total items: 4
18/08/2021 15:20
Borrow 4
Overdue: 0
Hold requests: 0
Ready for collection: 0

hank you for using the SelfCheck System.

'And perhaps I'll only think about recommissioning you if you stop being so bloody sharp with me.'

'Girl Guide's honour,' she said, trying to shift the conversation on to more light-hearted ground.

She felt the mood shift.

'Don't tell me *you* were a Girl Guide?' he smiled, pausing to light a cigarette.

'Why not? It's a positive social programme based on military principles. Chairman Mao would approve,' she said more knowingly.

'He wouldn't approve of you marching into church carrying the Union Jack every Sunday.'

'Well, I was exempted from all that church parade nonsense.'

Dominic nodded. 'Of course, you free-thinkers view religion as the opium of the masses.'

'Opiate,' she corrected. 'It's not that, though. My dad's Jewish, and my parents made a pact to observe customs from both religions once they had children. So we have Hanukkah and Christmas, Sunday lunch and a Sabbath dinner. In fact it feels weird being in a pub on a Friday night and not at home eating chicken soup and challah.'

'Even stranger that you're with a man you publicly attacked barely a week ago.'

She allowed herself a smile, and folded up her feature and put it in her bag.

'I reread your piece on Indian repatriation. It was interesting.'

'Is that an apology?' he smiled.

'Let's just say I don't generally share *Capital* magazine's views, but I was a little hasty with my protest the other day, yes.'

She looked at him and it was as if his grey eyes were dancing. They were certainly teasing her. Men like Dominic Blake were clearly used to women fawning over them, and she didn't want to be so obvious. But she couldn't deny that she liked this man.

'How long have you been involved with the DAG?'

'Two years in June. How long have you been editing *Capital*?'

'Six years. Since I raised the finance and launched it.'

'You *own* it?' she said with surprise.

'A slice of it. I had to borrow money to set it up, and when you do that, you have to give away your baby. But I always say it's better to fund a business with other people's money.'

'Well the DAG is a purely self-funded organisation,' she quipped, trying to impress him. 'We don't want to lose control of what we're doing.'

Dominic smiled at her. 'You don't have to. Not if you're clever.'

'I'll ignore the implication of that comment,' said Ros tartly.

Aware that things were not going well, she decided to keep quiet for a few moments and hear what he had to say, not her default setting by any stretch, but Dominic Blake, with his easy confidence and wit, made it easy for someone to sit back and listen to him.

He was not, it transpired, the editor of *Capital* any longer, but the more grandly titled editor in chief, handing over the more hands-on work to his former features editor Robert Webb. This apparently allowed him to spend more time schmoozing advertisers, keeping his backers happy, and doing what he actually loved most about journalism – writing. Plus he was able to do more travelling. He wasn't a tourist, but an adventurer, he explained as he told her about trips to the Bolivian salt flats and the African plains.

'Ever since I was a little boy I have always wanted to be a writer. But the problem with your passion being your job is that you need another hobby. Everyone needs something in their life that's not work, and for me that thing is travel. Not just Paris or Rome, but the bigger, undiscovered places. I love the excitement of the fresh and the new.'

He made it all sound so fabulous and exciting that Ros suddenly imagined herself on a boat, exploring some remote Pacific island, a warm breeze in her hair, the sun on her face and Dominic Blake handing her a cold beer at her side. She stamped out the image as quickly as it appeared and cleared her throat.

'I haven't travelled much,' she admitted. 'My parents came over from Hungary when I was three and we only ever went to Brighton after that. But I would love to travel the world.' Just saying the words out loud made her horizons feel very narrow indeed.

'What's stopping you?' asked Dominic.

'Money,' she said simply. 'Working for the DAG has meant sacrifice.'

'Then I'll have to send you somewhere.'

'Me?'

'You strike me as the sort of woman who'd just get on the elephant.'

For a split second she wondered if he was flirting with her; the idea both horrified and thrilled her.

'I should be going.'

'Don't be daft, it's not even ten.'

'I've had a really busy day,' she said, not allowing herself to be persuaded.

'Then hop in the car. We'll be back in thirty seconds.'

She looked at him, wondering if he was glad to wrap this up quickly, whether he was just being kind saying it was only ten o'clock. After all, he had put his coat on pretty quickly and was ushering her out of the pub before she even had the chance to be honest and say that she wanted to drag the night out as long as possible.

The barmaid called across before they were at the door; Ros didn't miss Dominic turning around and giving her a dazzling smile.

Outside, the temperature had dropped at least five degrees since their arrival. Ros pulled up the collar of her coat and started to walk.

'What are you doing?' asked Dominic, holding his car keys.

'Honestly, it's not far.'

'But it's freezing out here.'

'Speaks the man who's been to the North Pole,' she grinned.

He caught up with her and their strides fell into step with one another.

'I thought you were never going to ring,' he said finally. 'What changed your mind about writing for me?'

'The excitement of the fresh and the new,' she said quietly.

She glanced across but couldn't read his expression: amusement, disappointment? She didn't know what she had been expected to say.

She felt her teeth chatter and stopped to button up her coat, even though Sam's house was within sight.

'Here. Take this,' said Dominic, removing his scarf and putting it around her neck.

She tried to stop him but he just grinned.

'See. It suits you better than it suits me.'

She gave a soft snort and turned away from him, ready to start walking again. He touched her arm to stop her and she felt herself flinch.

'You know, it's not a crime to let people be nice to you.'

She focused her eyes towards the ground, afraid that under the bright sodium of the street light he would be able to see inside her. Would be able to see the truth: that Rosamund Bailey did not have many friends, certainly not any boyfriends. Her few short-lived flings had all ended due to some version of the same reason: that she was too shouty, too angry, too much, and as a result she had built a wall so thick around herself that it was almost impenetrable.

'Thank you for tonight. I didn't really want to be alone on my first night in London.'

'What are friends for?' he said as he walked her to the door.

'Goodbye, Dominic,' she said, folding her arms in front of her.

'Good night, Ros.' He smiled, then turned back towards his car.

She watched him go, his walk turning into a trot, the tails of his Crombie flapping in the wind, and when he didn't look back, she felt a sense of panic in the pit of her stomach, a sickening, thudding realisation that she might never see him again unless she did something that very second.

'Another night out?' she shouted suddenly after him.

He turned back, and she could just see his face, smiling in the dark.

'What did you say?' he yelled, his words echoing in the space between them.

'What are friends for? They're there for more nights out,' she said, her heart hammering.

'What did you have in mind?' he said, moving a few steps back towards her.

'How about the Rosamund Bailey guided blue plaque walk on Sunday?'

'You're on,' he shouted, giving her a thumbs-up.

'Excellent,' she whispered, and let herself into the house.

Chapter Ten

'Remind me who these people are again,' said Ros, looking up at the tall white stuccoed house in front of them, and smoothing down the red cocktail dress that she had borrowed from Sam.

'Friends from university and assorted others,' replied Dominic, tucking a bottle of champagne under his arm as he trotted up the stone steps towards the front door.

'Rabid Tories, you mean,' muttered Ros, wishing she weren't meeting *all* of Dominic's friends in one intimidating go.

Dominic paused before he rang the doorbell.

'Ros, I wish you'd stop insulting everyone who doesn't share your political views.'

'So what does he do, then? This Jonathon Soames.'

'He works in Whitehall.'

'There you go. A rabid Tory.'

He turned around and looked at her. 'So my friends are a little more conventional than yours. We've lived shallow, sheltered lives of little meaning. But they are generally very nice, so don't start badgering them to hand over the means of production to the proletariat, or whatever it was that Marx and Engels said. This is a dinner party. For my friend's birthday. I'm just asking that you don't turn things into a political debate.'

Ros smiled mischievously. 'I thought that was what every good dinner party needed. Lively conversation.'

'Not all-out war,' grinned Dominic, finally pressing the bell.

The door swung open, spilling warm light and the chatter of conversation on to the street.

'Blakey, old chap!' cried the man in the blue shirt and tie who stood there. 'So glad you could come.' He pumped Dominic's hand enthusiastically, then switched his gaze to Rosamund. 'And who is this, may I ask?'

'Jonathon Soames,' said Dominic, 'may I present Miss Rosamund Bailey?'

'Good to meet you, finally,' Jonathon smiled.

Rosamund felt a vague sense of triumphant excitement at being talked about. She didn't want to put too much meaning into the fact that Dominic had mentioned her to his friends, but secretly it thrilled her. In the six weeks since their night at the Primrose Hill pub, they had seen each other a handful of times, although they'd spoken on the phone almost every day.

Their afternoon walking the streets of London on Rosamund's blue plaque tour had been magical. They had lost interest in plaque-spotting sometime after John Logie Baird, and instead had got lost in a six-hour conversation that had covered their views on love and life.

At one point, Dominic had held her hand to cross the street, but instead of keeping hold of him, she had let go to scratch her leg, not because it was particularly itchy but because she had been so nervous and afraid that he would let go first. Looking back, as Rosamund had done many times since, she suspected it had been a turning point in their fledgling relationship. Were it not for that fateful scratch, the night could, she dared to dream, have concluded in a kiss in some dark, sultry corner of London.

Instead they had settled into a comfortable, combative friendship that made Ros think of what it must be like to have a particularly clever and confident brother. She tried to ignore the giddiness she felt whenever the phone rang at the Primrose Hill house, or the way her heart sometimes flipped when he smiled at her. But she was self-aware enough to know that Dominic Blake was out of her league, and that even if a drunken night out did lead to something romantic, it would be a fleeting involvement, a diversion before he moved on to a more exotic and beautiful woman, that wouldn't be worth the heartbreaking consequences. No, it was better this way. They were better as friends.

'No one's wearing a cocktail dress,' she whispered from the hallway, as she glanced into the house.

'I've got one under my jacket,' said Dom distractedly as he accepted a glass of champagne from a butler.

'I'm not joking. I feel overdressed,' she hissed, wishing she was wearing something plainer than Sam's Hardy Amies gown.

He turned his full attention back towards her.

'You look beautiful.'

He rested his hand on the small of her back and led her into a wide, stylish living space, where a dozen or so people were standing around drinking wine and talking loudly. There was modern jazz playing on the record player in the corner, and the butler circulated with a bottle of Pol Roger held in a crisp white linen napkin, topping up glasses.

'Everyone,' called Jonathon over the soothing noise, 'you all know Dom – obviously – but this is Rosamund. Be nice to her, hmm?'

'I love these paintings,' said Rosamund, indicating the bold graphic artwork on the wall.

'Roy Lichtenstein,' Jonathon said simply. 'Most people hate them. My mother threatens to send them to the tip every time she sees them. But I'm quite excited about the pop art coming out of New York. Time will tell if I've made a good investment or whether my mother was right.'

A sexy brunette approached, wearing a pencil skirt and a tight jumper that clung to her curves. Ros felt like a gaudy Christmas decoration next to her.

'So you're Rosamund?' she said in a husky voice that suited her. 'What a pretty name. Where did you find her, Dominic?'

'In the street, shouting insults,' said Dominic with a smile. 'Rosamund, this is Clara Barrett, she's an old friend from . . . Where did we meet, Clar?'

'At Bunty Willoughby's twenty-first, of course. Surely you couldn't forget that night?'

As Jonathon led Dominic away to view his latest artistic acquisitions, Clara continued to quiz Ros.

'So. How long have you been seeing Dominic?'

'He's just a friend. I work for *Capital*.'

'Ooh. A clever girl.'

Ros smiled thinly.

'I remember now,' continued Clara. 'You're the one writing those controversial think pieces.'

'I was brought on board to bring alternative viewpoints to the magazine, yes. Dominic likes to call me his polemic-in-chief.'

'Dominic is very good at making people feel special,' Clara said pointedly.

'So where do you stand on the nuclear question?' asked Ros, desperately casting around for something to say.

'The nuclear question?' Clara giggled.

'The United States' Polaris missiles have arrived on British soil. You must have read about it?'

'Oh darling, I try not to think about that sort of thing too much,' said Clara, waving her wine glass airily. 'I mean, if the

95

Russkies are going to drop a bomb on my flat, I'm not going to know about it until it's too late, am I? So why waste time worrying?'

Ros looked at her, not quite believing how someone could be so flippant about something so important. She was considering telling her about the Committee of 100's sit-in that was due to take place in Parliament Square that week when Jonathon clapped his hands to summon them for dinner.

'If you'd all like to follow me through to the dining room . . . I promise I haven't cooked any of it myself.'

The dining room was a smaller version of the living room, but the table was large enough to seat the dozen dinner guests, and it had been laid with white linen and silver.

'Boy, girl, boy, girl,' called Jonathon as they all filed in looking for a seat. 'You know the rules.'

'I didn't know you were so strict, Jonny,' quipped a red-cheeked man named Neville, to much laughter.

Dominic ended up sandwiched between Clara and Michaela, Jonathon's rather mousy girlfriend, while Rosamund found herself at the far end between the host and an art-dealing friend called Zander, who seemed intent on impressing his knowledge of abstract impressionism on everyone.

Jonathon, on the other hand, was more down to earth, despite his obvious riches. He told her that he and Dominic had met at Cambridge and had been friends ever since. They went pheasant shooting every Boxing Day, cycled together every fortnight and were currently working their way around the pubs of England that had the word 'cricketers' in the title. He told her that not only was Dominic the most social creature he knew, but also the most solitary. How he loved to travel by himself. How he had grieved alone after the death of his father, retreating to a remote woodland cottage belonging to the Soames family for over a month before returning to London.

The picture he painted was of a complex and contradictory individual, and to Ros, that made Dominic even more appealing.

'So, Dom, I hear you're heading out on another of your splendid adventures,' said Zander as coffee was served.

'Where's it to be this time?' smiled Jonathon. 'Borneo? Tierra del Fuego?'

Dominic smiled. 'Jonny, I know for a fact that you haven't the faintest idea where either of those places are.'

'Well *I* don't need to know where they are,' said Jonathon. 'You're the one who's going to get lost.'

'Fair enough,' smiled Dominic. 'I'm heading back to the Amazon, actually.'

'How thrilling,' said Michaela. 'Is it terribly dangerous?'

'Only if I forget my shotgun.'

The girl gave a little gasp, and Rosamund glanced over.

'What's the game this time, Dom?' asked Neville. 'I mean, why go all that way? Sounds damned uncomfortable for a start, riding on donkeys and rickety aeroplanes, and that's without all the snakes and the scorpions in your boots.'

'I suppose I like to see what's out there.'

'Well I think you're bally mad,' said Jonathon. 'All the gold in Shangri-La couldn't drag me there.'

'I think you mean El Dorado, and that's all very well for you to say when you've already got a vault like Aladdin's cave over at Coutts.'

'You're only jealous of Dom's daring,' purred Clara.

'I know it may seem crazy,' Dominic said. 'But there are still huge parts of the globe that have never been mapped – not accurately, anyway. Even somewhere as developed as America is so large that there are hundreds of miles of desert that no man has ever walked across. And the Amazon jungle is so dense it's almost impossible to penetrate, let alone say with any certainty what's hidden in there.'

'Do you think you'll find El Dorado?' asked Michaela breathlessly, directing her full gaze in Dominic's direction. 'Is it really there?'

'No, I don't think so,' smiled Dominic. 'I don't think it ever was. I think the first Westerners to South America misinterpreted local legends and rituals as fact because they wanted them to be true. However, the secret city of Paititi could very well be real.'

'Paititi?' asked Jonathon, looking more interested.

'It's a mythical lost Inca city. Stories from around the sixteenth and seventeenth centuries talk about a jungle settlement in the Amazon full of gold and silver.'

'I love Dominic's stories,' said Michaela. 'Last time he was here, he was telling us about the lost Fabergé eggs.'

'Dominic is actually going to liberate the oppressed peasants, aren't you?' said Zander with a wink.

'Really, old man?' said Neville, his brow furrowed. 'You haven't gone pinko on us, have you?'

'Actually, Zander is right,' piped up Ros, eager to join in the conversation. 'Dom believes that the native Indians are being exploited and that they should be left alone. Isn't that right?'

Dominic pulled a face. 'Yes, to an extent, but—'

'You were absolutely right when you said that they are relatively ignorant of international trade – large-scale commerce of any kind, actually – and there's a danger that their resources are going to be exploited by others,' continued Ros.

'And you think that's a bad thing?' asked Neville from his seat opposite her. She had learnt earlier that Neville's family had made their fortune in imports, historically sugar and oil. But in the fifteen years since the end of the war, they had lost almost all of it through the redrawing of borders, new interests in the

Middle East and, most importantly, the sudden feeling in many places that, frankly, they were better off exploiting their own sugar and oil.

'What about British companies like Moran Timber who are operating in the Amazon? Do you think we should force them out?'

'Ros wasn't saying that,' said Dominic quickly.

Neville didn't look placated. 'Principles are one thing, but not at the expense of British commerce. We're struggling enough abroad as it is.'

'But those resources belong to the people of Brazil and Peru,' said Ros, taking another sip of wine.

'No they don't,' scoffed Neville. 'They were bought fair and square by Western companies, who, by the way, are providing jobs for these so-called locals.'

Ros and Neville both looked at Dominic for support.

'What do you think, Dommy?' asked Clara, taking the role of provocateur.

Dominic shrugged diplomatically. 'I think that native people should benefit from their own land, their own crops, but letting them self-govern is perhaps a fast route to corruption and I don't think you'd be doing them a favour. You'd be throwing them to the lions of capitalism. And they're not ready. Not yet.'

Neville grunted his approval as Clara leant forward, her finger tracing the edge of her wine glass.

'And what do you believe, Rosamund? Capitalism or communism?'

Ros glanced at her, realising that her sudden interest in politics was simply for show.

'I think socialism is the only sane choice,' she said haughtily.

Silence fell on the room.

'Socialism?' said Zander finally, as if he were addressing

a child. 'But my dear, we have just finished fighting a war against it.'

'The Nazis were socialist in name only. We were fighting against totalitarianism. Hitler was a dictator. Whatever he said went, however terrible, or you would find yourself up against a wall. The Allies were fighting for the very opposite of that: self-government. Pure and simple.'

'Isn't self-government just a polite way of saying "give everything to the workers"?' laughed Zander.

'Not at all,' said Rosamund. 'Self-government is democracy, the ability to choose how your country is run. What's wrong with that?'

'You're saying you'd allow a lot of lazy, illiterate Peruvian peasants to run their own country?' laughed Neville. 'They'd never become a developed nation, no matter how rich they are in natural resources.'

'I think what Rosamund is trying to say—' began Dominic, but she cut him off with an angry shake of her head.

'I am perfectly capable of expressing myself,' she said.

'Oh, we can see that,' said Clara, rolling her eyes.

'Why shouldn't I be?' snapped Rosamund. 'If I'm able to form an opinion, it's because I am the product of the liberal school system in this country, which says that every child is entitled to an education regardless of background or sex.'

'Goody, at least we've brought sex into it,' smiled Clara.

'Why not? Aren't you glad we have the vote, Clara?'

'I certainly don't think we should go around burning our bras.'

'Oh, I don't think that's such a bad thing,' said Zander, his voice dripping with lechery.

'Shut up, Zander!' said Clara and Dominic simultaneously.

'All right, all right,' said Jonathon, standing up. 'No more politics, please. Let's all retire to the lounge and have another drink, hmm?'

'I should go,' said Ros through gritted teeth as she accepted a cup of coffee from the butler.

'Don't be silly.'

'I want to go,' she said more curtly.

She asked the housekeeper for her coat, whilst Dominic went to make their excuses. Ros gave a genuinely fond farewell to Jonathon – she had liked him – but the others didn't seem too upset to see her go. Outside, she and Dom stood in silence on the pavement.

'Go back in if you want to,' she said, wondering how far they were from the tube.

Dominic still didn't say anything, but she wasn't going to let him make her feel guilty.

'Well, do *you* think that went well?' she asked, hovering by the door of his car, unsure he was even going to offer her a lift.

He let out a long breath. 'Perhaps not the sparkling success I'd hoped, no.'

'We might have got on better if your stupid friends didn't insist on sticking to the ignorant, reactionary opinions of their parents,' replied Ros.

'Don't blame it on my friends,' said Dominic, looking suddenly annoyed. '*Or* their parents.'

Ros huffed.

'It was only a dinner party, Ros. There was no need to get so hostile or mock my friends or call them stupid.'

'I wasn't mocking them. I was trying to correct them.'

'*Correct* them?'

He gave a slight shake of the head, and Ros knew that she had crossed a line.

'Ros, why do people with such fervent views as yourself assume that any political position that isn't exactly the same as theirs is somehow flawed?'

'Because it is!' said Rosamund.

'Is it? And I suppose your dreamy principles are completely watertight? Do you really think that the socialist states in Russia and Cuba are these glorious idylls free from greed and self-interest? I know you care deeply about what is going on in Vietnam and the Congo. But by your own admission, you haven't been further east than Margate.'

'I was born in Hungary, Dominic. I've seen first hand what flawed politics can do,' she said, hating him at that very moment.

Another silence.

'I'm going,' she said finally, buttoning up her coat.

'Let me drive you home.'

'I'm not going home.'

'Where are you going?' he asked, his face clouding with concern.

'I'm going to the office.'

He glanced at his watch and smiled, the passing tension apparently over. 'It's nine thirty at night.'

'I won't stay long. I just have to catch up on a few things.'

'At this time?'

'We're going on a protest march tomorrow,' she explained.

'What are you planning on saving this time?'

'Stop making fun of me,' she said angrily.

'I'm not. I am genuinely interested in your work.'

She exhaled, a little cloud of breath mushrooming in the cool night air. 'All right then. We're protesting about the legalisation of betting shops.'

'The legalisation of betting shops?' he said, smiling.

Ros glared at him. 'I know how much you like a game of

blackjack, but this is sucking people who can't afford it into gambling.'

They both got in the car and Ros rested her elbow on the edge of the window, turning away from him and gazing out.

They drove in silence, South Kensington, then Knightsbridge slipping by, until they came to Piccadilly. Green Park was like a big gaping hole on their right. The car seemed tiny and vulnerable next to the red buses zooming past.

'I'm sorry you didn't enjoy yourself,' said Dom as he turned the Stag in to Soho. 'They should have been more welcoming to you, especially Neville.'

'I liked Jonathon and Michaela. The others . . . I think we were just not a very good social match.'

'If I'm totally honest, I thought you were going to shake up what might otherwise have been a bloody dull dinner party.'

'Ah, let's bring the pet tiger along for entertainment. No wonder you invited me.' As with everything she said to Dominic Blake, her words came out sharper and more sarcastically than intended.

'That's not it,' said Dominic more softly. 'I brought you because I think you're smart and funny and interesting and I wanted my friends to see all that too.'

'Oh really?' Rosamund met his gaze in a challenge. 'And why's that?'

'Because I like you,' he said simply.

'The office is just here,' she said, pointing towards the tired block on Brewer Street. 'Don't park up. You might be tempted to go to Raymond's Revue,' she added, nodding in the direction of the famous strip bar.

'You really think I'd do that?' laughed Dominic.

'You're a single guy . . .'

Dom stopped the car.

'So which one is the famous DAG office?'

'The penthouse,' she grinned.

He touched her on the sleeve before she got out of the car.

'Do you want to go to Ronnie Scott's next week?'

'Only if it's me and you, Professor Higgins,' she said rather daringly.

'I think that can be arranged.'

She hated leaving him like this, wished the evening had gone better.

'Friends again?' she said, extending her hand.

'Friends,' he smiled, and she stepped out on to the pavement.

Chapter Eleven

The stairs of the rickety old building creaked as she went up them. Remembering her outburst at the dinner party, she felt like the mad woman returning to her attic.

Why was she here? she asked herself, reliving Jonathon's soirée with each slow and steady step. Why hadn't she just grabbed Dominic by the collar and kissed him on the lips, which was precisely what she had wanted to do ever since that night in Primrose Hill when he had turned around and smiled at her.

It was at that moment that she realised the full force of her feelings for Dominic Blake. It wasn't that he was good-looking, or charming, or even her editor at an important and talked-about magazine; she did not want to admit to herself that she was so predictable. But here was someone who had bothered to look past her temper and her opinions and seen something to like. And she liked him. She liked him so much, she sometimes couldn't sleep at night for thinking about him. She imagined what it would be like to kiss him, to wake up next to him in his bed, to hear him say, I love you, Rosamund Bailey.

But that was the stuff of dreams, of fantasy. She hadn't kissed him, she never would. And the way she was sometimes so rude to him, so deliberately difficult, it was little short of miraculous that he hadn't stopped returning her calls.

Her steps slowed to a stop when she reached the door of the DAG office on the top floor, and she sighed as she fumbled around for her key.

She had hoped, secretly hoped, that the night might have ended somewhere more romantic. On Albert Bridge, holding hands at midnight, perhaps. But no. It was ten o'clock and here she was back at work, preparing for a protest march for an issue she cared very little about. Nor was she sure that the small rally outside the proposed site of a tote shop on Bethnal Green Road would make any difference to the gambling habits of the nation anyway.

She slotted the key into the lock but the door was already open.

Ros frowned. Ever since Sam's revelation about her relationship with Brian, she had been nervous about finding the two of them in a compromising situation in the office, and someone was certainly in there now. She crept inside and peered around.

The light was so low that she had to squint, and besides, the room was so full of files and boxes, it was difficult to make out exactly who or what was in here.

After a moment, she heard the flush of the loo at the back of the office and Brian came out of the cubicle zipping up his flies.

'Brian, you scared the living daylights out of me,' she laughed, holding her hand to her chest.

'It's only me,' he said, coming quickly back to his desk at the far side of the office. Two filing cabinets and a stack of books and boxes acted as a natural barrier between him and Ros.

'What are you doing here at this time?' she asked, moving towards him.

'I could wonder the same about you,' he replied, his words prickly and defensive.

She was immediately on edge. Brian had walked past his desk and was in her personal space.

'Where's Sam tonight?'

'Visiting her parents in Hampshire. She'll be back in time for the demo tomorrow.'

Ros already knew this but she'd wanted to test him.

'What are you doing?' she asked, craning her neck so she could see his desk.

'I was just typing out some literature.'

Ros nodded, her eyes subtly searching the room. On the face of it, there was nothing suspicious about what he was saying, but something was making her instincts bristle.

'Let's have a read.' She didn't miss him flinching.

'I'll show you when I've finished.'

'Come on, Brian, let's have a look.' She tried to get past him.

'Don't go over there,' he said, deliberately blocking her way.

'Why not?'

'Because it's private.'

'Brian, what the hell is going on?' she asked, her eyes darting around, her ears searching for noise.

She had heard stories from sleepy suburbia about postmen hiding in wardrobes, lovers being ushered out of back doors to avoid detection. She thought of those stories and felt instantly nervous for Sam.

'Just leave me alone. I'm only working.'

'Then why won't you let me see your desk?'

'Because there's nothing to see.'

'Now you've really made me want to have a look.' She laughed nervously.

'Piss off, Ros,' he hissed.

'Let me through, Brian,' she said, trying to squeeze around him.

He pushed her with such force that she tumbled back, her legs buckling under her, her head smashing against a table as she fell.

She cried out in pain and drew her hand to her skull, holding it there for a moment as she felt her palm grow wet and warm.

She could hear footsteps running up the stairs.

All she could do was moan, and then she felt a pair of strong arms lift her back to her feet. She sighed in relief when she saw Dominic.

'Ros, are you okay?' he said, holding her tightly for a second.

Brian tried to push past them and make a run for it, but Dominic stopped him. Brian swung a feeble punch; Dom grabbed his fist and twisted his arm until it was bent back behind his body.

'What the hell is going on?' he asked.

'The desk,' croaked Ros. 'He's hiding something.'

She staggered towards it, the pain in her head still throbbing like a heartbeat.

At first she saw nothing suspicious.

There was a roll of insulating tape on the desk, a large box of nails and a thick brown envelope. She picked it up and looked at the address label. She recognised the name instantly – a prominent Tory MP, known for his war-mongering ideals.

Peering inside the envelope, she saw that it was full of nails.

'Put it down,' growled Brian.

There was something else on the desk. Two sticks that looked like wax candles.

'Don't touch that,' shouted Dominic urgently as Ros reached towards them.

She dropped the envelope and a shower of nails fell out on to the floor.

'Brian, what's going on?' she asked, feeling increasingly panicked.

'Get off me,' he shouted, and charged forward like a dog on a leash, his chest pushed out, a bluish vein protruding on his forehead. Dom had to restrain him with both hands.

'What is going on?' Ros screamed.

'Two years we've spent doing this, Ros. Two years. And what notice have people taken of anything we have done? None.' Brian's teeth were bared, and there was spittle dripping from the corner of his mouth.

'What is that on the desk?' she asked, her voice shaking with panic.

'Gelignite,' replied Dominic quickly. 'Tell her, Brian. Tell Ros what you're doing here so late at night. You're making a parcel bomb, aren't you?'

'People need to take notice,' hissed Brian, his eyes angry and unrepentant.

'And you're prepared to kill to make yourself heard?' Dom applied more pressure to his restraint. He glanced at Ros, and she could tell by the look in his eyes that he was praying she knew nothing about this.

'I didn't know,' she whispered.

'We need to call the police,' said Dominic after a moment.

'The police?' she repeated, feeling panic swell in her throat. She started to sob. 'But they'll close down the group.'

'Where's the nearest phone?' asked Dom, his voice calm and clear.

'There's one in the hall by the front door, but I think we've been cut off.'

'Then find a phone box and call this number,' he said, reciting some digits.

She grabbed a pen, her hands shaking as she wrote down the number.

'Who should I speak to?'

'My friend will answer. Tell him I asked you to call. Give him this address and come back as quickly as you can, you understand me?'

Ros nodded, and headed out of the office.

She ran down the stairs, taking them two at a time, almost stumbling on her kitten heels.

The hall phone *was* out of order – she couldn't recall paying any bill for a very long time – but she knew there was a phone box fifty yards away on Brewer Street. She ran out of the front door and down the street, the lights of Soho passing by in tear-blurred stripes of red and hot pink.

She called Dom's friend. The conversation was short. She had no idea who he was, but he seemed to understand what was being asked of him with brisk efficiency.

When she returned to the DAG office, Brian was gone. She could hear banging sounds coming from inside the toilet. Dominic was rubbing his hand.

'Have you locked him in there?' she asked, noticing that there was a chair pushed up against the door.

Dom nodded.

'I bet he went in there willingly,' she said grimly. 'You've torn your jacket,' she added, touching a seam that had come apart.

He shrugged and pulled a cigarette packet from his pocket.

'I think I need one of those,' said Ros.

He lit one for her and then put one in his own mouth, getting a light from the glowing end of Ros's.

'Who's your friend?'

'Not the police,' replied Dominic quickly.

He wasn't looking at her and she couldn't detect any emotion in his voice.

'I was wrong to say not to call them. I was just scared. I don't care if the group has to be shut down. Brian is dangerous and he has to be stopped.'

Dominic turned his full gaze on her in the soft light.

'I don't care about the Direct Action Group or about Brian, but I care about you,' he said finally. 'If the police get involved, you will be investigated. Probably arrested and even charged.'

It was a possibility that Ros hadn't considered.

'But I've done nothing. I knew nothing about this.'

'In your line of business, I expect you've been in trouble with the police before,' he said quietly.

'There was a police caution last year . . .'

She didn't need to finish her sentence.

'We should let my friend deal with it.'

There was a noise at the door. Ros turned and saw two men in dark overcoats coming in. Dominic seemed to recognise them immediately and asked her to go and wait on the street while he spoke to them.

She nodded and went to sit in the doorway of the building. She stubbed her cigarette out on the pavement and closed her eyes.

A parcel bomb, she thought with a shudder.

It wasn't possible. Brian was angry at the establishment. Angry about everything if truth be told. But she hadn't suspected for one moment that he had been radicalised. That he was capable of hurting – of *killing* – someone for his beliefs.

She shivered in the cold and pulled her collar around her neck. The cut on her head was throbbing and she wished she had some aspirin to quash the pain.

Finally she heard footsteps behind her.

Standing up, she turned round, and as Dominic extended his arms, she allowed herself to be enveloped by them.

She closed her eyes, feeling safe, as if everything for that one moment was all right.

'I didn't know,' she whispered.

'I know,' he said, and she felt his arms squeeze her just a little more tightly.

'Your head is cut,' he said, pulling back in concern.

'It's okay,' she shrugged.

'We should go back to mine, it's only round the corner. We'll have a look at it, clean it up. You might even need a stitch in there.'

'I'm not going to hospital.' She flinched.

'You might not have to,' he said, putting his arm tenderly around her shoulder.

His flat on Tavistock Square was just a few minutes' drive away.

It had a red front door, and they went up a flight of stairs to the first-floor apartment.

She wasn't sure what she had been expecting, but it was a small space. A thin hall led to a square living room with a long window that looked on to the square. As Dominic switched on a lamp, she looked around, absorbing the details of the room, the details of the way he lived his life. There was a bookcase stuffed with novels, an olive-green sofa, pictures of far-flung places – deserts, jungle and mountains – lining the walls. The largest piece of furniture was a desk that stretched the length of the window.

There was a typewriter on the desk, together with a stack of *Capital* magazines and a pen pot. The place was sparse and ordered, a home that did not feel very lived in.

A small drinks trolley sat in the corner of the room. Dominic poured them each a whisky, then disappeared to the bathroom, returning with a wet flannel and a bottle of iodine.

'Stay still,' he said quietly as he stood behind her.

She could feel his breath on her neck, then the cold flannel on her crown and the iodine starting to sting.

'Who were those men?' she asked after a moment. 'The men that came to the office. Who were they if they weren't the police?'

'You don't want to know.'

'I do.' She winced as Dominic applied more iodine.

'They deal with problems.'

'Legally?' asked Ros with a jolt of concern.

'Yes, legally.'

'So they're Special Branch?' she said, feeling curious.

'Not exactly, but they're friends of mine and I trust them. They will know how to deal with Brian.'

'It was a good job you came up to the office,' she said finally.

'Yes, it was.'

'Why *did* you come?'

'I didn't want the night to end as it did,' he said, and she felt herself shiver.

'What am I going to tell Sam?'

'The truth.'

'I still can't believe it. I still can't believe Brian would want to do a thing like that.'

'I guess you never really know someone. Not truly.'

'I'm not the person you think either,' she said, turning round.

Dominic put the flannel on the desk.

'Oh yes?' he said, moving closer.

'You've been so nice to me, and yet sometimes I'm a bitch to you.'

He gave a low, slow laugh. She liked his laugh. It was one of the many things she loved about him.

'I don't know why I do it. I don't blame you for wanting to have nothing to do with me.'

He took another step towards her. They were so close now they were sharing the same air.

'Ros, I knew you were trouble from the moment I heard the words "fire Dominic Blake" drifting through my office window. I've given this a great deal of thought, and to be honest, I think there's only one way to shut you up . . .'

He tipped her chin up with his fingertips and then he kissed her, and it wasn't the bump on her head or the trauma of the evening that made her feel weak and delirious. And as she kissed him back, tasting him, feeling his soft lips against hers, Ros knew with absolute certainty that Dominic Blake was the love of her life.

Chapter Twelve

London, present day

The days after the exhibition went past in a blur. The press reviews had been sensational, not least Elliot Hall's piece in the *Chronicle* entitled 'The Last Goodbye: why the new RCI exhibition restores your faith in humanity', and Abby had been fielding calls asking for tickets, prints, even private views ever since. Just the day before, Christine Vey herself had called with the news that RCI membership had tripled literally overnight, and in return, Abby had told her that the limited-edition print run of *The Last Goodbye*, as she was now calling the photograph of Ros and Dominic, had entirely sold out.

She clicked on an email – another request for a copy of *The Last Goodbye* – and was just typing back her regrets when her phone started to ring.

She looked at it, forcing herself to wait before she picked it up. She had been anticipating a call from Nick since the exhibition, as she knew he read the *Chronicle* – at least he had done, when they were still together.

'Abby. It's Stephen. Can you just pop through a minute?'

Glancing at the clock, she hung up and walked across the basement to Stephen's little cubicle. If she left in five minutes and caught the first tube, she'd be at Piccadilly in plenty of time. Relax, she told herself, as she tapped on Stephen's door frame.

'Ah, Abby, come in,' he said. 'Take a seat.'

'You do remember I'm on a half-day today?' she said as she perched on a small fold-up chair; there wasn't really room for anything more in the cramped cubbyhole.

'Of course, don't worry,' said Stephen. 'This won't take long.'

'Now then,' he said, sipping his tea. 'I want you to know that we have been very pleased with your work here.'

She knew there was little room for promotion at the Institute, but a bonus would be very welcome right now. Nick was still paying money into their joint account, but with an uncertain financial outlook, any sort of cash injection would be appreciated.

'The exhibition has been a roaring success and Christine wanted me to pass on how impressed she was with its execution – and of course you were a part of that success, Abigail.'

'Thank you,' said Abby, feeling genuinely flattered.

'We're all very excited that the archive is showing it can be a commercial force as well as an important cultural resource,' continued Stephen, putting down his china cup.

'As you know, Christine is a very modern thinker. Her vision is that the archive should be a global resource available online, like AP or Getty. Genius. Absolute genius. Of course, future exhibitions are vital for marketing such a plan.'

Abby nodded politely, although she did have some reservations about their director's vision. Christine Vey had never so much as set foot in the archive, and probably imagined it as some sort of high-tech mechanised warehouse instead of a dingy cellar crammed full of cardboard boxes. Still, she was glad that people had recognised its potential.

'So is she going to allocate more funds to us?' she asked hopefully. 'If we had a newer scanner, maybe Photoshop, it would certainly help . . .'

Stephen dropped his eyes to his desk and the mood suddenly shifted.

'There's the rub,' he said finally. 'Our budgets are finite and we have to look at ways in which we can economise. Economise to expand, as it were.'

'Economise?' repeated Abby. They had so few tea bags in the kitchen, she had started to bring in her own.

Stephen shifted uncomfortably in his chair.

'Abby, an online archive of saleable prints represents the future of this Institute. But until we can make that work, really work, we don't need two senior full-time archivists. Christine thinks one person can oversee the archives and handle exhibitions, possibly with the help of someone junior. Then we need someone with real digital experience who can sort out the launch of a website.'

'I can do all of those things,' said Abby quickly. 'Okay, I haven't got much online experience, but the exhibition was a success, I'm a quick learner and I have lots more ideas . . .'

'Abby, you're keen. We both know that. It's probably why I gave you so much autonomy with the show. Too much, perhaps. It was naïve to put a limit on the prints. You know we can't extend the print run after we have sold them as limited editions, and Christine is particularly disappointed that we can't squeeze any more out of *The Last Goodbye*. The way my phone has been ringing off the hook, we could have sold ten thousand of them. But no. We had a ceiling of seventy-five and that has cost us.'

'But you agreed everything, Stephen,' said Abby, starting to fret. 'Numbered prints meant we could charge more for them . . .'

'Abby. I've done all I can to protect your position, but Christine insists that I take a more hands-on role, and I agree with her.'

Abby shook her head. The truth was that he was protecting his own position. She thought of Stephen's day-to-day work life. Swanning around the library, taking long lunches, hiding in his office reading back issues of the RCI magazine. There was no place for that sort of role any more, and he knew it.

'So I'm fired,' she said, disguising the panic in her voice.

'Fired? No, no, no. You're on a freelance contract. We just need to take another look at it. I've fought to keep you on for two days a week, and Christine has agreed to it. At least until the digital side is up and running.'

He looked at her sympathetically.

'Abby, I know this is disappointing for you, but we have to think about the future of the archive.'

'Clearly,' said Abby bleakly.

'Good,' said Stephen, obviously relieved that it had all gone so smoothly. 'Then that's settled. Why don't you get off early today, hmm?'

'I have the afternoon off anyway.'

'Of course, I was forgetting. Are you going somewhere nice? A long weekend?'

She stood up slowly.

'I'm going to see a divorce lawyer.'

Stephen's face fell.

'I see. Well, I hope it all . . . goes the way you want.'

'I can't imagine it will,' said Abby and walked out of the office.

Donovan's solicitors was a more modern-looking outfit than she had imagined.

She had met Anna outside dozens of times, but had never

gone into the building. She announced herself at reception, and within a few moments she was introduced to one Graham Kelly. Abby had not had a great deal of experience of solicitors beyond the many legal dramas she had seen on television. She imagined Graham playing rugby and hanging on Jeremy Clarkson's every word. She didn't suppose he was more than thirty, which was definitely a good thing. She knew that experienced solicitors meant expensive solicitors. She'd already broached this point gently with Matt, who had reassured her that an associate at the firm would do as good a job as he could.

'Come through,' said Graham, leading her down the corridor to his office.

'Are Anna or Matt around?' said Abby, hoping that seeing a friendly face might make her feel less anxious.

'Anna's in court, I think, and Matt is in a meeting. I'll give his secretary a call, though, and let him know you're here. Tea?'

'No. No thank you,' said Abby, taking a seat in front of his desk.

There was a buff-coloured file on the desk with the words Gordon/Separation written in bold ink at the top. She'd heard about things staring you in the face in black and white, but seeing the file made everything feel horribly real.

'So. Matt has given me an outline of your situation.'

'I want a divorce,' said Abby, ditching the mental script she had written for herself on the way here.

'Okay,' he said, sipping from his glass of water. 'I believe you are currently separated from your husband.'

Abby nodded, trying to keep her cool. 'I asked him to leave. Well, I didn't actually ask. I just sort of threw him out seven weeks ago. He had an affair. Sex. And now I would like a divorce.'

She expected him to pass judgement, to try and talk her out of it, but he just sat there writing everything down.

'How long have you been married?'

'Almost six years exactly.'

'Children?'

'None.'

'Do you work?'

'Yes. No. Sort of. I lost my job today,' she said sadly.

Graham continued writing in his yellow notebook.

'What is your husband's position?'

'He works. He has an IT consultancy business.'

'Assets?' asked Graham, beginning to sound like a robot.

'We have a house with a mortgage. It's in joint names. There's some savings. Not much, although to be honest, I have no idea how much Nick has in his personal account. His business is doing pretty well, actually, so I imagine he might have quite a bit.'

'How long has he had the business?'

'He set it up a few months after we got married.'

'Good.'

'Good?'

Graham looked up from his frantic scribbling. 'It means you'll have a strong claim there.'

She felt a knot of guilt at that one. The business Nick had worked so hard to build up. *The business that took him away from home so often. That took him to hotel rooms in the path of temptation . . .*

'Once we get the ball rolling, you will have to fill out some paperwork known as the Form E. We can work out the assets from there. Meanwhile, I believe you're in the family home.'

Abby nodded. 'I assume I can stay there.'

She thought of their Wimbledon terrace. They'd not had the

money to kit it out with anything more extravagant than IKEA furniture, but they had made it into a lovely, stylish place and it was tied up with so many memories. Happy memories if you discounted that final, high-octane showdown. An image of a Dune shoe flying – being hurled – down the stairs at her husband sprang instantly to mind, and she tried to blot it out as quickly as it came.

'You can stay there for now,' Graham said flatly. 'At some point, matrimonial homes may have to be sold, particularly when there are no children involved. I haven't established what your husband's financial position is, but perhaps you could buy out his share . . .'

Abby didn't care about the money. She just wanted this to be as painless as possible. She closed her eyes tightly at the thought of losing the house. Then again, she wasn't sure she wanted to stay somewhere that represented her life with Nick. Their marriage.

'I think we are looking at a fairly straightforward fifty-fifty division of assets. And provided your husband doesn't contest the divorce, it shouldn't take too long.'

'How long do you think?' she gulped.

'To decree nisi? Fifteen, sixteen weeks. Decree absolute another month after that.'

'So I'll be divorced by Christmas.'

She felt her hands shake and a wave of nausea pool in her throat.

'Would you like some water?'

'No, no. I'm fine,' she muttered, wondering if she had let out a moan.

'Divorce can be a very traumatic experience,' said Graham softly. 'Especially when you are the, uh, injured party, shall we say?'

'*Can* be traumatic?' said Abby, challenging him. 'Isn't it always?'

'I think it can be something of a relief in some cases. Not everyone has a good marriage, and sometimes divorce is the first thing a couple have agreed on in years.'

He sat back in his chair and put down his pen.

'You know, at this stage it's sometimes helpful to attempt a reconciliation before we get too far down the line.'

'Is that what's in the file? A key card to Babington House?'

She regretted her sarcasm when Graham looked confused.

'I assume you've spoken to Nick. He thinks we should try counselling.'

'Nick is not my client, Abby. I deal with his solicitor. But regardless of what most people think about lawyers, we're not out to ruin lives and screw everyone for money. If you can sort this out, get things back on track and that's what you both genuinely want . . . Well, I certainly think it's something you should try.'

'Do you mind if we stop there?' asked Abby, feeling emotional.

She looked at the clock behind him and puffed out her cheeks. She knew from Anna that lawyers didn't just work by the hour. Every ten-minute unit was clocked and billed. Time was money. It had taken her six weeks to decide against any sort of marriage counselling or mediation. She didn't want it to cost her another hundred quid to confirm that decision to her lawyer.

'How about I call at the end of the week?' said Graham. 'Give you a chance to mull everything over. Look, there's Matt. He'll want to say hello.'

She looked behind her and saw a tall, familiar figure waving from the other side of the window.

She picked up her bag, shook Graham's hand and left his office.

'Hello, stranger,' said Matt, giving her shoulders a reassuring squeeze. She hoped he hadn't noticed that she was shaking. 'Everything okay in there?'

'I think you should maybe offer vodka instead of tea,' she replied, glad to see his friendly face.

'Temazepam rather than biscuits . . .'

'Bring it up at your next board meeting,' she smiled, trying to keep the situation light.

'You'll get through it,' he said, reminding Abby that Matt wasn't just a divorce lawyer. He had been divorced too. A messy, emotional affair, according to Anna. A difficult wife who'd had an affair and walked out taking their young son with her. It had almost destroyed him, and yet Matt was now happy and about to marry Anna.

They were almost at reception when they heard a commotion at the front desk. A woman a little younger than Abby was struggling with a buggy and a small boy.

'Abby, this is an ex-colleague of ours, Sid Travers. She comes back to see us occasionally. Sid, this is Abby, a friend of mine and Anna's.'

'Matt. Phone,' called a PA.

'Abby, Sid, I'll see you later.' He waved regretfully.

The young woman was clearly harassed. The toddler in the buggy had started crying and the young boy was tugging desperately at her skirt.

'Can I help?' asked Abby.

'It's fine,' said Sid. 'He just wants to get out.'

She unclicked his harness and the toddler wriggled out of the buggy.

'Mummy, I need the toilet.'

'In a minute, Charlie,' she said to the older child.

'I need it now.'

The toddler was starting to sprint towards the other end of the corridor.

'Shit,' whispered Sid. 'Ollie, come back here.'

'Mummy, I need the toilet now.'

'I'll get him,' said Abby, setting off after the child. 'Bloody hell. He's like Usain Bolt.'

As she scooped him up, she couldn't resist pulling him close. She felt a soft wash of maternal instinct flood over her and started to smile.

'You cheeky thing,' she whispered.

A piercing scream ripped into her ear. She held the little boy away from her. He was red in the face, his tiny features scrunched up in pain.

'What's wrong, poppet?' she gasped before realising that the clasp on her bracelet had scored a long red scratch down his plump little arm.

'Come here,' said Sid, taking the child from her.

'I think my bracelet must have caught him,' Abby stuttered.

'It's okay,' Sid replied briskly.

Abby had no idea if she really meant it.

'I'm so sorry.'

'It's fine, honestly,' said Sid less sharply.

Abby felt hot and her breath had grown ragged.

'I should go,' she muttered, but Sid was so busy fussing over her child that she didn't even notice.

She stabbed the button to the lift, but when it didn't come immediately, she took the fire exit. As she emerged on to the street, her dress felt tight around her neck. She sank down on some stone steps next to the office, emotion rising in her throat and spilling out in loud sobs.

For such a long time she'd felt numb, as if her emotions had shut down completely and she was just existing on autopilot. But looking back at the time and effort she had thrown into work, into the exhibition, Abby knew that she had simply been keeping a lid on a simmering pot.

A suited man glanced at her uncomfortably before walking on. A second passer-by, a woman about her own age, stopped and asked awkwardly if everything was all right.

'Just getting divorced,' laughed Abby almost hysterically. The girl nodded with embarrassment and smiled weakly before moving on.

Abby's tears shuddered to a stop and she looked down at her trembling hands, her eyes drawn to the simple gold band on her finger. She had removed her engagement ring weeks ago; it was a symbol of the heady excitement and possibility of the early days of their relationship, and clearly, whatever magic that had held had been used up long ago. But the wedding band felt different, like it was part of her, something she had built and invested in, and even though her marriage had failed, that ring had still been important to her.

Her fingers touched the metal of the band. She twisted it around for a few moments and then removed it, putting it in the zip pocket of her handbag.

'I should go,' she told herself out loud, wiping her eyes with the back of her hand.

She heard a muffled sound coming from her bag, and for a moment she thought it was her wedding ring, come to life and struggling to get out. Realising it was her phone, she pulled it out and pressed answer.

'Hello?' she sniffed, trying to disguise the distress in her voice.

'Is that Abby? It's Elliot. Elliot Hall.'

'Elliot. How are you?' she said with surprise.

'Pleased that my journalism skills have managed to track you down.'

'What do you want?

She winced, realising how rude that sounded.

'We could start with lunch,' he replied, and suddenly Abby started to feel a little bit better.

Chapter Thirteen

'I just want to say how thrilled we were with your piece in the *Chronicle*,' said Abby, allowing a waiter to place a napkin on her lap with one fluid flick of the wrist. 'I think Stephen wrote to thank you properly.'

'He did. Much rather it had come from you, though,' smiled Elliot, taking a sip of the expensive wine he had ordered.

Abby smiled nervously. She still didn't know whether it was one of her better ideas agreeing to come to lunch with Elliot Hall. A solid morning of internet snooping, unfortunately carried out after she had agreed to meet him at London's fashionable and impossible-to-get-into Pont restaurant, had revealed that her lunch companion was a terrible womaniser. An interview in *Harper's* profiling London's '40 most beautiful under 40' had referred to him as 'the Don Juan of the Dorchester', and the endless Google Images snaps of him with his arm around pretty girls, and a Facebook page littered with photographs of parties and mini-breaks, each apparently attended with women more beautiful, tanned and skinny than Abby would ever be, had confirmed that they might have a point.

'How did you get a table here at such short notice?' she asked, looking around the room and recognising at least three celebrities.

'Special number,' he smiled as he filled her glass with water. 'Now, I suggest you try the linguine. They melt aged Parmesan over it, then grate truffles on the top. Literally the best starter I have ever had. I don't like to have it too often, though, in case it spoils it, so I keep this place for special occasions.'

'Right, yes,' said Abby nervously. From the moment she had arrived, she had tried to be as professional as possible, shaking hands rather than kissing him on the cheek, steering all conversation back to the exhibition. A little voice in her head was telling her to relax. That it was about time she had some fun with someone interesting and clever.

But the fanciness of the restaurant and the price tag of the wine was making this feel suspiciously like a date, something Abby hadn't been on for a long time with anyone other than Nick, and the whole thing was making her feel as jumpy as a box of frogs.

They ordered, and Abby told herself that it was only lunch. One she hoped to God Elliot was picking up the bill for, otherwise she was going to have to sell all her worldly goods at the next local car boot sale in order to pay for it.

'Well, I'm flavour of the week with my editor,' said Elliot, handing his menu back to the waiter. 'I think he's even ordered a copy of *The Last Goodbye* for his wife, although I hope there's no hidden meaning in the gesture. It's been rumoured for months that he's having an affair with someone in ad sales.'

He smiled again, his orthodontically perfect teeth reminding Abby that not all men were created equal.

'So what's the next big exhibition I can look forward to?' he said, meeting her gaze and not letting go. 'You're a brilliant curator. I get invited to a lot of these things, and Great British Explorers was the best I've seen in ages.'

'I wish everyone agreed with you,' sighed Abby, grateful for his words.

Elliot frowned. 'What's wrong?'

She was desperate to offload her problems, and Elliot Hall seemed like the sort of capable, can-do person who would know what to do about them.

She told him about the scene in Stephen's office and about how Christine Vey seemed to think the RCI could manage quite well without her.

She expected him to be sympathetic, but his expression was bullish.

'Well, let her,' he said, as their starters were placed before them. 'You're overqualified for that job, Abby. You're experienced, commercial, you're hot.'

She wasn't sure in what context he had used that last word, but it still gave her a little thrill.

'The RCI exhibition was a high-profile hit,' he continued. 'Now's the time for you to go out and find yourself another job, take the next step up. You might have to sit tight for a few months until the right opportunity comes along, but this is a blessing in disguise, I'm telling you.'

Abby looked at him. She knew that other people were looking at him too, women especially. Elliot had that star wattage that made people stare, and she felt uncomfortable just sitting in his glow.

'It doesn't work like that. Not for me. I separated from my husband recently. I have bills to pay, overheads, so I hate the insecurity of not being in work.'

'I'm sorry to hear that.'

Abby shrugged.

'I don't have the luxury of taking a few months out to con-sider my future, though I might not have any choice. The kinds of jobs I'm looking for, that I'm qualified for, are few and far between, and when people get in, they tend to stay there for life.'

'I'm sure my father knows a few dealers, gallerists . . .'

She appreciated the gesture, although she wasn't sure she was the type to get recruited by the fancy-pants galleries around Hoxton or Mayfair, no matter who had recommended her. She didn't have the right accent, the clipped RP vowels, and although she had often been complimented on her prettiness, she knew her looks were of the quiet, unremarkable sort. That her tidy brown hair and small hazel eyes were a far cry from the oddly beautiful girls with their choppy haircuts and Helmut Lang trouser suits or the blonde Sloaney show ponies who worked in the city's top galleries.

'Thanks for the offer,' she smiled. 'Truth is, I've really enjoyed working at the archives. Okay, it's like living in a cave sometimes, but I like digging out dusty old photos, bringing them into the light and finding the stories behind them.'

'Then why don't you come and work for me?' said Elliot bluntly.

'Sorry?' She felt her face flush with embarrassment and looked into her drink.

'Me. I could do with a researcher,' he repeated.

'Your researcher?' she laughed incredulously.

He flashed her a half-smile and she felt a little more confident.

'Actually, I think you'd be perfect. You're obviously good at finding interesting stuff. You'd just bring it to me and I can work on an angle, then you can help me fine-tune the details as the story unfolds.'

She allowed herself to consider it for a while, imagining herself as a glamorous newshound striding through a buzzing newspaper office, getting important phone calls from shadowy contacts and writing wild exposés that would make the front pages of papers the world over.

'So what are you working on at the moment?' she asked tentatively.

'See? I can tell you like the idea,' said Elliot, putting down his fork.

Abby laughed.

'Well,' he said more cautiously. 'This week I've been looking into the mysterious world of Dominic Blake.'

She felt her bubble of good mood pop, but Elliot didn't seem to notice.

'You know how much my editor loved the *Last Goodbye* story. Well, he asked me to have a poke around.'

'Elliot, you know how unhappy Rosamund Bailey was about it.'

'Rosamund is a dignified, probably too cynical old lady who doesn't want her private life splashed over the newspapers, and I can understand that. But it's Blake I'm interested in. His story is fascinating. I've only had a quick dig around, but there's a possibility he may not have died of natural causes.'

'What do you mean? Murdered?' she asked, aghast.

'It's pure speculation at this point, but I've been looking into his background. We know he was an explorer, of course, but that's not all he was known for back in 1961. I pulled some files down in the paper's cuttings library, and his name pops up again and again in the society gossip columns.'

'A man after your own heart,' she smiled.

'Cheeky. Anyway, reading between the lines, it appears he was squiring a lot of socialites and heiresses around town, possibly some of whom were already married.'

Abby couldn't believe he had found all this out in such a short space of time.

'And what? You think a jealous husband got to him?'

Elliot lifted his glass and smiled.

'Doubtful. Blake disappeared in the Amazon jungle, remember? That's a long way from Mayfair. I imagine the cuckolded Earl of Whatnot would have preferred to run him over crossing Piccadilly or something.'

Abby grimaced. 'So why do you think his affairs are relevant to his disappearance?'

'Well, ladies like that, married or not, they're not going to be a cheap date, are they? Expensive restaurants, hotel rooms, little gifts, it's all going to mount up. Our hero wasn't from money – he went to Cambridge on a scholarship, his father was a middle-ranking career soldier turned grocer after the war – but for his lifestyle, he seemed to need an awful lot of it. For a start, he's listed as the co-founder of *Capital* magazine. Setting up a magazine isn't cheap. My family knows that better than anyone. His expeditions, his playboy lifestyle. It doesn't add up.'

'And you have a theory . . .'

'Drugs,' he said bluntly.

'Drugs?'

'Blake spent a lot of time in South America – Bolivia, Colombia, Peru – just at the time when drug trafficking was exploding in the area. They were clearing huge swathes of the rainforest for cash crops – it was just that some had a higher cash value than others.'

She looked at him wide-eyed.

'You think Dominic Blake was involved with drug-running?'

'It would explain why he kept going back to that part of the world, and remember, it would have been much more straightforward to walk through an airport with drugs in those days. It was easy money really.'

Abby frowned, then shook her head.

'It just seems . . . wrong. It doesn't seem to fit.'

Elliot shrugged. 'Maybe. All I'm saying is we can't get carried away by the romance of that photo. The facts are that Dominic Blake was living the high life with no visible means of support. That money had to be coming from somewhere. And he was spending a lot of time going back and forth between Peru and Colombia and London.'

'And this is the story you want to write?' said Abby, feeling herself bristle. 'That Dominic Blake was a drug dealer?'

'No, that's not what I'm saying. The story I want to write is how and why Dominic Blake disappeared. And to know that we have to know a bit more about him. Because the answer to his death is right there in his life.'

She had to admit that what he was saying made sense.

'The answer could be something as simple as getting lost and sick in the jungle.'

'Perhaps,' he said, settling back into his chair.

'I can't get involved in this, Elliot. I feel as if I know Rosamund now.'

'Imagine you are Rosamund Bailey,' said Elliot slowly. 'You're old, you're wise, but you never knew what happened to the love of your life. Wouldn't you want to find out? Wouldn't you want someone younger, more dynamic, someone with twenty-first-century technology, resources and money to help you find out the one thing that has eluded you, tormented you, for fifty years?'

'Elliot, you should be on the stage,' she replied more playfully.

'I'm serious, Abby,' he said.

'All right,' she said, 'I'll do it.' As she spoke, she felt a rush of excitement, and something else – an unfamiliar sense of freedom, of abandon even. She hadn't done anything impulsive for years. It felt good.

'Excellent,' said Elliot, offering her his hand. She took it, and felt a current of complicity run between them.

'Welcome aboard, partner. You won't regret it.'

Chapter Fourteen

It was a fine morning as Abby walked up the hill, the sunlight slanting through the trees to her right, laying zebra stripes of shadow across the graveyard behind the railings. All she knew about Highgate Cemetery was that Karl Marx was buried there, but it looked overgrown and abandoned, with headstones leaning at crazy angles and the odd ivy-trailed angel peeping out from the undergrowth.

Don't think I'd want to walk through there at night, she thought, crossing the road. And I wouldn't want to live over-looking it either. She glanced up at the Victorian flats running at right angles to the graveyard; she supposed they preferred the view of tombs poking out from the trees to that of another building blocking their view of London. And what a view, she thought, turning to look as she reached the crest of the hill. The whole city was laid out there below her, looking surprisingly flat and curiously peaceful from this distance. She supposed that was why Rosamund Bailey had decided to move here. After a lifetime fighting her way through the choked streets of London, this comparatively sleepy backwater would seem like the countryside.

Catching her breath, Abby crossed the cute little square in front of her and walked up to the first house on the left, knocking on the red front door.

She wasn't exactly looking forward to this – she wasn't a naturally confident person – but if she was going to start this new career as a researcher, she needed to jump in at the deep end. She was raising her hand to knock again when the door swung open.

'Abby,' said Rosamund, beckoning her inside. 'Come in, come in.'

She was led along a dark corridor towards the back of the house, where it opened on to a large kitchen.

'Take a seat,' said Rosamund, gesturing to the rustic table. 'I was just making tea, and there's some cake as well if you fancy it. Not home-made, but I have my book group coming round this evening, and they get very tetchy if there are no carbohydrates on offer.'

Abby almost sat on the cat that was curled up on the chair. It sprang off with an angry meow.

'Harold, shoo.'

'Lovely, thank you,' she said, sitting down.

She rummaged in her tote bag and pulled out a large hard-backed envelope.

'The photograph,' she said with embarrassment. 'It's not an official one so you can't sell it or anything. But it will go nicely in a frame.'

'I won't sell it,' Rosamund said, putting a hand gently on top of the envelope.

She picked up her cup of tea.

'I assume the exhibition did well. I saw the piece in the *Chronicle*.'

Abby was waiting for a caustic remark. Rosamund had got a

name check in Elliot's Great British Explorers article. It had only been a passing mention, but it had gone against her express wishes, and Abby didn't think she was the sort to take it lying down.

'You don't work for the press any more, do you?' she said after a minute.

Rosamund shook her head as she bit into a biscuit. 'I officially retired a few years ago, although I'm still busy. I'm on the board of two charities and do the odd bit of writing, although the editors are all so young these days, no one really remembers me.'

'I saw you on *Newsnight*.'

'Ah, yes,' she smiled. 'Debating ageism in the media.'

'I bet you like keeping busy,' said Abby, looking at the older woman. Her brown eyes were bright and lively and her trim figure belonged to someone who was still active.

Rosamund nodded. 'I think I would go stir-crazy if I wasn't. I don't have family, but I have plenty of friends.'

'Did you ever marry?'

It was a personal question, but it felt like a natural one to ask.

'Almost. A couple of times,' she said frankly. 'As you know, I was engaged to Dominic. There was someone else a few years later. He was a friend, a colleague at the *Observer* who became something more, but my heart wasn't in it. My friends at the time thought I called it off because I didn't believe in marriage. I don't blame them; I was always railing against something when I was younger. The truth was, my heart belonged to Dom and there was never room for anyone else in it.'

She took the photo out of its envelope and went to prop it up on the mantelpiece.

'I suppose Robinson wants a follow-up piece,' she said, looking back at Abby.

'Who's Robinson?'

'Elliot Hall's editor. That's why you're here, I assume.'

'No, I'm here to give you the photograph.'

'I'm sorry. That sounded very ungrateful,' said Rosamund with a soft laugh. 'It's just that my phone has been ringing off the hook about the story. Friends feigning interest in other lines of gossip, but they all got round to it in the end. My relationship with Dominic.'

She came and sat back down.

'People have a fascination with the missing, don't you think? Whether it's Amelia Earhart or Madeleine McCann, these cases intrigue the world. I remember being dispatched to Cambodia in 1970, when Sean Flynn, Errol's son, disappeared covering the war. The story ran and ran and people used to ask me about it at dinner parties for years afterwards.'

Abby pictured a different Rosamund Bailey to the old lady sitting opposite her now; she could quite easily imagine her flying out to war zones, brave and defiant.

'What do you think happened to Dominic?' she said finally.

'Are you helping Mr Hall with a story?'

'Yes,' she replied honestly. 'We thought we might be able to help you find out the truth.'

Rosamund looked sceptical. 'I don't suppose Elliot Hall has such altruistic motives.'

'But I do,' said Abby.

Rosamund's look softened. 'Don't you think I did everything I could?' she said, her voice tinged with sadness. 'I spent two months in Peru trying to find Dominic. When you love someone and they leave you, you do whatever you can to bring them back.'

Abby felt a spike of guilt at her words.

'Your exhibition showed the romance of exploration,' continued Rosamund slowly. 'But let me tell you, there is no romance in that damned place.'

'How far into the jungle did you go with him?' asked Abby.

'On my first visit, when I went to send him off on his expedition, the visit when the photograph was taken, I just went to the fringes. But I went back a second time,' she said, her voice tailing off into the past.

'Dominic went missing two weeks after he set off. At first he used local tribesmen to relay messages back to Kutuba and he had a radio to keep in contact with Miguel, his expedition manager, who was based there. But after ten days, the messages just stopped. Miguel sent a party into the jungle to look for him, but the trail had gone cold.'

She took another sip of her tea and continued her story.

'I hadn't even arrived back in London by this point. Miguel got a message to my hotel in Lima when I was just about to leave for the airport. There was no doubt in my mind that I had to return to Kutuba and go and look for him. I hired a team, a small army really, and I helped them search every day for him.'

'What was it like?' said Abby, trying to picture it.

'It was hell,' said Ros, her eyes glistening. 'Not just the emotional torment, but the physical difficulties. Huge mosquitoes jabbing you day and night, insects burrowing into your skin, clouds of flies that are attracted to moisture and try to land on your eyeballs. There was no real trail, so you have to cut your own with machetes, and it's constantly wet, so there's no chance for your blisters to heal. But you trudge on and on, step by step, sinking into mud, torn by leaves, never being able to see more than about six feet in front of you, hoping that you might find something that will give you an answer, even if it's closure.'

Abby looked at the old lady with awe. She wondered if she herself would ever have done anything like that for Nick. Right now she wasn't even returning his calls, let alone subjecting herself to hostile conditions to save her relationship. Rosamund was describing the incredible things that people did for love. Ultimately her search had turned up nothing, but still Abby felt overcome with emotion.

'So what do you think happened?' she asked softly.

'The most obvious answer is that Dom's canoe overturned. That's fatal on an expedition; your food, equipment gone. He could have lost a boot. Sounds simple, but it can have devastating consequences. Perhaps he fell sick, delirious, and got lost. You can't appreciate the size, the density of virgin jungle unless you have been there. Or he was killed by one of the tribes.'

'Why would they kill him?'

'Because he upset or dishonoured them?' Ros suggested. 'He'd taken a selection of gifts along with him because he knew of those dangers, but perhaps it wasn't enough.'

'And perhaps he didn't die. Perhaps he survived,' said Abby, desperately wanting to say something to make the woman feel better.

Rosamund Bailey looked up, her brown eyes both soft and solemn.

'He died,' she said in a voice so fragile Abby could barely hear it. 'Because if he didn't, that would mean that he didn't come back to find me, and our love was too strong to let me believe that theory.'

Abby shifted in her seat as a thick silence settled around the room.

'Miss Bailey. You say you want closure. Well, this is an opportunity to get that. You are a journalist. You know what can be achieved. I read an interview with you yesterday and it said that you became a writer because of the power of words.'

'You've been reading up on me?' She smiled.

Abby didn't look at her.

'I suppose this investigation will go ahead with or without my cooperation,' said Rosamund finally.

'We want to help you,' said Abby with feeling. 'I don't know him very well, but I would say that Elliot Hall is the tenacious sort, and if anyone can find out what happened to Dominic, it's him.'

'Don't you think I did everything that was humanly possible to find out the truth?' Her voice rose with emotion and tears sparkled in her eyes. 'He's dead, Abby. Dominic is dead. For a long time, I tortured myself with the whys and the hows, but he's gone. It took me a long time to come to terms with that, but I had to, before it drove me insane, and at this point in my life I'm just not sure it's helpful to dredge it all up again.'

Abby's heart was thumping hard. She didn't want to add any more distress to Rosamund Bailey's life, but she didn't believe her when she said she had moved on.

'It's the twenty-first century. We have more resources, more technology at our disposal.'

'And what do you think you can do that I wasn't able to?' Rosamund said more fiercely.

'Perhaps the jungle is easier to navigate these days.'

'Even if it was, I doubt you could find Dominic's trail. We travelled in a dozen different directions from his last known whereabouts and found nothing. Besides, do you really think Elliot Hall is going to go to Peru for the sake of a story? You'd be lucky to get him as far as the Groucho Club.'

Abby cleared her throat.

'I know you have issues with Elliot's father, but Elliot is one of the good guys.'

'Just be careful with him,' said Rosamund more kindly.

Abby glanced up and noted the woman's look of maternal concern.

'Oh no, no. It's nothing like that,' she said, waving her hand. 'I separated from my husband just a couple of months ago. Men are the last thing I need right now. My relationship with Elliot Hall is purely professional.'

'That's what we all say, Abby my dear.'

Chapter Fifteen

The taxi drew up to the kerb and the driver nodded towards the open gates and the neat semicircular drive.

'You want me to take you inside?' he asked.

'No, that's fine,' said Abby, leaning forward to hand him three ten-pound notes. 'We'll walk from here.'

She waited as Suze uncoiled herself from the car, wobbling on her five-inch heels.

'Walk?' she hissed. 'I can barely stand.'

Abby slammed the taxi door and grabbed her arm.

'Lean on me until we get to the front door, and I'll remind you next time to wear trainers.'

They paused and looked up at Elliot's impressive home, a large detached white Victorian stucco in Barnes. Stretching in either direction along the road was a line of top-end cars: BMWs, Range Rovers, Mercedes.

'What sort of people are going to be at this party?' asked Suze as they reached the door. 'I thought it'd be Elliot's journalist friends, but the journos I know can barely afford to run a Fiat.'

'I'm guessing Elliot runs in fairly high-society circles.'

'Should we just go to the pub?' she asked, looking away from the house.

It was rare that Suze was intimidated, and it made Abby giggle.

'I thought you wanted to come. "I wonder if Elliot's got any rich mates", remember.'

'That was before I felt like the Little Match Girl standing in the street.'

Abby had to admit that she felt quite anxious too.

'It's rude not to turn up, but I think we just might have to get very, very drunk. We only have to stay an hour, then we can go to the Olympic for some food.'

'By the way, you look amazing tonight,' grinned Suze, looking at the tight little black dress that Abby was wearing. 'Are you sure you don't fancy him? I saw his picture in the paper the other day and he looks like Rupert Penry-Jones.'

'Suze, we've been through this,' replied Abby.

'Then what are we waiting for,' smiled Suze, knocking on the door as if it was the home of an old friend.

'Good evening, ladies,' said Elliot warmly. He was dressed in indigo jeans and a navy cashmere jumper, sleeves pushed up: casual, relaxed, but you still had the feeling that he could run off to interview royalty at the drop of a hat. He looked like a man completely used to such grand surroundings. He stepped forward to kiss Abby's cheek.

'You look great,' he said into her ear.

Abby stepped away from him, smoothing down the black dress self-consciously.

'Thanks for inviting us,' said Suze above the noise. 'What's the occasion?'

'Summer,' smiled Elliot.

They followed him through the double-height hallway

dominated by a wide staircase and a glittering chandelier. Abby was surprised; for some reason, she had imagined Elliot would live in an ultra-modern bachelor pad, all chrome and leather and exposed brickwork, but the house was tastefully decorated in what she assumed was period-correct style, with deep carpets, ornate furniture and oil paintings on the walls.

Abby had lived in London, the so-called global centre of international wealth and commerce, for over a decade, but she had never seen anything like this. She'd heard local couples boasting that their Wimbledon homes were worth well over a million, a sum that would have seemed a dizzying amount when she was growing up on Skye, particularly as they were just south-west London terraces decked out in IKEA and B&Q. So she couldn't begin to imagine the value of Elliot Hall's home.

Suze caught her eye, grinning and mouthing 'nice' behind Elliot's back. He led them through into a large sitting room where around a hundred people were standing holding glasses and chatting over the sound of a young man playing a grand piano at the far end of the room.

'That's my nephew Michael,' said Elliot, following Abby's gaze. 'Just started at the Royal College of Music. He'll play all night for a bottle of wine.'

'So who's single?' asked Suze.

'Suze!' scolded Abby.

'What?' said her friend with a pout. 'Why waste time?'

She turned to Elliot. 'Look, I'm thirty-five, I've just come out of a shitty relationship, and my biological clock has practically stopped ticking, so what's wrong with wanting to cut to the chase?'

Elliot laughed. 'At least you're honest,' he said. 'Remind me to introduce you to my friend Adam. Filthy rich, in property, had a pretty tragic love life that's put him off dating. But I think he might like your direct approach.'

He waved to a handsome man standing behind a makeshift bar. 'Marco, can you rustle up something for the ladies here?' he called. 'Be back in a tick, Abby,' he added, disappearing into the crowd.

Marco was late twenties, dark and brooding, the sort of man you'd expect to see pouting from a Dolce & Gabbana advert.

'What can I do for you, madam?' he said, with a half-smile and a heavy accent.

Abby found herself blushing.

She had dressed up for this evening, had even tried to blow-dry her own hair, and she knew that she looked better than she had done in recent weeks. But Marco was looking at her and Suze as if they were a pair of Greek goddesses blown in on the wind.

'Ask him to make the thing with lime, vodka and angostura bitters,' said a voice behind them. 'I had one ten minutes ago and I'm not sure I'll ever want to drink anything else again.'

Marco nodded, picked up a silver cocktail shaker and spun it around in his palm.

Abby turned to see a man, late thirties, receding hair, but a friendly smile.

'Thanks for the tip.'

'Sorry . . . Will Duncan,' he said, juggling his glass and a plate of canapés before thrusting his hand forward. 'I'm a friend of Elliot's at the *Chronicle*. Well, we sit next to each other – not sure that's the same thing, but . . . anyway. Are you Abby? Elliot's told me all about you.'

'Good or bad?'

'The fact that he's mentioned you at all is tantamount to an engagement in my book, but don't quote me on that.'

Abby chuckled, warming to him immediately.

'Yes, Abby Gordon, hello. This is my friend Suze Donald.'

'Who's here, then?'

'A who's who of London society,' said Will flippantly. He turned and surveyed the room. 'There're a few people from the *Chronicle* by the fireplace. The ones with the red cheeks are Elliot's school friends from Radley mostly. Stockbrokers, lawyers, bankers . . .' He lowered his voice. 'Deathly dull, only ever want to talk about the state of the yen or their new Aston Martin. I'd avoid them if I were you, unless the only alternative is the wives and girlfriends. I'd give them an even wider berth, because they'll almost certainly hate you on sight.'

'Us? Why?' asked Suze.

'Young, gorgeous, invited by Elliot? Are you kidding me? They'd poison your drink if you got close enough.'

He carried on pointing.

'The leggy ones are models, TV presenters or both; the group by the window go sailing with Elliot every summer. And over there you've got Lord Shah, Elliot's dad, and a couple of his mates.'

'How come he invites his dad to his parties?' asked Abby.

Will laughed. 'To keep him sweet, I suppose. After all, he pays for all this.'

Elliot returned and slipped a casual arm across Abby's shoulder. She felt her stomach flutter and avoided the temptation to edge closer to him.

'There's dancing in the Oasis,' he announced.

'The Oasis?'

'The conservatory.'

'You have a conservatory?' asked Abby.

'Posh greenhouse stuck to the back of the kitchen, that's all. There's a DJ in there sweating under the potted palms. I think we should go and support him.'

'Well I'm up for a boogie if I can get rid of these shoes somewhere,' laughed Suze.

Abby danced with Suze and Will until her head began to spin. She saw Elliot standing in the doorway to the kitchen, watching her. Grinning and giddy from the alcohol and music, she went over to talk to him.

'Enjoying yourself?' he asked, still holding her gaze.

She nodded. 'Lost my shoes ages ago, though.'

The corner of his mouth curled upwards, and she felt a prickle of something between them. If she was less drunk, it might have unnerved her, but she was just happy to be relaxed and enjoying the party.

They were interrupted by a tall, silver-haired gentleman in a sharply tailored suit.

'Elliot. What's the chance of you getting out that bottle of fifty-year-old Talisker I know you've got hidden in the basement?'

'Dad, that was a present. From you. You know it's a special release. I'm keeping it as an investment.'

'Go on, crack it open,' the older man chided.

'Sorry, no.'

Andrew Shah snorted with disapproval.

'Abby, meet my father. Dad, this is my friend Abby Gordon.'

'Hello,' said Shah, looking her up and down.

She took a moment to observe him. He looked more like an ageing matinee idol than one of her friend's dads.

'They make Talisker down the road from where I grew up,' she said nervously.

'Skye?'

She nodded, glad to have found some common ground with the wealthy, intimidating man.

'It's why it has such a smoky taste. The ground around Skye is very peaty.'

'I like this one,' said Shah with a wink. 'A girl who knows her whisky.'

He turned his attention to his son.

'Nice piece about the RCI exhibition, by the way. I never knew Rosamund Bailey had such an interesting past.'

'Abby works at the RCI. She found the *Last Goodbye* image in the archive.'

'You get even better.'

'So you know Rosamund?' asked Abby.

'Know her?' huffed Shah, his dark eyes narrowing. 'Bloody woman made my life a misery for the best part of a decade. That column of hers, that left-wing soapbox, well, I was her favourite whipping boy just because I'd made some money and acquired a voice. She tried to trash me. I needed a stable of my own newspapers just to keep my reputation intact.'

Abby knew all about Lord Shah, enough to know that his wasn't exactly a rags-to-riches story. His father had owned a successful advertising company in the 1950s, and although Andrew had started off at the bottom of the Fleet Street pole – obits, quizzes, researching, fact-checking – he'd been able to buy a small chain of local newspapers when his father died and bequeathed him a large windfall.

Family money had given Andrew Shah that first break, but ruthless business smarts helped him convert his initial media portfolio into an empire. When the ailing *Chronicle* came up for sale in the early 1970s, he quickly bought it, turning it around and launching its tabloid sister paper *The Post* five years later.

'Right-wing buffoon, capitalist pig,' said Shah, still muttering to himself. 'They were just some of the things she called me. One week, I'll never forget, she said I'd done more damage to democracy in this country than Mussolini in thirties Italy.'

'Did you sue her?' asked Elliot defensively.

'Only makes a situation worse,' said Shah, shaking his head.

'What I should have done was repeat some of the rumours that were flying around about her in the sixties.'

'Rumours?' asked Abby quickly.

'A whole raft of Fleet Street journalists were under suspicion of being Soviet assets and spies. Rosamund Bailey was one of them.'

Abby looked at him wide-eyed. 'Surely not?'

'Don't be naïve, Abby,' smiled the older man. 'Just because you've met her and liked her doesn't mean to say she's a saint. In my time I've met dictators, criminals, and CEOs who would crush entire companies before breakfast without blinking, and believe me, most of them were perfectly charming company. That's generally how they got to where they were in life.'

He focused his attention back on his son. 'Now then, Elliot. I was just telling Paul that we need more images like that *Last Goodbye* picture in the *Chronicle*. Tug-at-the-heartstrings stuff. I don't know about you, but I'm sick of reading about bad news in the broadsheets. All these so-called news websites are making a killing peddling pictures of cute kittens. See what you can come up with, all right? You too, Miss Gordon. You've clearly got a nose for a story. And persuade my son to crack open the Talisker and we'll see what else we can do to further your career.'

Chapter Sixteen

The thin line of sunlight crept slowly across the floor, up over the bedspread and finally, inch by inch, onto Abby's face. When it reached her eyes, she twitched, flinched, then rolled over, groaning. She tried to block the glare with her pillow, but it was too late: she was awake. Well, conscious anyway. 'Awake' suggested being alert, bright-eyed, ready to meet the day, none of which described Abby at that moment.

'Urrssh,' she hissed through her teeth, pressing the heel of one hand to her temple as she tried to sit up and focus on the room. As she did so, her heart jumped. This was not her bedroom. Not even her house.

'Oh no . . .' she whispered, as a series of images leapt into her mind. Endless cocktails, the fifty-year-old whisky, laughing with Suze, dancing with Elliot, dancing with Andrew Shah. God, dancing on a sofa. And then . . . nothing.

Heart bumping now, Abby quickly examined herself: no, she was fully clothed and there was no sign of Elliot or any other man. In fact, this was a single bed in a cramped space, the classic spare room. Elliot's spare room? The decor seemed to fit with the rest of the house – expensive and elegant-looking – but she couldn't be sure. She couldn't be sure of anything.

Suddenly she was seized with a strong desire to get away. She swung her legs out, then stopped as zigzags of light flashed across her vision, accompanied by a pounding at the front of her skull.

'Ouch,' she whispered.

How many cocktails did I have exactly? she wondered, silently cursing Marco the barman. They had been so delicious, she hadn't been able to refuse when they were placed in front of her.

She pushed herself up, wobbling a little and grabbing for the bedside table. There she noticed a telling detail: someone had put a glass of water next to the bed.

Well it wasn't me, I think we can be sure of *that*, she thought.

Which suggested someone had been looking after her last night. Had it been Elliot, putting her to bed, coaxing her to drink water to offset her hangover? That was somehow worse: the embarrassment of being treated like an invalid.

For a moment Abby felt a stab of disappointment that there hadn't been a drunken lunge – well, none she could remember, anyway. But what if she had thrown herself at Elliot and he had rebuffed her? She squeezed her eyes shut and tried to remember, but she was met by an inky blackness.

'I've got to get out of here,' she muttered to herself, picking up her shoes and inching towards the door.

She reached the corridor and looked around as she tiptoed towards the stairs.

She was definitely at Elliot's – she could tell that now. She recognised the mouldings, the chandeliers and the black-and-white-checked tiled floor in the hall. But how had she got into the spare room, and more importantly, what had happened in there?

She felt sick, and it wasn't just her hangover. Here she was, still a married woman, she reminded herself, creeping around the aftermath of a house party like a randy teenager.

She grabbed the banister and a floorboard creaked loudly.

Elliot came out of a nearby door, rubbing his damp hair with a towel. At least he was fully clothed, she thought, noticing his grey T-shirt and dark jeans. Different clothes from yesterday, she realised with relief.

'Morning,' he said, draping the towel around his neck.

'I was just leaving,' she replied, pointing her thumb towards the front door. 'I apologise for whatever I've done. Whatever state I managed to get myself in to end up in your spare room.'

He gave a slow smile. 'You were a bit the worse for wear.'

Abby looked away in embarrassment.

'How did I end up . . . you know, staying over?'

'I suggested it, you agreed.'

'I did that?' she said soberly.

Elliot laughed.

'What's so funny?'

'You just look so angry with yourself.'

'I am.'

'For ending up in my spare room?'

She couldn't tell if he was flirting with her. She hoped not, and was determined to get rid of any frisson that might be in the air.

'I'm sure most women would be pretty miffed to end up in your spare room, Elliot, but not for the reasons I am,' she said, trying to recover some dignity. 'I should have gone home, I wanted to go home . . . I mean, I came with my friend.'

She looked at Elliot urgently. 'Oh no. What happened to Suze?'

'I think Suze can look after herself. If not, she had Will Duncan to help her.'

'The Will you work with?'

'They left together.'

Abby raised a hand to her mouth.

'Come on. Let's go downstairs,' he said, his words sounding intimate. He touched the small of her back to direct her. 'I'll make some breakfast. Full English and a bloody Mary. That might make you feel better.'

Downstairs, the house had been miraculously transformed back into an elegant living space. Abby wandered through into the conservatory, marvelling at the fact that the dozens of empty bottles had been cleared, the stickiness mopped up from the floor, the cushions on the sofa plumped and put back in place. In fact there was no indication that a party had ever been held there.

'Look at this place,' she said, coming back into the kitchen. 'Have you got cleaning fairies?'

'Sandra must have come in early.'

'Sandra?'

'Housekeeper. She has a key. I warned her I was having a party.'

'I thought you had a secret wife.'

'You'd have known about that,' he said, looking up from the blender.

Something shimmered in the air between them. Abby knew she shouldn't be here, but the thought of a delicious breakfast in this incredible kitchen was irresistible.

'It was a good party. I think,' she said, sitting at the breakfast bar.

'I had no idea you were such an expert at the limbo.'

'The limbo?' said Abby awkwardly.

'Yes, don't you remember?' replied Elliot. 'You stretched Will's tie between the backs of two chairs and organised everyone to join in, shouting "How low can you go?"'

'You're joking . . .'

'I am,' he teased. 'There was no limbo, but there was a spot of Beach Boys-inspired surfing on the couch.'

He put a Bloody Mary in front of her, and for a second she just looked at it.

'Go on, drink up. Hair of the dog is the best thing for you.'

'I never believed that line.'

'Trust me, I'm a journalist.'

The room fell silent.

'So what else can't I remember?'

'Well, my dad was rather taken with you.'

'I hope you don't mean in a sexual way.'

'So do I. But he liked you.'

He caught her gaze again and held it. 'I'm surprised he spilt the beans like that. About Rosamund Bailey.'

Abby sipped her drink slowly. She had never been much of a fan of Bloody Marys – she'd always thought it was like drinking cold soup – but this was a good one. Her stomach was objecting, but she kept swallowing until the glass was empty.

'You know, I think that's why I got so drunk,' she said finally.

'Don't say my dad tried it on with you. His last secretary left the company because she said he pinched her bum. He swears it was just his cufflink that caught her, but it's gone legal.'

'No, not your dad,' said Abby softly. 'What he said about Rosamund. Being a spy.'

Elliot went over to the hob and started frying some bacon.

'It's not a stretch of the imagination, though, is it?' he said, looking over his shoulder. 'Have you read her columns? She's pretty left-wing.'

'But not a commie. Or a spy.'

'Dad didn't know for sure. I pumped him for info when you were sofa-surfing and he said Clive Desmond would know more about it. It pained him to admit he didn't actually know much.'

'Who's Clive Desmond?'

'Editor of the *Chronicle* in the sixties. He only lives in Kew. I think we should go and see him.'

Abby let her silence register her disapproval.

'Abby, this is the gig. If we want to find out what happened to Dominic, then we might have to dig up things that aren't exactly palatable about him and the people around him.'

She agreed he had a point, even though she hated thinking anything bad about Rosamund. She had found the older woman both smart and inspiring on the two occasions they had met. She didn't want to be disappointed by another person in her life.

'You should probably get in touch with him then, if only to prove that your dad was talking whisky-fuelled nonsense.'

'Already have,' replied Elliot, sipping his black coffee. 'I called him this morning. Says we can pop over at midday if it suits us.'

'Us?'

'Come on, Abby. Next best hangover cure after a Bloody Mary is a brisk walk.'

'Elliot, I've got three-inch heels on.'

He walked over to the kitchen door and picked up a battered pair of green Hunter wellies.

'Sandra's,' he said. 'But I'm sure she won't mind you borrowing them for a while. I'll get you one of my jumpers as well. You can put it over your party dress.' He winked. 'That is, unless you want people to know you stayed over.'

'So did you enjoy last night?' asked Elliot as they snaked through the quiet, leafy streets, turning left at Barnes Bridge station and taking the Thames towpath.

'I had fun.' She smiled, enjoying the warm sun on her face. 'You've got a perfect house for parties.'

'It's why I bought it. I have to keep reminding myself that otherwise I might as well be living in a studio in Knightsbridge.'

'I remember one of the reasons we bought our house in Wimbledon was because it was a great entertaining house. I mean, it's tiny compared to your place, but it's got this big kitchen diner and doors that open on to the garden. But we were there three years and never threw one party. It probably won't ever happen now.'

'Not necessarily.'

'I'm not really in the mood for parties.'

'Could have fooled me last night,' he smiled.

'I needed cheering up. It's probably why I drank so much of your posh whisky.'

'No, that was my dad's fault.'

There was a pause.

'Is it amicable?' said Elliot after a moment. 'The divorce?'

'How do you know about that?'

'You told me you were separated. At lunch.' He looked at her as if he had logged every single detail about her.

Abby felt her cheeks colour.

'I'm trying not to think about it, but it's hard. I'm just getting on with things, but every now and then, even when – *especially* when – I'm doing something really mundane like the supermarket shop or walking to work, I just stop and have this sense that things are not the same. That my life isn't right. It feels like a magician has come along – you know, the ones you used to get on TV variety shows – and whipped off the tablecloth, leaving the plates and cutlery in place, leaving everything the same, but actually it's all so very, very different.'

Elliot nodded. 'It is strange. You have this intense relationship with another person. You share the detail of your life with them, you're intimate with each other in every conceivable way, and then, boom, you never see them again. They're gone but you can't get rid of their imprint.'

'Has it happened to you?' she asked. His words seemed heartfelt, like an honest expression of an experience they had shared.

'I was engaged a few years back,' he shrugged. 'And don't look so surprised.'

'What happened?'

'I was stupid. I was unfaithful.'

'Hmm,' said Abby disapprovingly.

'It was a few weeks before the wedding and I felt trapped. She didn't forgive me. Moved back to Argentina. And I regret it. I regret my selfishness, which came back to bite me on the arse because I lost the person who really meant something to me. I would never do it again.'

'Men,' muttered Abby.

'You told me about Nick, last night.'

'He was unfaithful too.'

'I know.'

She didn't want to know what else she had told him last night, so instead she kept quiet and concentrated on the path.

They left Barnes behind and walked through Mortlake towards Kew. Sometimes the path was muddy and overgrown with dandelions and nettles, other times it was smooth and tarmacked. Although she only lived a few miles away, Abby had never done this walk before, and Elliot pointed out some places of interest along the way. The finish point of the Oxford and Cambridge boat race, the National Archives, and Oliver's Island in the middle of the Thames, where rumour had it Cromwell once hid during the Civil War. She enjoyed his knowledge, liked the way he didn't patronise her, but threw comments into the air as an equal and made her feel smart and interesting in the process.

'I love London,' sighed Abby as Kew Gardens came into view.

'Why did you leave Scotland?' He gave her that look again. As if he was studying her.

'I moved down to London after graduation with Nick.'

'Would you ever go home? Skye's a beautiful part of the world. I went climbing once in the Cuillin – it was incredible.'

'It doesn't feel like home any more,' she said, kicking a pebble with her boot. 'My dad died in a motorbike accident when I was a baby, and my mum became a very heavy drinker from that point on. That's how I know a lot about whisky,' she said with a note of irony. 'She got cirrhosis of the liver and died the summer of my A levels.'

'You were brave going to university after that.'

'There didn't seem much alternative,' she shrugged. 'I went back to Portree in the Christmas holidays of my first year, but it seemed strange. I had no other family in Skye, and with Mum not there, I didn't feel as if I belonged. I don't think anywhere feels like home once the people you love have gone.'

They carried on walking in silence. Abby liked the easy companionship between them. It was nice not feeling lonely on a Sunday. The other days she could cope with. Since her separation, she'd worked late at night during the week, and spent her Saturdays shopping, popping into the West End, Westfield or Wimbledon, either on her own or with friends. But Sunday was the day when she felt Nick's absence most keenly. It was the day people spent with their families and lovers. It was the day she had got used to spending on her own.

She glanced at Elliot and felt sure that he was never lonely on Sundays. She wasn't entirely convinced that these were the house-keeper's wellies, and she wondered how many other women had borrowed this cashmere jumper to take a walk along the towpath.

'Here we are,' said Elliot finally, stopping outside a double-fronted villa set back from the river. Clive Desmond's house too reeked of class and money.

'Have you ever met him before?'

'A couple of times. He's a good friend of Dad's, though,' replied Elliot as he banged an impressive brass door knocker.

An elderly woman came to the door and greeted them warmly. She introduced herself to Abby as Connie Desmond and led them both through to a large study that overlooked the back garden of the house.

Clive Desmond looked to be in his mid-eighties. He was wearing blue cords and a pinstriped shirt, and half-moon glasses that seemed to have been fixed halfway down his nose. He peered over the top of them and smiled at Elliot.

'How are you, young man? Heavens, you're the image of your father when we worked together. How is he?'

'Hungover, I dare say. He came round last night and liberated the fifty-year-old malt he got me as a thirtieth birthday present.'

'Ha. That sounds like Andrew,' laughed Clive, easing himself back into his armchair. 'Coffee? Tea? Something a bit stronger? It's the afternoon. Almost.'

They both shook their heads and took a seat on a leather chesterfield opposite.

'You wanted to see if I could help you with something,' said Clive, stroking his chin and looking statesmanlike.

'I'm investigating the death of Dominic Blake.'

'I remember that,' nodded Clive.

'You do?'

'I was deputy news editor of the *Chronicle* at the time. I measure my life in news stories. It was around the time that Connie and I got married.'

'Did you run a story about it?'

160

'It was a long time ago, Elliot. But I doubt it. It was '61, wasn't it? That was a busy year for news, I can tell you, so smaller items got pushed aside for the big international stories. The Cuban Missile Crisis, Bay of Pigs. I didn't know whether to edit copy or stay at home and dig a nuclear bunker.'

'Did you see the photo of him with Rosamund Bailey in last week's *Chronicle*?'

'I did.'

'I was discussing it with Dad and he said there were rumours that Rosamund was a Soviet asset.'

'I can guess where that came from,' smiled Clive, accepting a cup of tea from Connie.

'Office gossip?'

Clive sat back and crossed one leg over the other so that his slipper dangled off the end of his foot. Abby noticed that the air smelt of Earl Grey.

'Back in the sixties, most of the major Russian newspapers were state-controlled. One of the main players, *Soveyemka* published a list of thirty British citizens who they said were Russian spies. It was largely propaganda, but as it was considered incendiary and dangerous, there was a media blackout on the story being published in the UK. We had a visit from a member of the Foreign Office, Jonathon Soames – Lord Soames as he is now – telling us to let it drop.'

Abby looked at Elliot.

'I recognise that name. I was looking at some old society party pictures of Dominic, and Soames was in a couple of them.'

'So you think Dominic got his friend in high places to wade in and protect his girlfriend?' said Elliot.

Desmond shook his head.

'No. *Soveyemka* printed the spy list in 1962, after Dominic's death. And as far as I can remember, Rosamund's name wasn't even on it. But Blake's was.'

Abby looked at him in shock.

'Dominic Blake was listed as a spy?'

Clive shrugged.

'As I said, who knew what was the truth. The Russians wanted us to believe that there were traitors in every sector of our ruling elite. They wanted to destabilise us.'

'So you think Dominic might have turned Rosamund?'

'Or vice versa. If it's true.'

Chapter Seventeen

Abby couldn't find her swimming costume anywhere. She wasn't entirely sure she needed it, but she'd googled the name of the hotel that Elliot had given her and it looked swanky enough to have a pool.

The only thing suitable that she could find in her drawers was a tiny pink bikini she had worn on her honeymoon. There was no way she wanted Elliot Hall to see her in that thing, but knowing that the taxi was due to arrive at any moment, she threw it into her wheelie case anyway.

The doorbell rang and she threw her hands up in frustration. She half zipped up her case and struggled with it down the stairs, losing a bottle of shampoo and her hair straighteners along the way.

She answered the door expecting to see Raj, her local cab driver, then blinked hard.

'Ginny! What on earth are you doing here?'

Her sister-in-law didn't wait to be invited in.

'I sent you three messages this morning and you didn't reply. I was worried about you.'

'Worried about me?' asked Abby in puzzlement. 'What – you thought I'd done something stupid?'

Ginny gave her a withering look.

'Yes – like forgetting our brunch date,' she said, putting the bundle of weekend newspapers she was carrying on the console table in the hall.

Abby felt her shoulders sink.

'Oh Ginny. I'm sorry. My phone's been charging so I didn't hear it. Besides, I've been running around like a lunatic this morning.'

'Well I'm here now,' Ginny said, clapping her hands briskly. 'Come on. Chop, chop. If we leave it much later, we won't get a table. You know how busy the Village gets.'

Abby looked at her sister-in-law and winced in apology.

'I can't come. Something has come up.'

Ginny frowned.

'Really?'

'I'm going to Russia.'

Her friend looked at her as if she had gone totally mad.

'Russia?' she said incredulously.

'St Petersburg.'

'What on earth for? A mini-break?'

Abby didn't miss Ginny's look of disapproval, of suspicion, and she didn't blame her.

'It's work,' she said quickly.

'For the RCI?'

Abby shook her head.

'I have a new job. I'm freelancing for the *Chronicle*.'

'What as? Cultural attaché?'

'I'm doing research for them.'

Ginny didn't need to say anything. The perplexed frown between her brows said it all.

'How on earth did all this happen?' She took a piece of Nicorette gum from her pocket and started chewing it.

Abby waved a hand, not wanting to look her sister-in-law in the eye.

'The *Chronicle* ran that big story on the Great British Explorers exhibition. The editor loved one of the photos so much he wanted me to look into it a bit more.'

'Isn't that a job for one of their journalists?'

'Apparently I'm the expert.'

She hated lying to Ginny, but she didn't want to tell her the truth either.

'So have we got time for a quick coffee?'

'I think the taxi is outside,' said Abby, hearing a car horn and glad of the excuse to leave.

'I'd better push off then,' Ginny said tartly.

'Gin, don't be like this. I'm so sorry I forgot to cancel brunch, sorry you've had a wasted journey over here, but this trip was really last minute and I've been up to here getting my visa sorted, making all my travel arrangements . . .'

'Don't worry about it. I know what it's like.'

'Look, Ginny. You know better than anyone what a shitty few weeks I've had. This is good for me, even if I'm so far out of my comfort zone it's not even funny.'

Ginny came and put her arms around her.

'I know, I know. You take care, okay.'

Abby nodded and prayed that her sister-in-law hadn't seen the contents of her wheelie case spilling out on to the floor: a sliver of pink bikini string, a glimpse of black sparkly T-shirt, a high-heeled shoe.

'Are we still on for starting this Pilates course on Thursday?' said Ginny. 'I thought we could go for dinner afterwards. My treat.'

'That would be nice. I'll email you in the week to make a plan.'

'When are you back?'

'Monday.'

'Great,' said Ginny seeming reassured. 'I'm proud of you, you know that.'

Abby nodded, not feeling especially proud of herself.

Abby sat in the back of the taxi watching the streets of west London slip by and asking herself what the hell she was doing. It had all happened so quickly, and at the time it had seemed to make perfect sense.

No sooner had they left Clive Desmond's home the previous Sunday than Elliot had made an action plan. Abby was to speak to as many of Dominic's friends as a) were alive, b) she could track down, c) were willing to speak to her. Elliot meanwhile was going to look into the more specific allegation of his involvement in espionage.

By Tuesday she had only managed to contact three of Dominic's associates, and that was with the assistance of Andrew Shah. Elliot, meanwhile, had not only tracked down a former employee of *Soveyemka* newspaper, but had arranged a meeting with a KGB colonel. By Wednesday he had flown to St Petersburg; within another twelve hours he had arranged for Abby to fly out to meet him, calling her and telling her the plan in so casual a way that he had made it sound as if they were going to the British Library for the afternoon.

Despite her anxiety, Abby slept for most of the three-and-a-half-hour flight to Pulkovo airport, landing late in the afternoon. Elliot was waiting for her at arrivals, and she almost sighed with relief to see him.

'Remind me what I'm doing here again?' she asked him as he brushed his lips across her cheek to greet her.

'Working,' he smiled, taking her case and leading her to a waiting chauffeured vehicle – a black giant of a car that looked as if it was used to ferry dignitaries around.

He refused to tell her much on the short journey into the city centre, and his semi-paranoid silence made her feel like a spy herself, putting her on edge.

When the skyline of St Petersburg came into view, however, she felt a flutter of energy that was pure excitement rather than nerves. Her gaze trailed the rooftops. The turrets and domes were more beautiful than anything she had ever seen, like something out of a pop-up fairy-tale book.

'Have you been to St Petersburg before?'

She shook her head.

'There's a lot of water,' she said, thinking it looked like a cross between Venice and Amsterdam, even though she hadn't been to either place. She smiled to herself at how you could pick so much up from movies.

'It's coastal for a start,' said Elliot. 'The Gulf of Finland is over there. As well as that, the city is built on about a hundred islands. There are fewer than that today, because some have been linked by bridges, but most of them have got their own individual personalities. Kammeny used to be the island for the ruling elite, so it's full of run-down dachas, the great mansions they built for themselves. Aptekarsky is home to the botanical gardens, Petrogradsky has the universities. In fact the city was called Petrograd for a little while before it was changed to Leningrad after Lenin's death. Some of the islands even have drawbridges that come up at night. We should watch for that if we go exploring.'

The car pulled to a stop.

'And this is where we're staying,' he said, as Abby looked up at the grand white baroque facade in front of her.

'Wow,' she whistled through her teeth.

Inside, the hotel had the quiet grandeur of somewhere very expensive. The atrium was a high, vaulted space with a chandelier the size of a small car, twinkling golden light around the reception. Abby checked in – this instantly reassured her that she and Elliot were not sharing a room, a thought that had crossed her mind on the flight over – and they took the lift to the fourth floor.

She pushed her key card into the lock of room 406 and gasped when she peered inside.

It was a suite, definitely a suite, she thought, clocking the small separate sitting room. She went into the bedroom, where there was a four-poster bed and double doors that opened to a balcony with views across the city. A silvery thoroughfare headed to the north, busy with traffic. Either side of the road she could see gorgeous medieval buildings, the Arabic influence evident in the pillars and carvings.

She heard the door of the suite close behind her, and out of the corner of her eye she could see Elliot standing in the doorway of the bedroom.

'This is amazing,' she laughed, trying to dissipate her awkwardness. 'It's like a palace. I'm amazed the *Chronicle* let you put this through on expenses. Things are obviously better than they are at the RCI.'

'Back in the glory days I could have stayed somewhere like this,' said Elliot. 'Nowadays we'd be lucky to be in the local Travelodge, so I thought I'd sub the trip before I put you off journalism completely.'

She kicked off her shoes and almost moaned as her feet sank into the carpet, then scooped up a fluffy robe and held it to her face; it was as soft as cashmere. 'Can we live here?' she grinned. 'I love it.'

He smiled as if he was enjoying watching her.

'I'm not sure even my dad's expense account stretches to that. Besides which, we're here to work, remember?'

She felt a knot of disappointment and the intimate mood seemed to shatter.

They went through to the sitting room, where there was a bottle of water and two tumblers. Elliot poured them both a glass, then sat back in one of the chairs. She watched him, how relaxed and confident he was, and thought how utterly bonkers it was her being here. She had known him barely two weeks and here they were in a city that quite clearly had romantic connotations. Even if it was for work.

'So who have you spoken to?'

'I met Jonathon Soames for lunch yesterday.' She said it as casually as she could, but she still couldn't believe she had pulled it off, even though Elliot himself had greased the wheels, getting his father to secure the meeting through his contacts at the House of Lords.

'How was it?'

'I was nervous as hell. I've never interviewed anyone before, but I just told myself to see it as two people having a chat.'

'Good,' smiled Elliot with approval. Abby felt herself blushing. She sipped her water as she told him about the events of the previous day, part of her not wanting to relive the minutiae of the encounter, wondering if she would reveal some terrible faux pas. Yet another part of her felt a bubble of pride that she was desperate to share.

She had almost laughed as she arrived at the entrance of Wiltons restaurant on Jermyn Street, amusing herself with the thought that she'd waited thirty-one years to meet a lord, and now two of them had come along in one week.

Knowing that her lunch date was Lord Soames, she probably shouldn't have called him Sir Jonathon for the first twenty minutes of the conversation, after which he was gracious enough to insist that she call him Jonny.

She had liked him immediately. Unlike the po-faced portraits of world leaders and military dignitaries that lined the walls of the restaurant, Jonathon Soames was good-natured, putting her at immediate ease with the skill of someone who'd had a long career in the upper echelons of government.

They'd discussed the history of the restaurant, the subject matter of his latest non-fiction book – a biography of the explorer Ferdinand Magellan – and Abby's work at the RCI. He confirmed he had been a good friend of Dominic Blake's and had been particularly interested, intrigued, to learn of Abby's recent acquaintance with Rosamund Bailey, asking all sorts of questions about her welfare and whereabouts that she could barely answer.

He was a little more sombre when the subject turned to Dominic, but still spoke of him with warm, if slightly sad nostalgia.

It had taken her the best part of the lunch to ask him the question that really mattered, and her heart had been thumping so hard she'd thought the maître d' was going to pull her to one side and ask her to quieten down. In the end she had decided there was no easy way to broach it and had just blurted it out.

Jonathon hadn't denied arranging the media blackout to stop coverage of the *Soveyemka* spy story. 'Not just for Dominic, but for our country,' he had noted quite passionately.

Nor did he deny the rumours that Dominic could have been spying for the Russians. She remembered what he'd said almost word for word, remembered the sadness on his face as he discussed it with her.

'To this day, no one knows with any certainty who was and who was not spying for the Russians,' he'd told her. 'One thing's for sure, the sixties was a very volatile time. Everyone was an idealist and the KGB were masters of recruitment. You only have to look at the Cambridge spies: Kim Philby was hands-down the most successful spy in history. He was head of MI6's counter-espionage division, privy to the secrets known by the Secret Service, the CIA and the FBI, yet all the time he was passing everything on to Moscow. Do you really think he was the only one?'

'What did Soames say about the specific allegation about Dominic?' asked Elliot in a natural pause in her recollections.

'He said he thought it was possible, but highly unlikely. He said he'd known Dominic since Dom's first day at university and they were as close as brothers. Not only did he never see anything to suggest that Dominic was working for the Russians, but he just wasn't the sort.'

'Who knows who has it in them to be a traitor?' replied Elliot cynically.

'I think he meant that Dominic wasn't that sort of political idealist.'

'*Capital* was a political magazine.'

'Jonathon said that Dominic was interested in politics insofar as it got people talking about his magazine. But he just didn't have the political zeal of someone like Ros. Apparently he was a *terrible* gossip, couldn't keep a secret to save his life. That's why people loved talking to him: he always had a story – usually a filthy one – about someone or other.'

She looked up at Elliot, who was staring out of the window thoughtfully.

'One thing Lord Soames did say, which puts paid to your theory about the drug-running, was that it was his dad who funded the start-up money for *Capital*.'

'We couldn't have expected Soames to admit to anything, even if he did know Dominic was a spy,' said Elliot, as if he were thinking out loud. 'It's not James Bond we're talking about. There's a certain glamour about espionage, but this is out-and-out betrayal of one's country, one's friends, colleagues. Take Philby: he was responsible for the deaths of dozens of Western agents.'

She told him about a phone call she'd had with Robert Webb, a former editor of *Capital* magazine, and an email conversation with another journalist associate of Dominic's, both of which Elliot said he would follow up, even though the communication had been fairly fruitless.

'So what about you?' she asked, sipping her water.

'Most of the *Soveyemka* press team from the period are now dead. But the list of spy names is fairly well documented if you know where to look, and I had it backed up by a member of the news team who was a junior reporter at the time.'

'It's hardly conclusive, though,' said Abby.

'I agree. The person I really wanted to track down was Dominic's handler.'

'Handler?'

'If you're an agent, your handler is your boss, the one who gives you your assignments, your point of contact. Have you never seen *Tinker Tailor Soldier Spy*?'

She shook her head, remembering Nick buying the DVD and ending up watching it alone while she had a bath.

'Bearing in mind that Dominic would have been in his eighties now, it's no surprise that any handler of that generation of spies is no longer with us. But we have a meeting tomorrow with Alexei Gorshkov, the former KGB colonel, who I think is going to confirm Dominic's activities.'

Abby laughed nervously.

'I'm just an archivist from Wimbledon. This morning I was supposed to meet my friend for brunch, and tomorrow we're off to meet the KGB.'

'You're not just an archivist, Abby. You're a journalist for the *Chronicle*,' Elliot said in a way that made Abby feel a little bit bigger and bolder.

She couldn't stop a yawn escaping from her mouth.

'Tired?'

She nodded, and their eyes met for a brief, electric moment.

She looked away, part of her willing him to leave the room, part of her hoping he would stay.

He stood up and walked towards her. Abby's heart started beating fiercely. He touched her shoulder with his fingertips as she held her breath, wondering what would happen next.

'You'd better get some sleep. You've been travelling all day and we've got a big meeting tomorrow.'

He left the room without even a kiss on the cheek good night, and Abby couldn't help but feel disappointed.

Chapter Eighteen

Abby was just about to reluctantly swing her legs off the bed and slip her feet into white fluffy slippers, helpfully put there by the housekeeping fairy at some point she hadn't even noticed, when the bedroom phone rang.

'Are you up?' asked Elliot.

'Just about,' groaned Abby. 'Although I could have stayed in that bed for ever.'

'Gorshkov has put back our meeting until five p.m. That gives us a chance to get out and see the city.'

'Well it's an awfully long way to come just to stay in a hotel room, however much I could happily sit out on the balcony all day nibbling blinis.'

Abby didn't know whether Elliot had inside knowledge of the city or whether the concierge had guessed her taste correctly, but their day had been planned to perfection.

They had breakfast in a nearby café, another grand space, with the feel of a Vienna tea room, where they ate *butterbrots* and *tvorog*.

Many of the great sights of the city were within walking distance of their hotel: the Mariinsky Theatre, St Isaac's Cathedral and the Church of the Saviour on Spilled Blood with its gold and turquoise onion-shaped domes that soared into the crisp blue sky. Just a glimpse of each one of them made Abby feel like a Romanov princess, although the many designer boutiques, expensive restaurants and chic fashionistas on the street made her realise that this was very much the twenty-first century.

They spent the afternoon in the Hermitage Museum, set in the spectacular Winter Palace, an enormous mint green, white and gold villa that had once been the royal residence of the tsars and was quite possibly Abby's favourite building in the whole city of architectural treasures. Inside was just as incredible. They saw golden thrones and dozens of *objets d'art*: clocks, crockery, caskets that had once belonged to Catherine the Great. As an art history graduate, Abby almost wept with joy at the museum's collection. Room upon room was stuffed with works from the great masters: da Vinci, Raphael, Michelangelo and Titian. Elliot couldn't have been a better companion, surprising her with his knowledge of Italian Renaissance art but not taking it all so seriously that they didn't have fun.

'Come on,' he said, glancing at his watch as time slipped away from them. 'We'd better get a move on. I can't imagine the KGB are too tolerant of poor timekeeping.'

'Ex-KGB,' said Abby hopefully.

The Mianovitch Building stood in the middle of a park, surrounded on all sides by hedges and fountains, as if it had been dropped into the middle of the city from the air. Such old-world elegance was an incongruous sight out in the suburbs, half an hour's drive from the city, where rows and rows of grey tower blocks − 'the people's housing' − pressed in on all sides. Abby peered out of the window of the taxi − an Eastern European town car with leather seats and rusting chrome bumpers − as it slid past a row of shops, some of them boarded up, a queue of sullen people outside one. What were they queuing for? she wondered. She leant forward to the driver.

'That shop?' she said, pointing. 'Is it a bakery?'

The driver, a thickset man in a lime-green Adidas top, shrugged and pulled a face to indicate he didn't understand.

'Bread?' said Abby, miming eating.

The man laughed. 'Bread? No, this.' He held up his mobile phone and chuckled to himself.

'The Russian Apple store, clearly,' said Elliot.

As they got closer to the Mianovitch Building, they could see that it was in a similar state of disrepair. The mouldings were cracked and a colony of pigeons evidently lived in the gutters, if the stains on the once white walls were anything to go by. But it still had a sheen of bygone glamour, with fluted columns and tall windows.

'Was it some sort of mansion, before communism, I mean?'

Elliot turned a page in the guidebook open on his lap.

'Built in 1897, apparently, as the country residence of one of Tsar Nicholas's relatives,' he read. 'At one time the gardens stretched for miles, but the city grew up around it, and after the revolution it became a possession of the Politburo, used for parties and visiting dignitaries. Sort of like the Russian equivalent of Chequers, I suppose. Or at least it was at one time.'

The driver pulled up outside the grand arched entrance.

'You wan' here?' he asked, gesturing to the building doubtfully. 'No tourist no come. Just old men.'

Elliot raised his eyebrows at Abby.

'I think what he's trying to say is that this place has seen better days.'

The driver nodded towards Elliot's laptop bag, then over to the nearest tower block.

'Bad men steal this. Bad men here.'

'We'll be careful,' Elliot said, handing the man a fistful of currency.

He touched Abby's arm reassuringly. The gesture made her feel safe as she followed him through the high doors and into a huge lobby.

'Wow,' she said, looking up at the domed ceiling. Sunlight was pushing in through dirty windows, winking off the dust motes in the air. 'I bet this was amazing.'

'Still is, in a faded sort of way,' said Elliot, heading for the wide marble stairs that curved away on either side of the hall. 'Second floor, room thirty,' he said over his shoulder.

At the top of the stairs, they turned into a dingy corridor. There was a smell of overcooked vegetables and floor cleaner, although Abby was fairly sure it hadn't been used for a while. She looked at the doors as they passed: all heavy oak, all tightly closed. It was intimidating, like a hotel shut up for the winter.

'How are we supposed to know which room it is?' she whispered as they turned a corner. 'It's all in Russian.'

'Don't think it matters,' murmured Elliot, nodding towards the end of the passageway.

A man was standing there watching them.

'Mr Hall, I presume?' he said with a faint accent. He was tall, with a slight hunch to his shoulders and white hair combed straight back from his temples. 'And Miss Gordon too, I believe?'

'That's right,' said Elliot, putting his hand out. 'And you are Mr Gorshkov?'

The man did not reply; instead he gestured to the open doorway to their left. 'Please, step inside. It is best if we do not talk out here.'

He gave Abby a slight smile, then stepped through into a large apartment. Like the rest of the building, there were echoes here of its previous use – thick carpets and heavy polished furniture. Perhaps it had been a reception room or a suite for guests. But the thing that struck Abby was the amount of books: in tall bookcases, in piles on the floor, stacked on tables; there was even a tower of them in the stone fireplace.

'Please, excuse the disarray,' said the Russian. 'I'm afraid history is one of my hobbies and there never seem to be enough books about any one subject.'

He moved an armful of volumes, clearing space for them to sit in two large velvet armchairs.

'This building is amazing,' said Abby, still looking around.

'Yes, but it was once magnificent. A venue for important affairs and people, everything polished and gleaming. There was a string quartet permanently employed to play in the drawing room, did you know that? Imagine!' He shook his head sadly. 'And look at it now. Reduced to the status of a boarding house for retired servants of the state.'

He perched on a wing-backed armchair and bent over a tray of tea things.

'I hope you don't mind, I anticipated your arrival – it's already brewed.' He smiled up at Abby. 'I spent some time in your country, you see, and developed a taste for the English way of things – at least when it comes to tea.'

Abby smiled back as she took a bone-china cup and saucer from him. Alexei Gorshkov wasn't at all what she had been expecting. She had imagined a stern, granite-jawed soldier with a stiff back and a gruff demeanour. The real Gorshkov was more like a slightly distracted Oxford don.

'Mr Gorshkov . . .' began Elliot.

'Alexei, please. I've had enough of formality to last me a lifetime.'

'Alexei, then. You said this place was a home for retired

servants of the state. Am I correct in thinking that you were a senior member of the KGB?'

Gorshkov smiled. 'If I was, you wouldn't expect me to answer that question directly, would you? Let's just say I was a faithful servant of Mother Russia.'

'A faithful servant who worked in the field of intelligence,' added Elliot cautiously.

Alexei nodded. 'Oh, I think I can say that much, yes.'

'You say you spent time in the UK. Was that in conjunction with this work?'

Gorshkov nodded. 'Of course.'

'And did you ever employ British operatives?'

Abby looked at Elliot and frowned. At this rate they wouldn't get back to St Petersburg until midnight.

'Were you a spy, Mr Gorshkov?' she asked. 'Did you know another spy, a British spy, called Dominic Blake?'

Elliot flashed her a surprised and slightly irritated look, but Alexei seemed to soften and started to laugh.

'I was very active in espionage in your country for many years,' he said. 'But I was never a field agent myself.'

'Then what were you?'

'A spymaster.' He looked over at Elliot. 'But then Mr Hall already knows all this, don't you?'

Elliot frowned. 'I'm sorry. What do you mean?'

'I mean that you asked your friend Paul Jacobs to put you in touch with a senior KGB operative. Once you had my name, you researched me from your terminal in the *Chronicle* building, making three telephone calls to contacts in the security services before you emailed me.'

He smiled at Abby's astonished expression. 'No need to look so startled, Miss Gordon. I even sent Tomas to drive you. It was his job to make you believe you were flagging a random taxi.'

He held up a hand to silence her questions.

'It's no secret who I am. The security services on every side always know their counterparts – that's the easy part. The hard part is finding out what your opposite number knows.'

He paused to pour himself more tea.

'So now we're all introduced. The only question remaining is why have you come all this way? Or to put it another way, why is Dominic Blake so important to you?'

Abby and Elliot exchanged a look.

'You knew we were coming to ask about him?' said Abby.

Gorshkov gave a gentle good-humoured snort.

'Give me a little credit. I searched for Mr Hall's name on the internet; the first thing that pops up is a story about the Great British Explorers exhibition, alongside a picture of a man kissing his fiancée. And of course I recognised Mr Blake immediately.'

'You knew him, then?' said Elliot.

'Of course. That's why I agreed to meet you.'

'Were you his handler?'

'I wasn't his handler. That was Vladimir Karlov. He died in 1993. But I knew Blake well. We met on many occasions and I found him to be charming on every single one of them.'

'What was his role?' said Abby.

'He gathered information. Information that Vladimir would assess and pass up the chain. Very simple, very efficient. For the most part, anyway.'

'Who recruited him, and when did it happen?' asked Elliot.

Abby looked at Alexei, praying that he would not name Rosamund.

'Dominic was recruited at Cambridge,' said Gorshkov simply. 'His college had a legacy of producing good men for Russia.'

'I don't understand why he would do that,' said Abby. 'What persuaded him to join? What made him betray his country?'

'Burgess, Maclean, Philby . . . no one believes what they are doing is wrong, Miss Gordon. There are any number of reasons why a man may join the other side; greed, lust, fear – all can be powerful. But can you guess the strongest of all?'

'Ideology?' said Elliot. 'Belief in the cause?'

'God, no. Politics is far too objective and far too prone to change. For example, you might be happy to give up secrets to undermine a certain government, but what if that government changed? Would you simply stop passing us information? No, contrary to what people think, spies are rarely motivated by belief – unless it's in their particular God, of course.'

'So what is the strongest motivation?' asked Abby.

'Hate, of course. Hate will drive men to do anything. And it keeps burning and burning, usually for ever.'

'And what did Dominic Blake hate?' asked Elliot.

'The British establishment. I forget the details, something to do with his father and the way they treated him during the war. It was a common theme in recruitment at that time; a lot of grudges were held after the war. Either way, Dominic came to our notice in his final year at Cambridge, practically breathing fire at the local Communist Party meeting. We soon put a stop to that, of course.'

'Why?'

'An outspoken communist shouting about the evils of the establishment? Hardly subtle, is it? No, we explained that he could further the cause far more effectively by playing a role, being the stereotypical public school cliché, joining the rowing club, making friends with the right sort.'

'The right sort?' asked Abby.

'The sort who might one day be in the Cabinet.'

Alexei's gaze trailed out of the window as if his thoughts were lost in the past.

'Dominic was special, I can say that after many years of experience. Most agents are opportunists. They get themselves in a useful position – a border control officer, say, or a worker at an aerospace factory – then they wait for interesting information to come their way. But Dominic was proactive. He'd think about what information could be useful to us, then he'd seek it out, talk to people, take out the guesswork.'

'Working as a journalist must have helped him.'

Alexei nodded.

'He joined one of the broadsheets straight out of Cambridge, but he realised it would take him years to climb up the Fleet Street ladder and have the ears of the rich and powerful. So he decided to set his own pace and launched *Capital*.'

Abby's shoulders slumped in disappointment. She imagined Dominic charming Soames's father with his vision for an exciting new magazine, getting him to invest and support him, and all the while he wanted to peddle a secret communist agenda.

'He was also a sexually attractive man,' continued Gorshkov, choosing his words carefully. 'Some of his most useful pieces of information were obtained not through idle tittle-tattle, but in the bedroom. Breathless embassy secretaries, personal assistants to Whitehall bigwigs, politicians' wives. One affair was particularly useful. The wife of a War Office minister, Gerald Hamilton.' He allowed himself a little chuckle at that one. 'It is amazing what you can find out second-hand.'

Abby shook her head, not wanting to believe any of it.

'How do we know you are telling the truth?' she asked recklessly.

Alexei didn't look offended. 'My dear, the Cold War is over. My life too is in its final act. You asked me a question, I will tell you what I know. When you are eighty-five years old, there is no point keeping things to yourself.'

'Alexei, what we really want to know is what happened to Dominic Blake, not whether he was a spy or not.'

'And why is this important fifty years after his death?'

'Because the people he loved deserve to know.'

Alexei gave a slow, soft exhale.

'The problem with being in the intelligence services is that it can make you reckless. You spend so long leading a double life, avoiding detection, taking greater and greater risks, that you believe you have become invincible. Dominic Blake was such a man. A charmed individual in so many ways, a thrillseeker who thought he could do anything.'

'Like the solo trip into the jungle.'

'Perhaps today it would be possible. With technology, GPS . . . In 1961 it was a death wish.'

'Rosamund said he had done a similar trip twelve months before.'

'And had been luckier. My friend, the life of Dominic Blake was somewhat complex, but his death was relatively straight-forward.'

'He simply ran out of luck,' said Abby grimly. She glanced at Elliot, who didn't look convinced.

'And you're sure that the KGB or the GRU didn't have anything to do with his death?' he asked pointedly.

Alexei hesitated.

'I don't know for sure. I doubt it. There were grumbles in the organisation when Dominic became close to Rosamund Bailey. His usefulness depended on the establishment thinking he was one of them, and his relationship with Rosamund put that in danger. But regardless of what you might see in Hollywood spy movies, we do not get rid of our comrades for no apparent reason.'

* * *

183

Alexei had recommended Café Musica for dinner, and eventually they found it, hidden in a warren of alleyways by the river. Apparently he had phoned ahead and told the staff they were coming, as Abby and Elliot were greeted with a smile and led through the restaurant to a terrace at the back overlooking the dark, shimmering water of the River Neva. Abby took a seat and drank in the view. The lights of the ornate buildings opposite twinkled as if tiny bonfires had been lit inside their depths.

'I can't believe we've taken a restaurant recommendation from a member of the KGB,' she smiled as she accepted a glass of Russian wine from the waiter.

'It's nice to step off the tourist track, regardless of how we got here,' said Elliot, holding her gaze.

Abby looked away, unsettled by the romance of their surroundings. She wondered if Alexei had chosen this place deliberately. Whether he had thought that her relationship with Elliot was more than professional, a question she did not want to think about too deeply.

'So what's the GRU?' She didn't doubt that Elliot would know.

'The KGB collected information on behalf of the Soviet government. The GRU was military intelligence. They were actually rivals. The KGB doesn't exist any more. It's called the SVR now, although the GRU still very much exists.'

'Do you know everything?' she asked, glancing up from her menu playfully. She caught herself, aware that she was flirting with him.

'No,' he smiled, tipping back his wine. 'I don't know that much about you.'

She shut the menu and put it on the table in front of her.

'What do you want to know?'

'What made you want to be an archivist?'

'I fell into it.' She shrugged quickly.

'How?'

She felt awkward talking about her past, not because she had anything to hide, but because she never thought anyone would be interested.

'My mum's drinking got so bad that I was almost taken into care. We avoided it, but I pretty much had to bring myself up. Mum didn't work. We had no money, no support network. I worked weekend shifts at one of the hotels in Portree, and the owners kept me on the straight and narrow. They were wonderful, big travellers before they decided to settle in Skye. The hotel was full of books and photographs of all the places they had been: Venice to see the Doge's Palace, Florence to visit the Uffizi, Canada for the Native Indian art. I was interested in it all, and they encouraged me to apply for an art history degree. After that, it was a short hop to thinking about careers in galleries or museums. I got an internship at the V and A. It went from there.'

Saying the words out loud made her think about whether she had been proactive enough in her life. Whether she had let decisions make themselves, or perhaps had been too influenced by others.

The waiter stopped her dwelling on it as he took their order, while Elliot topped up her wine glass. The light was starting to fade and the waiter lit the candle on the table between them. The terrace suddenly became even more magical, and looking up, Abby was caught unawares by how handsome Elliot looked in the soft, flattering glow.

'So did you believe everything Alexei told us?' she asked, wondering for one moment if the restaurant might be bugged.

'Why on earth would he make up such an elaborate lie?'

She didn't know the answer to that one.

'I think he was right that Dominic craved excitement,' she said thoughtfully.

Elliot nodded. 'That was probably his original motivation, regardless of what Alexei said about hate. I mean, come on, you're twenty years old, you like beautiful women and fast cars and someone asks you to be a spy. You're going to take the offer. Or at least seriously bloody think about it. It fits with everything we know about Dominic. His love of danger, his pursuit of glamour.'

'Can we not talk about it any more?' said Abby softly. 'At least not today. It makes me sad, and we're here in this beautiful, magical place.'

She watched a boat cruise along the Neva, the soft ripple of music radiating from below deck.

'You know, if we'd come a few weeks earlier, we would have caught the white nights,' said Elliot as they finished their main course of veal and potatoes and waved away the dessert menu in place of the bill.

'White nights?'

'The sun hardly sets and the air is so milky. You could stay up all night and not notice.'

Abby smiled at the romantic image.

'I have really got to travel more,' she said, taking a long, wistful swig of wine.

'No reason not to. Not in this day and age.'

'Well, I've had a passport since I was sixteen, but I've only ever used it four times before this week.'

Elliot sat forward, an amused but fascinated look on his face.

'So where *have* you been, Gordon?'

She started counting them out on her fingers.

'France on a school trip, a girls' package holiday to Tenerife, New York, and Turkey for my honeymoon.'

'Well, the Canaries are practically Africa, New York is the centre of the world and Turkey straddles Asia, so you're more cosmopolitan than you think,' he said, a smile pulling at the corner of his mouth.

'You're laughing at me.'

'I'm not. Did the travelling stop once you got married?'

'Not really. We go to Cornwall twice a year,' she said, suddenly aware that she was using the present tense. 'Nick is really into surfing and I just love the colour of the sea down there. We always had this dream that we would move there one day, open a café with a surf school. It was a bit of a pipe dream really, because Nick's business started to do so well that giving it all up to run a hobby horse seemed out of the question. But for four weeks of the year we went and lived the fantasy. This year has been the first year we haven't done it. Understandably,' she added quickly.

She fell silent and played with her napkin.

'Are you okay?'

'I can't stop thinking about Dominic. What are we going to tell Rosamund?'

'We don't tell her anything yet.'

She glanced up and saw that Elliot was watching her intently.

'Do you regret finding the picture? Agreeing to work with me?'

'Not for a minute,' she said quietly. 'It's fortified me.'

She let her eyes drift out across the river and took a sip of her wine before turning back to Elliot.

'I haven't had a great time recently. I've hidden myself away, not gone out, not really even spoken to anyone, hoping I could avoid the glaring issues in my life that need sorting out but not quite having the confidence to do that, to move forward.'

'Throwing yourself into work definitely helps,' he said, moving his thumb and forefinger up the stem of his glass.

'But this work, your work, has done more than that. You asked why I became an archivist. When I was younger, I loved the idea of being a journalist, but it always felt beyond me. I remember in my first week of uni I went down to the student paper. I put my face against the window of the office and I just stood there, looking in, too afraid to open the door. To be honest, that could be the story of my life.'

Elliot glanced at the bill and put a handful of roubles on the table.

'Abby, believe me when I say you're a bloody good journalist. The way you were with Gorshkov . . . direct, fearless. People with ten years' experience, let alone ten minutes', couldn't charm the pants off him and get him to talk the way you did. I was proud of you.'

'Fearless. I like that word.'

She noticed a frown line between his eyes.

'Come back to the hotel with me.'

For a moment she almost missed what he had said.

His eyes challenged hers and her heart started beating faster, and before she knew it, she was nodding.

He stood up, and held out his hand for her to take. She felt her cheeks flame with shame and desire as they weaved through the tables out into the alley, where the crisp night air cooled her cheeks but not her longing.

Still holding her hand, he spun her round and kissed her, his moist, wine-scented lips pressing against hers and pushing them apart. His hands were holding her face now and she could hardly breathe as they stepped back against a wall.

'Let's hope the hotel isn't too far from here,' he said, nuzzling her ear lobe. 'I've no idea what the Russian laws against indecency are like.'

There was time to think about what she was doing during the

five-minute taxi ride to the hotel, but she didn't let herself. She felt as if she were being carried along by the breeze, like a crisp autumn leaf turning and bobbing helplessly in a gust of wind.

They walked through the lobby holding hands, not saying anything, not even looking at each other. But as soon as the lift doors closed, they came together and kissed once more, softer but still impatient. Heady with the promise of what was to come.

There was a 'ping' and the doors opened on the fourth floor. Elliot put his arm around her shoulders as they walked and then ran to the door of her room, forcing the key card into the lock until they fell inside, not bothering to switch on the lights.

This time, she kissed him. She drank him in, enjoying the faint smell of his aftershave, the raw sensation of his tongue in her mouth. She couldn't ever remember a kiss like this. Pure longing and heady desire.

She could feel his fingers unbuttoning her jeans, and the only way she could respond was to do the same with his. Pulling her T-shirt over her head, he unclipped her bra and rubbed his palm across her nipple.

'Why didn't we do this sooner?' he whispered, rolling her knickers over her hips with one smooth movement.

She groaned as a fierce tingle seared between her legs, but the noise was lost in his mouth.

By the time they got to the bed, they were both naked. His body was as incredible as she had suspected. Sculpted torso, wide shoulders that narrowed to his hips. She lay back and he straddled her, scooping down to kiss her neck, her belly and her breasts. She tipped her head in pleasure, and he parted her thighs, licking his fingers and pushing them inside her, stroking her and then easing himself into her until she was dizzy with pleasure and all she could think about was how good he felt, how good he made her feel. She felt the sweet swell of orgasm gather in her belly, drawing it tight and making every nerve ending contract in desire. He quickened his pace, kissing her with hunger, with longing, and she grabbed his hair, pulling him closer, desperate to feel him deeper and deeper inside her. She gasped as her body seemed to lift higher and higher, exploding into one almighty release of pure, undiluted pleasure that made her cry out loud.

'That was good,' moaned Elliot, collapsing on top of her.

'Sensational,' she agreed, realising at that moment that nothing could ever be just sex.

Chapter Nineteen

Abby and Ginny had signed up for a course of ten Pilates lessons. It had sounded simple enough. Fifty-five minutes long, a smiling, benevolent-looking fifty-something teacher – or so she had seemed from her photograph on the website – and a bunch of testimonials confirming how it had improved people's posture no end. But the hour-long class that Abby had just taken with her sister-in-law could only be described as torture – leg pulses that seemed easy enough after the first couple, but after sixty repetitions fired a burning sensation from thigh to toe.

Abby couldn't help but think that it was some sort of punishment for what had happened in St Petersburg. Of course she had woken up feeling guilty in that gigantic four-poster bed in the Russian hotel. That was what happened when you opened your eyes and found yourself lying naked next to a man when you were still technically married to someone else.

When she thought back to it, as she had done almost every hour of the intervening four days, the idea of sleeping with Elliot Hall was as alien as the weird Cyrillic letters she'd seen on signs and posters all over St Petersburg. Girls like her – normal, ordinary, nice girls – just didn't have nights like that with men they barely knew in exotic hotels a thousand miles away from home.

But guilt wasn't the only emotion she had felt when she'd woken up in bed with Elliot. Abby didn't really have anything to compare it with – she had only slept with two men other than Nick Gordon, both of those brief sexual liaisons occurring in her first year at university, boys rather than men – but her catalogue of experience was enough to tell her that the sex and the chemistry she had experienced with Elliot was pretty potent. So she hadn't just felt guilty; she had felt exhilarated, she had felt sexy, she had felt like a completely different person, as if she had shed a dour and weathered old skin, and for that, the Scottish Presbyterian in her felt as if she needed to be punished. Pilates style.

'I enjoyed that,' smiled Ginny, rolling up her mat and pushing it into her Louis Vuitton tote.

She hadn't even broken sweat, whereas Abby could feel perspiration dripping down her temples and the back of her neck. She wanted to go home, have a cold shower and go to sleep, but she knew that escape was not an option.

They showered and dressed and walked out into the balmy evening sun that was shrouding the South Bank in soft golden light.

'So how was Russia?' asked Ginny, fastening back her shoulder-length hair as they left the studio. They hadn't had a chance to talk properly before the class; Ginny, being Ginny, had turned up minutes before it was due to start. As a consequence, Abby had felt tense for the entire hour, wondering where any conversation with her sister-in-law might lead.

'Revealing,' she said, instantly regretting her choice of words. She imagined Elliot's mouth on her nipple, his hand between her thighs, and felt a flush of colour.

'Get what you want?'

She nodded tightly, offering a silent prayer of thanks that the workout had been tough, otherwise her colour would have been a dead giveaway.

'So who was it you had to meet?'

Abby knew that Ginny was not going to let it drop.

'You're not going to believe it, but a member of the KGB. It was fascinating. He lives in this old people's home for retired intelligence.'

'The KGB?' said Ginny with a look of disbelief. 'What was this all for?'

'We're tracking down the story behind a Peruvian jungle exploration,' Abby replied, not wanting to link her trip to the *Last Goodbye* photograph too closely. Ginny was a wily fox. It was just a couple of short hops between seeing the photo in the *Chronicle*, noticing that the story had been written by the celebrated Elliot Hall and wondering who on earth she had gone to St Petersburg with.

'Still up for dinner?' Ginny said, as Abby breathed a silent sigh of relief that this line of conversation was not going to be pursued.

'How about Mexican?' said Abby, pointing in the direction of Wahaca.

'How about a drink first?' In true Ginny style, her words were more like an order.

'We can drink at Wahaca. They have those delicious *caipirinhas*.'

'I haven't been to the BFI bar for ages,' said Ginny as they walked past it. 'Let's just pop in for one.'

Abby agreed. She liked the BFI. When they'd first moved to London, she and Nick had become members, and spent every weekend watching specially curated programmes, from Jim Jarmusch movies to Hitchcock classics to world cinema gems.

She pushed open the door and walked to the bar area. She was still thinking about the old days, how she couldn't even remember the last time she had been to the cinema with Nick, and that was when she saw him.

At first she thought it was a mirage, before it dawned on her what Ginny had done.

'It's an ambush. I'm guilty,' said her sister-in-law, holding up her hands. 'But you have to talk to him, Abby. You owe it to each other to at least try before it gets all legal.'

'It's already got legal,' Abby said, panic in her voice and a knot of fear in her stomach. She didn't want to see him. Couldn't see him. Not now, only four days after she had woken up in bed with another man. All week she had been asking herself over and over again how this made her any better than her husband, and had come to the conclusion that it didn't. Her moral high ground was gone, and without it she felt vulnerable, exposed and culpable.

'Even your solicitor has recommended you try counselling,' hissed Ginny, standing behind Abby so she had nowhere to go but forwards, into the bar.

'How do you know?'

'Because Nick's solicitor has told him exactly the same thing.'

Abby turned round and looked at her with surprise, a stab of panic the only sensation she could register.

'Nick has been to see a solicitor?' she repeated.

'What did you expect? He's not going to wait around for ever.'

The bar was busy but Nick had found a table. Nick was always the type to find a table. He gave a tense smile as they approached, as well he might after their last confrontation in Hyde Park, and Abby had to fight every instinct not to run away.

She was glad to see he had dressed up, even if there was a series of creases in the arms of his suit. Abby imagined him pressing it on the creaky ironing board they kept in the airing cupboard. The old Abby would have done it for him, tutting a little perhaps, but doing it anyway, because that was what a wife did, wasn't it? But that was the old Abby. Not the one who flew to St Petersburg alone and got secrets out of former Soviet spies.

'What are you drinking?' said Ginny, her breeziness an attempt to hide the awkwardness of the situation.

'Just a lime and soda,' said Abby. She could have done with a stiff vodka or two, but she knew she needed to keep her head straight.

'Yes, the same,' said Nick cordially.

What are we doing? thought Abby with a sinking feeling. They were already talking like complete strangers after a matter of weeks. She wanted to grab him and yell, 'It's me! Your wife!' But it wasn't that simple.

'Ginny told me about your job,' said Nick, when she had gone to the bar. 'I called you and left a message. Twice.'

'To commiserate?'

'Well it's pretty shitty. I can't believe Stephen would do that to you. You keep that place together.'

'I haven't lost my job,' she said with as much dignity as she could manage. 'I've only had my hours cut. Besides, I'm making them up with some freelance work.'

They fell into silence and were saved by Ginny arriving with two glasses, which she put down in front of them.

'Well, you both know why you're here. I'll make myself scarce,' she said, slinging her bag over her shoulder.

'You're leaving?' said Abby and Nick simultaneously.

Ginny smiled. 'See? You still think the same way. No point me getting in the middle of it, is there?' She reached out and squeezed their hands. 'For God's sake, sort something out. You love each other too much to let this get the better of you.'

Abby grabbed her drink and took a gulp, wishing she had gone for the vodka after all.

Ginny handed them both an appointment card.

'Before I go, you're booked in here. Dr Naylor. Six thirty on the twenty-fifth. She's in Clapham, so it's convenient for both of you.'

'Who is Dr Naylor?'

'Nick will explain. Now I have to go.'

They watched her leave, watched her browse the book stalls under the bridge, turning to look back at them before she faded away.

'Dr Naylor. Is she putting us up for psychiatric evaluation?'

'She's a marriage counsellor.'

'An overqualified one,' smiled Abby, looking at the long list of initials after her name.

'Ginny says she's the best, but I bet she's just got her name out of the back of *Tatler*.'

'Nothing but the best for Ginny,' Abby replied.

'So was your trip to St Petersburg the freelance work?'

Abby didn't doubt that Ginny had told him every single detail she had revealed on the morning she had gone to the airport.

'Sort of,' she said, searching his expression for any suspicion. 'Interest has picked up in the archive after the exhibition the other week. I needed to do some more research on one of the photos.'

'Did you go on your own?'

'Yes,' she said with another stab of guilt. She felt sick at the ease with which the lies started. A little fib at first that snowballed until you didn't even know the correct version of the truth. A voice in her head pointed out that she had travelled to St Petersburg alone, even if she was met at the airport by the man she had gone on to have sex with three times in one night. But it only made her feel a tiny bit better.

Nick smiled. 'I have to admit, I had visions of you on a romantic break with Stephen.'

'Can you imagine?' she said, laughing nervously.

There was a brief silence, and Abby felt herself soften, not so much from relief as an unwillingness to have another confront-ation.

She knew that couples could have the same arguments again and again – sometimes for the entire duration of a marriage – but she didn't want a rerun of their angry, accusatory confrontation in Hyde Park. Not only was the thought of it exhausting, she wasn't entirely sure she could continue avoiding the truth about St Petersburg.

'You'd like Russia,' she said eventually. 'I was apprehensive about going, but it was pretty amazing. The architecture is incredible: all these fading baroque facades and peeling gold leaf. I'm not sure it was real gold leaf, but it looked beautiful and shiny and majestic. It's a city for princesses. And the Metro! Some of the stations even had chandeliers.'

'They were designed as palaces for the people, so they're full of marble and glass. They look old and elegant, but the network only opened in the 1950s.'

She looked at him in surprise, though she wasn't sure why. Nick had always been able to teach her things. His general knowledge was vast, but he was never pompous with his inform-ation. She couldn't help comparing him to Elliot, who sometimes seemed to assume that he was there to educate her.

'I've always wanted to go to St Petersburg. We should have gone,' said Nick, looking at her.

'Nick, we never used to go anywhere other than Cornwall.'

'I thought that was what we both wanted.'

'Clearly not. I never knew you had this burning desire to go to Russia.'

'Well, perhaps we stopped communicating a long time before we separated,' he said, not unkindly.

'You know I love Cornwall,' she said, remembering the beach barbecues they used to have: the little metal tins, the Lincolnshire sausages bought from the Co-op, the banana ketchup that made them laugh every time they bought it but which they both found secretly delicious.

She saw him glance down at her ring finger and notice that her wedding band was no longer there. Without thinking, she put her left hand on her knee under the table.

'We got into a rut, didn't we?' she said, feeling a knot of nostalgia. 'I mean, look at us now. A few weeks ago we'd never have done this, would we?'

'Done what?'

Abby gestured around the bar.

'This. Met for a drink by the river. Most of the time you were working in town, and I'm only a couple of tube stops away. Why did we never do this? We could have had lunch, gone to the Tate. I'm a bloody art history graduate and how many times have I been to the Tate?'

'I bought you membership for your birthday last year.'

'Yes, you did.'

She looked at him and their eyes locked, and suddenly she wanted to make sense of everything that had happened.

'When was the last time we came into a bar just to talk? That was all we used to do before we were married.'

'Things change, Abby. Priorities change.'

'What do you mean?'

Nick shrugged. 'Well, you stopped drinking for one thing.'

The comment hung in the air between them. To an outsider, it would have seemed innocuous, but within their private language it said everything.

'It wasn't all about getting pregnant, Nick. You changed too.'

He'd become quieter, more serious. The quirky, spontaneous side of him, that had made him jump off a cliff in Turkey or buy that horrible lime-green VW beetle, that part of Nick had silently slipped away. She looked across at the man she had promised to spend her life with and saw a stranger. Perhaps he saw the same thing too.

'Abby, I've worked twelve-hour days for the past six years. Spontaneity tends to go out of the window.'

'It doesn't have to. I flew to Russia with forty-eight hours' notice; I got a fast-tracked visa and everything. And do you know what? It felt brilliant.'

He looked at her with a chink of hope, like a Monopoly player just handed a get-out-of-jail-free card, and pushed his hand into his pocket, pulling out a piece of paper. Abby recognised the name of the Cornish estate agency immediately, because she'd been on this website a hundred times, dreaming of their little cottage, their business, their shabby-chic hotel.

'Remember that old B and B we always used to walk past in St Agnes?' he said, his green eyes shining. 'It's for sale.'

The price was there for all to see at the top of the page.

'I've spoken to a financial adviser, and we can afford it. Someone is interested in buying my business. They want to tie me in for three years as a consultant, but I could work remotely, one day in London, four in Cornwall, until my contract is over.'

Abby looked at him, not believing what he was suggesting.

'It just seems like the time is right, Abs. With your job being downsized at the RCI, and me selling the business, it could be a fresh start for us both.'

Three years ago this would have been her dream. The conversation they'd had every time they walked past this B&B had been an annual ritual; an electric, excited discussion of what they would do with the property if it ever came on the market. There would be an art gallery in the stone outbuilding, an organic café at the front, and an office for the surf school somewhere among their living quarters upstairs.

'How is it the right time, Nick?' she said with sadness. 'We're here to discuss the breakdown of our marriage. After your affair. We've both instructed solicitors. Mine wants me to get the house valued, and not so that we can cash in our chips and buy a Cornish B and B together.'

'It wasn't an affair,' he said, his voice choked. 'It was one night. One stupid, idiotic night.'

'It only takes one minute to betray the person you love, to destroy the bond of trust between two people. One minute to break everything.'

Not for the first time, she imagined him in some corporate hotel, his eyes meeting a woman's across a half-empty bar.

It was a scenario that had played over and over in her head. A Stockholm hotel with smart teak interiors, soft subdued lighting. She wondered how many drinks they had imbibed on expenses. When had their conversation turned flirtatious, and who had initiated that first loaded, intimate touch? Who had said 'Come back to my room', in the way that Elliot had taken charge of the sexual tension?

'Are you at least going to come and see Dr Naylor?' he asked more soberly.

'I don't know,' she replied, and she honestly didn't.

He pushed his hand across the table, trying to stretch out and touch her fingers.

'Abby, please. I will do anything to make this right again.'

It was a gesture so loaded with love and hope that it seemed wrong to accept it under false pretences.

'Nick, I've met someone,' she said finally.

She expected him to look furious, to accuse her of hypocrisy, at least to come back tartly with 'That was quick.' Instead he looked as if his heart was breaking.

'Is it serious?'

Abby had no idea herself what the answer to this question was. Yes, she enjoyed Elliot's company, yes, they'd had sex, and yes, they'd eaten breakfast on the balcony like any self-respecting mini-breaking couple the morning after. She didn't want to dwell on where this was leading back in England, especially since they hadn't seen each other since they'd parted at Heathrow. Elliot had a hectic work schedule, including a five-day trip to San Francisco to interview the wunderkind founders of the latest billion-dollar Silicon Valley start-up. But he had phoned three times, sent dozens of text messages – inconsequential chat, most of it: a man he had seen with a silly hat at the airport, a great restaurant he had discovered in Pacific Heights, a novel he recommended about the Russian Revolution – and a dinner date was pencilled in for his return to London on Monday. She didn't know whether this meant nothing, or everything; either way she suspected that she should be economical with the truth before she knew where their relationship was going.

'No. We've just had dinner. A date,' she replied, willing herself not to blush.

'But you like him?'

'I like feeling good about myself,' she said honestly, realising that that was exactly what had attracted her to Elliot Hall. Not his obvious good looks or his public school charm, but the way he made her feel like the most interesting person in the room, whether he truly believed it or not. 'I haven't felt good about myself for quite a long time now.'

Nick folded the B&B particulars carefully into a square and pushed it back into his pocket.

'I know approximately what the house is worth,' he said, adopting a more formal tone, the tone she had heard him use with clients when he took calls at home. 'I've done some back-of-the-envelope sums and I don't think we'll have to sell it, so I don't want you to worry about anything like that. And I've also put extra money into the joint account, so try not to get too bogged down about your hours being cut at the Institute.'

'Nick, you didn't have to . . .'

He drained the dregs of his drink and stood up to leave.

'Are you going to see Dr Naylor?' she asked, suddenly not wanting to leave.

He nodded, but didn't ask her again if she was planning to go too. He left without another word, and it was another minute before Abby realised she was crying.

Chapter Twenty

In the dream, Abby was running. She was on a road that looked familiar, but she couldn't quite place it. And why was she running? She knew she was scared; was something chasing her, or was she late for something – an exam perhaps? Slowly she became aware of a clanging noise; that was it. She was running for a bus, and there it was, bright red in front of her. But wait! Buses didn't have clanging bells. And suddenly she knew what it was: a fire engine, and it was going to her house. Her house was burning down with everything in it. 'Nick!' she cried, sitting up, her fists clutching the bedclothes.

There was no fire. The house was still there, the morning light leaking underneath the bedroom curtains. But the ringing was real. It took her a second to realise it was the doorbell.

She blinked hard to wake herself up and rolled out of bed, glancing at her bedside clock to check the time. Pulling on her dressing gown, she went downstairs, snapping the Sunday papers from the letter box before she opened the door.

'Rosamund?' She frowned with confusion as she recognised her visitor.

'Can I come in?'

Abby registered something clipped and impatient in the tone of her voice.

'Are you all right?' she asked.

It was 8.45 in the morning. A Sunday morning. Abby had no idea how the older woman had tracked her down or what was so important that she had.

Rosamund said nothing as she stepped inside the house. Abby tucked the papers under her arm and ushered her through into the living room.

The two women stood there for a moment without saying anything.

'How did you know where I lived?'

'Fifty years as a journalist teaches you a few tricks,' Rosamund said crisply. She nodded towards the newspaper. 'I expect you're going to frame it.'

'Sorry?'

'The newspaper.'

Abby put the copy of the *Sunday Chronicle* down on the table. 'Why would I want to do that?' she asked in bemusement.

'Isn't your first byline a big thing for any new journalist?'

'Byline? What?' She rubbed her face. 'I'm sorry, Rosamund, I'm not following you.'

She was met with an icy silence.

'The lead story in the News Review section of today's *Chronicle*.'

'What about it?' she asked slowly. Rosamund's expression was making her nervous. She saw a glimmer of steel, the tough patina of a hardened journalist, not the benevolent wise owl she had previously encountered.

'I take it you didn't know the story was to be published today.'

'What story?' said Abby, now utterly confused.

'Have a look,' said Ros.

Abby picked up the paper, tossing aside the various sections until she found the News Review. There, splashed across the front page, was the picture she had found in *Bystander* magazine of Rosamund and Dominic, alongside a smaller version of *The Last Goodbye*. The headline above it all read 'The Playboy Spy – Mystery Explorer Sold Secrets to KGB'. Her wide eyes shot to the top of the page: 'Reporting, Elliot Hall and Abigail Gordon'.

'You're kidding,' she whispered, opening the paper to see that the story ran to a double-page spread on pages two and three.

'My thoughts exactly,' replied Rosamund sharply. 'I assume the timing of the feature has surprised you, if not its content.'

Abby looked up at her.

'Honestly, Rosamund, I had no idea about this,' she said quickly.

'Abby, please don't take me for a fool.'

'You have to believe me,' she said, trying to catch her breath. 'Elliot hired me to be his researcher.'

'So you *did* know all about it.'

Abby felt caught out, cornered.

'As you know, after the feedback about the *Last Goodbye* photograph, Elliot wanted to look into Dominic's disappearance. I told you that.'

'And I told you it was against my wishes.'

'But he thought he could solve it,' said Abby more passionately. 'He had a lead and we went to St Petersburg to follow it up. We got back on Monday and I haven't seen him since. He certainly didn't mention that he was writing this story.'

'Enough,' said Rosamund, raising her hand to stop Abby in full flow. 'I thought better of you, Miss Gordon. I trusted you. You seemed decent.' She spoke so softly that Abby could barely hear her. 'My memories are all I have left of Dominic, and this feature, this feature has just set out to trash them.'

Abby looked at her, at the hurt in her eyes, the bottom lip that quivered with emotion, and had to glance away in shame.

'I'm going to call him right away,' she said, her heart pounding.

Rosamund blinked hard to recover her poise, the vulnerable woman gone and the firebrand returned. 'If you do see him, could you tell him to expect a finely worded note from my lawyers, and pass on the observation that karma is bound to catch up with you both in the end. Oh, and that I very much hope it's sooner rather than later.'

'Lawyers?' said Abby, her embarrassment now replaced by panic.

'I may be old, but I'm not dead. I believe libel laws apply to the living.'

'Look, maybe we can get it removed from a later edition or something.'

'I doubt you'll get through. I've been trying since just after seven.'

'Couldn't you call another of your contacts in the media, maybe do a story on your side of things?'

'And what would be the point?' said Rosamund. 'The damage is already done and another story would only fan the flames. Besides which, I'm not worried for myself; my lawyer will encourage me to sue, but I'm sure my reputation, such as it is, will survive. I'm just angry that Dominic Blake will now forever be seen as a traitor to his country, when nothing could be further from the truth.'

Abby shifted with discomfort and looked down at the feature again.

'But Gorshkov . . .' She trailed off, suddenly paranoid about using the Russian's name. 'The KGB contact, he claimed that Dominic worked for him. Do you think he was lying?'

'I don't have time to discuss my thoughts with you right now,

Miss Gordon. Perhaps you should have thought to include them before Mr Hall filed the piece. Right now I've got to get to the newsagent and buy up all the copies of the *Chronicle*. My national reputation is one thing, but I don't want people talking about me in my local shop.'

'Rosamund, I'm sorry. I'm so sorry,' Abby said, but the older woman had already turned to leave.

When the front door had clicked shut, Abby closed her eyes and puffed out her cheeks. She stayed still for a moment, then went to the kitchen, made herself a coffee, and returned to the paper, curling her fingers around her mug as she read and reread the story from start to finish. There was, she had to admit, a tiny kernel of excitement at having – on paper, at least – become a journalist, at seeing her name in print, but it was squashed flat when faced with the arrogance and presumption of Elliot Hall.

How dare he file the story without consulting her? How dare he even write this story? She had always understood that they were looking into Dominic's death, but the story in front of her was a textbook example of press sensationalism.

It was, however, a riveting read, and any other Sunday morning, before the exhibition, before Elliot Hall, Abby would have relished it.

From what she could gather, reading the article carefully, Elliot hadn't said anything they knew to be untrue, but he had turned up the dial to make everything that little bit more salacious. Dominic Blake was portrayed as a decadent Oxbridge toff who used his contacts to seduce the wives and daughters of the aristocracy in order to pump them for information, which he would then gleefully feed back to his Soviet paymasters. According to Elliot's account, Dominic was simply a traitor with an unspecified grudge against the establishment, who betrayed his country for the buzz of being a spy. Rosamund hardly came out of it much better; Elliot insinuated that her 'dangerous left leanings' meant she was fully sympathetic to her boyfriend's line of work. In his conclusion, he implied that Dominic had been assassinated by MI5 before he could do any more damage. No wonder Rosamund had been upset.

Abby picked up her phone and began to dial Elliot's number, stopping when she realised it would be past midnight in San Francisco. They were close, but not that close. Even if she was phoning with a bloody good reason, she knew enough from listening to the banter between Nick and his friends that midnight calls were likely to get you branded mad or a stalker. A darker thought also troubled her. What if she heard the sound of giggling in the background, or got the polite brush-off that suggested he had company? In the early hours of the morning that was not a good sign.

She would send him an email, she decided, folding the newspaper and walking across to the coffee table to get her lap-top. Perching on the edge of the sofa, she balanced the machine on her knee and turned it on to the sound of a low, soft gong. For a minute she sat staring at the blue screen, wondering what to say. She was still furious, still shocked and bruised from her encounter with Rosamund, and she knew she should give it to him with both barrels, but as she sat there crafting her words, it all sounded hollow and naïve.

Yes, Elliot was wrong to file the story without telling her, but it wasn't as if he had pretended to be anything other than a journalist. What did Abby really think was going to happen? It was inevitable he'd print something eventually, even if it was only to justify the expense bill for their trip to St Petersburg. Besides, it was a very, very good story. An exposé. Dominic Blake, friend of the establishment, had betrayed them all.

In the end she decided to keep things simple.

Elliot, I know it's late, but if you haven't gone to bed, please call me. The Chronicle *piece is out and Rosamund has just been to see me.*

That was it. No kisses, no smiley faces, just the bald facts. She congratulated herself on her restraint.

But as she closed the laptop, she felt deflated and unsettled. The threat of some vague and future legal action obviously troubled her, but it was more than that. She had been let down, tricked and lied to by another man, and for that she felt an utter fool.

Chapter Twenty-One

Paris, May 1961

'Why does French bread taste so good?' said Ros. They were strolling down the rue du Bac, and the taste of their supper – a huge pot of mussels laced with garlic and white wine and served with an enormous chunk of soft baguette – was still dancing on her tongue.

'I think it's the flour,' said Dominic, his answer typically decisive and culturally knowledgeable.

'We should take some back with us,' she decided, imagining herself reliving this moment from Sam's kitchen in Primrose Hill.

'But it will be stale by the time we get back to Calais.'

'Then I'll stand it in a vase. Put it on my mantelpiece as a reminder of simple yet exquisite pleasures.'

Dominic laughed, and she grinned into space.

She still couldn't believe she was here in Paris. They had caught the early-morning ferry from Dover; Dom's Stag clattering up the metal gangplank had been like something from a sci-fi movie, but by the time they reached the Arc de Triomphe

at a little after four o'clock that afternoon, she had felt like Jean
Seberg in *À bout de souffle*.

'Ice cream,' she shouted, running up to a shopfront, leaving
Dominic in her wake.

'I can't believe you are still hungry,' he called after her.

She looked over her shoulder and grinned playfully at him.
'We can't come to Paris and not have ice cream.'

'I think you're thinking of Rome,' said Dom, catching up with
her, by which time Ros had ordered two *boules de glace* and
handed him one.

She took a lick, her giddiness subsiding, and turned to
Dominic with a more sober expression.

'What's wrong?' he asked.

'It feels wrong to be so happy.'

'We're on holiday.'

'No we're not. We're here to work,' she said, reminding herself
that Dominic had officially commissioned her to write a thousand
words on the Algerian situation in France. 'I should be
interviewing members of the FLN, not eating ice cream.'

'I told you you could write about the Monaco Grand Prix.'

Ros waved a hand. 'That's your story. You do frivolous so
much better than I do.'

'Oh, I'm sure I can squeeze some pro-Tory rhetoric in there
somewhere,' he teased as she slapped him on the shoulder.

Whatever conflict there was between herself and Dominic
Blake – wildly differing political views, social circles and outlook
on life – had settled down into affectionate banter.

They still rarely agreed on anything, but Ros doubted she
would ever meet anyone who understood her like Dominic. He
was the only person who knew how to handle her moods, the
person who made her a better version of herself. She wasn't sure
if that was why he made her so happy, but right now she didn't

think she had ever been happier.

Paris was everything she had imagined. They had parked the Stag on a side road on the Left Bank and walked a long stretch of the Seine from the Pont Neuf towards the Gare d'Orsay before looping round and weaving back through the streets of the fifth arrondissement.

Dominic had given her a guided tour, pointing out the famous Parisian sights, but in truth she hadn't really needed it. She knew all about Les Deux Magots, where writers such as Sartre and Simone de Beauvoir had sat in a corner booth and discussed the issues of the day, and the political history of the Café de Flore, a 1920s hangout for Zhou Enlai when his communist fervour had been ignited. Her information had only come from books – it was the first time she had ever been to Paris – but the spirit of her literary heroes felt alive on the streets of the Rive Gauche.

Butterflies collected in her stomach as they approached the hotel, tucked away on a side street near the Sorbonne. She had not had a chance to feel nervous when they had checked in three hours earlier, even when Dominic had announced them to the reception desk as Mr and Mrs Blake. They had gone to their room, thrown their suitcases on the bed and headed straight out, desperate to explore, their stomachs grumbling after the long drive down from Calais.

But now Ros realised that she was excited and terrified in equal measure. Although she and Dominic had been dating for almost two months, although they went out three or four times a week and spoke constantly on the phone, they had not yet made love, a situation that was surely set to change within the next few hours.

Ros did not see herself as particularly old-fashioned, but stepping up her relationship with Dominic to a sexual and intimate one was something she had subconsciously tried to avoid since their first kiss at his flat. She was not an experienced lover, and Dominic most certainly was. She did not want to suffer in comparision with the dozens of women who had no doubt fallen like dominoes into his bed, didn't want to break the spell of their compatibility. And deep down there was the lingering thought that he saw her as another notch on his bed-post, a challenge he would quickly lose interest in once it had been conquered.

Their hotel was elegant rather than grand. Dominic waved at the desk clerk, who informed him that he had a telegram, which he collected along with their key.

'I can't believe we're only here for a night,' said Ros, kicking off her shoes and perching on the bed.

'Don't sound too disappointed. We've got Monte Carlo to look forward to at the weekend,' replied Dominic, scanning the telegram.

'Do you think they'll check our bank balances along with our passports?'

'I hope not, not unless they take overdrafts into consideration.'

He folded the telegram, put it back in his pocket, then glanced at his watch. Ros felt it was like a countdown.

'I'm sticky and smelly,' she announced, instantly realising that this did not sound very sexy or seductive. 'I'm going to have a bath.'

'Can I join you?'

She wasn't sure if he was joking and she felt herself blush.

'I just need to pop out for cigarettes. How about I pick up some champagne?'

'My sort of bubble bath,' she grinned.

He went to the bathroom and she heard him running the water.

'Any other requests?'

'Only that you hurry back.'

She smiled as she watched him leave, going over to the window as he stepped out on to the street, her eyes following him until he disappeared from view.

Her thoughts drifted to the Amazon expedition he was currently planning. He was due to leave in less than three months and she was worried sick about him, particularly as he insisted that it was to be a solo trip. It was like a black cloud that would occasionally drift in and block out the sun, ruining her mood – although she was determined not to let it spoil this holiday.

She opened her suitcase and looked for her toiletry bag. Pulling out her toothbrush and paste, she went to the sink and brushed her teeth, blowing into the palm of her hand to check that her breath didn't smell of garlicky mussels.

The sound of the telephone on the bedroom table filled the room. The noise made her drop her toothbrush in the sink, but she left it to go and answer the phone.

She picked it up and said *Bonjour* in her best accent, but there was nothing but the sound of silence down the receiver.

'*Bonjour*. Hello. Hello. Is anyone there?' she said, not wishing to attempt the question in French.

Still silence. Ros put the phone back in its cradle and looked at it for a moment. At the back of her mind she wondered if they had been found out – an unmarried couple sharing a hotel room – but reminding herself that she was in France, one of the more liberal countries on earth, she giggled and dismissed the thought as soon as it had occurred to her.

The bath was run and Ros was ready for it. She stepped into the tub and sank back in the water, the heat snaking up her back like steam from a kettle. She lathered a bar of lavender soap in her hand and massaged it into her skin, submerging herself entirely under the water to wash it all off. As she resurfaced, wiping the bubbles from her face, she felt ready, reborn.

There was another flutter of nerves, but Ros wasn't going to dwell on sex a second longer. Wasn't going to worry if their bodies would move in tandem, wasn't going to fret if Dominic could tell she hadn't been intimate with anyone since . . .

Well, she could hardly recall when that occasion was. An under-the-blanket fumble with an unreliable economics postgrad student was the last sexual encounter she could remember, and it still made her cringe.

But tonight, for the first time in her life, she felt like a sophisticated woman. Not an angry student, or a bitter spinster, but someone who liked to travel, and talk; someone who could love and be loved.

Stepping out of the tub, she wrapped herself in a towel. Her pot of Nivea was on the bathroom cabinet and she scooped up a big dollop with her fingers and smoothed it on her skin.

As first, it turned her almost totally white – Dom's going to find me here looking like a tub of lard, she thought, trying desperately to rub it in – but within a few minutes her skin was silky soft. She lay naked on the cool white sheets and almost wanted to purr.

Folding her arms behind her, she arranged herself on the mattress, feeling like an artist's muse.

She didn't know whether Dominic would love seeing her like this when he walked back through the door, or whether he would die of shock.

After ten minutes she began to get restless. She was cold, with the beginnings of cramp in her leg. There was still no sign of Dominic; she didn't know exactly how long he had been gone, but it had to be over half an hour.

How long did it take to buy a packet of cigarettes? she asked herself, trying to remember the streets they had walked through, mentally locating a *tabac*.

The window was open, letting in a chill. She pulled a pillow over her and rubbed her arms to get rid of the frosting of goose pimples.

The phone rang again, sending spearshots of anxiety around her body.

She leant over to answer it, conscious of her nakedness.

There was a click and then a silence.

'Hello?' she said nervously when there was no sound at the other end. 'Dom, is that you?'

Straining her ears, she thought she heard the faint sound of breathing, which made her drop the phone back on to its cradle as if it were hot.

She could feel her pulse in her chest. Outside she heard a woman's laugh, and then a male voice trying to impress her. She imagined it being Dominic and some secret Parisian lover – she had seen the way women looked at him in the street – but she told herself how ridiculous she was being. He had just popped out for champagne and cigarettes.

She put on the thin cotton robe she had packed and took a packet of Gauloises from her handbag. Hadn't Dominic remembered that she had bought some near the Gare d'Orsay?

She perched on the edge of the bed, not wanting to feel like this. She wanted to feel as carefree as she had done when she was eating her ice cream in the rue du Bac, absorbing the sights and sounds of Paris and feeling as if they were the only thing that mattered.

She stood up, and was about to pace the room when she heard the heavy sound of footsteps on the stairs. The door creaked open and Dominic stood in the frame, smiling and holding a bottle of champagne. She no longer had the taste for it.

'Did you get what you wanted?' she asked, not even looking at him.

'I had to make a couple of calls,' he said, approaching her and kissing her on the neck.

She turned her head away from him. 'Why couldn't you have made them here?'

'Because this room is about me and you. Not about work.'

'We got a call to the room. Two, actually.'

'Who was it?'

'I don't know. They rang off.'

'Nothing important then,' he smiled, coming up behind her and wrapping his arms around her waist.

'You smell lovely.'

She flinched away from him.

He sat on the edge of the bed and looked up at her.

'Ros, what's wrong?'

'You were gone ages.'

'Time ran away from me. I had to find a *tabac*, a phone box . . .'

'You left me here. It got dark outside.'

'Dark outside?' He smiled.

'I was worried,' she scolded him. 'When the phone rang I thought you'd been knocked over or something else terrible.'

'I'm sorry,' he said, taking her hand.

'So am I,' she said briskly.

She didn't want to sound like a lunatic. She didn't want to admit that his thirty-minute absence and the two phone calls to the room – wrong numbers most likely – had made her paranoid and suspicious, and had trawled up every single feeling of inadequacy she had inside her.

'Ros, talk to me, please,' he said pulling her closer until she sat beside him on the mattress.

She felt unwelcome tears spring to her eyes.

'This is hard for me,' she said finally.

'What's hard?'

'Being here, in Paris, in this room. Alone with you. I know what that means. I know it means the next step, and I'm scared of that.'

'It's not meant to be scary,' he said, stroking her hand.

She took a breath to summon her courage and the words that had been trapped inside her since they had first kissed.

'Dom, I think you know me by now. You should know that when I care for something, I really care and I give my heart and soul to it. That something used to be politics, the cause. It still is. But now I care you for too. I care for you so much, more than anything, and it terrifies me that I'm going to get hurt. That you're going to walk off for a packet of cigarettes one day and realise that you've just been wasting your time with the shouty girl with frizzy hair who brings you nothing but trouble.'

'You're not the shouty girl,' he said quietly.

'Then who am I?'

'The beautiful, brilliant woman I have fallen in love with.'

The power of his words stunned her into silence.

His hand brushed her shoulder and pushed back the thin cotton of her gown, exposing a pale scoop of flesh. He bent down and kissed it and she shivered at his touch.

She got up slowly and stood between his legs, knowing, but not caring, that she was about to cross a line.

The space between them seemed to take on an electrical charge. Dominic looked up at her, seeking her approval, then gently untied her gown. The flaps fell open, exposing her naked body.

He pulled her closer, and as he kissed her belly, she pressed her hands against the back of his head.

When they pulled apart, she slipped off the gown and it rustled to the floor.

Dominic stood up and she undid his belt, his shirt buttons, stroking her fingers across his downy chest hair.

When he was naked, he kissed her again, this time on the lips, his hands running through her hair.

They fell back on the bed and he positioned himself on top of her. She gasped at his closeness, nerves melding with the excited sensation of skin against skin. She closed her eyes and tried to feel every inch of him: coarse pubic hair, the roughness of his stubble, the softness of the lips that brushed against her breast. She kept her eyes closed, wanting to feel the surprise of where his mouth would go next.

His tongue connected with her nipple and she felt it harden in his mouth.

She tipped her head back in abandon, desperate to heighten every sensation, the pleasure and wantonness, the feeling of being desired.

She had always known that Dominic would be a good lover, but his touch was instinctive, knowing all her sweet spots without her needing to guide him.

A line of soft kisses traced down her abdomen. She knew where his mouth was going and it thrilled and terrified her. She had never been so intimate with another person before, but as his hands parted her thighs and he kissed her, right there in her most secret place, his tongue pushing itself inside her, she groaned in delight.

His sweet strokes sent a pleasure pulse around her body. She didn't want it to stop, and when he pulled away to put on a condom, she felt maddeningly bereft.

Needing him back inside her, she pushed her knees further apart, and he entered her. She felt her body resist him at first; a short stab of pain that reminded her how closed off her body had been from all touch. But as she relaxed, feeling him sink deeper and deeper into her core, she gripped herself around him until they felt exquisitely bonded.

They moved in rhythm, bodies and breath, until she felt the pressure build in her core, every nerve ending alive. She felt as if she was climbing, higher and higher, her breath getting faster and more desperate, every ounce of passion and emotion she had ever felt compressing into a wild, sweet abandon that ripped through her body like a tidal wave.

His own pleasure was etched on his face and he collapsed on top of her, groaning with release.

Her heart was thumping wildly in her chest. And as he clasped her hand, all thoughts of his earlier disappearance, of their differences and her inadequacies, vanished completely.

Chapter Twenty-Two

'I think you're going to like Les Cyprès,' said Dominic as he indicated left through a pair of stone gate posts and down a long drive lined with cypress trees.

'You mean I'm going to love it more than Monte Carlo?' replied Ros, remembering the way the Côte d'Azur sparkled in the sun, and the yachts bumped together in the harbour.

'Even more than Monte Carlo,' grinned Dominic as he glanced across at her.

'Even more than that little B and B in Lyons with the world's flakiest croissants and the courtyard that smelt of lavender?'

'Even more than that,' said Dom, pressing his foot on the accelerator so that they picked up speed, the breeze ruffling her hair.

'I want to live here,' declared Ros, feeling as if life had been sweetened by the sun and the smells of the Côte d'Azur.

'We haven't even got there yet.'

'I don't mean Les Cyprès.' She sighed wistfully. 'I mean the South of France.'

'Speaks the socialist . . .'

She shifted in her seat and looked at him.

'I'm not saying I want a mansion. I'd be happy with one of those little cottages we saw at the turn-off to Antibes. All I want is a bed, a table, a bowl for my peaches and a window that overlooks the Med. That's got nothing to do with politics. It's about appreciating nature.'

'I hope that bed sleeps two,' smiled Dominic, taking his hand off the gearstick and putting it on her stockinged knee.

'Oh gosh,' she gasped as Les Cyprès came into view.

'I don't want a mansion . . .' he teased as he removed his hand.

'Just look at it,' she whispered, her mouth dropping open. 'How many families live here?'

'Just the Harbords. And they don't even have kids.'

'Do they want to adopt me?' she asked, swooning at the low Latin-style finca, wild jasmine growing unchecked over its whitewashed walls.

They pulled to a stop at the front of the house and knocked on the door. A housekeeper answered, and Dominic went to get their cases out of the boot, leaving them in the hall.

They were led to the back of the house, down a short flight of stone steps to a kidney-shaped pool that stretched the width of the ornamental garden.

Ros could just make out that the woman standing in front of the pool wearing a bathing costume and wide sunhat was holding up a crystal decanter.

'Drink?' she called. 'I'm making martinis. Or daiquiris, haven't decided yet.'

'Your call,' replied Dom, turning to Ros.

'Ooh, I think it's the weather for something fruity, don't you?' she giggled.

Dominic made the introductions. Up close, Lady Victoria Harbord, his old friend, a woman whose name cropped up regularly in his conversation, was every bit as glamorous as the picture he had always painted of her.

'Darling Ros, I can't believe we haven't met until now,' she said, putting down her silver cocktail shaker.

'You're never in the damn country,' quipped Dominic, taking off his driving gloves and putting them in the pocket of his cream linen jacket.

Victoria shrugged, and her chiffon kaftan fell off one tanned shoulder.

'When the sun starts shining, I just want to be by the coast.'

'I don't blame you. The view is magnificent,' smiled Ros, looking out towards the shimmer of blue in the distance.

'Dommy, did I tell you we've just bought a place in the Hamptons? It's a bloody long way, but Tony says it's the new Newport. The sunsets over the ocean are stunning, and it's so handy for Manhattan.'

She focused her attention back on Ros. When she looked at you, Victoria Harbord made you feel as if you were the only person in her orbit.

'So, Ros. Tell me about Monaco,' she began, pouring out the daiquiris.

'I thought you'd be there,' said Dominic, helping himself to an almond from a bowl on the drinks trolley.

Victoria shrugged. 'Tony went to meet some of his frightful boring Texan friends. I stayed here and topped up my tan. Frankly I couldn't think of anything worse than spending an entire afternoon watching souped-up tin cans zooming around Monte Carlo.'

She took a sip of her cocktail.

'But darling, tell me. Did you see Grace Kelly?'

'Sadly not,' said Ros, shaking her head.

'She's done wonders for the principality. Princess Margaret

should have married Cary Grant. Maybe we'd have got our empire back.'

'Well, we enjoyed it,' said Dom, taking off his jacket and throwing it on a sunlounger.

'You enjoy anything that involves fast cars and alcohol. I want to know what Ros made of it all.'

'I thought it was like a weird zoo for millionaires,' she smiled.

'A sound observation. They go to avoid tax and feel they've succeeded in life because they pay an obscene amount for spaghetti.'

Ros laughed. 'You're not joking. It cost us over a guinea for two bowls of pasta.'

She glanced over at Dom and noticed how relaxed he looked. Relieved. She had known he had been nervous about her meeting more of his friends and had seemed to be particularly bothered that she and Victoria get on. After all, the hostess of Les Cyprès was one of his oldest friends.

'Darling Ros. Do you have a swimming costume?'

'I have three in my case.'

'Three?' asked Dominic.

'A girl needs options,' Ros replied. 'Two bikinis and a one-piece.'

'A *maillot*,' smiled Victoria, putting down her cocktail glass. 'We're in France now.'

'I didn't think feminists wore bikinis,' said Dominic playfully.

'Why not?' Victoria winked at Ros.

'Don't they demean the movement or objectify women or something?'

'Feminism is about choice, Dommy darling. And if Ros chooses to show a bit of leg, screw the movement.'

Dominic grinned at Ros wolfishly.

'Hear, hear.'

Ros went to the cabana to change. She felt washed-out and pale compared to Victoria with her smooth bronzed skin, and her navy blue one-piece was a little school-regulation, but she was too self-conscious to try the bikini.

Peering through the wooden slats of the cabana, she saw Victoria do a perfect swallow dive off the board. She entered the water with an elegant splash, and when she surfaced, rubbing her eyes, she turned and watched Dominic do the same.

Ros remembered a line from a short story she had read by Scott Fitzgerald, about the rich being different from you and me. It had never seemed more appropriate.

She finally emerged from the cabana and inched her way into the water.

Dominic swam up behind her, wrapped his arms around her waist and pulled her under.

She screamed, and then they were all laughing, and before she knew it, her face felt slightly burned and her fingertips were crinkled from their time in the water.

They dried off and changed, just as a short, squat man emerged at the doorway to the house. He was wearing sunglasses, pale trousers and a bold coloured shirt that made his face look even redder.

'Tony!' Victoria waved as she slipped her kaftan back on over her bikini. 'Where have you been?'

'Cannes,' he replied in an American accent.

Victoria slipped a loving arm around her husband's shoulders. 'Darling, you must show Dommy your new plaything.'

'What have you been buying this time?'

'Come and have a look,' Tony said with pride.

Ros followed them back through the house to where a bright red sports car was parked in the drive. Dom was already sighing with envy before they had even got up close.

'Ferrari Testarossa,' said Tony, opening the driver's door. 'Fewer than forty of them have ever been made.'

'And you've got one of them, you lucky devil,' replied Dominic, drawing his hand across the paintwork. 'She's beautiful.'

'Why don't you take her for a spin?' said Victoria.

Dom looked at Ros but didn't say anything.

Victoria linked her arm through Ros's, understanding the situation immediately.

'Don't mind us,' she smiled. 'We can go for a walk to the cove.'

'Is that okay with you?' asked Dom.

'You know I get carsick if we go over thirty miles an hour,' grinned Ros.

'That's settled, then,' said Victoria. 'We'll go and change, and boys, make sure you're back in time for dinner.'

The housekeeper showed Ros to their room, and she threw on a rustic blouse and a navy skirt, tying her hair back into a ponytail. She bent to the mirror on the dresser, touched up her lipstick and blew herself a kiss, realising with some concern how easy it was to get accustomed to this luxury.

'You look lovely,' said Victoria, waiting for her at the bottom of the stairs. 'I'm glad you're wearing plimsolls. Some guests arrive with just a bag of high heels and they wonder why we can't go and explore.'

Ros followed Victoria to the far edge of the grounds, where there were stunning views over the Mediterranean. She could immediately see what a spectacular location the house was in – perched in a sheltered hollow of coastline above Antibes, surrounded by lemon trees and wild flowers.

Victoria pointed out a herd of goats, which had been known to eat through the only telephone line linking them to the outside world. She described them as 'pesky things', but Rosamund found the idea of such splendid isolation quite heavenly.

As they talked about the literary heritage of the area – how Scott Fitzgerald had written *The Great Gatsby* from a rented villa in Saint-Raphaël, and how Dick and Nicole Diver from *Tender is the Night* were based on the Harbords' friends, the wealthy ex-pats Gerald and Sara Murphy – Ros realised that Lady Victoria was not the glamorous trophy wife she had first thought. At one point she asked her how someone who was so obviously intelli-gent and educated could be happy just enjoying herself and throwing parties. Victoria answered the question in the spirit in which it had been asked.

'People who think I'm a silly socialite are completely missing the point,' she confided. 'There is great value in bring-ing people together. I'm sure Tony wouldn't be half as successful as he is without the currency I bring to the table. And I'm confident enough in myself not to have to trumpet my con-tribution.'

They picked their way along the coastal path and chose a spot to sit down at the top of a bluff, looking towards the sea, not a building in sight, only the cries of the birds and the breeze rustling the grass to break the serenity.

'I'm glad that Tony and Dom are getting to spend some time together,' said Victoria.

'How so?' asked Ros, peering over the top of her sunglasses.

'Tony's frightfully jealous of Dominic. Always has been.'

Ros didn't ask her to be more specific. She didn't want to know the answer. She supposed that many men would be envious of Dominic's easy charm and good looks. After all, Tony wasn't a particular looker. She wasn't surprised that he had reservations about his wife's obviously close relationship with the *Capital* editor.

'So how's it going with Dominic?' Victoria asked, more playfully.

'Rather well,' said Ros guardedly.

A smile played on Victoria's lips. 'I have to admit, I have never seen him like this with anyone else before.'

'How do you mean?' Suddenly Ros wanted to know everything.

'He's brought girls to meet us before. Mainly to parties at Batcombe. But you're different. He's different with you. He's in love with you.'

Ros smiled. She was desperate to tell her new friend about their night in Paris. How they had spent half the night kissing and making love and telling each other how much they loved one another. But at the same time, she wanted to keep those details a secret between herself and Dominic.

'No, I've seen Dominic Blake with dozens of women, hundreds. And he's never been like this with anyone else, not even close,' mused Victoria. 'But . . . Dom's life is complicated. You have to be sure you're prepared to take that on.'

'The jungle, you mean? The adventuring?'

'That's part of it, yes, but . . .' She paused, seeming to search for the words. 'Look, life is not a fairy tale and neither are relationships. You have to work at them, set boundaries.'

'Boundaries?'

'Ros, you're an intelligent woman and I am not going to insult that intelligence by saying that Dominic isn't extremely popular with the opposite sex. No matter what his feelings for you are, men are men; if some strumpet opens her legs right in front of them, what do you think they're going to do?'

She leant forward.

'You've seen their faces when they're about to pop. It's a primordial urge; they're not in control of themselves.'

'You think I can't trust him?' she asked defensively.

'I thought I could trust Tony. At the beginning. Although I love him, although I fell in love with him, he's not an obviously attractive man,' she said, choosing her words carefully. 'Not like Dominic. And yet there were at least two affairs in our first three years of marriage. What he lacks in matinee idol looks, his wallet makes up for. If you have something to offer – sex, excitement, money – people will always be interested in you.'

'So what did you do?'

'I laid down the law. I told him what he had to lose. And I made some rules. I vet his secretaries, limit his time abroad . . .'

'And you think that helps?' said Ros, imagining Tony like a panting dog on a tight leash.

'I do what I can.'

A bird was circling overhead, and Victoria tipped back her head to listen to its song.

'You didn't answer my question,' said Ros softly.

'Whether I think you can trust Dominic?'

Ros nodded.

'Dominic Blake is a remarkable man. He's climbed unclimbable mountains, mapped unmappable rivers, he's brave and resourceful and on top of that he's a very good writer. And one of the reasons he's done all that is because he is a free spirit. He's unfettered, curious.'

'So if a girl falls in love with the dashing pilot, she shouldn't be surprised when he flies off into the sunset the week after the honeymoon. Is that what you're saying?' Ros could feel tears building in her eyes.

'Left to his own devices, he isn't going to change. Why should he? But he has to know that he can't have his cake and eat it,' said Victoria decisively.

Ros admitted she had a point. Of course she had been

229

apprehensive about Dominic's popularity with women. Every time he went out was a reason to get suspicious. London, Paris, Monaco – they were stuffed with beautiful women. There was temptation at every corner, every bar, restaurant and party, and Ros knew that many of those temptations were far more attractive than she was.

'What if I bring it up? What if I tell him he can't go careering to the furthest corners of the globe any more, or to every party he's invited to? What if he chooses his old life? What if he chooses not to change? What if he doesn't choose *me*?'

'Then at least you'll know,' replied Victoria bluntly. 'And at least you can decide if that's an arrangement you are prepared to accept.'

Ros was glad her sunglasses were hiding her tears.

'Darling, don't get upset. You're a strong woman who won't be walked all over. Let him know that.'

Victoria held out her hand and pulled Ros to her feet. They walked back in silence. Ros had a lot to think about, and she didn't even glance at the view – the wooded hillside that fell steeply down to the cliffs, and beyond that, the bay sparkling silver and blue.

The men were back by the time they reached Les Cyprès. Dominic was still discussing the Ferrari and wanted to share his excitement with Ros. Although she did not care for cars, she tried to get involved, listening with manufactured enthusiasm to the history of the car and how it had won the race at Le Mans.

They went to change and Ros delighted in their bedroom. It was decorated in shades of cream and pale blue that reminded her of hydrangeas; French windows trimmed with wisteria led out on to a small balcony.

Dom was in a particularly good mood and seemed to relax

even more when Bellinis were served on the terrace. Victoria had also changed for dinner and looked ravishing in a salmon-coloured knee-length gown that showed off her waist and her tan. Ros discreetly observed her boyfriend's reaction, but if she was expecting him to cast lascivious glances in Victoria's direction, she did not see any.

They ate dinner outside, on a round table underneath a citrus tree.

'Just the four of us tonight, Vee?' asked Dominic as he dug into cold avocado mousse.

'Aren't you glad? I thought you'd had enough polite conversation in Monaco.'

Ros laughed, thinking about the countless drinks receptions they'd had to attend both before and after the Grand Prix.

'You know what I'm saying, don't you, Ros? Free parties? They come at a price.'

'Dom did spend half the time drumming up business for the *Capital* ad team, but still, I was happy to people-watch.'

'Well now is the time for close friends,' said Victoria, and Ros gave her a grateful glance, remembering the last time she had met Dominic's friends en masse.

Victoria and Tony were happy to talk about politics and the issues of the day, but not in the confrontational way they had been discussed at Jonathon Soames's house. Victoria conveyed her distress that a bus carrying civil activist Freedom Fighters had been fire-bombed in Alabama, and Dominic predicted that this would lead to race riots.

'Dom tells me you run your own pressure group,' said Tony as the starter was cleared away.

'I've scaled it back a little recently,' replied Ros.

'How so?' asked Victoria with interest.

'We didn't seem to be pressurising anyone into doing anything.'

She meant it as a joke, but Tony and Victoria looked at her seriously.

'What was your cause?' asked Tony, lighting a cigar.

'Lots of things. Anything we cared about.'

'Perhaps that's your problem,' said Victoria.

'That we lacked focus? You might have a point.'

'Never spread your interests too thinly,' nodded Tony. 'Always worked for me in business.'

He looked at Dominic.

'You need to promote Ros to editor of *Capital*.'

'*Capital* has an editor, Robert Webb.'

'He's a decent guy, but the two of you heading up that magazine would be dynamite.'

'I don't think it's a good idea to mix business with pleasure too much, Tony,' said Victoria.

'But you're never in the office, are you, Dom?'

'I don't know about that.'

'Vee says you're off to the Amazon. Where are you thinking of going after that? Harbord Industries could chip in a few dollars if it was somewhere interesting.'

'Interesting?' grinned Dominic.

'Go on, give me your ultimate challenge.'

He looked thoughtful for a minute.

'I've always fancied trying the Bering Strait. Crossing the water when it's covered in ice. You know it's only sixty-five miles from Alaska to Siberia, although the Russians won't let a Westerner anywhere near their borders. Not officially, anyway.'

Tony laughed. 'Would they notice one man and his husky? You could go, plant the old Union Jack and come home.'

Dom grinned. 'As I said. Not officially.'

'It sounds absolutely treacherous,' said Ros, sensing an

opportunity to make her feelings known. 'Anyone doing that alone would be signing their death warrant.'

'In this case, I think you'd have to,' replied Dominic. 'It would be the only way to go under the radar.'

'Besides, I thought you preferred solo adventures these days,' added Tony. 'What was it you said about the romance, the peace of discovering the undiscovered all by yourself? I can't remember his exact words.' He turned his attention to Ros. 'Your boyfriend's the wordsmith. I'm just a dull finance guy. Still, it made me want to run off to Tangiers all by myself and have a religious experience.'

'Religious experience?' scoffed Victoria, sipping her wine. 'If you went to Tangiers, you'd get drunk and find the nearest socialite throwing a party.'

Ros was determined to hold her ground, safe in the knowledge that she had an ally in Victoria.

'Dom, I just worry about you. The Amazon adventure is bad enough.'

'Bad enough?' he said with surprise.

'One man and his canoe, in the heart of the Amazon. I mean, I was reading about Percy Fawcett the other day. The adventurer who went looking for the Lost City of Z, not far from where you're going. He went missing and was never found again, and he was one of the celebrated adventurers of his day. No one knows what happened to him. People say he was eaten by cannibals or murdered by one of the jungle tribes . . .'

'I'm aware of Fawcett's disappearance and the theories surrounding it,' said Dominic more coolly.

'I just don't want it happening to you,' said Ros, getting more worked up at the idea of him leaving. Already he was in the final stages of preparation, his flat littered with boxes and equipment, making the prospect of his departure seem very real.

'What are you saying, Ros?' He sat back in his chair and studied her.

'I'm saying I don't like it. I know the Amazon trip is arranged, but for your next adventure can't we go away on safari or something?'

'You're saying you don't want me to do any more expeditions?'

'Yes, I suppose I am,' she said, folding her arms in front of her.

An awkward silence settled around the table.

'We should talk about this later,' said Dominic quickly.

'Good idea,' replied Victoria.

Glancing across at her host, Ros was upset that Victoria hadn't backed her up, hadn't offered anything to the conversation to support her. Their heart-to-heart, the female solidarity she had felt on their clifftop walk, suddenly seemed hollow.

Ros didn't feel hungry for the rest of the meal. She struggled through the main course of *Beef Provençal*, and her apricot tart went untouched.

Tony steered the conversation towards their new house in the Hamptons, and when the sky had finally turned dark and the stars started glittering above them, Ros took it as an excuse to say good night.

Dominic got up to join her, but she shook her head.

'You stay,' she said as light-heartedly as she could.

'No, I'll come.'

'Don't be silly. You three have a proper catch-up.'

This time he didn't object.

Victoria got out of her seat to give her a hug.

'I hope you don't think we are too bohemian putting you in the same room,' she giggled. 'But it is the best suite in the house.'

'I'll be up soon,' promised Dominic.

Ros nodded and left them to it.

The bed was incredibly comfy, and the wine with dinner and the heat of the day conspired to make her fall asleep very quickly.

When she opened her eyes again, she was momentarily disorientated. It was still dark, just faint silvery light creeping through a crack in the shutters. Rolling over, she saw that the space beside her had not yet been slept in.

She glanced at her watch and saw that it was just after midnight. Her mouth was dry and the alcohol had given her a headache. She got out of bed to get some water, knowing this was really an excuse to see where Dominic was.

Opening the bedroom door, she could hear Tony's deep baritone coming from the study to the left of the hall. The thought of Dominic and Victoria left alone sent shivers of dread around her body.

Dominic loves me, she reassured herself. Victoria, one of his oldest friends, had noticed it too.

She went to the bathroom and filled a tooth glass with water, enjoying the sensation of the cold liquid sliding down her throat. It was a warm, clammy evening, so she went to open the French windows and stepped out on to the balcony.

The Mediterranean shimmered in the distance – a dark blanket threaded with silver – and she sighed at its beauty. Closing her eyes, she let the soft evening breeze stroke her face.

She knew that you were meant to remember moments like this for the rest of your life, but she felt too unsettled to take in its magic.

The South of France was a place to fall in love. Oh, and she had. She had ignored the voices in her head, the voices that had warned her from the start that it was unwise to lose her heart to Dominic Blake. That blind optimism that had made her think she could change the world had convinced her they could be happy and grow old together.

'You fool,' she whispered out loud.

She opened her eyes and was about to go back inside when she heard a noise in the grounds, a voice, soft and low, carried on the breeze.

Stepping to the edge of the balcony, she looked around, the gardens of Les Cyprès a series of shapes and shadows in the dark.

And then she saw them, Dominic and Victoria, walking across the grass, deep in conversation. After a minute they stopped and turned to face each other. The moon had gone behind a cloud; a minute earlier and they would have been spotlit like actors on a stage, but in this light Ros could not make out any detail in their faces. She strained her ears and could hear the low grumble of conversation. Not the laughter and joking of two people trying to impress one another. It sounded serious, sombre, which at least gave Ros some small comfort. But still, they looked so perfect together, even in silhouette, *especially* in silhouette.

They turned to face the house and Ros retreated quickly inside, not wanting to be seen.

She returned to bed, pulling the sheet right up against her chin, and started to count sheep, desperate to fall asleep before Dominic came back into the room.

Chapter Twenty-Three

The Direct Action Group had, to all intents and purposes, ceased to exist. Officially they were on a sabbatical, to regroup and refocus. Ros remembered what Tony Harbord had said, his suggestion that the group was directionless, and she had to admit he had a point. How was it possible to change anything when you wanted to change everything?

Some days she felt a fierce longing for the Brewer Street office, whose lease had long been surrendered; other times she felt ready for new challenges. She was now writing for the *Manchester Guardian*, and the *New Statesman*, whose editor John Freeman was both a journalist and a Labour politician, a CV that Ros greatly admired and aspired to.

'Oh Ros, what's the matter?' said Sam, putting a steaming cup of coffee in front of her on the kitchen table.

Ros took a breath before she opened her mouth. Although she could shout louder than most people, was the first to voice her opinions, she saw herself as a private person.

'It's Dominic,' she said finally, wrapping her fingers around her cup.

'What's wrong? Have you two had a fight?'

Ros hesitated before she spoke, knowing that she had to be sensitive. She wasn't sure whether Sam was over her own heartbreak. Brian had disappeared off the face of the earth after the night of Jonathon Soames's dinner party, leaving Sam utterly distraught and bewildered. Ros had been forced to explain what had gone on at the DAG office, which had led in part to Sam deciding to step back from their activities. But what had upset Sam just as much as Brian's vanishing act, the fact that she had been lied to, and that he had put them all in danger, was that she hadn't really known her boyfriend at all. Right now, Ros could sympathise.

'A fight? Not exactly,' she said quietly.

'Then what is it? You don't think he's still upset about that row you had at Miss Fancy Pants' villa in Antibes?'

Ros didn't like to think about that. The entire holiday had been so magical, but that last night at Les Cyprès had caused unmistakable tension in the subsequent days.

'I don't know. He certainly doesn't like me talking about the expedition.'

'Because he knows you disapprove.'

'Thanks to Victoria,' said Ros.

Sam settled forward and looked her friend in the eye.

'Trust no one,' she said finally. 'I'm not convinced Victoria had your best interests at heart when she gave you the lecture about keeping him on a leash.'

'I don't want him on a leash. I just don't want him going off with other women, and I certainly don't want him to get killed in the jungle. But you're right, I don't trust Victoria.'

Ros felt embarrassed to admit the next thing, but Sam was the only person she could talk to.

'Victoria warned me that Dominic might stray,' she said, voicing the suspicion she had kept down inside her. 'But I think he might be straying with her.'

Sam gasped. 'Surely they wouldn't be that brazen?'

'Who knows what people are capable of.' She cast her friend a glance, and they both knew they were thinking about Brian.

'Something just doesn't feel right,' Ros said finally. 'He hates taking phone calls when I'm around. And on at least half a dozen occasions I've picked up the phone and the person at the other end has just hung up. I've brought it up with him but he dismisses it as wrong numbers and crank callers. Apparently he gets a lot of those at the *Capital* office because of the polemics they run.'

'I can understand that,' shrugged Sam.

'The other day I wanted to meet him for coffee. He was very cagey. One minute he said he had to go to a meeting. An hour later he mentioned he was going somewhere else. So I followed him.'

'Ros, you didn't.'

'Look, I'm not exactly proud of myself, but if he's having an affair with someone, with *her,* I have to know.'

'What happened?'

'He left his office and got the tube to South Kensington.'

'Doesn't she live around there?'

Ros nodded. 'In some enormous pile on Egerton Crescent. The London house,' she said with a hint of sarcasm.

'Is that where he went?'

'Well, no,' said Ros, her shoulders slumping. 'He went into the Brompton Oratory. He was in there about ten minutes, then he came out and disappeared down Knightsbridge.'

'Did you follow him into the Oratory?'

'No.'

'Then why are you suspicious?' Sam gave a little laugh to lighten the mood. 'Don't say you've got visions of him having nooky with Victoria on a church pew.'

Ros sipped her coffee. She didn't know whether Sam was

being incredibly naïve, or whether her own feelings for Dominic were sending her mad. It was her default setting to see conspiracy everywhere. She thought the Russians were in league with the Chinese, that the World Bank was more like a global dictatorship and that, quite possibly, the Americans had had prior knowledge of the attack on Pearl Harbor but had allowed it to happen to justify an attack on the Japanese. But when it came to affairs of the heart, she had always been quite uncomplicated. Previous relationships had failed to take root because she hadn't been in love, and she was certainly not the sort of girl to be with someone for the sake of it.

'Look, I know it sounds silly. But he just seemed a bit shifty, a bit guilty, when he came out.'

Sam stretched her hand across the table reassuringly. 'Ros, listen to yourself. I was expecting you to tell me that you'd spotted him necking with some blonde. He was probably lighting a candle or praying for luck for his expedition.'

'Dominic isn't at all religious,' Ros said, though she knew Sam had a point.

'He loves you. I've seen it with my own eyes. And if you think he's being distant, I'm not convinced it's because of an affair with Victoria Harbord.'

'Then what is it?'

'He's off to the jungle. On his own,' said Sam quietly. 'There's anacondas and angry pygmies. You know, pretty much everything out there can kill you.'

'I'm not sure that's helping me much, Sam,' Ros said grimly

'My point is that perhaps he's deliberately distancing himself from you because he knows how dangerous it is. He's trying to protect you in case he doesn't come back.'

'Oh Sam. That's just what I'm scared of. I'm terrified of losing him.'

'Then don't give up.'

Ros scoffed. 'Don't you start. I followed Victoria's advice and look where that got me. '

'You're Ros Bailey,' said Sam firmly. 'Everyone in the socialist movement respects you because you're—'

'A bitch?'

Sam shook her head.

'Because you know what you want and you go out and get it. You're a doer, a fighter, and we all follow you because you never say die.'

Rosamund looked down, slightly taken aback and a little embarrassed.

'So why should Dominic be any different?' Sam continued. 'If you were running a campaign against the injustice of Dominic Blake ignoring his girlfriend, what would you do?'

'Start a demonstration? Print up some posters?'

'No, Ros,' she said, wagging a finger. 'That's what other people would do; you would think of something clever. Lateral thinking, isn't that what it's called?'

Slowly, a smile crept over Rosamund's face.

'You're right. In fact I have an idea that might just kill two birds with one stone.'

'Then what are you waiting for, Ros Bailey? Go and get him.'

For a moment Rosamund wondered if she had walked into the wrong flat. She was tired and preoccupied and had barely paid attention to anything on the walk from the tube, so it was entirely possible. But no, it was definitely the right place; it was just that everything looked different. When she had left this morning, the narrow passageway from the front door had been crammed with boxes and equipment; now it was empty save the sideboard, which had a neat stack of envelopes and a vase of fresh flowers on it. *Flowers?*

The flat even smelt different: some sort of cooking coming from the kitchen. And was that singing?

'Hello?' she called, walking forward uncertainly, glancing into the bedroom, which, like the hallway, was uncluttered and tidy. *What on earth?*

The singing stopped and Dominic put his head around the door. 'Hello,' he smiled, stepping over, wiping his hands on a tea towel. He had a smear of something white on his right cheek and he was wearing an apron. He bent to kiss her on the lips.

'Good timing,' he said. 'Dinner will be five minutes. I'll just pour you a drink.'

Frowning, she peeked into the small living room.

'Dom, where are all the boxes? What's happened?'

'I saw you trip over a hurricane lamp last night.'

'Class act, aren't I?' she smiled.

'No, no. The flat's in chaos, so I've sorted it out. Some of the stuff has been shipped out to Peru. At least we'll have a bit more space to sit, have dinner. Oh shit. Something's burning.'

'Supper?' said Ros with a grimace.

Dom disappeared into the tiny galley kitchen and returned holding a blackened pan.

'What was that?' she asked, peering into its depths.

'Chicken à la King.'

'No longer looking too royal.'

'Let's go out,' he said grabbing her hand.

Twenty minutes later, they were in a quiet French restaurant on a side street in Covent Garden. As the light outside faded and the waiter lit the candle placed between them, Ros thought she could be back in Paris.

Dom smiled at her, and his expression was so loving, she felt guilty for doubting him.

'Thanks for cooking,' she said as the waiter poured them glasses of crisp white wine.

'Thanks for putting up with me,' he replied, clinking his goblet against hers.

She raised her eyebrows. 'The expedition?'

He nodded. 'I've been thinking a lot about what you said in France, and you're right. For so long it has been just me. I haven't had anyone or anything else to think about in any decision I make, except maybe the readers of *Capital*. But now there's you. You are the most important thing in my life and I want to make some changes to accommodate that. To accommodate you.'

'You make me sound like a four-poster bed you've got to squeeze into a studio room,' she laughed. Ros never felt comfortable with compliments or emotion, but secretly she was thrilled with his words. After the tension at Les Cyprès, she had never imagined he would say them.

'I don't want you to do anything you don't want to do,' she said, treading carefully. Half of her was still imagining it was a trick. 'Travel, adventure, it's your lifeblood. I don't want to change you. The only thing I want is for you to be happy. For *us* to be happy.'

'We could go and live in Paris. Or the South of France. Get that shack you liked the sound of, with the bed for two.'

'What about *Capital*?'

'We could set up a French sister publication. For English-speaking ex-pats. Robert can run the London edition, I can become international chief, and you, Rosamund Bailey, rising star of the industry, can be editor-in-chief, *Capital Paris*.'

'Now that sounds like an adventure,' she said grinning.

The enthusiasm on his face softened.

'But first I need to go to Peru. I can't pull out now.'

It was the first time she had ever heard him talk about the expedition with anything other than excitement.

'I don't want you to pull out,' she said softly.

'You don't?' he said with surprise.

Ros paused as the waiter brought their food. Then she took a fortifying mouthful of boeuf bourguignon and looked at Dominic.

He frowned. 'What is it?'

'I went to the Foreign Office today.'

'The FO? Why?'

'Because I've decided to come with you to the Amazon.'

'You want to come with me,' he repeated slowly.

She locked eyes with him, her expression stony. 'I won't come into the jungle, if that's your decision. You are the expert on this and I will respect your opinion. But I am going out to Peru with you because there is a chance you may never come back and I want to spend every possible moment with the man I love. Is that clear?'

'That's not the most optimistic way to view my trip.'

'But it's true,' she said frankly. 'You know it, I know it. That's why you want to go to Blackpool for our next holiday.'

'Not exactly,' he smiled.

'I've been to the Royal Geographical Society, the Peruvian embassy and the Foreign Office,' said Rosamund. 'All the paperwork is in. I am signed on as your logistics manager.'

She gulped, trying to stay composed, knowing he had every right to be furious with her.

'You would do that for me?' he said finally.

'You should have realised by now that I'm an all-or-nothing kind of girl.'

'I've realised that you're even more remarkable than I thought.'

'Stop getting mushy. I'm just protecting my investment, even if you can't cook a meal without burning it.'

'Let's get out of here.'

'Hang on. I haven't finished my potatoes.'

He had already asked for the bill and thrown down a ten-shilling note to pay for their food.

'Where are we going?'

'Let's just walk,' he said, taking her hand.

He was quiet for a few moments, as if he was thinking. They crossed the road at Aldwych, exiting the dense streets of Covent Garden, and she felt her shoulders relax as they came within sight of the river.

'Waterloo Bridge,' she smiled. 'I remember what you said about this place on our first date.'

'Our first date?'

'At the pub in Primrose Hill. I know it wasn't actually a first date. I know you just wanted to talk about my article, but still . . .'

'It was a first date,' he said, squeezing her hand.

She gasped when she saw the view. As a former student of the nearby LSE, it was a vista she knew well, but it never ceased to astound her. The majestic Houses of Parliament, an always inspiring symbol of democracy, was to her right, whilst St Paul's Cathedral and the twinkling lights of the City sparkled to her left.

Dusk was settling over London, streaking the sky with gold and violet, and it sent shivers of emotion coursing through her body.

'I don't think I've ever felt more excited about life and the promise it held than when I walked over Waterloo Bridge,' she said softly.

Dominic put an arm around her shoulder and drew her close.

'You said that on our first date, and now I know exactly what you meant,' she said, looking up at him.

'I'm feeling it again now, aren't you?' he said, nuzzling the top of her head.

As she nodded, he took hold of her hand and turned her around so that she was facing him. She thought he was about to kiss her, but he looked suddenly nervous, a tic pulsing under his left eye, those grey eyes she loved.

'Marry me,' he said.

At first she wasn't sure she had heard him properly.

'I don't just want you to come to the Amazon with me. I want to be with you for ever.'

Her heart was racing, and then she started laughing, the sound carried away on the riverside breeze. And finally she said, 'Yes.'

Chapter Twenty-Four

Nobody was particularly surprised when Dominic Blake insisted on throwing a party to celebrate his engagement to Rosamund Bailey. If cooking wasn't his forte, then throwing an intimate bash for a hundred of their closest friends was what he was certainly good at.

Ros walked into the stucco apartment in Belgravia and gasped. It was a huge lateral space with a bank of almost floor-to-ceiling windows on one side of the room looking out on to Eaton Square. The polished walnut floors and the elegant grey furniture gave it a glamorous Art Deco feel, and as she accepted a glass of champagne from a man in a dinner jacket, she felt like Audrey Hepburn in Billy Wilder's *Sabrina*.

'If this was my house, I'm not sure I'd lend it to anyone,' she said, looking around the room, searching for breakables.

'It's a good friend and they are never in the country,' said Dominic, taking a guest list out of his pocket and checking it.

'Do they know how many people you've invited?' asked Ros, peering over his shoulder at the long list of names.

'Everyone's well-behaved,' he whispered, sipping at his champagne bowl.

'We'll see about that,' laughed Ros cynically.

She was glad to see Jonathon Soames and his girlfriend Michaela, who brought her an enormous bunch of peach-coloured roses. Accepting them, she felt like a movie star on stage at the Oscars, but told them not to expect a speech. There were others in the room that she was only meeting for the first time – more university friends, old colleagues from a broadsheet where Dominic had worked straight out of Cambridge.

Her heart fell when she saw Victoria Harbord arrive, especially as she looked more stunning than usual. Ros had seen her without make-up in the pool, and knew she was a natural beauty, but she couldn't help thinking that Lady Harbord had made a special effort this evening. An emerald-green silk dress with a boat-cut neckline showed off an expanse of tanned shoulders, and her dark blond hair fell in waves down her back.

She waved when she saw Ros and headed over.

'Ros, you look as ravishing as ever. I love this dress.'

Ros looked down at the blue shift dress she had bought specially for the occasion; it looked very dowdy and ordinary compared to Victoria's.

'How are you, Vee?'

'Good, good. I've been following your journalism. I saw your piece in the *New Statesman*. Do you really think they're going to build an actual wall through the middle of Berlin?'

'That's the rumour. It was denied in a press conference, but East Germany wants to stop the brain drain to the West, and I think they're going to take quite drastic steps to do that.'

Victoria sighed and looked around the room, clearly no longer interested in discussing politics.

'Enjoying the party?' she asked, playing with a gold pendant around her neck. 'I can't say I ever thought it would come to this,' she added.

'You sound surprised,' replied Ros thinly.

'I have never doubted Dominic's love for you. I just didn't think we'd see him at the altar. How on earth did you do it?'

'Well, I didn't need a leash.'

'Then why are you going with him to Peru?'

Ros glanced at Dominic with annoyance, wondering how much her fiancé had told his friends.

'Why are you here, Victoria, if you're not happy for us?' she said, unable to contain herself any longer.

Victoria put a reassuring hand on her forearm. It was a trick that Ros had seen time and again among Dominic's high-flying circle of friends. She wondered if it was something they taught you in the fancy schools these people went to.

'Ros, please don't be sensitive. Dominic is one of my dearest friends. Of course I am happy for you.'

'But you don't think I'm good enough for him, do you?'

Victoria's expression hardened.

'I don't think you're right for him. There's a difference,' she said in a quieter voice.

Ros felt her back stiffen. She knew how easy it was to be intimidated by these people, but she was not going to let it happen.

'And why would that be, Victoria? Am I too Jewish? Too working class? Too opinionated for a trophy wife? How do I not quite fall into your very narrow view of what is good marriage material?'

'I don't care who you are or where you came from,' said Victoria, keeping her tone light. 'Tony was a butcher's son, born in the slums of New York, but he has made his mark in society in spite of where he came from.'

She took Ros's hand and wrapped both of hers around it, her self-assurance softening to concern.

'You excite Dominic, Rosamund. You madden him, you intrigue him. You are as exotic as the jungle and as familiar as the girl next door, and believe me, that is quite an intoxicating combination. But you are just too different to make it work. I mean, do you ever socialise with his friends?'

'Like who?'

'His friends! These people?'

'I've seen them,' she said stiffly.

'Occasionally, by all accounts.'

Ros knew they were both aware that it had happened just a handful of times.

'Ros, there is a difference between a marriage of opposites and an incompatible partnership. Dominic keeps his worlds separate, you and them, because he knows you just don't mix. He will never let go of his friends, so his solution is to keep you apart. But how is this anything other than a temporary solution? At some point he will have to make a choice. And even if he does choose you, which I suspect he will, there will be a part of him that will be forever resentful. I should imagine the same goes for your friends. How much do they like hanging out with Tory boy? They don't, and so never the twain shall meet.'

'We love each other, that's what counts.'

'Does it? I thought you of all people wouldn't have such a rose-tinted view of life.'

'What are you saying, Victoria? What are you *really* saying here? That I shouldn't marry Dominic?'

'Have you set a date?'

'Not yet, no.'

'Well, I wonder why,' said Victoria, taking a glass of champagne and wandering off into the crowd.

* * *

Not even another couple of glasses of champagne, downed in rapid succession, could calm Rosamund.

'I'd say the party's a success,' said Dominic, slipping his hand around her waist.

Ros nodded and smiled with as much enthusiasm as she could manage. But whilst she knew she had no loyalty to Victoria Harbord, she could not tell her fiancé about the conversation they had just had and how much it had upset her. For a moment she was reminded of an episode with bullies she had experienced at school; for weeks she had been too scared to speak out against the girls who had tormented her for being too ethnic, and too smart. Even though she had stuck up for herself in the playground, it was only when she spoke out and canvassed support around her, teachers and other pupils, that the bullies went away.

And yet still she could not tell Dominic about Victoria. He loved his friends, she knew that, and she didn't want to create a wall between them.

'Right, I want to meet some of your friends,' said Dominic, taking hold of her hand. 'Sam. Where's Sam? I want to introduce her to my friend Edward.'

'She's definitely on her way,' said Ros, scanning the room. The party had started at 7.30, and all of Dominic's friends seemed to have arrived by eight o'clock, yet none of the people Ros had invited – Sam, Alex, George, the manager of the café where she used to work and three new Primrose Hill friends – were yet here.

She breathed a sigh of relief when she saw her parents standing awkwardly at the door, the first of her fashionably late contingent. Her father was in his smartest suit; her mother was wearing something that resembled a saucer on her head.

'Mr and Mrs Bailey,' said Dominic, squeezing Ros's fingers as they went over to greet them.

'Dominic, what a beautiful place,' said Valerie, almost speechless as she looked around.

'Sadly it's not mine,' said Dominic, making sure they had drinks.

'In which case, I'm going to have to take you into my study and talk about your prospects,' said Samuel, already looking giddy on the champagne.

Ros laughed. She knew how well Dominic got on with her father. When he had gone round to officially ask for Ros's hand in marriage, the two men had disappeared to the pub and returned three hours later laughing like old friends, which had only impressed upon Ros how badly she wanted to marry him.

A few more of Ros's friends arrived, and Dom announced that he wanted to make a speech, banging a teaspoon against a crystal glass.

'Gather round, everyone. I'd like to say a few words.'

'There's a surprise,' shouted Zander from the back of the room.

Everyone laughed, then made a semicircle around Dominic and Ros. He thanked them all for coming, and gave a few special mentions to those who had helped with the arrangements.

'Ever since I was a little boy, I've wanted to be a journalist,' he told the sea of faces. 'I've always been fascinated with words, and what they can do. Words can make you laugh, they can make you cry, they can alter your opinions by giving you hope and wisdom and knowledge. They have an alchemic power to change things. Words changed my life,' he said, clutching Ros's hand tighter. 'One day earlier this year, I read a blistering, roughly typed attack on *Capital* magazine, and I knew I had to meet its author. Words brought Ros Bailey through my door. And then one word made me happier than I have ever been in my life. That word was "yes".'

He turned and took both of her hands.

'Ros Bailey, I love you so much. I can't wait to marry you and I am honoured that you want me as your husband.'

A cheer went up around the room. Ros found herself beaming at everyone until she spotted Victoria Harbord standing at the back, unsmiling, just sipping her champagne. Their eyes met, and Ros felt not triumph, but a sweet, overpowering sense of relief that everything was going to be okay.

'I missed the speech,' said Sam, throwing her arms around her.

'You came!'

'You didn't think I'd miss a party in Eaton Square, did you? Gosh, I haven't been here since I was a deb in '55.'

'Your natural habitat, then,' laughed Ros, imagining her free-spirited friend navigating the social mores of the Season.

'Put it this way, I know half the girls in the room from Cheltenham Ladies',' whispered Sam.

'They must be glad to see you,' replied Ros honestly.

'Absolutely. They look at me, listen to what I do, and feel grateful for all their life choices.'

Ros laughed. 'Well I'd rather be you than them any day of the week.'

'Your sparkler. Let me see it,' said Sam, grabbing Ros's left hand and lifting it up to inspect it.

Ros fluttered her fingers to show off the beautiful ruby ring that Dom had presented her with the day after his Waterloo Bridge proposal.

'It's gorgeous,' sighed Sam. 'It makes me want to meet a man who loves me as much as Dom loves you. Is it terribly unfeminist of me to think like that?'

'There's absolutely nothing wrong with wanting to love and be loved,' smiled Ros, touching her arm. 'Speaking of which,

Dom wants to introduce you to his friend Edward,' she said, waving him over.

'Oh good. Is this a set-up?'

'Just call him Cupid,' whispered Ros.

Dom was feet away from them when the butler tapped him on the shoulder.

'Excuse me, Mr Blake. There's a phone call for you.'

Dominic frowned in puzzlement.

'Ladies, I'll be back in a minute.' He winked.

'Go on, then. Charm us out of trouble.'

'What do you mean?' asked Sam when he'd gone.

'The flat belongs to some American friends who I swear don't know the scale of the party. The complaints from the neighbours have probably started.'

'Mr and Mrs B. How are you?' said Sam, turning to Rosamund's parents.

'I could get used to this sort of night out,' laughed Ros's dad.

'If this is the engagement party, what did the pair of you have in mind for the wedding?' asked Valerie, a crease of concern appearing between her brows.

'Something small. Intimate. I had something half this size in mind,' replied Ros.

'Good, because your father has been terribly worried. I understand our responsibilities and we fully intend to pay for the wedding, but there has to be a limit.'

Sam's brows shot up with the excitement of an idea.

'I know. You can use my parents' place.'

'Sam, don't be silly,' said Ros.

'I'm being serious! It's just ninety minutes out of London and we've got a huge terrace for drinks and a ballroom for dancing. I'm afraid the sofas smell a bit of cat pee and you'll probably have to invite Mum and Dad, but buy them a crate of gin and they'll be delighted to host the wedding.'

'Sam, that's so generous of you. Too generous, in fact,' said Ros, putting an arm around her friend. 'I couldn't possibly make that sort of imposition.'

'I agree,' said Samuel awkwardly. Ros looked at her father, knowing that his unwillingness to accept Sam's hospitality was rooted in pride.

He didn't need to worry. She and Dom had already discussed the broad strokes of their wedding.

Ros had no desire for a big white dress, nor the religious conviction to exchange vows in church. Instead she fancied Chelsea registry office for a handful of their closest family and friends, and a meal afterwards of roast chicken and lemon tart; things that reminded her of Provence. She had already seen the perfect dress: a cream knee-length shift in Bazaar on the King's Road.

'You should at least think about it,' said Valerie, sipping her champagne. 'I think it would add something special having the celebration at such a good friend's home.'

'Well the offer's there, but you'd better hurry up and make your mind up,' said Sam with a shrug. 'You should at least have a date and a venue in place before you leave for your trip. You can't leave the crowds hanging.' She winked.

'Trip?' asked Valerie, peering up at them from under her hat.

'The Amazon trip.'

'What Amazon trip?' asked her mother in disbelief.

'I'm going to Peru,' replied Rosamund sheepishly. 'With Dominic. I'm the logistics manager for his next expedition.'

'I thought you'd settled on journalism, love,' said her father with concern.

'There are cannibals in Peru,' said Valerie, her mouth wide open. 'Is this Dominic's idea?' she frowned.

'All mine.'

'And is he happy about it? He's your fiancé. It's his duty to protect you.'

'I've made my mind up, Mother. I'm going.'

Valerie pulled her hat off in anger.

'Where's Dominic? This is outrageous. I must speak with him this instant.'

She put down her champagne and ploughed into the crowd. Ros followed her.

'Mum, please,' she said as Valerie stopped at the entrance to the kitchen, where Dominic was talking to Jonathon Soames.

'Young man, I need a word with you,' said Valerie briskly.

Dominic turned to her, his expression serious.

'What's the matter, Mrs Bailey?'

'What's the matter? You're taking my only child into the jungle. Endanger your own life with your flights of folly, but don't risk the safety of my little girl. I thought you would know better than this.'

There was a long, awkward silence.

'You're right,' said Dominic finally.

Ros glared at him in horror. 'What are you talking about?' she snapped. 'It's all arranged. I thought you were excited that I was coming with you.'

'That was before I realised how upset your parents would be.'

'It's my mother. She's had too much drink.'

'No I have not,' blustered Valerie.

'Let's talk about this later,' said Dom.

'No,' said Ros with passion. 'Let's talk about it now. Jonathon, help me out here.'

'Mrs Bailey, perhaps we should leave these two alone for a few minutes,' said Jonathon diplomatically.

Valerie looked as if she was about to object, but Jonathon

guided her out of the room and closed the door behind them.

'I can't not go,' Ros said with panic. 'I've spent the last few weeks looking at maps and charts and atlases – I even went along to the Royal Cartography Institute to read up on anything and everything they've got on the Amazon. I'm going to be the best expedition team member you've ever had.'

'You know how dangerous the trip is going to be?'

'I've always known that. It's why I'm coming with you. Right until the bit where it starts getting muddy and jungly and full of flies.'

She thought he would laugh, but his expression remained sombre.

'Are you sure you're up for that? Waving me off when there's every chance I might not come back?'

'You are coming back. You promised me. I trust you. I believe in you.'

Dominic nodded but didn't quite meet her eye.

'I'm not going to change your mind, am I?' he said quietly.

'And neither is my mother,' she said, taking his hand and holding it as if she would never let go. 'We're a team, Dominic Blake. That's what we're here to celebrate. You and me. And I'm not going to let anyone or anything change that.'

Chapter Twenty-Five

God, it was hot. Rosamund didn't think she'd ever been this hot. She pulled at her collar and untied her damp scarf, dabbing at the beads of perspiration on her forehead. Not that she had much experience of heat beyond a sweltering family holiday on the Isle of Wight when she was fourteen. This was something else; the heat seemed to get inside your skin, and the air felt thick and soupy, like you couldn't draw enough into your lungs. Ros had long ago given up worrying about her clothes: they stuck to her from morning to night, as though she'd just run through a shower. She looked up at the corrugated-iron roof and willed the fans to turn faster.

'I'm guessing they don't have ice,' she said, pressing her tin cup against her cheek.

'I don't think there's been a refrigeration unit since Lima,' said Dominic. He was sharpening one of his knives with a flint.

'But at least we're off the boat,' quipped Willem, the half-Peruvian, half-German translator, who had met them at the airport and who was apparently making some additional cash by taking a series of photographs for the Royal Cartography Institute back in London.

Ros and Dominic nodded in agreement, thinking of the *Santa Ana*, the rusting steamer that had been their transportation from the regional capital of Tarapoto, upriver to Kutuba, the furthest outpost of civilisation, little more than a tiny shanty town, before the jungle closed in around you.

It had been an awful journey but the only practical option. There was no railway in Peru, at least not in this remote part of the country, where the lumber and the various cash crops could be moved much more easily by river. The geography and meteorology of the country made roads impractical for the most part, with the fast-growing vegetation able to close in on a highway in a matter of days, and flash floods and mudslides washing them from the map in hours. And while seaplanes occasionally made the journey into the interior, the only reliable way to reach Kutuba was on the painfully slow steamer, which had taken ten days to limp the 150 miles.

Ros could still envisage each hellish moment. During the day, the humidity and the thumping diesel engines would force them up on deck, then the pitiless sun, the clouds of insects or the sudden Biblical downpours would force them back inside. At night, they had no option but to swelter in their quarters, reading or talking in low voices in the orange light of the hurricane lanterns as moths the size of crab apples swooped around.

Rosamund had been travel sick almost every day, and had been glad to get to dry land. Kutuba, with its single dusty street haunted by skinny dogs and seemingly abandoned Indian children, now seemed an oasis of civilisation compared to the boat.

Miguel, Dominic's guide, who had met the team in Tarapoto, had taken them to his home on the edge of the village. It wasn't exactly the Ritz: more like a large timber-frame shack with palm matting underfoot. But at least it had electricity, when the generator was working, and clean sheets in the lean-to rooms out the back, courtesy of Miguel's feisty Indian wife Quana.

Rosamund, Dominic and Willem went out to the patch of dry, parched grass behind the hut. Two of their Peruvian porters came to join them, both of them puffing on cigarettes, followed by Miguel, who sat cross-legged on the floor for the briefing.

'When are the other guides arriving?' asked Dominic, taking a long swig of water from a bottle. He was pacing around anxiously, like a caged animal.

'I spoke to Padre this morning and I am assured today. We shall see,' said Miguel with a shrug.

Ros shot a glance at Dominic, but he didn't look unduly concerned; in fact she knew he had been expecting this. The guides for the final leg of the journey, the leg before he was to be left completely alone, were two Indian tribesmen from a settlement close to Kutuba. They had more specialist knowledge of the jungle than Miguel, who looked and acted like the locals she had seen in Lima. Dominic had had extensive dealings with the tribe before, living with them for six weeks of jungle training, learning how to survive and live off the land, before he had launched out on a previous expedition in the Amazon. And he knew them well enough to know that they moved at their own pace. That 'today' could mean tomorrow, or even next week.

'Can I come with you to their settlement?' asked Ros, looking out to the thick line of trees beyond the village.

'She is brave,' laughed Miguel, and Ros was not sure if his expression was one of respect or concern.

'You've come this far. What's a few more miles?' Dominic winked at her, and she felt her heart do a little flip.

Dominic and Miguel walked away to talk more. Willem relaxed with the porters, smoking and tugging on a bottle of beer, as Ros stood up to stretch her legs.

She didn't like to eavesdrop on their conversation, but Miguel's voice was loud, as if the volume might make up for the comprehensibility of his heavily Spanish accented words.

One line of conversation was quite clear: there were 'bad men' in the forest.

She also caught the word 'drugs', and she knew full well what they were talking about. She had submitted a feature idea to the *Sunday Chronicle* a few weeks earlier about global drug trafficking. She felt sure that the issue was set to explode, and that it needed talking about immediately, but the piece had been turned down by a sceptical features editor who argued that illegal drugs had no place in Western society beyond its most bohemian fringes.

Ros thought otherwise. Her research had revealed that cocaine manufacture was a huge growth industry in the coca-farming areas of South America, despite, or perhaps because of, the recent criminalisation of the drug. Illicit trade in the substance was widespread, peasant farmers supplying their coca to a new and ruthless brand of smugglers, who were carving trade routes through the jungle.

'Are you sure you've had enough jungle training?' asked Ros when Miguel had gone. She walked into their room and perched on the end of the makeshift bed.

'It's a bit late to be asking that,' replied Dominic, rubbing the sweat from his face with a towel.

Silence fell between them.

'I'm prepared,' he said softly. 'As prepared as I'll ever be.'

She nodded. 'Well if you've forgotten anything, it's a bit bloody late to turn back and get it.'

It was meant to be a joke, but Dominic looked thoughtful.

'I hope I've brought enough gifts.'

'Gifts?'

'For the tribes. If I anger them, gifts might placate them. Plus it's good etiquette to arrive with something.'

'Well at least you've got a gun,' she smiled, looking at his shotgun propped up next to a long machete. Ros considered herself a pacifist, but the sight of the two weapons gave her some reassurance.

He reached into his bag and pulled out a buff-coloured envelope.

'What's this?' she asked.

'My will.'

Her face fell. 'Your will?'

'I said I was prepared.'

'Of course. You have to be practical about these things. Should I read it?'

He shook his head. 'Just put it somewhere safe. But you should know that Jonathon Soames and Robert Webb are the executors of my estate should anything happen. As we're not married yet, I've changed a few things around to accommodate my wishes.'

'Dom, don't talk like this.'

'If anything happens to me, I want you to have my shareholding in *Capital* magazine,' he continued. 'The Tavistock Square flat too. There's a small mortgage on it, but nothing the hottest journalist in London shouldn't be able to handle.' He smiled at her softly, the corners of his eyes creasing into fine lines she hadn't even noticed before.

'I don't want to talk about it,' she said, putting her hands dramatically over her ears. 'You're here now. You are going into that jungle, coming out again, and in the week before Christmas we are getting married. Me and you. I've even found a cream velvet cape, so you can't let me down.'

Dom's eyes were shining. She thought she saw a glint of

emotion, but when she looked closer, his tears had gone.

'A cape?' he said finally.

'Trimmed with silk. You'll like it, but I'm not saying anything else. It's bad luck for the groom to know too much about his beautiful bride's gown.'

'Miguel's wife is cooking,' said Dominic, deliberately changing the subject. 'Do you want to eat with the others, or just us?'

'Just us.'

He grinned and instructed her to wait in the room, returning a few minutes later with a cast-iron pot, which he held by its handles with some sacking cloth.

While he'd been gone, Ros had lit three storm lanterns and placed them around the room. The light was low, soft and glorious, but the air was still humid, and for a second she felt like a fly trapped in amber.

Dominic put the pot on the table, which she had set with plates and two tin cups. She smiled to herself, deciding that she had some potential as a homemaker, while Dominic poured red wine into the cups.

She didn't have to ask how he had sourced a decent claret in the jungle. It was one of the many things she loved about him: his competence and cleverness, the easy way he just got things done. That confidence in his ability to do absolutely anything was the one thing that had kept her sane over the past few weeks. If anyone could do a solo adventure into the Amazon and make it safely back, it was him. He had made similar journeys before and come back with stories for his dinner parties, rather than broken bones and tropical diseases. He was blessed. It was as if God was smiling on him.

'Do you know what? I think the world would be a better place if it was lit only by candlelight,' she said, dipping her spoon into her stew.

Dominic started to laugh.

'Whatever do you mean?'

'Look around,' she said, her eyes shining. 'Look how intimate it is. It's a light made for sharing secrets, for complicity, for honesty.'

'Maybe we should recommend it to Kennedy and Khrushchev the next time they meet.'

'Perhaps the Cold War would be a little less chilly,' she agreed.

'Tell me a secret,' she said after a moment.

'I can play the ukulele.'

'I didn't know that.'

'You wanted a secret.'

'All right, all right,' she said, sensing that he did not want to play. She couldn't help but think he was being a little distant; then again, it was probably just nerves, the excitement and the prospect of what was to come. 'We have a lifetime to get to know one another. I want to be still talking, still finding things out about you when I'm seventy-five. The last thing I want to be is one of those couples who run out of things to say to one another after two years of marriage.'

'I'd like that,' he said softly.

Ros wanted to know more about his survival training, about his last time in the jungle with the Lampista tribe, and Dominic seemed to relax as he showed her how to make a bow and arrow out of twigs, twine and stone. He told her how the tribe leader had given him a shot of venom from a poisonous Amazonian tree frog, and how he was hoping the procedure didn't have to be revisited once they reached the camp.

At some point Miguel knocked on their door, and Dominic disappeared for half an hour to meet the Indian guides, who had just arrived. In his absence, Ros changed into her last clean nightdress, enjoying the feeling of fresh cotton on her skin, although when Dominic returned, it was not long before it was removed.

Their lovemaking was tender but intense, and when it was done, she did not want him to pull out from inside her. She wanted to stay absolutely connected to him for as long as she could, as if it would help her to lock in his scent, his touch, the sensation of him, until he got back.

The sound of the bullfrogs woke her.

Dominic was already awake and standing on the far side of the room getting dressed. She could see his muscular tanned back, and wished she was close enough to touch it.

Yawning, she wondered how tired he was. She herself had woken at various points in the night and she could tell he had been awake. The first time she had rolled towards him and put her arm across his chest, at which he had given a barely audible sigh of satisfaction. The other times she had left him with his thoughts.

Miguel's wife made them some breakfast – a version of what they had eaten the night before – and at nine o'clock they set off, Dominic, Rosamund and the guide in one small boat, Willem, Miguel and their two porters in the other. Ros's water bottle was strapped across her body – Dominic had given it to her that morning, reminding her that more people died from dehydration in the jungle than from poisoned darts.

The engines of the boats were not powerful, and progress was slow. She dipped her hand into the brown water to cool down, but Dominic pulled her back immediately, warning her of carnivorous fish.

Watching the turtles scramble across the riverbanks, Ros could understand why this sort of adventure was so seductive. It was like another world. Ignore the heat and the humidity and it was as if they had been dropped in Paradise.

A bird circled overheard. It was large, black, with a broad wingspan and a thick, vicious squawk. She knew from her research at the RCI and the Royal Geographical Society that the Amazon rainforest was home to some of the most brightly coloured birds on earth: macaws in shades of hyacinth and scarlet, toucans, and turquoise-hued cotingas. But this wasn't one of them. She remembered a story she had read about the evil bird that lived in the jungle and sang on the rooftop of someone who was going to die, and as she watched it fly wide, low circles above them, it made her shudder.

The tribal settlement was only a few miles from the edge of Kutuba, but it was slow going reaching it. This was still officially the edge of the jungle, but the vegetation was dense, and thick vines and branches dangled over the boat, scratching their arms and faces.

They steered the boats towards the riverbank and clambered on to shore, pulling the equipment and medical supplies away from the water.

Padre, the tribal chief, was waiting for them in a clearing, smoking a cigarette.

'We'll make camp here tonight,' announced Dominic. 'Amando will stay,' he said, gesturing to one of the porters.

'What about me?' asked Ros.

His look softened. 'You should go back with Miguel.'

The reality of what was happening started to suffocate her. It was as if the jungle was closing in around her.

Miguel had his hands on his hips. He looked up to the sky and announced that they should go within the next half an hour. One of the guides nodded.

Ros watched the scene unfold around her. Willem took

some photographs. Miguel, Dominic and Padre conversed in rudimentary language.

She waited until Dominic was alone, then went over to talk to him.

'Don't go,' she said.

'Ros, please.'

'I mean it. It doesn't feel right.'

Miguel was clapping his hands.

'It is time. Rosamund. Please, in the boat.'

Amando was already chopping leaves and branches from the surrounding trees to build a fire and a shelter for the night.

The crow was still overhead, Ros wasn't sure where, but she could hear it, and the angry squawks now felt like a warning.

'Don't go,' she said more urgently. 'I just have a bad feeling.'

'Ros, don't. You're not helping.'

She took hold of his hands and squeezed them.

'Dom, it's not too late to say no. The power of words, you talked about it at our engagement party. Just stop this now, please. You can stop all this in thirty seconds.'

'I know you're scared. I'm nervous too, but I've done this before. I'm taking a radio . . .'

'It doesn't feel enough. I don't know why the guides can't stay with you for the entire trip. Take one of them with you, it's not too late. One of Padre's men. They know the jungle better than you. Better than anyone.'

Dominic raised his hand to her cheek. Her skin absorbed his warmth and instinctively she placed her own palm over his.

'I love you,' he said simply.

Behind her she could hear the click of the camera.

She turned and saw Willem taking a photograph of them. She knew that it was one of the reasons he was here, but still, she felt angry at his intrusion.

She turned back and looked at Dominic.

'I'll be waiting for you,' she said softly.

He nodded, his nostrils flaring with stoic emotion. He put his arms around her, and held her as if he never wanted to let her go.

'It's time,' he whispered into the top of her hair.

She pressed her cheek into his shoulder, the thick fabric absorbing her tears.

'I love you, Dominic Blake,' she whispered, and he turned and headed off into the jungle.

Chapter Twenty-Six

London, present day

Chelsea Physic Garden smelt amazing. It was pretty too, of course: a maze of criss-crossing gravel paths leading you through an array of flowers, plants and trees, each one of them begging you to bend down and examine its leaves, shoots or blooms. But it was the smell, especially on a bright summer morning like this, that overwhelmed you. Abby could barely believe she had lived in London for so long and never stepped through the gate, because inside the high stone walls it was like being in a cocoon of calm. If you cared to look, you could see the tall Georgian residences outside the walls, but once inside the garden, it was as if London had momentarily slipped away.

She looked at her watch: she was early, but that was good. She wasn't exactly looking forward to this meeting, and it gave her time to relax and soak up the atmosphere. She sat down on a bench and pulled out her phone.

The little screen was crowded with messages from the men in her life: Elliot, Nick and Stephen. She ignored them for the moment and opened one from Suze.

Second date with Will last night – amazing, must talk. Call me! Sx

There was another, sent two minutes after the first.

Didn't shag him! First time THAT's ever happened! Sx

Abby smiled. At least someone's love life was going well. Sighing, she clicked on Stephen's message – the lesser of three evils.

Hi, Abigail, congrats on piece in Chronicle, Christine very impressed. Could you give me a ring? Have an idea. Stephen

She could just imagine what the idea was: more free publicity for some other exhibition he could take all the credit for masterminding. She took a deep breath and clicked on Elliot's message.

Are we still on for dinner tonight? I know you're pissed off, but we can fix this.

She frowned to herself, wondering if she should cancel, and indeed whether she wanted to. Elliot had called her the day the *Chronicle* story had run – mid-afternoon, but 7 a.m. West Coast time – and had spent over half an hour explaining himself. How he'd mentioned the story and their St Petersburg findings to his editor, how his editor had wanted to run with it immediately, while *The Last Goodbye* was still hot, how Elliot had spent twenty-four hours solid writing the piece, not sleeping, only drinking and smoking. And not telling Abby that he had filed the story because he feared her reaction, knowing that the editor would want to run with it whatever her objections. 'I didn't want to deceive you, Abs. So I just didn't tell you,' he had said over their long-distance phone call.

Abby wasn't sure if the two things were mutually exclusive.

Finally she opened Nick's message.

Are you going to Dr Naylor's? I am. Let me know. I love you. Nx

Another one who wants to talk, she thought dismissively,

noticing the 'x' at the end and thinking that wasn't like Nick at all. He was always critical of people who signed off with a kiss; it wasn't real, he used to say, then would grumble about how social media were destroying people's ability to actually connect with each other. All this upheaval must have brought out his feminine side. About time, thought Abby with a grim smile.

'Something funny?'

She looked up to see Rosamund standing there; she had been so wrapped up in what she was doing, she hadn't heard her approach.

'Oh, no. Just catching up on my messages,' she said, standing up, wondering if they should shake hands or air-kiss or something. No, she decided, looking at Rosamund's face. She was clearly here for a purpose, not socialising. Abby could hardly blame her. In her shoes, I wouldn't exactly be my first choice for a friend right now, she thought.

'Thank you for agreeing to see me so quickly,' Rosamund said. She had called Abby earlier that day.

Abby didn't like to point out that her lack of work and the desire to sort out – indeed, scotch – any potential legal proceedings had facilitated their prompt meeting.

'I was just glad you got back in touch,' she said quickly. 'I still feel terrible about what happened. I've spoken to Elliot. He was under pressure to run the story and didn't tell me because he knew how angry I'd be.'

'And I'm sorry for coming round unannounced like that,' was Rosamund's surprise response. 'I shouldn't have been so abrupt, although you can understand my initial shock and anger when I first read the piece.'

'Of course,' said Abby, still feeling guilty.

Ros glanced over at her as they began to walk, a look of good-humoured complicity on her face.

'I should imagine it's quite easy to fall into step with men like Elliot. They are rather seductive.'

'I think he's just ambitious,' said Abby, feeling herself blush at the thought of herself being quite literally seduced.

Rosamund nodded. 'I have always found the third-generation children of wealthy families quite fascinating. They tend to go one way or the other. Either they are lazy, complacent, unmotivated. Everything in life has been given to them on a plate, and instead of building on that success they squander it. Or they can be even more ruthless and driven than their parents or grandparents because they have something to prove. Let's give Elliot the benefit of the doubt and say his absence of morals is simply a reaction to the achievements of his father. But that's in the past. Let's move forward, hmm?'

They walked on, their feet crunching on the gravel, Rosamund pausing every now and then to admire a plant or to stoop to read one of the name labels.

'Beautiful, aren't they?' she said, rubbing a leaf between her fingers then holding them to her nose. 'But everything in this garden has a purpose. Some plants can cure stomach upsets, some can even stop bleeding. Before modern science, with its pills and powders, this was essentially a giant pharmacy.'

They stopped at a group of plants with a wooden sign reading 'Neurology and Rheumatology'.

'Now I think I could do with a few of those,' said Rosamund, indicating a nearby bench.

'Sorry, not quite as sprightly as I was,' she sighed when they were seated. 'It's true what they say, you know – everyone feels much younger inside. Some people claim to feel eighteen, but I suppose I think of myself as about twenty-eight, twenty-nine. It's always a surprise to me when I look in the mirror in the morning, or when I have to sit down quickly.'

She tapped her temple and her wistful expression dissolved.

'But I'm every bit as sharp up here, however weak the flesh. And frankly, Abby, I don't buy it.'

Abby looked at her, realising the time had come for Rosamund to explain the purpose of their meeting.

'You don't buy it? The story about Dominic?'

Rosamund nodded.

'Now, I believe you spoke to one Alexei Gorshkov,' she said after a moment.

'How did you know?' asked Abby with surprise.

Ros's grey brow arched knowingly.

'I've been doing a little research of my own.'

Abby could imagine her on the internet, on the phone, calling her contacts, calling in favours, the years rolling away as if she were back in the Fleet Street newsrooms.

'Gorshkov is who he claims. He was a senior member of the NKVD during the war, moving up into the KGB and achieving the rank of colonel. No one could tell me if he ever retired, which suggests that he still has "juice", as I believe the Americans put it.'

'So if he's legit, why don't you believe what he said about Dominic?'

'Don't you think I heard the espionage rumours in the sixties, Abby? Dozens of journalists were under suspicion, myself included. There were a few instances when I suspected Dominic of *something*: an affair, even keeping the wrong company, although as a connected magazine editor he knew everyone from lords to gangsters. But I never believed he was a Soviet agent because I *knew* my fiancé,' said Ros more fiercely.

'And so did Gorshkov. He knew Dominic was working for the KGB.'

'We only have his word for it.'

'And the *Soveyemka* newspaper article that named the Soviet spies operating in England,' replied Abby quickly.

Rosamund let out a snort.

'Propaganda.'

Abby softened her tone of voice.

'But why would Alexei lie about it? He's an old man without an agenda.'

'People like Gorshkov always have an agenda,' said Ros quietly.

She opened her handbag and pulled out an envelope, handing it to Abby.

'I loved Dominic. I don't believe he would have betrayed his country. But I'm not the only one. Read this,' she said.

Glancing quizzically at Rosamund, Abby pulled out a small white postcard, the sort you could get in any post office. Written in small black letters were the words *Trust Dominic*.

'Who sent this?' she asked.

'No idea,' replied Rosamund. 'It arrived yesterday. First-class stamp, central London postmark. I assume someone read the *Chronicle* at the weekend and posted this sometime on Monday. Although look, my address seems to have been written in different handwriting to the postcard.'

Abby looked up. Ros's expression was animated, resolute.

'Trust Dominic. What do you think it means?' she asked, handing back the card.

'That he was innocent,' said Rosamund with passion. Abby noticed that she had clenched her fist.

'Or that whoever sent it believes he was innocent.' Abby's mind was whirling.

Rosamund gave her a stern look.

'Whose word do we really have that Dominic was a KGB spy? Gorshkov's? He admits he wasn't Dominic's spymaster.'

'But he knew him. Apparently the spymaster died over ten years ago, and that's why we couldn't speak to him.'

'That's convenient.'

Abby let her shoulders slump. She knew how desperately Rosamund wanted Dominic to be innocent of the charges he was posthumously facing, but she was growing frustrated that she refused to see the facts.

'Ros, I know Elliot's story was sensationalist and perhaps he didn't speak to enough people—'

'You can say that again,' said Rosamund over the top of her. 'Journalism was a whole different ball game in my day. Things had to be corroborated and re-corroborated. Nowadays any old source can give you a nod and a wink and it passes for investigative journalism.'

She sighed and looked at the envelope.

'I always trusted Dominic,' she whispered. 'He was no traitor. He was a good, good man.'

Abby wanted Dominic to be innocent too. Just as she had hoped that when Nick had told her about his infidelity, it had all been an unpleasant joke. Like Ros, she had believed in the man she loved, right up until the moment that tears had welled in her husband's eyes and she had seen the guilt in his expression.

'What do you want me to do, Ros? Why are you showing me this? As you said yourself, the story has run, the damage has been done.'

'We have to find out what this means,' Ros said, her voice going up a notch. 'Dominic is innocent and I want you to help me prove it.'

'Me?'

'Don't worry, I will pay you.'

'How can I help you?' said Abby desperately. 'I'm an archive assistant, not a bloody detective. I have a divorce to sort out, a

275

job to salvage . . . I want to help you, and that message you've been sent is definitely intriguing but what can I do?'

Ros waited a few seconds before she spoke again.

'Why do you think the *Last Goodbye* story was so popular? Why have so many copies of the picture been sold?' she said finally, locking eyes with Abby and not removing her gaze. 'Because it represents hope,' she went on without waiting for an answer. 'Love and hope. Whether it's in someone's misty past, or somewhere in their future, everyone wants to believe that someone loves them that much too. But if Dominic was a Soviet spy, that picture, our love, would have been a fake, a lie. No one wants to feel deceived by love.'

'You can say that again,' mumbled Abby softly. She glanced at the postcard in Ros's hand.

'Abby, please. I did everything I could to find Dominic. I was this far from a breakdown,' Ros said, putting her thumb and finger together to indicate the smallest of margins. 'In the end it was my parents who forced me to call off the search. They made me see that Dominic would not want me to destroy myself looking for answers I was never going to find. It was why I resisted your attempt to investigate his disappearance. Because I knew it was futile. Not just because you're unlikely to find anything even if you did go to the Amazon, but because whatever you do isn't going to bring him back.'

'Then why are you here now?' asked Abby softly.

Rosamund's eyes trailed to the white card.

'Because somebody knows something. Not Gorshkov or Elliot, but the person who sent this. The man I love is gone, but I have to prove his innocence.'

Abby looked at her, wondering if what she really meant was that she had to prove his love. Ros's faith in Dominic seemed un-shakeable, but Abby knew first-hand what it felt like to be betrayed.

'And you think I can help you?'

'You've got a head start on anyone else.'

'Anyone except Elliot.'

Ros gave her a soft smile.

'You remind me of myself when I was starting out in journalism. You have that same belief in the truth.'

Abby nodded to accept the compliment.

'If only we knew who had sent the card. But how on earth are we supposed to track them down? It's got a WC2 postmark. Hundreds of thousands of people send letters from this postal area. It's one of the busiest in the world.'

'Maybe that's the point. The person who sent this didn't want to be found out.'

'Graphology?' said Abby weakly.

'My CIA contacts aren't particularly up to date,' smiled Ros.

A couple of Chelsea Pensioners walked slowly past, their red jackets as vivid as summer poppies bending in the wind.

'I bet Elliot knows someone,' said Abby. 'I'd say it's acceptable to dance with the devil when he's got something you want.'

Rosamund laughed.

'I'm seeing him this evening,' said Abby, realising that her decision about whether or not to meet Elliot had been made for her.

'See? You're good at this,' said Rosamund.

Abby grinned. 'I'm working on it.'

On their way back to the gate, they made their plan, a checklist of people to contact and places to go. As they talked, Abby could see Ros becoming more alert and alive. Abby glanced at her watch and flagged a black cab. She wasn't going far, but she was in a hurry to get started. 'Can I drop you anywhere?' she asked Rosamund, who was buttoning up her jacket.

'Thanks for the offer, but no, I think I'll go for a stroll by the river.' She smiled. 'Rivers always remind me of Dominic. We spent ten horrendous days trapped on a boat once. You see, it's not always the good things that you remember.'

'What if it turns out that you're wrong?' said Abby as the taxi drew up by the kerb. 'What if Dominic really was a traitor?'

'Then I will live with it. But if the two of us are half as smart and resourceful as I believe we are, I don't think I will have to.'

Chapter Twenty-Seven

'Abigail,' said Stephen, looking up from his laptop quizzically. 'What are you doing in today? I thought we'd decided on Wednesdays and Thursdays.'

'We did. I'm not here to work. I'm here to pick your brains.'

'Oh,' he smiled, looking rather flattered. He took off his glasses and put them in his top pocket. 'Congratulations on your *Chronicle* piece, by the way. I trust you received my message? Both Christine and I were most impressed.'

'Yes, thanks,' she said, cutting him off. 'Actually, Stephen, I think you might be able to help me get a follow-up story. Paul Robinson, the *Chronicle* editor, asked personally for us to get involved.'

She watched as a proud smile spread across his face. She knew from experience that the only way to get her boss to do anything was to flatter him into it; clearly the possibility of a personal link to a high-profile media figure like Paul Robinson was exactly what he wanted to hear.

'You're going to write more for the *Chronicle*?'

Abby had to suppress a smile. There was nothing like looking popular to make others see the error of their ways.

'I am. And I wondered whether you'd like to assist.'

'Of course,' he said eagerly. 'I'm keen to help however I can.'

'Great,' said Abby, sitting down and pulling out her notebook. 'Obviously I'll do this on my own time . . .'

'No, no,' said Stephen, lifting a hand. 'If your story is promoting the archive and our exhibitions, then of course you may do it from here. As well as your other duties, obviously.'

Abby smiled. 'All right, down to business. You are, of course, one of the most respected archivists in the country, if not the world.'

She said it as if it were fact; there was a good chance it was true anyway. The Institute had a huge amount of prestige in the small yet incredibly nerdy archive community, and Stephen certainly didn't go in for false modesty.

'But if I were looking for documents, possibly classified government documents, who would you say your opposite number would be?'

Stephen's mouth pursed. 'I'm not sure I would call him my opposite number, but that would be Tobias Harding over at the National Archives. All documentation in the public domain – anything declassified or available under the Freedom of Information Act – will be held there. I worked with Toby for a little while at the British Museum. I could certainly arrange an introduction.'

Abby smiled back at him. 'Thanks, Stephen. The editorial team at the *Chronicle* will be thrilled.'

Stephen puffed up his chest like a turkey. 'But if the documents you're looking for are of a genuinely sensitive nature, you probably won't find them in Kew.'

'Where will they be then?'

'I do believe there's an intelligence archive.'

'Where's that?'

'Oh, the MI5 building in Vauxhall.'

Abby felt her heart drop – clearly it showed on her face, because Stephen gave a sympathetic smile.

'Indeed. Even if you could get in there, the word is they've been scanning classified files on to encrypted servers. It actually is all rather James Bond.'

Toby Harding was waiting for Abby and Rosamund in the lobby area of the National Archives, a lumpen 1970s concrete carbuncle chipped from the same block as the National Theatre on the South Bank. Unlike Stephen, who looked perfectly suited to the role of archivist, Toby seemed pleasant and efficient, like a strait-laced dad at the school gate.

'Ms Gordon?' he said, extending a hand. 'Pleased to meet you. Stephen has told me all about you.'

'All good, I hope?'

'Oh yes, I rather think he sees you as his protégée – quite an honour.'

Yes, now that I'm getting Stephen's name in the paper, thought Abby cynically. She wasn't so much of a protégée when he was slashing her hours in half.

She introduced Ros, who extended her hand with a smile, and Harding led them into the bowels of the building. Abby listened with admiration to Ros making small talk. To a casual observer it was just polite chit-chat, but Abby could tell it was cleverer than that. That Ros was subtly working out how useful Toby and the archives could be.

As they walked through the building, Toby pointed out the various sections: documents, certificates, photographs, communications, all filed down a maze of corridors. Occasionally Abby would see staff pushing trolleys stacked high with buff-coloured files, requested by members of the public or researchers waiting upstairs in the reading rooms. Finally Toby ushered them into his office, and she was struck by how similar it was to Stephen's cramped cubbyhole: just enough room for a desk and a few filing cabinets.

'Now then,' he said. 'How can I help?'

Rosamund quickly outlined Elliot and Abby's *Chronicle* story about Dominic.

Toby glanced at Abby.

'Stephen did give me a heads-up that you were looking for some sort of confirmation of Dominic Blake's involvement with the KGB. He also said that you were in something of a hurry – so I took the liberty of having a ferret about for you.'

Abby and Ros glanced at each other in anticipation.

He opened a drawer and slid a slim file across to Ros. He must have sensed their excitement, because he stood and walked around to her side as Ros opened the file.

'As you will see,' he said, 'the declassification of files is never entirely straightforward.'

Abby peered over Ros's shoulder and could immediately see that the documents inside were woefully incomplete. The one on top began with a series of inscrutable code designations, then a subject line, *Surveillance by XXXXX, 24 October 1958*, followed by a dry description: *Following information from XXXXX, as detailed in report XXXXX, the subject DB XXXXX was observed leaving his flat in Tavistock Square at 19.23. He then hailed a taxi cab, registration XXXXX. We followed in XXXXX to XXXXX, where he was observed entering the premises at 19.45.*

'A DB who lived in Tavistock Square. Do you think that's Dominic?' she asked as she scanned the text.

'Dominic did have a flat in that square, yes,' said Ros.

She flipped through the papers, deep in thought.

'Are all the files like this?' she asked, with obvious disappointment.

'It is rather frustrating, isn't it?' replied Harding. 'These documents are released to the public after the prescribed time, but anything the authorities deem sensitive is either withheld or redacted as you see here. So even though we've got reports on DB's movements, as well as transcriptions of his conversations on the telephone or overheard in restaurants, there are huge sections blacked out and we're left speculating about what has been withheld or withdrawn. Indeed, his very identity.'

'So they're not that transparent after all,' said Abby quickly.

Toby gave a sympathetic shrug.

'But the fact that a DB of Tavistock Square has been monitored, that there are MI5 files on him at all, is quite revealing.'

The implication of his words settled around the small room.

'Is there likely to be anything more specific than initials here?' asked Rosamund, looking up.

'Possibly,' nodded Toby.

Ros's back straightened in her chair.

'If you persevere, you can occasionally stumble across the odd nugget,' he added, taking the file from her. 'There are often inconsistencies, you see, little secrets that slip through the net. Have a look at the back page, for instance.' He pulled out a single sheet and handed it to her. 'Portions of this document should have been removed, but for whatever reason, they missed the chop, as it were.'

Abby stared at him.

'Isn't that a security blunder?'

Toby nodded again. 'It's hardly surprising. There are hundreds of thousands of documents to get through, and to make accurate assessments about which should remain secret would require both a vast knowledge of Cold War espionage and the highest level of security clearance. Anyone fitting that description is hardly likely to be sitting in a basement with a marker pen.'

Abby looked at the page.

Report from agent XXXXX, line tap designation XXXXX.
11 March 1961, intercept 08:40 GMT.
Discussion between Soviet agent EZ and DB. Translation transcript can be found at XXXXX.

'The translation transcript. Where do you think it could be found?'

'At the registry, I expect.'

'The registry?'

'In the 1960s, the surveillance of Russian spies or suspected operatives was dealt with by Division E of MI5, I believe. All MI5 files were kept at Leconfield House, in Curzon Street.'

'And the chances of me accessing those are zero.'

He winced with sympathy.

'You know, there has been a wealth of information written about the Cold War: the main players, the rumour, the scandal. A whole slew of books have come out in the last few years, now that most of the major players are dead. Our libel laws may be fairly draconian, but they don't stretch as far as the deceased. Why don't you go down that route? Maybe you can work out who EZ is.'

'I know just where to start,' said Rosamund softly.

Chapter Twenty-Eight

Abby stood outside Elliot Hall's front door and took a deep breath. She flicked her hair over her shoulder and it bounced, reminding her of the blow-dry she'd had this afternoon. A blow-dry that now made her feel obvious, made her look, in the words of some forgotten teenage lexicon, as though she was gagging for it.

She wondered what Rosamund would think of her standing here in her little black dress and matching underwear, a lacy bra and knickers set from La Senza that was very much date underwear, underwear designed to be seen and removed. She was here to persuade Elliot Hall to help her clear Dominic's name, and yet she was dressed for a booty call. Too late now, she thought, pressing the bell.

When Elliot answered the door, she knew exactly why she had spent so long getting ready. In khaki chinos, a navy polo shirt and bare feet, he looked even sexier than she remembered.

'Abby, come in. You look amazing,' he said, kissing her on the cheek.

Abby wasn't sure which was making her blush more – the thought of her carefully chosen underwear or the memory of that perfect, erotic night-and-morning in St Petersburg.

'Are you hungry?' he asked, leading her into the kitchen.

'What's with the spoon?' She nodded at the wooden spatula he was holding.

'I'm cooking dinner.'

'There's more than great bacon sandwiches in your repertoire?'

He grinned over his shoulder. 'I blame my mother,' he said, sprinkling sea salt over a Dover sole that had just come out of the oven. 'In my gap year she packed me off on every self-improvement course she could think of. Art history in Florence, cooking in France, sailing in Brazil. All I wanted to do was go to Spain with my mates and get pissed.'

'You'd make someone a good wife,' Abby said, watching him drain the potatoes. She couldn't help comparing him to Nick, whose culinary talent extended as far as calling the Indian takeaway down the road.

'Is there a compliment in there somewhere?' said Elliot, leaving the fish and pouring her a glass of wine.

She inhaled the delicious warm and homely smell of the kitchen, and found herself forgetting that she was cross with him.

'So how was San Francisco?'

'I love it out there. It's so dynamic. I got approached twice to set up a new media venture.'

He handed her the plates and grabbed a cocktail shaker from the marble worktop.

'I thought we'd eat upstairs, on the roof terrace. You take the food, I'll bring the martinis. There's wine and water already up there.'

She hated martinis, but now didn't seem the time to bring it up.

Following him upstairs, she glanced across the landing and

saw the doorway to the room where she'd slept after Elliot's party. It was hard to believe it had only been two weeks earlier. So much seemed to have happened in the interim.

The roof terrace was a wide balcony that led off Elliot's bedroom. She took in the details of the room: a blue shirt folded across the arm of a captain's chair, a bookshelf full of books, a MacBook Air on the small table next to a king-sized bed, neatly made up and inviting. She felt nervous being in its orbit. Nervous about where the night might lead, and not sure how she felt about it.

Elliot seemed not to notice that they were in such an intimate space. He took the chair that looked back towards the house, whilst Abby had a view of the gardens growing dark in the fading light.

For a minute she couldn't believe that she was living this life. In their flat in Clapham, the one she and Nick had bought when they had first got engaged, there was a patch of roof over the downstairs extension accessed by crawling out of the bathroom window. That first summer as homeowners, there had been a stretch of unusually warm weather, and they had gone out there most evenings, sitting cross-legged on cushions, drinking beer, laughing and swapping gossip about their days. This was a more grown-up and sophisticated version of that memory, although she couldn't help feel a pang of nostalgia for the old days.

Elliot poured a martini into the empty glass on the table.

'So your mate Suze is seeing Will tonight, so I hear.' He looked up and grinned. 'What's she like?'

'Why do you ask?'

'She just looks as if she might eat him for dinner. I'm simply looking after the emotional well-being of my colleague.'

'Yeah, right,' she smiled. 'You men are just as much gossips as women.'

'I'm a journalist. I'm nosy. Besides, I like to think I played Cupid.'

'Actually, she says she's approaching this one differently.'

'You mean they've not had sex yet.'

Abby fumbled the water jug and spilt liquid over the tablecloth, which she quickly mopped up with a napkin. Clearing her throat, she took a long swig of her cocktail. As she tipped her head back, she could feel Elliot's legs, stretched out under the table, resting ever so gently against hers. His toe grazed the back of her calf, and she wondered if she should shift position, whether he would shift his. Seconds ticked by, and she predicted that if he hadn't moved his feet away by the count of ten, they were going to end up in bed together. The idea both excited and bothered her. So far, their night in St Petersburg had been a one-off. She could put it down to a moment of madness, but tonight was crossing a line. If they had sex, if she slept with him in that big, expensive-looking bed behind her, they would be in a relationship and that made her different to Nick.

Eight, nine, ten . . .

'I saw Ros today,' she said, changing the subject and the position of her legs under the table. She had expected Elliot to mention the Dominic Blake debacle, expected a few more apologies perhaps, but his silence on the matter suggested that it was over and done with. But she couldn't let it go. She was here for a reason, even if the bedroom looked tempting.

'Ah. I wondered when you were going to bring this up again.'

'Of course I'm going to bring it up, Elliot. That's why I'm here.'

'Not the only reason, I hope.'

'I'm still pissed off,' she said, not entirely honestly.

'You're very beautiful when you're angry,' he said, leaning back in his chair and watching her.

'And sometimes you sound like a total sleazeball.'

'You bring out the best in me,' he replied, his mouth curling roguishly. 'Look, Abs, I explained all this on the phone. I had to file the story, but I didn't want to upset you. I was going to tell you in person. I thought they were going to run with the story next week, but things just didn't work out. I'm sorry if Rosamund Bailey gave you a hard time about it. She should have taken it up with me, but she didn't, and I think that says a lot about her, don't you? I wouldn't go feeling too sorry for her. She's a tricky customer.'

'She's an old woman, Elliot, who found out that the love of her life was a Soviet spy simply by reading her weekend news-paper. You should have let her know.'

'You know what you need?' he said, topping up her wine glass.

'What?'

'A holiday.'

It wasn't what she had expected him to suggest.

'I know we've just got back from Russia, but that was work. My father has a house in France. It's lovely. In the Luberon, Ménerbes, the village from *A Year in Provence*. There's a pool, and the air smells of lemons and lavender, and we don't even have to get out of bed if we don't want to. I think it's what you need to unwind.'

She laughed nervously. Elliot wasn't just asking her to go to France; he was asking her to take their fledgling relationship to the next step, a step far beyond just spending another night together. She had to admit that it was more than she'd expected from him, but whilst she was flattered by the offer, it didn't seem the most important issue on the table.

'Ros doesn't believe that Dominic was a spy,' she said, deflecting the conversation away from mini-breaks.

'Of course she doesn't,' replied Elliot, smiling. 'She loved him.'

'I met her today and she showed me a postcard she had received. It said, "Trust Dominic."'

'And what does that prove?' He said it with a laugh, but there was a note of scorn in his voice.

'Maybe nothing, but don't you think it's strange? It was anonymous. "Trust Dominic." As if someone knows something and wants to reassure Ros that what she read in the paper isn't true.'

Elliot frowned dismissively.

'You were there with me in St Petersburg. You heard what Gorshkov said. That's as near as we're going to get to any official confirmation. Yes, we were wrong not to tip Ros off about the story, but our facts were right. Now, what do you think about Provence?'

'What about Ros and Dominic?' said Abby, feeling as if all the romance had been sucked off the terrace.

'What about them, Abby?' he said, putting his fork down in annoyance. 'What do you want me to do here?' She could hear a familiar tone in his voice. The fractious souring between couples.

'She thinks Dominic is innocent. She's convinced he wasn't working for the Russians and she wants us to find out for sure. She'll even pay us for any investigation, though I'd feel uncomfortable taking money from her.'

Elliot gave a small shake of his head.

'You're connected, Elliot,' pressed Abby. 'You know how easily your dad got in touch with Jonathon Soames. He probably has a hotline to the Prime Minister if you ask him. A few calls and we could sort this out, clear Dominic's name. Then you can write another piece in the *Chronicle* with the real story.'

'Abby, how do we prove that Blake *wasn't* KGB? Send Putin an email and ask him? Break into the Kremlin HR department to have a peek at their records? Besides which, it's not a story I would want to write even if we found out that he was just a journalist and explorer after all.'

'Why not?' asked Abby, shocked.

'Because I've just filed a bloody four-thousand-word article saying he *was* KGB. How's it going to look if a couple of weeks later we admit that we were wrong and our original story was completely bogus? How credible is that going to make me look as a journalist?'

'But someone's reputation is on the line here.'

'Yes, mine,' he said fiercely.

Abby wasn't hungry any more.

'So you don't want to help me?'

'Abby, stop. Listen to yourself. Think about it. We wanted to find out about Dominic Blake. And we did. Not how and where he died, but we did find out that he was a Russian spy and we had good sources to back that up. *The Last Goodbye* was a beautiful photo, and Blake was a romantic, charismatic character. Anyone remotely interested in him was going to be disappointed about what we found out – us, the readers, certainly his friends, and especially Rosamund. But it doesn't mean it's not true just because you want him to be something else, something different.'

She found herself thinking about Nick. She'd found out a truth about him and it wasn't something that she'd wanted to hear.

'I trust Dominic,' she said with feeling.

Elliot sighed and threw down his napkin.

'Abby. Grow up.'

She shook her head with frustration. 'You really don't care, do you? It's job done. Story filed. Glory received. You don't care about what you've left behind in the slipstream. Don't care who you've hurt.'

Elliot's voice softened. 'Maybe you should see someone.'

'Someone who could help us?' said Abby, perking up.

'A therapist, Abby. I mean a therapist. You know, I think I know what this is. Your marriage has broken down. You're looking for meaning, for some romantic truth, some vindication that love exists. I think this could be depression.'

'You think I'm depressed?' she said, trying to control her emotion.

'I'm saying it's possible. You've been under a lot of stress. Hell, this story was a roller-coaster ride. I got quite an adrenalin rush from it myself.'

She took a breath to compose herself. She did not want to put herself under the microscope. She had come here to talk about *The Last Goodbye*, and Elliot was making her feel like some sort of fruitcake. She felt tears welling up in her eyes. It was as if every emotion she had experienced over the past eight weeks was crystallising into this one moment of rejection.

'Abby, don't get upset. It's only work.'

'Is it?' she choked. 'You know, I thought that what happened in Russia might have meant something.'

'We had a great weekend, and we're here now, aren't we, taking it slowly. I've just invited you to Provence, for goodness' sake. I don't do that with everyone.'

She could see the panic in his eyes and it actually made her laugh.

'Don't worry, Elliot. I don't want a ring on my finger. I just thought you cared. About me. About Ros and the story . . .'

'Why does everything have to be about the bloody story?' he said, throwing his hands up in frustration.

'It's about doing the right thing,' she said, getting to her feet. 'And right now, this doesn't feel like it.'

'So that's it?' His handsome face suddenly looked cold and aloof.

She'd been talking about the story, about Dominic and Ros,

but she realised that Elliot had been asking about their affair. Suddenly she knew the answer to that question too.

'I should go,' she said softly.

Elliot sat there shaking his head.

'After everything I've done for you.' His mouth curled into a sneer. The smooth, charming Elliot gone, in his place the petulant rich boy who always got what he wanted. Rosamund had been right about that.

Abby knew how easy it would be to rise to his bait. For the evening to turn into a confrontation, an embarrassment. But she didn't want to slink away. She was not that girl any more. She went round to his side of the table and kissed him courteously on the cheek.

'Thank you, Elliot,' she said as her last goodbye, as he looked at her with complete surprise.

Chapter Twenty-Nine

'So what's going on with your chap?' asked Rosamund as they turned off the dual carriageway on to a country lane.

'I don't want to talk about Elliot Hall,' said Abby, trying to follow the GPS in the car.

Out of the corner of her eye she could see Rosamund raising an intrigued brow.

'I was actually talking about your husband. You said you were separated.'

'Ah,' replied Abby, squirming in her seat. She felt herself fall under Ros's penetrating stare. 'Honestly, I don't want to talk about him either.'

'Why not?' asked Rosamund.

'It's complicated,' she said finally.

'Relationships always are.' She paused. 'Are you getting divorced?'

'I think so.'

'So you're not sure you want to.'

'I'm sure I can't pick up where we left off with our marriage. I'm not sure that I can ever trust Nick again.'

'So I assume he – Nick – had an affair.'

'A one-night stand.'

'I see.'

Abby glanced across at her.

'You don't think that's enough, do you? You don't think that's enough of an excuse to get divorced.'

'You don't have children?'

'No, we don't.'

'So it should be a fairly clean break.' It was a statement of fact rather than a question.

'Yes, I suppose it will be.'

'And have you thought about what it would be like never to see him again?'

'Of course. But it's not like you and Dominic. I know that's what you're thinking.'

'No, Abby. Nick would not be dead, but he'd still be gone, and you have to ask yourself how you'd feel about that. How you'd feel about seeing him across the street one day with another woman, his new wife, children. How you'd feel seeing him live a life that was nothing to do with yours.'

Please turn right in one hundred metres, said a robotic voice, as Abby's hands gripped the wheel of her Fiat 500 and she tried to dismiss the image that Ros had planted in her head. An image of the B&B in St Agnes, the shutters painted bright blue, a shabby-chic shack built on to the side of it. She could see Nick, his hair a little longer than it was now, waxing down a surfboard, a woman in a bikini rubbing suncream into a small tanned child, an adorable genetic mix of the two of them. A perfect family living a perfect life by the coast. The life she had always wanted.

She mounted the kerb, the car shaking as she navigated it back on to the road. Ros jolted in surprise and flashed her a look to say that now was not the time to be thinking about it.

* * *

Appledore was a care home, but unlike any other Abby had seen around London – those huge converted Victorian houses on busy main roads that always struck her as depressing places to see out your final days. This home was as pretty as its name – a large Arts and Crafts building in endless acres of manicured grounds. Driving the Fiat down the long approach, she saw a sign to an orchard, another to a walled garden, and when Ros wound down the window, letting in the scent of freshly cut grass and roses, Abby thought it smelt as good as it looked.

As they approached the house, she turned her stereo off, as she did when she drove past a church or a cemetery. It was something she had learnt from Nick; a little sign of respect, he used to say.

'So when was the last time you saw Victoria Harbord?' asked Abby as she slowed the car to park outside the house.

'Over fifty years ago,' said Rosamund quietly, her eyes trailing out of the window, her thoughts lost in time.

'Were you close?'

Ros shook her head. Abby had suspected that would be the answer. When they had left the National Archives, Ros had immediately suggested that Dominic's good friend Victoria Harbord might know the identity of the EZ mentioned in the archive document. Victoria apparently knew everyone in the heady days of the fifties and sixties. But the pinched and cold way in which Rosamund had spoken about the great society hostess had suggested that she did not like her very much.

Abby turned off the engine and stretched her arms out in front of her. She expected Ros to make a move, but the old woman just sat there with her handbag on her lap, staring out in front of her.

'I think you should probably talk to her,' said Ros finally.

'What's wrong?' frowned Abby, turning to look at her and

noticing an unfamiliar look of nervousness in her expression.

'Vee and I never saw eye to eye,' Ros said quietly. 'She might be confrontational, obstructive if I'm there. It's best if you conduct the interview.'

Abby waved a hand. 'Come on, Ros. It was all a long time ago. I'm sure she'll be glad to see you.'

'No,' said Rosamund, shaking her head.

Abby looked at her with exasperation. She knew that Ros had spent the past twenty-four hours trying to track down Victoria; she couldn't believe she had cold feet now that they were minutes away from meeting her.

'Ros, we've come all the way to Kent to see this woman.'

'Victoria Harbord tried to sabotage my relationship with Dominic. I was convinced she was a little in love with Dominic herself and didn't like the Jewish interloper making off with the grand prize. I always swore that if I ever saw her again in my life it would be too soon.'

'But she might know who EZ is,' said Abby, feeling duped and angry. She felt more confident with Ros by her side, in the same way that she had enjoyed the *Chronicle* investigation working alongside Elliot. Anything else made her feel painfully aware of her position as a novice, a fraud.

'Come on, Ros. If you want to find out the truth about Dominic, you have to come with me now.' Her stern tone surprised even herself. She had no idea what had happened to the mousy archivist; Abby felt as if she was kicking ass.

'You speak to her,' said Ros just as firmly. 'I'll wait in the car.'

'Ros, please. We'll only be ten minutes.'

'Just go,' she said with a look that told Abby she was not going to budge.

Abby sighed as she got out of the car, and looked back at Ros sitting defiantly in the passenger seat. She knew she might have a point. If there was bad blood between the two women, that might colour the interview. As she studied Ros's expression – the lines on her face creasing a little deeper, the anxious downturn of her mouth – her reluctance to come face to face with her old rival was clear to see. It made Abby think about what it would be like if she were to confront the woman that Nick had had sex with in Stockholm.

She walked into the house and announced herself at the nurses' bay. A woman in a blue uniform introduced herself as Tracey and asked Abby to follow her down the corridor.

She knocked on a door at the far end of the house.

'Lady Vee, you have a visitor,' she said, popping her head around the door.

Abby was glad that she had phoned ahead. Not wanting to turn up at Appledore unannounced, she had rung and arranged an appointment with Victoria Harbord, explaining that she was a journalist friend of Rosamund Bailey's.

At first she could see no one in the room. Her eyes moved around the space, taking in long French windows, a small double bed with a floral duvet, a desk covered in a dozen silver-framed photographs. Finally her gaze rested on a wing-backed chair facing the garden, and she could just make out the profile of a tiny woman, so pale that she almost faded into the background.

'Er, Lady Harbord. Hello. My name is Abby Gordon.'

The old woman appeared to be hard of hearing and took a second to register Abby's voice.

'Ah, yes. Come and sit. Get a chair and move me around a little.'

Abby adjusted the position of Victoria's chair and put her own opposite so they could talk.

'What a pretty girl you are,' Victoria said in a soft, plummy voice. 'I like the colour of your dress.'

Ros had supplied Abby with a few details about Victoria Harbord. Apparently she had been quite the glamour puss in her day, with an exotic house in the South of France, a country estate in Buckinghamshire and closets stuffed with haute couture. Abby was quite shocked at how geriatric the woman looked, though it wasn't really surprising considering she was touching ninety years old. Unlike the much younger Ros, who was mature but well preserved, everything about Victoria Harbord was ancient. She was so slender she looked as if she might snap. Her skin was crêpey, a series of lines and contours on her face like the ageing maps in the RCI archives. But she was immaculately dressed, with a huge diamond ring on her finger and pearls the size of petit pois in her ear lobes.

'So, a journalist begs to see me,' she said more archly. 'I haven't had that since *House and Garden* persuaded me to do a cover story on Batcombe in the seventies.'

'Did you say yes to them too?' asked Abby.

'Oh yes. It was a glorious twenty-four-page spread. Then again, Batcombe was worth it. They described it, quite rightly, as one of the most beautiful homes in Europe.'

Her wistful eyes rested on Abby.

'Still, I'm glad to have visitors these days. Batcombe was always full of people, but things are a little different for me now.'

She paused.

'So you work for the *Chronicle*,' she said. 'I recognised your name. You wrote the piece about Dominic, didn't you?'

'Actually, I work at the Royal Cartography Institute. But I did find the photo of Dominic and Ros in our archives, and I collaborated with the *Chronicle* to promote our exhibition.'

'It was a beautiful photo,' nodded Victoria. 'I was never aware of it.'

'The Royal Geographical Society and the RCI have a huge collection of photos from hundreds of expeditions over the years,' explained Abby. 'Generally, if an expedition had some sort of sponsorship or financial support, a photographer would be sent along to get pictures. You knew Dominic well?'

'Very well,' smiled Victoria, with a hint of smugness. 'People used to joke that the two of us should marry. Perhaps that would have happened except for two minor details. I was already married to Tony, and I don't honestly think Dommy ever thought of me like that.'

She looked at Abby, her expression sharp, pointed.

'Aren't you going to pull out one of those dreadful dicta-phones?'

Abby hadn't thought to buy one. She had brought a notebook and pen, though goodness only knew if she could keep up with what Victoria was saying. Remembering that her phone had some sort of recording device, she plunged her hand into her bag, pulled out her Galaxy and fiddled around with it.

Victoria smiled as she waited.

'I thought you young people knew all about new technology,' she said, appearing genuinely fascinated.

'So,' said Abby finally, pressing the record button, 'did you read the *Chronicle* story about Dominic?'

'I did,' said Victoria, taking on a more self-important look.

'And do you believe he was a Russian spy?'

Victoria Harbord frowned. 'Miss Gordon, this was all such a long time ago, I wonder what the purpose is in dredging it up again. You've sold your papers, your photographs . . .'

'But do you believe that Dominic Blake was a spy? You knew him better than anyone,' Abby said, flattering the old woman.

She expected Victoria to vehemently deny it, but she did not.

'Perhaps. There were rumours about a lot of our crowd.

I mixed with influential people, Miss Gordon.'

'Do you know who EZ was? He was Russian. I found his initials and mentions of espionage in a document in the National Archives.'

Victoria gave a tiny shrug. 'That could have been Eugene Zarkov. He was a naval attaché at the Russian embassy. He was a bit intense but rather dishy. Came to my house a number of times.'

'I think he was a Russian spy,' said Abby flatly.

'Entirely possible.'

'Is he still alive?"

'You're the journalist.'

Right now, Abby felt wholly ill-equipped and out of her depth. It was fine in St Petersburg, when she'd had Elliot at her side leading the interview, but she really didn't know what to ask. She felt a grudging respect for him.

'Do you have any idea where I could find Zarkov?'

'No,' said Victoria simply.

Abby felt a flutter of panic, as if sand were running through her fingers. She couldn't come away from here with nothing. If Victoria, one of Dominic's closest friends, couldn't shed any light on his involvement with the KGB, she wasn't sure where she could turn next.

'So you've met Rosamund?' said Victoria finally. 'When you called, wanting to meet me, you said you were friends.'

Abby nodded, not wanting to give away that Ros was waiting in the car. As old and withered as she was, Victoria's poise and sharp tongue were still intimidating, and Abby could understand why her friend did not want to be here.

'How is she?' asked Victoria.

'She is a wonderful woman.'

'Yes, she is.' Victoria nodded, her expression full of emotion.

'You know, she's desperate to know what happened to Dominic.'

'We all were. Dommy was one of my dearest friends. But I think perhaps we should just remember him the way he was. I know you want to help, Miss Gordon, but it's better that those who loved him accept that he's dead and cherish the memories that we have. Including Ros. *Especially* Ros.'

Tracey popped her head around the door to tell Victoria that she needed her walk, and Abby knew that their meeting had come to a close.

'Send her my very best regards,' said Victoria slowly.

Abby nodded, shook the old woman's thin hand and left the room with a heavy sense of disappointment. Wandering down the dark corridor, she thought about what she should do next. She had a sense that Eugene Zarkov could be the key to finding out what she wanted, and she wondered how she could go about tracking him down.

She stopped as she saw Rosamund standing by the nurses' station. She was reading a selection of birthday cards propped up on the shelf that Abby had noticed on her arrival.

Abby smiled as she approached. Clearly the older woman had had a change of heart. She'd known Ros was not the type to stay in the car; no matter how difficult it was going to be for her, she had decided to come and confront Victoria. Abby felt a flutter of pride for her new friend as she stopped in front of her and watched her take one of the birthday cards off the shelf.

'What are you doing?' she asked in surprise. She had expected a barrage of questions from Ros about Victoria, about their meeting, about EZ. Instead her eyes were transfixed on the card.

'I should talk to Victoria,' said Ros finally.

'I think she has to go for a walk, but I'm sure we could pop back in,' said Abby.

They headed back towards Victoria's room, but were stopped by Tracey coming out of the loo.

'Where are you going?' she asked, putting her hand on Abby's shoulder. 'Victoria needs her exercise now.'

'We'll be five minutes,' said Abby with as much charm as she could manage. 'Five minutes, that's all we need. My friend wanted to say hello.'

'You'd better be quick,' said the nurse with a weary shrug.

Abby knocked on the door. Victoria's voice summoned them inside.

Victoria was out of her chair, and was standing holding a cane. Her face visibly paled when she saw Ros. As the two women looked at each other, Abby could see the years melting away, a bristle of rivalry vanishing as quickly as it had come, softening to a look of nostalgic complicity.

'Ros,' said Victoria quietly. 'I didn't know you were here.'

'Hello, Vee. It's been a long time.'

They stood in silence.

'I saw this card on the nurses' bay,' said Ros finally. 'Your birthday card to Tracey, I believe.'

Abby didn't miss the sharp look that darted between the two women.

'You sent me the postcard, didn't you, Vee?' Rosamund's voice started to crack.

'What's going on?' whispered Abby.

Ros handed her the birthday card and Abby read the message inside.

Darling Tracey. Wishing you much happiness on this special day, best wishes, Victoria H.

At first she didn't understand its significance, until Ros rooted around in her handbag, pulling out the postcard that she had shown Abby in the Chelsea Physic Garden.

'I recognised the handwriting, Vee,' said Rosamund slowly.

'Victoria sent the card?' said Abby.

'Should we walk?' said Victoria after a moment. 'I have to do a lap of the garden every day. Not the easiest thing with two artificial hips.'

'We'll take it slowly,' said Rosamund, holding her arm.

The sun was out and Victoria's cane sank softly into the grass as they stepped through the French doors on to the manicured lawn.

'Perhaps you'd like to close the door,' said Victoria, turning to Abby. 'Most of the residents are stone deaf, and the staff only seem to be interested in celebrity tittle-tattle, if the publications behind the nursing station are to be believed. But still, what I am about to tell you is private.'

Abby did as she was told and then returned to the two older women.

'What's going on?' she asked as she caught up with them. 'Why did you send Ros the card, Victoria?'

'Because I didn't want her doubting Dominic,' she said, turning her full attention to Rosamund. 'I know how much you loved him, Ros. We both did. I didn't want you to believe that he was a traitor.'

'What do you know, Vee?' said Rosamund desperately. 'Tell me everything you know.'

It was several seconds before Victoria spoke again.

'A few minutes ago, your friend Abby asked me whether Dominic gathered intelligence on behalf of the Russians. The answer to that question is yes. Yes, he did.'

'So he *was* a spy?' Abby turned to her in surprise. 'And you knew that?'

Victoria nodded, her tiny head bobbing like an apple. 'But he was also gathering intelligence for the British government.'

Rosamund stopped walking.

'You mean he was a double agent?'

Victoria smiled and gripped her cane a little harder, her knuckles turning white.

'Dominic was the perfect English gentleman, but he was also the perfect spy,' she said slowly. 'No family, beyond his war-veteran father. Well connected, intelligent, but considered a bit shallow, too interested in the pleasures of the flesh to be taken seriously. He operated very publicly, but completely under the radar. The Soviets thought he was working for them for years. He fed information back to them through contacts in London or through the letter drops at Brompton Oratory.'

'Letter drop?' asked Abby.

'It was a way of transferring intelligence, usually through letters or microfiche. The Oratory was a popular drop-point because people filed in and out all day and it was close to the Russian Embassy.'

Abby watched Ros nod thoughtfully.

'He was taken into their trust, but that only enabled him to feed information back to MI5,' continued Victoria, rubbing the handle of her cane.

'And how do you know all this?' said Abby, picturing Sean Connery as James Bond.

Victoria laughed.

'Because I was his handler.'

'Handler . . .' said Abby, suddenly remembering Alexei Gorshkov.

'It was the perfect arrangement. My husband Tony and I could invite all these well-connected and influential people to our gatherings, and Dominic could befriend them and pump them for info.'

'Was Tony a spy too?' asked Ros quickly.

'Heavens, no. I don't think he ever knew my secret either. I loved him dearly, but he was a dreadful misogynist underneath it all. I don't think it ever occurred to him that a woman could be so clever.'

She paused and turned to Ros.

'I know you might think we never saw eye to eye, Ros, but believe me when I say it was nothing personal.'

'It felt like it,' whispered Rosamund. 'I felt as if you wanted to sabotage our relationship.'

'Dominic was a successful spy because no one ever suspected him,' said Victoria. 'But then he starts dating a left-wing radical, and suddenly he's drawing attention to himself, inviting investigation from British intelligence. At the same time, you, dear Rozzie, get him frozen out of party land, so he's no use to Moscow.'

'Do you know what happened to him?' asked Ros, gripping her old rival's arm.

Victoria shook her head sadly.

'We – the more discreet elements of the Security Service – made enquiries after his disappearance. We were told that someone Germanic-sounding had been spotted in the villages around Kutuba asking about the British adventurer. We never found out who it was, but we believe Dominic was assassinated before we could get to him.'

Abby heard Ros give a slow, sad exhalation.

'But why would he be assassinated?' she asked quickly.

'He wanted to leave the intelligence service. Had done for a while, but once he met Ros, he made his mind up that he definitely wanted out. I assume he said this to the Russians too, but I'm not certain how easy it is to leave the KGB.'

'Surely they wouldn't have killed him for that?' said Ros, looking up.

'No. But they take a more dim view of double agents.' Victoria's face was hard, efficient, as if she had turned off her personal feelings like a tap.

'How did the Russians know he was a double agent?'

She closed her eyes.

'I ask myself that very same question every single day. Could we have done more to stop the leaks? What more could we have done to protect our colleague, our friend?'

'So what happened?' asked Abby.

'There must have been a mole. Someone who knew about Dominic's position in MI5 and tipped off the Russians. He wasn't the first to be sold out in that way.'

'Have you any idea who it might have been? How it might have happened?'

A tiny tear slipped down Victoria's cheek.

'I had my suspicions about Jonathon Soames. Call it women's intuition rather than fact-gathering intelligence, but he was too nice, too good to be true, and I never trusted him. He had a very senior but rather vague role in Whitehall. And he was influential, connected, a member of various security think tanks, the perfect recruit for the Russians. I mentioned it to my superiors and they laughed in my face. Upper-class men stick together like glue, whereas I was always viewed with suspicion, not because of my background, but because of my sex. They dismissed me as a gossip-monger, a troublemaker, and because I had no proof, I began to doubt my own instincts and stopped pushing. Six months later, Dominic was dead.'

'So you think Jonathon found out that Dominic was a double agent and shopped him to the Russians.'

She nodded, the movement so slow and sad it was as if it was painful to do so.

'Jonathon made all the right noises when Dominic disappeared.

He even organised a small memorial service for him a few years later. Seven years later. That's how long you have to wait before you can declare someone dead in absentia. I didn't go. Not because I didn't want to remember Dominic, but because I couldn't stand the hypocrisy of Jonathon weeping crocodile tears.'

She sat down on a bench, and Abby didn't know which was too much for her: her dodgy hips or the weight of the story.

'Dominic loved you, Ros,' said Victoria, her words barely a croak. 'He loved you so much. I told him how dangerous it was for him to keep seeing you, but he said that you were non-negotiable. As for me? Yes, I tried to break up your relationship, but not totally out of love for queen and country. It was more than that. I was jealous. He loved you. Not me. I may have won the battle, but I didn't win the war.'

'No one won,' said Rosamund painfully. 'Dom's gone. I loved him, but I didn't even have the chance to show him.'

Chapter Thirty

An appointment with Dr Melanie Naylor was the last thing Abby needed. She still couldn't believe she was here. It was only out of nostalgia and the emotion of the previous day's events at Appledore that she had agreed to attend when Dr Naylor's secretary had phoned to confirm the appointment.

The clinic was in a double-fronted house in Clapham Old Town. It was smart and expensive-looking – there was clearly money in the high-end marriage counselling business, noted Abby on her arrival. She was asked to sit in a small waiting room, which was like a particularly chic friend's study, with comfy sofas, glossy magazines on a walnut table, and a jug of water with slices of cucumber floating in it. It was all a bit too informal for her liking.

After a few minutes, she heard a ring on the bell and a familiar voice introducing himself to Dr Naylor, who had answered the door.

'Mrs Gordon? Do you want to come through?' said the doctor, popping her head around the door and smiling at Abby.

Melanie Naylor was about forty. No white coat, just a smart navy wrap dress that looked like DVF. Abby glanced at Nick.

He was wearing suit trousers and a pale blue shirt. She always laughed at what men wore in hot weather – shorts and brogues, suits with sandals, Lycra or board shorts – but Nick got it just right. She wondered if he had been to see a client. She wondered if he fancied Dr Naylor, pretty and perfectly poised as she held the door open for them.

Abby sat down on a fashionable-looking orange sofa and glanced up at the certificates on the wall. According to her website – which Abby had googled and read at length – Dr Naylor was a halfway house between a counsellor, which sounded truly terrifying, and a divorce mediator, which didn't sound much better. Throw in the doctorate and Abby had started to feel as if she had some sort of problem, when her only problem was the cheating husband sitting next to her.

There was a desk in the corner, but Dr Naylor didn't sit at it, instead choosing an Eames chair opposite the sofa. Abby assumed this was a therapist's trick, a removal of boundaries to create the most open environment possible.

'So you two separated several weeks ago?' said Dr Naylor after taking down a few details.

'That's right,' said Abby, deciding that now she was here, there was nothing for it but to be as honest and transparent as possible. 'I found a text on his phone from another woman. Nick admitted being unfaithful and I asked him to leave the marital home. The problem, and it's always been Nick's problem, is that he does things without thinking about the consequences. He always has. I mean, the first time we met, he turned up to Glastonbury without a tent, because his had been stolen. Who does that? Nick does, because he believes that things will always work out in the end. But it can't work itself out this time.'

She'd said more than she had wanted to, but she felt like a Duracell bunny that had been wound up and was ready to go.

Nick looked uncomfortable. She could feel him squirming on the seat next to her and she was glad.

'Have to tried to talk about it? Have you tried to work things out?'

'There was an argument at the time, but it was very emotional,' said Nick sheepishly.

'Have you spoken since?' asked Dr Naylor.

'I've tried,' replied Nick.

'There's nothing to say,' said Abby flatly. 'The facts are pretty simple. Infidelity is non-negotiable in our marriage. I can't get past it. I can't get past the betrayal.'

She thought of Elliot Hall and her bubble of self-righteousness popped. She flushed, and felt her shoulders sag a little in shame. She hoped Nick wouldn't bring up her own recent admission that she'd had dinner with someone.

'I think there's plenty to say, to talk about,' said Melanie Naylor reasonably. She turned to Nick. 'Do you want to tell me what happened?'

'It was just a one-night stand. Not just,' he corrected himself quickly. 'I know how bad that sounds. But it wasn't an affair. I went away on business and I slept with a client. Someone I had known for a few months, and one thing led to another.'

Someone I had known for a few months.

Abby felt sick at that image of intimacy. He hadn't told her how well he had known the woman before. Abby had imagined that she had been a sexy stranger, and that had been some small consolation. But now she could picture them talking and laughing together. Knowing little things about one another. Things perhaps as simple as how he liked his coffee. Whether he preferred French or Italian food for lunch. Had Nick got excited every time he knew they were to have a meeting? Had he worn a favourite suit on the days he was going to see her?

'I read the text, Nick. She wanted to see you again and it sounded as if you had discussed it. When was that? The morning after? You can't blame it on alcohol then.'

'Yes, we discussed it,' he said quietly. 'And I wasn't that drunk.'

It was like a punch in the guts. She couldn't bear to look at him and focused her eyes on the far wall.

'We're here to be honest,' said Nick, trying to catch her eye. 'I want to be totally honest with you.'

'I don't want to hear it,' she said, wrapping her arms around herself.

'Let him talk,' said Melanie softly.

There was silence, and then Nick spoke again.

'I've never stopped loving Abby, but I didn't like the state of our marriage, not since we started trying for a baby.'

'Did you want children?' asked Melanie. It was a reasonable question.

'Yes. Eventually. We married young, but I loved being married to Abby. I loved spending time with her. Talking to her, just reading the newspaper lying next to her, made me happy. Then she wanted to try for a baby. I wasn't really ready but I agreed because I loved her, and because it was something I wanted too. Maybe not at that minute, but when is it ever the right time to have a family?'

He paused and crossed one leg over the other, and started pulling awkwardly at his trousers.

'We tried for a long time but nothing happened. Two IVF attempts were unsuccessful. Whatever we did seemed to make it worse. We went to more fertility experts, which made us more frustrated. We weren't getting on so I spent more time at work. We had tests. Lots of them. Turns out we have sperm and egg incompatibility. If there's a medical term for that, I don't know what it is, but the long and short of it is that Abby and I are unlikely to ever have children together. Ironic for two people who fell head over heels in love the first time we met.'

She didn't want to look at him, didn't think she could bear it.

Nick puffed out his cheeks and even Dr Naylor looked emotional.

'I thought we could handle it, I thought we'd get through it. Then my sister Ginny told me Abby had said she couldn't be in a marriage where she couldn't have kids. Apparently they'd had some conversation about it. I sort of lost it. I felt totally rejected, worthless. I went away on business a few days later. A client showed some interest and I slept with her. It was madness, but when I think about why I did it, it wasn't because I was drunk and reckless. I wanted to feel like a man. I wanted to feel wanted.'

He shifted in his seat so that he could look more directly at Abby.

'I know that's little consolation for you now, Abs, but believe me when I say that I don't want anyone else but you. I never did. If you want a divorce, if you want to move on and find a man who can give you what you want, then that is something I am going to have to accept.'

'Ginny said I didn't want to be married to you?' Abby was trying to process everything he had just said.

'If we couldn't have children. She said it was making you question our marriage. I can't remember her exact words, but that was about the sum of it.'

Abby desperately trawled through her memory bank. She couldn't believe she had ever said that.

'Nick, I was in love with you. I wanted to grow old with you. I honestly don't remember saying that to Ginny. Even if I did, it wasn't what I meant.'

Dr Naylor reached for a box of tissues and handed it to her.

She took one and blew her nose, then looked up at the counsellor, who seemed to understand that they had probably had enough emotion for one afternoon.

'I think another session within the next few days would be useful,' she said briskly. 'But first you need to go away and digest everything that has been said. You should do that separately, and then we can reconvene.'

Neither of them said anything until they were outside on the street.

'That wasn't so bad,' said Nick, pushing his hands into his pockets.

'Other than the part where you admitted that you'd known that woman for ages, and that you weren't drunk when you slept with her. Oh, and the fact that your sister lied about the way I feel about our marriage.'

'You said you couldn't remember what you'd told her.'

'I don't need babies to make our lives complete, Nick. I want children, yes. Trying for kids felt like the next stage in our relationship, and I admit, I would be very, very sad if I never had them. But I don't miss something I've never had. And from the minute I met you, all I ever wanted was you.'

She thought she could see the hint of a smile pulling at his lips.

'Does that mean you'll give Melanie another go? I thought she was pretty good.'

'She didn't say much.'

'Not sure that's the point. She's there to make us talk.'

'Why didn't you tell me all that before?' said Abby after a minute. 'The stuff about feeling rejected.'

She had always known that their infertility had driven a wedge between them, but she'd never suspected that it had made him feel unloved, unwanted. Was that enough of a reason to condone or forgive what he had done? Abby wasn't sure.

'Because it would have sounded like an excuse.'

He paused and looked up at her.

'Did you ever feel like that too?'

Abby gave a little shrug. 'Sometimes, when it all seemed so difficult, the IVF and the hormones and the moods and the arguments we used to have. I thought it might have been a sign that we shouldn't be together. But then I remembered all the good times . . .'

'There were a lot of good times.'

There was a loud grumble, and Abby realised with embarrassment that it was her stomach.

'Was that you?' asked Nick.

She couldn't help but laugh.

'I haven't eaten since breakfast.'

'Want to have dinner? Alba is just around the corner.'

It used to be their favourite restaurant when they lived near Clapham Common. They'd go there every Friday night and laugh and chat till closing time. She smiled at the innocence of it all. The calm before the storm.

'I don't think that's a good idea,' she said quickly.

'Abby, we're still husband and wife. I think that just about qualifies us to share a pizza.'

'I want my own pizza, thanks. I'm starving.'

A black cab rumbled past, and before she knew it, Nick had got the driver to stop.

They were there within a minute, and as they found a table on the patio area, the waiter recognised them, which surprised Abby, as they had been gone from the area for three years.

'I miss this place,' said Nick casually as his eyes scanned the menu.

She missed *this*. She missed the small simplicities of their life.

She thought of the Joni Mitchell track that Nick used to play on the drive down to Cornwall, 'Big Yellow Taxi', with its lyrics that reminded you that you don't know what you've got till it's gone.

She thought about Ros and Dominic, who had never had the opportunity to grow old together, to laugh, to row, to eat pizza together on a Friday night, to do all the things that couples did, and suddenly her heart ached.

As if he was reading her thoughts, as if he could look into her mind and see *The Last Goodbye*, Nick spoke.

'So Dominic Blake was a spy.'

She nodded.

'KGB. Who'd have thought it?'

'Well he was. But it turns out that he was working for the British all along.'

'What do you mean? He was a double agent? Or is that a triple agent?' he asked, trying to work it out. 'It didn't say that in the piece.'

The pizza arrived and Abby lowered her voice. She was glad that the patio was empty as she told Nick everything she had discovered about Dominic Blake, glad to share it with him, safe in the knowledge that he wouldn't judge.

'So you think Jonathon Soames dobbed Blake in to the Russians?' he said, leaning back in his chair when she had finished.

'That's Victoria's theory.'

'Bloody hell,' said Nick sipping his beer. 'With friends like that, who needs enemies? So Dominic Blake is dead, probably murdered, and Soames get a peerage and a stately home . . .'

'It isn't fair, is it?' said Abby, glad of Nick's support, glad that he saw this the way she did, glad he had spotted the injustice of it all.

'Can't you out Soames?'

'How?'

Nick shrugged as if he was thinking out loud.

'Elliot Hall wrote the piece. I thought his dad was Andrew Shah.'

'He is,' she said, wondering how he knew that.

'Shah owns one of the largest newspaper groups in Europe. The press have come under fire recently, but remember all the attention the *Telegraph* got for breaking the expenses scandal. Every newspaper in the world wants a bit of that kudos. If one of Shah's papers outed Soames, as a Russian asset, a traitor, that's big news. That sells papers.'

Abby shook her head. 'Soames is establishment, Nick. So is the Shah family. They're all going to protect each other. That's how it works. I've learnt that much recently.'

Nick picked up the last bit of pizza and stuffed it into his mouth.

'Shah cares about profit. He cares about the reputation and power of his newspapers.

'Look, I've discussed this with Elliot, and he reckons it's not in his interests to admit he was wrong about Dominic.'

'But Elliot is just a writer,' he said with pointed dismissiveness. 'Bypass him. Take it straight to the editor.'

'Which would be a kick in the teeth for Elliot.'

Nick looked slightly gleeful at her remark. She wondered if he had guessed. Guessed what had gone on between them.

'So take it elsewhere,' he said simply. 'Take it to the BBC. Take it to the *Times* or Sky News.'

'I can't,' she said softly. She heard the old Abby creep back into her voice. The Abby who thought her place was to stay in the archives and hide away from everything.

'Do you want to?' asked Nick.

She nodded. 'If Soames betrayed Dominic, I want to prove that. Not just for Dominic or for Ros, but for me,' she said honestly. 'You know, I really felt kicked to the floor when you were unfaithful, Nick. You were my world, the only family I've got, the one person I trusted. Writing this story helped me through that. It made me think about other people, not just myself. It taught me I could be a little bolder, in life, in love.'

She thought about Elliot Hall and looked away.

'Then do it,' said Nick simply.

'How on earth do I do that after so many years?'

'Ask him.'

'Ros has already threatened to go round and have it out with him but I persuaded her to bide her time. As if he'd tell her anything anyway. I've already interviewed him for the *Chronicle* piece, and he didn't give anything away.'

'He wouldn't. Not unless he had to,' replied Nick, not taking his eyes off hers.

'But how am I going to make him? Wheel out the thumbscrews?'

'Flush him out.'

'Flush him out?'

'Don't you ever watch spy movies?' he grinned.

'No, I was always upstairs in the bath.'

The waiter came over to clear away their plates, and Nick ordered a coffee.

'Speak to him again. Accuse him of everything you've just told me. He'll deny it. Then you wait, watch, listen. See what he does next.'

'Wait, watch, listen . . . What are you suggesting, Nick? That I put on a flasher mac and follow him?'

'You'd look good in a flasher mac.'

'Nick, please . . .'

'I could help you.'

He said it slowly, as if he wasn't sure what her reaction would be.

'Abby, what do you think I do for a living?'

'You're in IT.'

She felt a pang of guilt that she didn't know the specifics. She didn't really understand IT and Nick didn't talk about it much. Who would? It wasn't a job like Elliot Hall's, where you flew around the world, met celebrities and attended international summits about important global issues, and then wrote about it.

Nick gave a wry smile.

'You think I spend all day playing computer games, don't you?'

'You're an IT consultant. A hi-tech troubleshooter. You fix people's servers. You are the technology fairy.'

She smiled, but Nick remained serious.

'Abby, I break into companies' computer and telecommunication systems.'

Her expression faded as she took it in.

'You're a hacker?' she said incredulously.

'No. I am not a hacker or a criminal. I am an IT security consultant.'

'I thought you had a legitimate business,' said Abby, aghast.

'Of course it's bloody legitimate,' he said fiercely. 'Cybercrime is big business. Every company in the world wants secure technology. To test out how safe their systems are, I get people to try and hack into them. It's proactive security.'

'It's hacking, Nick. You're a hacker!'

'No. I break into their systems with their permission. But for that, I have to know and employ people who do know how to hack.'

They were both silent. They could hear the roar of traffic and the grumble of a train.

'What's wrong?' he asked as she blinked back tears.

'With everything that's happened, there have been times when I really feel as if I don't know you, Nick. And do you know what has felt far worse than being cheated and lied to? It's being made to feel utterly stupid, naïve and foolish. Right now is one of those times.'

He leant in to look at her.

'It's not my dream job, Abby. I'd rather be a surf instructor, a photographer, something that gets me outside with the sun on my face. But what I do pays well, I'm good at it, and I provide a service that people need. If you want to write this story, if Jonathon Soames is KGB or a Soviet asset and helped destroy his friend, and if you want to nail him, then I think I can help you. Because from the moment I saw you, all I have wanted to do is be by your side and do just that.'

It took a few moments for Abby to realise she was crying. She blinked hard and took a sip from her glass of tap water.

'So what do you say?'

She didn't know what to say. All she knew was that she wanted to try and make things right.

Finally she nodded.

'Is that a yes?' he smiled.

'My very own James Bond,' she said quietly.

Nick's expression turned sad.

'We let it go, didn't we? The fun, the excitement, the adventure. When did we let it all get so difficult?'

The waiter came over with the bill on a tiny silver platter. Nick took out his wallet and put three ten-pound notes under the money clip.

'He's the one, isn't he?' he said before they stood up to leave.

'You said you'd met someone and it's him, isn't it? Elliot Hall.'

'It's over,' she said quietly.

'Is it?'

When it came to affairs of the heart, Abby wasn't sure if she knew anything any more.

Chapter Thirty-One

'Anna, this place is amazing,' said Abby as her friend's hen party posse arrived at the hotel suite on the South Bank. She ran over to the window, from where she could see all the way down the dark ribbon of the Thames: the London Eye with its egg-shaped pods glowing blue against the night sky; the bright lights of the City.

'Matt's treat,' smiled Anna as a bare-chested butler appeared out of nowhere with ten glasses of champagne on a silver platter.

'It must have cost him a flipping fortune. Did he even throw in the butler?' said Abby, dropping her voice to a whisper. 'If he did, that's what I call a modern marriage,' she giggled.

'Actually Matt's dad, Larry, knows the owners and got it at a very good rate. And I hired the butler. You can never have too much of a good view,' Anna said, eyeing his rippling torso.

Abby flopped back on to the bus-sized sofa feeling very, very tired. It had been a long day. They'd had spa treatments at the Aveda Institute, taken a Thames boat cruise from Westminster to Tower Bridge and had afternoon tea at the Shard. Anna was still dressed in a pink tutu, which she claimed made her look more like Peppa Pig than Sarah Jessica Parker, and except when she'd been having the deep moisturising facial, Abby didn't think she'd stopped laughing all day.

She'd managed to forget all about Nick and their separation, forgotten about Rosamund, Dominic and Elliot Hall, and had spent the day having fun with her friends.

'What's for dinner?' asked Suze, popping a Parma-ham-wrapped fig into her mouth. 'Will Sophie be cooking?' Sophie was Anna's famous TV chef sister.

'No, she's got her assistant to cater for us,' replied Anna diplomatically. It was common knowledge that Anna had a difficult relationship with her sister, after Sophie had had an affair with and subsequently married Anna's ex-boyfriend.

Suze rolled her eyes. 'Assistant does cooking shocker. Does Sophie ever do anything for that show of hers? I've heard of a dumbwaiter, but she's like telly's dummy chef.'

'Ssh, she'll hear you,' said Anna, stifling a giggle.

'You'd better get out of that tutu, Anna Kennedy,' grinned Abby, popping open a tube of Pringles.

'We should probably all change,' she agreed. 'There are two bathrooms, one over there, another on the far side, if anyone wants to freshen up. Dinner should be in about half an hour.'

'Drink, madam?' said the butler, offering Abby a glass of champagne.

'Don't mind if I do.'

'So,' said Suze, curling her feet up on the sofa. 'How's it going with sexy Elliot Hall?'

'How's what going? We filed the story. End of story,' Abby said with a dismissive wave of the hand.

'I know you said nothing happened after his party, but Will told me you went round to his house for dinner the other night. He seemed to think there was something going on.'

'I thought men only talked about beer, work and football,' said Abby.

'Come on, Abs,' said Suze, nudging her. 'I've told you everything about Will.'

'I didn't realise it was a competition.'

'There is something going on, I can tell,' grinned Suze.

Abby took a deep breath. She hadn't told anyone about the night with Elliot in St Petersburg. It seemed too personal, and far too confusing to discuss it before she had decided what she felt about it herself. But she also knew that Suze was unlikely to let the matter drop.

'Okay, okay,' she hissed quietly. 'I slept with him, all right? We went to St Petersburg for the story and I slept with him. Are you happy now?'

She wasn't expecting Suze to be judgemental, but nor was she expecting her to respond with such enthusiasm. Suze clapped her hands with glee.

'St Petersburg. How romantic! So when are you seeing him again?'

'There's no plan,' she whispered, hoping her friend would simmer down.

'Text him. Text him now,' said Suze excitedly. 'Arrange brunch for tomorrow.'

'I can't. We had a row at dinner.'

'You see, you're like a couple already!'

The sound of a doorbell disturbed their conversation.

'I hope nobody has ordered strippers,' said Abby, glad of the distraction.

Suze winced. 'I had one of those when I left my last job. He had one ball hanging out of his posing pouch.'

'Someone must have thought you liked that kind of thing,' Abby giggled.

Suze slapped her playfully.

The bare-chested butler went to open the door and Ginny came in holding two big pink parcels.

'Ginny!' called Anna from the bedroom door.

Abby felt her back stiffen. She had been glad that her sister-in-law had such a high-flying job that she'd had to miss the bulk of Anna's hen do, as uncharitable as that felt even thinking about it. But she didn't want a confrontation with Ginny tonight. It was Anna's special day and she didn't want to do anything to jeopardise that.

She slipped out on to the balcony and breathed in the cool evening air, letting the sights and distant sounds of London calm her. By the time she came back inside, everyone was seated around the long dining table in the middle of the room.

Thankfully, the only space was nowhere near Ginny, but she blew Abby a kiss from the other end of the table.

Abby sat quietly as Ginny told the girls about her work trip to New York, and how she was sorry to have missed most of the hen night fun but had brought two big boxes of Magnolia Bakery cupcakes to make up for it. They polished off their dinner quickly, and moved on to the cupcakes, while Suze whipped a pack of cards from her handbag.

'Right. Showtime,' she announced. 'I found this game in Ann Summers.'

Everyone groaned.

'It will be fun,' she laughed, flicking through the cards. 'We'll start with this: how often do you have sex? Anna, you go first.'

Anna pulled a napkin up to her face and giggled.

'No! This is private stuff!' she protested.

'This is tame,' replied Suze. 'You should read some of the questions on these cards.'

'Suze, please.'

'Come on. Chop, chop. We've got a whole pack to get through.' She was drunk, and the volume of her voice had gone up several decibels.

'All right. Once.'

'Once?' said Suze at the top of her voice.

'Once last week, but Matt's been away. Usually it's three or four times a week.'

'Ooh! You pair of goers,' smiled Suze, satisfied with her answer.

'Is that normal? I thought that was normal,' said Anna, looking for reassurance.

'Three times a year, more like,' laughed Caroline, one of Anna's married friends from work.

They went round the table.

'Abby. Your turn,' said Suze mischievously.

'Come on. I think we should have coffee to sober up,' said Anna, flashing Suze a warning look.

'No, I think Abby's got something to say. Come on, Abs. Tell us about St Petersburg,' pressed Suze, taking a sip of her mojito and looking mischievously over the rim of the glass.

'Suze, please,' she said, desperately regretting telling her friend about her night with Elliot.

'Abby had a romantic interlude with one of London's sexiest men the other day,' announced Suze. 'In Russia, no less.'

'You shagged a Russian?' said Sophie, Anna's sister.

'No,' said Abby with exasperation.

'Abby is seeing Elliot Hall,' explained Suze expansively. 'Gorgeous journalist. Blond. Rupert Penry-Jones lookalike.'

'I know the one,' said Caroline approvingly. 'The bloke you wrote that spy story with. His photo is always in the *Chronicle*. No wonder. He's hot.'

'And loaded. You should see his house.'

'Money isn't everything,' muttered Abby.

'Abby, I am so pleased for you. Glad you're back in the saddle, so to speak,' said Sophie.

The only person who looked more furious than Anna at the way the conversation was going was Ginny.

'Right, coffee,' said Anna.

The bare-chested butler stopped adjusting his dickie bow and ran to the Nespresso machine.

'And let's not forget this,' laughed Suze. 'Anna Kennedy. This is Your Life . . .'

'What on earth . . . ?' Anna smiled, untying the white ribbon, then gave a peal of delight. 'A photo book! Look at this,' she said, leafing through the pages. 'Where on earth did you get all these pictures?'

'Your mum and dad came up with loads, and we tracked down some school friends. Cath supplied those debauched university years . . .'

Abby was still aware of Ginny glaring at her. She excused herself under the pretext of getting some fresh air, and had only been on the balcony a few moments when she heard footsteps behind her.

'Anna seems to be enjoying herself,' said Ginny.

'I think we're all a bit knackered, though. Spa treatments, afternoon tea, river cruises, it's thirsty work.'

'It's all one big laugh,' said Ginny pointedly.

They were both silent, and Abby looked out at the view. It was dark now, and London was lit up like a celestial map in front of her.

'Everybody in that room knows Nick, Abby. I think you should have kept your love life out of the hen night fun and games. At least until you're divorced.'

'Suze shouldn't have said anything. She's off her head on mojitos.'

'Yes, Suze was wrong, but perhaps you could have been a bit more discreet and not told her about your celebrity screw in the first place.'

'Celebrity screw? Thanks for that.'

Ginny raised an eyebrow.

'You know, you're still married.'

'No thanks to you,' muttered Abby.

Ginny paled.

'What do you mean by that?'

'I think you know,' she said quietly.

Ginny turned to go back inside, but Abby did not want to let her escape.

'Why did you lie to Nick?' she asked as a cool breeze slapped her face.

'What about?'

'You said I didn't want to be married to him if we couldn't have children.'

'I never said that.'

'Nick told me you did.'

'And now you trust him?'

Abby did not believe for one second that Nick would have lied to her.

'What *did* you say, Ginny?'

She looked guilty, caught out.

'I was only repeating what you said.'

Abby gripped the stem of her glass so hard she thought it was going to crack.

'Ever since Nick told me, it's been going round and round in my head. In a low moment I might have asked you if it was a sign that we shouldn't be married, and boy, did I think that sometimes, but I loved him. I wanted children with Nick precisely because I loved him so much. I would never say I didn't want to be married to him.'

For a minute Ginny said nothing. Abby glanced across. Her sister-in-law's gaze was fixed on the London Eye, turning slowly in the dark night sky.

'All my parents want is grandchildren, and it doesn't look like they're going to get them from me,' she said at last. 'My brother would be a brilliant dad. He's from a happy, secure family and that's what he has always wanted for himself. But you and him together . . . it's not going to happen, is it? You can't have children.'

'So you stirred up trouble,' said Abby.

'I made Nick think about what it is he really wants. You, or a family,' she replied more fiercely.

'So you think we should split up? You think Nick should find someone new, someone who could give him children? Is that what you're saying?'

'What I want is for my brother to be happy,' she said vehemently.

'We *were* happy.'

'Were you? You had a funny way of showing it.'

Ginny turned and looked at her friend directly.

'Do you know how long I've been single, Abby? Ten years. And for half of that time, I liked it. I loved it. It was my choice. I was independent, my own woman. I could have dinner with friends in Soho every evening, and every night out was full of possibility. And then I woke up one day and realised that I was lonely. I had the job and the flat and the money in the bank to go on holiday with, but all I wanted was to find someone to share it all with. And I've not been able to. Whereas you and Nick . . .' She shook her head. 'You had what everyone wants. But you were constantly sniping at each other, you never seemed to appreciate one another.'

Abby had to admit she had a point.

'Things got difficult when we had fertility problems,' she said more quietly.

'Or is that just an excuse to cover up the fact that you got married too young and you'd just grown apart?'

'I love Nick,' Abby said, clenching her hand into a fist. 'I love him more than anything. I would do anything, *anything* for him.'

'Then why are you getting divorced?' said Ginny simply.

Chapter Thirty-Two

Abby couldn't believe the time when she opened her eyes. She pushed herself back on the hotel pillow and glanced at her watch. It was gone 10 a.m. Her dress was in a pile on the bedroom floor and her mouth felt dry and prickly like wool. After Nick left, she'd made sure she wasn't that woman who sank into a heavy-drinking depression, but last night she had really imbibed too much, she thought, crawling out of bed.

She went into the big living space of the hotel suite, expecting it to be littered with bodies and wine bottles, but Anna was already up and tidying. She had done a good job and the suite almost looked like a show home again.

'You shouldn't be doing this, Anna,' Abby said, picking up an empty Pringles tube, shaking it, then throwing it in a black bin liner. 'I'm a bad and ungrateful friend.'

'You are my friend who had way too much to drink last night. How are you feeling?'

'Felt better. Where is everyone?' Abby said, looking around.

'Most people have gone home.'

They remained silent for a moment.

'So what time do we get thrown out of here?'

'Eleven, I think. Just enough time for some breakfast.'

'What have we got? Left-over Magnolia Bakery cupcakes?'

'Have a look. The butler helpfully left some stuff.'

Still in her pyjamas, Abby shuffled into the kitchen. She put the kettle on for a big pot of tea and poured two large glasses of orange juice, then rustled up some toast and poached eggs.

'That looks great,' said Anna, sitting down at the dining table, which looked terribly big for just the two of them.

'What a great night,' smiled Abby, sticking her fork into the runny yolk.

'It was a brilliant day. I loved it.'

'Good. You deserve it.'

'Did you have a good time?'

Abby grinned as she nodded. 'I haven't laughed so much in ages.'

Anna sipped her juice and looked at her friend.

'So are you going to tell me what was going on with you and Ginny?'

'What do you mean?' said Abby, glancing away.

'Did you two have an argument? I just noticed an atmosphere.'

'It was nothing.'

'Really?'

Abby didn't want to tell her. She still couldn't believe that Ginny had tried to sabotage her marriage, and didn't want that information to get out to their mutual friends.

Ginny had finally apologised for what she had done and admitted that all her attempts at orchestrating a reconciliation between Nick and Abby were, in part, to do with her guilt.

It was small comfort to Abby, who couldn't help wondering whether Nick would have been unfaithful if he hadn't taken what his sister had said as gospel. Ginny's words had cut deep in another way too.

Then why are you getting divorced? she'd asked, and that question had echoed around Abby's head as she'd finally fallen asleep.

'Pass that book over,' said Abby, wanting to change the subject. 'I didn't have a chance to see it last night.'

'Let's sit on the sofa and have a proper look,' said Anna, grabbing her mug of tea.

The two women sat down and opened the photo book between them.

'I can't believe how thin I was at university,' screamed Anna, flipping through the earlier pages.

'I can't believe someone put a picture of Sam Charles in the bloody book,' said Abby, pointing at a photo of the Hollywood movie star Anna had had a fling with just before she got together with Matt.

'I think it's Suze's idea of a joke, but I can't show the damn thing to Matt now.'

Abby grinned. 'You don't have to feel guilty that you still find Sam sexy. He did appear in *People* magazine's most beautiful in the world list. Twice.'

'Is it that obvious?' Anna winced. 'Gosh, I'm horrible. Here I am, a very happily about-to-be-married woman, and I'm secretly leching over a Hollywood superstar. I don't know if I'm immoral or a middle-aged cliché.'

'I'd say you were just human,' smiled Abby.

'So's Nick,' said Anna quietly.

'Is he coming to the wedding?' asked Abby after a moment.

'Of course not.'

'He was invited.'

'He was your guest.'

'And he's still your friend.'

'He sent me a really lovely note, but he doesn't think it's

appropriate for him to be there.'

Abby was aware of a vague sense of disappointment, but dismissed it by carrying on flicking through the pages, smiling wistfully at some of the images: a young Anna in pigtails running through a stream in the Lake District; on a girls' holiday in Spain, laughing in a bikini and holding a bottle of wine; graduating from university in her cap and gown; on various twenty-something mini-breaks in Prague, New York and Rome. Abby had spent many nights listening to Anna complain about the lack of decent men, but now she wondered if her friend hadn't got it right. Years of wild and adventurous singledom, then getting married in her thirties to the man she loved. She couldn't help but think that she herself might have got it the wrong way round.

Towards the back of the book were more recent pictures. One was a shot of Matt lying on a sunlounger wearing Mickey Mouse ears, another a cute snap of them skiing.

'Remember this?' said Anna, pointing to a picture of them all outside a Cotswolds cottage.

Abby wondered if Anna remembered that this was the weekend before she had found out about Nick's unfaithfulness. He had returned from Stockholm on the Friday and they had driven directly to Chipping Campden, to a big stone farmhouse with a thatched roof and a hot tub in the garden.

It was Matt's dad Larry's latest purchase, and he had lent it to Matt and his friends for the weekend. They had gone for long walks, stopping off in various country pubs, and had cooked a big supper together in the evening.

There was a collection of photos from that trip. Matt and Anna laughing in the hot tub, Suze and Ginny making big jugs of cocktails, Abby and Nick sitting out on the grass in the sun. Abby was leaning against her husband's shoulder, while Nick was looking down at her and kissing the top of her head.

'Cute picture,' said Anna, tracing her finger over the page. 'He looks so in love with you there.'

Abby gave a small ironic laugh. 'You know this was a couple of days after he slept with her?'

'It wasn't?' said Anna, looking embarrassed.

Abby looked closer, imagining that she had her glass loupe, imagining that she was back at work inspecting her archive of images.

'You know, you can see it in his eyes,' she said finally.

'See what?'

'The guilt,' replied Abby softly.

Anna took a moment.

'I think he looks like he loves you. I think he looks like he's sorry.'

Abby studied the photo again. Something about it unsettled her. Not Nick's wistful, faraway look of shame, of fear that he was about to lose something. It was something else. It was an expression she had seen before, and with a jolt she remembered where.

'I have to go,' she said quickly.

'I know. We should check out before they get security to physically remove us. What are you up to today?'

'I need to go into work,' said Abby.

Chapter Thirty-Three

The tube had just pulled in to the platform, and Abby ran to catch it, although getting to South Kensington took another forty minutes, thanks to weekend engineering works. When she reached the RCI, the main gates were closed, but Abby had a key to a back entrance and let herself in. It was quiet and eerie, and the sound of her heels on the marble floor echoed around the building.

Mr Smith, the security guard, was on his rounds.

'What are you doing in on a Sunday, Miss Gordon?' he asked.

'Something important,' she said, giving him a thumbs-up.

She went down into the archives and punched in the code to open the door. Once she was inside, she crossed straight to the filing cabinet that contained the Blake expedition photographs. She could remember every line, every inch of *The Last Goodbye*, but it was the others in the set she was interested in. Flicking through them quickly, she discarded the scenic shots – an ancient steamer on the river, a group of natives standing outside a straw hut – and concentrated on any she could find of Dominic or Rosamund until she got to the one she'd remembered. It had been taken in Kutuba, in a quiet, unguarded moment. Rosamund and Dominic were standing outside a hut, and the way he was looking at her . . . it spoke to Abby.

'You knew,' she said. Then, louder: 'Dominic Blake, you knew!'

Nick lived in Kennington now. Abby hadn't been to his flat before, and she was a little shocked to see the small one-bedroom place in the eaves of a slightly scruffy Georgian town house.

Nick answered the door in sweat pants and an old T-shirt, his dark hair particularly tousled. He looked as if he had just tumbled out of bed, and that thought stirred something inside her.

'Come in,' he said, looking a little embarrassed. 'A pot of coffee is on.'

'I need it. It was Anna's hen night yesterday.'

'I hope Suze was suitably badly behaved,' he grinned.

She looked at him, wondering for a moment if he had heard from Ginny about their showdown, but he clearly hadn't.

'Speaking of badly behaved, I have just stolen something from the archives.'

Nick frowned. 'Fancied wearing Livingstone's pith helmet for the wedding?' he asked.

He went to fetch the coffee and Abby perched on the edge of a new-looking sofa. Everything in the place looked temporary, as if it had been furnished on the cheap. She knew it had been hurriedly rented and probably chosen for its proximity to Nick's office, which was close to the Imperial War Museum. But she didn't miss the stack of estate agents' particulars peeping out from under a music magazine on the table. She wondered if the details for the Cornwall B&B were among them. She doubted it.

'Do you want me to make you a fry-up?' he asked, running his hand through his hair.

'It's fine. I just wanted to talk to you about something. About what we discussed at Alba the other night.'

He sat down next to her, and as his bare forearm brushed against hers, she flinched away.

'So what have you found?' he smiled.

'A picture of Dominic Blake.' She took it out of its envelope and showed it to him. 'I think he knew he was going to die,' she said, pointing at Dominic's expression. The same expression of guilt and sadness she had recognised on Nick's face in the Cotswolds photo.

'He knew he was going on a dangerous expedition,' said Nick, sipping his coffee. 'He knew there was a chance he wouldn't make it out alive.'

'Soames gave me his business card when we met for lunch, so I'm going to call him,' she said more urgently. 'This afternoon. You said you could trace his calls . . .'

She expected him to laugh at her, or to dismiss her suggestion. She suspected that he regretted volunteering his help at the pizzeria, but she felt she was so close to discovering the truth, and Nick, not Elliot Hall, was the person she trusted to make that happen.

'Don't call him this afternoon,' said Nick, glancing up. 'Wait until tomorrow.'

'Why?' said Abby. She just wanted to get it done now.

'It's going to take me twenty-four hours or so to set this up.'

'Of course. How much will it cost?' she asked suddenly. She hadn't stopped to think about that, and whilst Rosamund had said she would pay for any expenses incurred in the investigation, Abby knew she couldn't take anything from her.

Nick rubbed his stubble. 'Don't worry about it. There are some people who owe me a few favours.'

'So you'll call me when it's okay to phone him?'

338

He nodded.

'I'll email you later with everything I can find out about him. When I went for lunch with him, he mentioned that he still lives where he did in the sixties. I'm going to call Ros now and see if she knows his address.'

'It's not hard to find these things out,' Nick said with quiet confidence.

Abby put the photo back in its envelope and into her bag, and they sipped their coffee in silence. Nick seemed anxious, on edge, and she knew she should go.

'What are you doing today?' she asked as she stood up to leave.

'Not much. I might go for a run.'

He opened the front door and she turned around to say goodbye. It seemed a natural thing to hug, and for a minute they just stood there holding each other.

She felt Nick rest his chin on her head, and the air that she breathed in seemed to smell of him. His clean, soapy scent. She closed her eyes and remembered how good it used to be, how happy he used to make her feel. A thousand memories ran through her head. Waking up next to him in her little flowery pink tent in Glastonbury, holding his hand as they jumped into a lagoon on their honeymoon, spending lazy Sunday mornings together in bed, the duvet covered with toast crumbs and newspapers – all the good memories in her life seemed to involve Nick.

For a second she wanted to suggest that they spend the day together. She wanted to ask him if he was as lonely as she was. But she pulled away and said goodbye. After all, she had things to do, and so did he.

Chapter Thirty-Four

Abby called Jonathon Soames' mobile number as soon as Nick had phoned to say that everything was in place. She had also contacted Ros, who had given her Jonathon's address, although Abby had been vague with her about the details of what she and Nick planned to do with it. She was aware that what they were doing was illegal, and while she knew that Ros was anxious to find out anything she could about Dominic, she didn't know her well enough to guess how she would feel about breaking the law to do so.

Her fingers had actually trembled as she punched the digits into her Galaxy. Abby hated the phone, always had done. Although it was something she'd had to overcome – even archivists had had to 'work the phones' more in recent years – she still felt uncomfortable speaking to people she didn't know, and she'd needed a stiff vodka before ringing Lord Soames.

She couldn't remember the exact words she'd used to accuse him of telling the Soviet intelligence services that his friend Dominic Blake was a British agent. A double agent. There was no easy way of saying it, and of course he'd denied it, laughing it off and telling her with a theatrical guffaw that she'd been given 'bad information'.

Now it was done, Abby felt feeble and hollow. She'd called him over four hours ago, and nothing had changed. She'd pottered around the house, doing the washing, tidying up. She'd watched a little television, paid some bills. It was business as usual, and that had made her feel even more unsettled.

She sat down at the kitchen table and stared out of the window. What had she expected to happen? she asked herself. And what was the point? A few days ago, seeking justice for Dominic Blake had seemed like the natural thing, the *only* thing, to do. Nothing could bring him back, but at least someone could pay for betraying him.

But with just a little bit of distance, it all seemed like misplaced revenge. And what business of Abby's was it anyway? Yes, she liked Rosamund Bailey and wanted to help her. Yes, she'd felt empowered, useful, trying to find out the truth about her fiancé's disappearance. But sitting here, she wondered if it was just a way of distracting herself from her own domestic and professional problems.

'What's done is done,' she whispered sadly.

She decided to go for a walk to her favourite deli, Bayley & Sage. Good food always cheered Abby up. She could almost taste the big vine tomatoes, fresh burrata and home-made truffles she knew they stocked.

Pulling on her trainers, she hurried out of the house. It was gone 6.30, so she power-walked up the hill to make the shops before they closed. It was still light, but the sun was already starting to dip behind the horizon. She had just turned on to the high street when her phone rang.

'Hello,' she said, already feeling in a better mood with some fresh air in her lungs.

'Abby, it's me,' said a familiar voice at the end of the line. 'You need to get in touch with Anna as quickly as you can. I think I'm about to be arrested.'

She had no way of getting back in touch with Nick after that. Numerous calls to his mobile had gone unanswered, and the only information she had to go on was what he had told her in his first, hurried communication, when he was apparently still at home and had managed to make a quick call as detectives had entered his flat with a search warrant.

She had called Anna immediately, who had reassured her that Nick would be allowed to make contact again if and when he was taken into custody. Neither Anna nor Matt were criminal solicitors, but between them they had enough legal firepower. Abby was grateful that Anna had also promised to get Larry Donovan, Matt's father, involved. He was a man of legendary reputation and sometimes dubious morals, just the sort of character to have on your side at a time like this.

She curled up on the sofa and drew her knees close to her chest. She could see her watch in this position. Almost eight o'clock. Anna had promised to come over as quickly as she could, but the minutes seemed to drag out endlessly. She felt totally powerless just sitting here, but she wasn't sure what else she could do. Resting her chin on her knees, she started to sob.

When at last the doorbell rang, she wiped her eyes and went to answer it, desperate for Anna's comforting presence.

The chain was still on the door as she unlocked it. Peering through the thin space, it took her a moment to recognise Jonathon Soames.

She felt her heart start to beat faster; a sense of unease made her shiver.

'Lord Soames?'

'Hello, Abby. Can I come in?'

Instinctively she gripped the handle on the back of the door, as if some fight-or-flight instinct had kicked in at the sight of Dominic's nemesis.

She made a quick assessment of the situation and decided that the old man was not strong. If she pushed the door in his face she was sure she could shut it. Her mobile phone, meanwhile, was just a few feet away in the kitchen.

'Abby, don't worry. I just need to speak with you. It's about your husband.'

'Where is he?' she said, feeling her palms grow sweaty against the cold metal of the door handle. 'Where's Nick?' she repeated, her voice fierce.

'Just answering a few questions,' said Jonathon more calmly. 'There are a few things we need to discuss too.'

'My lawyer is due round any minute,' Abby said, trying to disguise the fear in her voice.

'This will only take a few minutes. Please, Abby, let me in. It's important. It's about Dominic. It's about what happened to him.'

Abby summoned her courage, and slowly her grip on the door handle relaxed. She slid the chain off the door and stepped back to allow Jonathon Soames into the house. She looked behind him, half expecting to see snipers in bulletproof vests, but he seemed to be alone. A voice at the back of her head wondered if this was the point where she disappeared, never to be seen again, just like Dominic Blake, but she felt oddly brave and defiant.

Looking at Soames, a white-haired old man, his hands frail and veiny, it was difficult to believe that she had anything to be scared of at all.

They moved into the living room. Neither of them sat. For a moment, neither of them spoke. Was she supposed to offer him a drink – coffee, a glass of wine – before he brought out his poisoned umbrella and killed her?

'Where is my husband?' she said finally in a low, calm voice. Right now, it was all she cared about. The longing to see Nick, to just hear that he was okay, made her feel sick.

'I assume you know what he's been doing this afternoon?' said Soames, an unmistakable archness in his voice.

'Please don't charge him with anything,' she said desperately. 'I asked him to do it. This is all my fault and I take responsibility.'

'That's very noble of you,' said Jonathon, raising an eyebrow. 'But I had a phone call just a few minutes ago, and apparently Nick Gordon insists that you've got nothing to do with the hacking of my phone and email.'

She thought of him being interrogated at that very moment. He'd be cool, unruffled. He was smart, so smart, she thought with a pang of emotion. But was he smart enough to know what to do?

'Please,' she said, starting to cry. 'Everything he did was because I asked him to. He was just doing it because . . . because he's my husband and . . .'

'And what, Abby?'

And because he loves me, she thought silently.

Jonathon put his hand in his jacket pocket. She was half expecting him to pull out a gun, but he handed her a tissue.

'I have come here tonight because I owe it to someone to tell the truth.'

She felt herself relax, as if a non-specific danger had passed and she was back in the company of someone who was on her side.

'The truth?' she said, rubbing her eyes.

'You've caused a lot of trouble, you know that?'

'I thought that's why you were here,' she said sheepishly.

'Don't worry about Nick,' said Jonathon, shaking his head reassuringly. 'He'll be fine.'

'You promise?' she said, her voice quavering between desperation and hopefulness.

'He's not in any serious trouble. I think they just want to frighten him a little.'

She didn't ask who *they* were – she doubted that Jonathon Soames would tell her anyway – but she believed his assurances.

'According to my housekeeper, Ros came to my house yesterday.'

'She did?' asked Abby. She might have known that Ros wouldn't listen to her recommendation not to confront him directly.

'Fortunately I was in Oxfordshire. Otherwise I think she might have throttled me.'

He looked up and met Abby's gaze directly.

'So you think I killed Dominic?' he said quietly, his voice sounding sad and raspy.

'Not with your own hands,' replied Abby, her own voice shaking as she willed herself to keep calm. 'But I wonder if you sold him out. I wonder if you tipped off your friends the Russians. Told them exactly where Dominic would be on his Amazon expedition. You knew all the details, where he was going, how long for . . .'

'I did not,' said Soames with absolute finality.

He sank on to the edge of her sofa, like an old bird on a telegraph wire. When he looked up at her, Abby saw that his eyes were glistening.

'Where to start?' he muttered to himself.

'At the beginning . . .' replied Abby more softly.

'That seems a very long time ago. Another lifetime.'

Jonathon rubbed his chin, as if he was hesitating about what he was going to say next.

'Dominic was my friend. My best friend. Of course, you know by now that he worked for the Security Service, but have you stopped to wonder how he was recruited?'

'I thought you got the tap on the shoulder at university,' said Abby, with her limited knowledge of the world of espionage.

'I recruited him,' replied Jonathon with a certain amount of pride. 'Dominic was the star of his year at Trinity. Clever, charming, going places. I was a postgraduate when we met, but I had already joined the service.'

Abby watched his face become more animated as he was lost in the memories of his youth.

'I spotted his potential the very first time I met him in the college bar. I knew we had to get in there before the Russians did, and Dominic came on board quite readily – the world of intelligence was perfect for him and he didn't shirk away from the plans we had for him.'

'Which were what?'

'We *wanted* him to be recruited by the Russians, right from the get-go. Dominic Blake – double agent. You can imagine how much he loved the danger and adventure of it all, and he played his hand brilliantly. A communist-leaning girlfriend here, a left-wing polemic in the student rag there. And the KGB came calling.'

'I thought *Capital* was a right-wing magazine?'

'That was later. That was cover for his Russian allegiances and a double bluff for us.'

'I know Victoria Harbord was his handler.'

'A very smart woman,' nodded Jonathon.

'She thought you had been turned by the Russians and that you betrayed Dominic.'

Soames smiled as he shook his head.

'Nobody trusted anyone in those days,' he chuckled. 'And

with good reason after the Cambridge Spies. But yes, I had a powerful position in Whitehall by then, and the Russians did try to turn me on a number of occasions. Two heterosexual attempts, one homosexual.'

He saw the look of confusion on Abby's face and smiled.

'That was a common ploy. Getting someone to seduce you, and then using it as leverage against you. I'm afraid my sex drive was never particularly high. Ask my wife Michaela.'

'So you didn't tell the Russians that Dominic was a double agent?'

'I would never have done that. I loved him like a brother,' he said passionately.

He seemed to switch into a more efficient, statesmanlike mode.

'The Russians had their doubts about Dominic. We were never sure how much they knew about him, whether they knew for sure he was a double agent. Besides, there was a bigger threat.'

Abby frowned. Jonathon started to cough, and she went to get him a glass of water.

'Have you ever heard of the missile gap?' he asked, taking a sip from the tumbler she handed him.

She shook her head.

'The Cold War was based on the assumption that both sides could blow the other to kingdom come. By the end of the fifties, the Americans thought they were lagging behind the Soviets, who were showing their might with all their space technology, and Kennedy made promises to change that when he came into office. But the Americans had overestimated the Russian nuclear capability.'

He took a breath before he continued.

'Dominic was friends with a Russian intelligence officer called Eugene Zarkov. Zarkov knew that Dom was working for the

KGB, and he shared some highly sensitive information with him about the Soviets' true number of weapons and how he suspected it fell far short of what the Americans had. This information put both Zarkov and Dominic in danger.'

'Why?' said Abby. 'Danger from whom?'

Jonathon didn't speak for another few moments.

'There were people in America who wanted to inflame the arms race,' he said finally, looking as if a weight was being lifted from his shoulders. 'Industrialists, arms manufacturers, money men . . . A few weeks before Dominic disappeared, I received information that Zarkov had been found dead in Moscow. I remember that night quite clearly. It was the evening of Ros and Dominic's engagement party. Officially Zarkov died of a heart attack, but he was only thirty-five. I knew then that Dominic was in danger.'

'Did you tell Victoria?'

He shook his head.

'Everyone knew the service was compromised. Burgess, Maclean . . . No one knew who to trust. I certainly couldn't trust Victoria, as much as I admired her.'

'You thought Victoria was also working for the Russians?'

She remembered the old woman's words at Appledore. *There must have been a mole . . .*

Victoria had laid the blame at Jonathon's door, but maybe she had been the one who had betrayed Dominic. Perhaps she wasn't even formally working for the Russians, but her love for Dominic had made her lash out when he had announced he was marrying Ros. Perhaps her betrayal had been a moment of madness that had had terrible consequences.

'I didn't trust Victoria because I didn't trust Tony,' said Jonathon slowly.

'Tony? Victoria's husband?'

'Tony Harbord was linked to the cartel of industrialists that wanted Dominic dead.'

'But Victoria said she didn't think Tony knew about her espionage activities.'

'Tony was one of America's wealthiest men, all of it self-made. He was a smart and ruthless businessman who was solely concerned with the pursuit of money. He'd have known about Victoria's link to the intelligence services, even if Victoria thought otherwise, and would have used it to his advantage.'

Jonathon paused before he continued.

'Once I had seen intelligence that Dominic was, essentially, a marked man, I knew that the only way to stop him from being assassinated was to take matters into my own hands.'

He let the words hang in the air for a moment.

'What are you telling me?' asked Abby, not daring to even think it. 'You murdered Dominic? You killed your best friend because he was a liability, because he knew too much?'

A ghost of a smile pulled on the old man's lips.

'I didn't murder him, Abby. I saved him. He didn't die in the Amazon rainforest in 1961. Dominic Blake is still alive.'

Chapter Thirty-Five

He was late, of course he was. There was a time, many years before, when he used to be late for everything, when his life had seemed so fast, so exciting, that there were barely enough hours in the day to fit everything in. But things were different now, thought Dominic Blake, squinting at the wheel of his Land Rover Defender as he navigated the dark Irish country roads. Today it had seemed to take him forever to have a shave, find his only blue shirt that wasn't faded from too many washes, and get out of the house, not because he had so many other things to do but because everything seemed to require more effort than it had ten, even five years earlier.

He reminded himself that he had much to be thankful for. Just the other day he had been reading how one person in six over the age of eighty had dementia. He had friends who could no longer recognise him, acquaintances now reliant on family members to dress and feed them. Besides which, he lived in a particularly magical part of the world that had brought him a considerable amount of pleasure over the years. The west coast of Ireland lacked the dizzy excitement of the bright lights of London, it was not as exotic as some of the places he had visited as a younger man, yet there was wonder of a different sort in the place he had called home for over forty-five years. A walk along the wild and rugged Connemara coast always lifted his spirits; he would never tire of the thick taste of Guinness on a cold winter's night; the sight of the ocean sparkling silver in the sunshine took the edge off his regret.

'Dammit,' he muttered as he misjudged the corner and swerved his old Defender up a grassy verge, bumping it back down again and through the gates of Dunlevy Farm. As he brought it to a stop, he puffed out his cheeks with relief and clenched his fingers tighter around the wheel, wondering nervously when he was due to renew his driver's licence. The thought of not being able to drive, being stuck, immobile, in his cottage a mile away from anyone, made him shiver.

His friend's farmhouse glowed in the darkness in front of him. He turned off the engine, picked up a bottle of red wine from the passenger seat and opened the door, steadying himself by holding on to the car until his boot hit the driveway. The sound of music drifted from the building. He took a moment to compose himself, a little nervous, not used to big social gatherings, and tuned in to the more familiar sound of the sea in the distance, waves crashing against rocks and gulls squawking overhead.

He smiled to himself, remembering the good old days, when he'd have bounded into a party, eager to scour it for the most attractive woman in the room, impatient to seek out anyone who might be useful to him as a contact or a source. Sometimes he had to remind himself that he had actually lived that life, that he hadn't dreamt it or read about it in a pulp fiction novel, but fragments of memory were still there, and for a split second he felt as if it was the sixties again and he was turning up at one of Victoria Harbord's parties, not knowing where the night would take him.

He knocked on the door and a red-faced, smiling woman answered it.

'Dominic, you came!'

'Finally.' He smiled at his friend and neighbour Julia. 'I'm sorry I'm so late. I hope everyone isn't sitting down already.'

'Don't you go worrying. Pete's lamb has been cooking since lunchtime and it's still not done to his satisfaction. Come in, come in,' she said in her sing-song voice.

Dunlevy Farm was one of the largest properties in the area, the sort bought with money made from downsizing from one of the bigger cities – in Pete and Julia's case Cork. It was warm inside, and a comforting foodie smell wafted around the hallway, the sort that rarely permeated his own cottage now that his culinary repertoire had contracted to tins of sardines, potatoes, eggs collected from his chickens and soda bread baked by a neighbour.

'Come and meet my sister. She's over from England with her husband for a few days,' said Julia.

Dominic smoothed down his tweed jacket anxiously as she led him across to a couple around twenty years younger than himself.

'Paula, David. This is our good friend and neighbour Dominic Bowen.'

He was stranded by his host and left to make small talk.

'So where's home?' he asked.

'London,' smiled Julia's sister, pouring him a glass of wine. 'Actually, Esher, but now the kids have left home, we're thinking of moving into London proper. Becoming those trendy OAPs who spend all their pension on the theatre and restaurants.'

'Where were you thinking of? Which area?'

'Why? Do you know London?' said David with a faintly

superior expression, or at least one reserved for old people and those he did not consider quite as sophisticated as himself.

'Not really,' smiled Dominic, playing the role that was now second nature.

'We were thinking Pimlico or Borough for the food market,' said Paula more kindly. 'I love Bloomsbury, very Charles Dickens, loads of history. The British Museum is there too, but prices have gone through the roof.'

Dominic nodded politely, longing to tell how wonderful he thought the area was too. He wanted to tell her about the secret gardens, and the overlooked pockets of the British Museum. About the house that had inspired the setting for the Darling residence in *Peter Pan*, and how it only took twelve minutes to walk to Soho, another fifteen to get to the river, which always made Bloomsbury in his opinion not just the centre of London but the centre of the world. And he longed to tell her husband that he was not Dominic Bowen, a simple man from the local village, but Dominic Blake, Cambridge-educated magazine editor and intelligence officer, a man who could offer so much to the conversation if only he could be bothered to listen.

'Lamb's ready,' said Julia, returning to the group and putting a hand on Dominic's shoulder. 'Hang on. Someone's phone is ringing.'

For a moment Dominic couldn't hear anything and made a mental note to get his hearing aid checked.

'Dominic, I think it's you,' said Paula, nudging him.

He looked up in surprise, unused to the tinny ring of his mobile phone. He'd only had it a few months, a present from Julia for Christmas, and although he'd jokingly dismissed it as new-fangled technology, Julia insisted he keep it on him, 'just in case'. He knew exactly what she was hinting at. He did not like to see himself as an old man, but with a phone in his pocket, he felt just a little less vulnerable.

He made his excuses and went to take the call in the study.

'Hello. Dominic?'

'Yes. Hello,' he said, struggling to hear the caller over the rise and fall of party chatter.

'It's Jonathon.'

He was not completely surprised to hear his old friend's voice. Even though the two men seemed to have very little to say to one another these days, their deep and long-standing bond eroded and weakened by time and space, he still heard from Jonny Soames every two or three weeks, in what he could only suppose was a duty call.

'How are you?' he asked.

There was a long pause that made Dom nervous. His first thought was whether Michaela and Jonathon himself were both okay.

'Ros knows,' Jonathon said finally. 'She knows you're alive.'

Dominic felt his breath shudder and almost stop in his throat. He went over to the study door and closed it.

'What has happened?' he asked, summoning the words to speak.

'A news story ran about your disappearance a couple of weeks ago,' replied Jonathon.

Dominic hadn't seen the piece. He had long ago given up reading the British press, which reminded him too much of a life unlived. He frowned, trying to work out if there was some significance in the date. Whether it was any particular anniversary or had any other news-worthy importance.

'Why on earth would anyone want to run that story now?' he asked, his old editor's instincts twitching.

'A photo of you and Ros surfaced in an RCI exhibition. There was some interest in it and the *Chronicle* followed it up.'

Dominic held the back of an old leather chair to compose himself.

'What did the article say?'

'It accused you of being a Soviet spy.'

'And you chose not to tell me about this?' he replied, feeling a shot of anger. 'You could have warned me. You *should* have warned me.' He could hear his voice trembling.

'I didn't tell you because I knew it would make you want to seek out Rosamund. And I didn't think that would be helpful at this point in your life.'

'And don't you think that was for me to decide?'

There was silence for a few moments.

'The woman researching the story. The story of your disappearance. She wouldn't let it go and was causing all sorts of trouble. She even recruited a hacker to tap into my calls, my email . . .'

'And this was all for the *Chronicle*?' Dominic asked, hearing his old heart thud in his chest as he waited anxiously for his friend to answer.

'It appears that she was helping Ros.'

He thought he felt something inside him dance.

'I have always wanted what's best for you, Dom. I didn't tell you because I wanted to protect you.'

'It's not your place to play God, Jonny.'

'I know. I realise that now,' he said. 'So I told Ros. I've told her everything.'

Dominic felt his palms grow sweaty.

'I should see her.'

'We're coming. We're coming as soon as we can sort out a flight.'

He closed his eyes, a thousand memories firing around his

mind like bullets. He could see her now, laughing and splashing in Victoria Harbord's pool in Antibes, the beautiful, elegant woman who had held his hand in Paris, the girl full of passion and promise and delight who had stormed into his office and demanded his resignation, the girl with whom he had pretty much fallen in love on the spot.

Another memory popped into his head unbidden. A more recent memory, but still one that belonged to another lifetime. Rosamund on her way to a literary event in Dublin, 25 October 1969. He remembered that date so well because it was the day that really had changed his life for ever. Not the evening of Vee's party when Eugene Zarkov had told him about Russia's true nuclear capabilities. Not the night of his own engagement bash, when Jonathon had revealed that Eugene had been found dead in mysterious circumstances. Not even the day he had waved goodbye to Rosamund in the Amazon and set off to fake his own disappearance.

No. It was 25 October 1969 when his life has been set irretrievably in another direction, when he had finally closed the door on his old life, and broken his own heart in the process.

For Dominic Blake had never intended to disappear for ever. He had known that his life was in danger, agreed with Jonathon that he had to drop off the grid for months, even years, until the risk of assassination had passed, and at first, everything had gone to plan.

The timing of his trip to Peru had been fortuitous. It was a dangerous expedition to a place where people really did go missing. Two mercenaries known to and trusted by Jonathon had helped Dominic escape north out of the Amazon into Colombia and then Central America. A new identity was arranged for him, and the next five years were spent moving around the United States and Canada: Idaho, Wyoming, Nova Scotia; big empty spaces where English-speaking loners could blend in and not be noticed.

Throughout this period he had kept in very sporadic contact with Jonny Soames – anything more was risky – and by the late sixties, his friend had reluctantly agreed that he could find somewhere more permanent to settle down. They had chosen the remote west coast of Ireland, close enough for it to feel like home, far enough to be out of any possible danger, and after twelve gloriously uneventful months in Connemara, Dominic had begun to dream that he could make contact with the woman he loved, the woman he had never forgotten about, even though Jonathon had warned him that she had moved on, found a job, a good job, a boyfriend, and that it was foolhardy to make contact with her directly in case she was being tracked.

He would have taken the chance and gone to London anyway, but she had come to Ireland. He had read in the *Herald* that she was speaking at a prestigious literary event in Dublin, and even the cynical journalist in him couldn't help but think that it was a sign, a sign that it was time to stop hiding and start living, because even though he had dodged the assassin's bullet, he had felt dead inside since that moment he had kissed Rosamund Bailey goodbye and disappeared into the Amazon jungle.

It had taken him seven hours to travel from Connemara to Dublin by bus. He had a letter in his pocket and had worked out how to get it to her in the course of the evening. They were the most important words he had ever written, explaining his decision and his reasons for leaving her, but setting out a plan for how they could be together. How he remembered her dream of living in a cottage in Antibes with a bowl of peaches in the window and a view of the sea, and although Connemara wasn't exactly the South of France, he could glimpse the ocean from his bedroom and there was nothing quite like the simple pleasure of collecting mussels from the beach and cooking them for lunch.

He had stood opposite the theatre where she was due to appear for over half an hour, waiting for her to show up. It had been raining and at first he couldn't make out whether it was her, stepping out of a taxi on to the street. She had turned to face the vehicle, and when she had smiled, he had thought for one glorious moment that she had seen him, and that her smile had been for him. But someone else had got out of the taxi. A man, who snaked his arm around her waist and then kissed her lightly on the lips as she giggled and touched his face in a way so warm and tender that Dominic had barely been able to watch them for a moment longer.

Right then, he had understood the true meaning of love. It was not the way your heart fluttered when you saw the object of your affection, how their conversation could make you feel alive, or their absence make you desperate with longing. No. True love was simply the desire to make that person happy, no matter the cost to yourself. And right there, on that cold, wet street in Dublin, Dominic knew that Rosamund Bailey would have a better life, the life she deserved, without him in it.

'Are you still there?' Jonathon's voice shook him from his thoughts.

'Yes,' he said quietly.

'Expect us on Thursday.'

After Jonathan had hung up, Dominic stood in silence until there was a knock on the study door.

'Dom. Are you coming through to eat?' said Julia, poking her head into the room.

'I think I should probably go,' he said, hardly glancing up at her.

Julia pushed the door open and came inside.

'Is everything okay?' she asked, putting a reassuring hand on the sleeve of his jacket.

Dominic nodded gratefully.

'Are you sure? The phone call . . . it wasn't bad news, was it?'

He looked at her and felt as if a fog was lifting.

'It's the call I've been waiting for my whole life,' he said with a smile.

Chapter Thirty-Six

Rosamund Bailey had never been to the west coast of Ireland before, and standing at the window of her small hotel in Clifden, Connemara's largest town, she wondered why. After Dominic's disappearance, all she'd seemed to do was travel, from California to Kathmandu, mostly in the name of work, sometimes to simply broaden her horizons, but now, letting her gaze settle over the gentle misty hills, she realised that sometimes you ignored the beauty and pleasure on your own doorstep.

A faint knock on the door shook her from her thoughts and sent a flutter of nerves coursing around her belly.

'Come in,' she said, knowing that it was unlocked.

Abby Gordon was holding a piece of toast and smiling at her. 'We should go,' said the younger woman reassuringly.

Ros glanced at herself in the mirror. She didn't feel ready. She was wearing a red dress, bought specially from Jaeger the previous morning, because she knew how much Dominic had liked her in the colour. It had seemed a bold and passionate choice when she had tried it on, and in the changing rooms it had looked flattering. But this morning, as the cool Irish light cut through the window pane, she felt old and gaudy, mutton dressed as lamb.

'Are you ready?' pressed Abby. 'Jonathon is waiting for us in the breakfast room.'

Ros had heard the expression 'run for the hills', but never had it felt more apt.

She took her coat from a hook on the door and put it on. It was now too late to change her dress, so she fastened the buttons to cover it, grateful for the tepid early August weather.

Abby was waiting patiently. Ros was grateful that her new friend had travelled with her to Ireland. She knew Abby had her own life, her own problems, but she had been there every step of the way.

Not much surprised Ros any more. She'd been a Fleet Street journalist for fifty years: she'd watched a man set foot on the moon, witnessed a wall go up – and then come down – through the middle of Berlin, and seen a black man become President of the United States of America, something that had seemed quite unthinkable that summer of 1961, when race riots raged in the Deep South. But never had she been more taken aback than when Abby Gordon had phoned her thirty-six hours earlier with the news that Dominic was still alive. At first she thought it was some cruel trick, or that Abby had gone mad through the stress of her divorce. It was only when Jonathon Soames had also contacted her to confirm the news that she had believed it, and felt a tide of joy so strong she thought it would knock her over.

'Before we go, I just wanted to say thank you,' she said, touching Abby on the arm. 'Thank you for finding the photograph, for helping me, for believing in Dominic and for making an old woman happy.' She felt her eyes moistening. 'You didn't have to do any of that, but you did, and I will never forget it.'

Abby didn't say anything. She just smiled and nodded, like a sage old owl, then made her way down the stairs, checking every few seconds that Rosamund was following her.

Jonathon Soames was waiting for them in the lobby. Ros was still mad with him, of course. She had fallen out of touch with him many years before, but she still couldn't believe that he had known all along that Dominic was alive and had not put her out of her misery. She'd asked him about it a dozen times on the flight over to Ireland, but he had been frustratingly vague and had simply said that it was for Dominic to explain.

He linked arms with her as they walked outside, and any anger that she had felt towards him began to soften. They were here now, and she was going to see Dom; that was really all that mattered. It mattered so much.

'Should I drive?' asked Abby after helping Ros into the back seat.

'Yes, I suppose that's best,' smiled Jonathon wearily. 'People get nervous seeing an eighty-six-year-old at the wheel.'

'Where are we going?' asked Ros as Abby started the engine.

'Just a few miles along the coast,' replied Jonathon. 'I've called him to say what time we'll arrive.'

Him. She felt light-headed. A wave of nausea hit the back of her throat, and she opened the window to let in some fresh salty air.

The road hugged the coast, and Ros tried to relax as she took in the view: broad white sandy beaches studded with rocks that stretched into clear blue ocean; fields and bog in every shade from moss green to ochre. Clouds gathered in the sky until they smudged into the rugged hills known as the Twelve Bens on the horizon. It was quite magical, a land of lochs and legend, and Ros thought it appropriate that she should be meeting him here.

She talked about the old days with Jonathon, and the recent deaths of some of their mutual friends: her wonderful flatmate Sam, who had moved to Cape Town many years before, and the glamorous art dealer Zander whom she had met at Jonathon's dinner party.

'We just need to turn left here,' said Jonathon, not entirely convincingly, after twenty minutes or so. He looked at his watch and frowned. 'I do believe we are a little early. The drive didn't take as long as I thought it would.'

They stopped outside a small single-storey house. Ros had seen many of these properties since her arrival in Galway – typical Irish low-slung cottages with rough whitewashed walls and slate roofs. Wide lawns stretched on either side and down towards the sea. She sighed at the view. She was glad Dominic lived with a view like this.

They all got out of the car. The iron gate creaked as Jonathon pushed it open.

Ros held back for a moment, a thousand questions whirling in her mind.

She had practised her opening line to Dominic countless times since Jonathon had told her that he was still alive, and every single word now seemed inadequate. She remembered the woman she once was, smart and opinionated and – yes, she could admit this now – attractive, but she wondered how much of that woman existed now, how much of her was left to love.

'Well, what are you waiting for?' asked Jonathon, smiling.

Feeling a swell of panic, Ros looked at Abby, then back at Jonathon, who gave her an encouraging nod and knocked on the door.

They stood and waited, but there was no reply. Ros hardly dared to breathe.

'He's probably round the back,' said Jonathon quite casually.

They took the path around the house to the garden. Ros saw him immediately, standing with a spade at the far end of the lawn.

One of the few benefits of old age was that her distance vision was very good. He turned and wiped his brow, and she could see the look on his face as he spotted her. His expression of pure joy fortified her so that she did not turn around and run away.

As they began to walk towards one another, everything else slipped away, until she could see only Dominic.

He was wearing a worn navy sweater, dark trousers and gardening boots. He was still tall; age had done nothing to diminish his impressive physique, as it had with so many of her contemporaries. His hair was thin and white, his face deeply lined, but as he came closer, she could see that his clever grey eyes, those eyes that she loved, were as clear and alert as she remembered.

'Ros,' he said simply, his eyes glistening.

'Hello, Dom,' she replied, feeling a single cold tear escape down her cheek.

He exhaled, and she could hear his breath shuddering, as if he was choked with emotion.

'I suppose you have a few questions.'

She couldn't remember a single one of her over-rehearsed lines. She could only feel a strong surge of love and frustration.

'A few,' she nodded, biting her lip to stop more tears from falling.

'You're beautiful,' he said, touching her jaw with his fingertips.

'Not any more.' She wanted to unbutton her coat and show him the red dress.

'I'm old, not blind,' he smiled, keeping his hand against her face.

She closed her eyes, unable to rid herself of that sharp and sour sense of injustice.

'Why did you leave me, Dom?' she said, opening them again, her hand curling into a fist. 'Why didn't you at least let me know that you were alive? I've spent over fifty years mourning you. You left me in the dark, believing you were dead.'

Her anger swelled like an ocean wave that peaked then crashed as it hit the shore. Her breath stuttered and she looked into his eyes, and she couldn't be angry for a second longer.

'I was recruited into the Security Service at Cambridge,' he said finally.

She nodded and smiled softly. 'I know. Jonathon told me. He told me that he was British Intelligence too. Who'd have thought it?'

'I always said Jonny had missed his calling. He would have been an incredible actor.'

'And you liked the adventure,' she said, trying not to sound bitter.

He was silent for a few seconds.

'I was fifteen years old when my father returned from the war,' he said eventually. 'He was sick, injured, mentally traumatised from a six-month spell in a prisoner-of-war camp. But he used to tell me and my mother that everything he had been through was worth it in the fight against oppression, and that was something I took with me to university. I wanted to be part of the struggle against whoever it was – fascists, communists, anyone – who wanted to keep people down.'

She could imagine him – young, handsome and brave. She hadn't known him then, and she sighed with regret, realising how much she wanted to.

'I didn't even think you cared,' she said with a touch of humorous complicity, that familiar banter between them returning.

'I cared very much,' he nodded, not looking away from her for even a moment. 'That was the first thing I loved about you, Ros. The first thing I loved when I heard you protesting under my office window. I loved the fact that you cared.'

'But why didn't you tell me about your other life?' she whispered. 'I often suspected that there was something going on behind the scenes, I just didn't know what. For a long time I thought you were having an affair with Victoria. I don't know why you couldn't trust me.'

'It was nothing to do with trust, Ros,' he said, taking hold of her hand. 'I was a double agent. That compromised me, and the people I loved. I wasn't sure how you'd feel about me working for the establishment and I didn't want to jeopardise our relationship. And besides, I was desperate to leave.'

'Why didn't you?'

'The Russians considered me useful. Leaving wasn't that easy.'

'But there were so many things we could have done. I could have helped you think of a way to get out.'

'I didn't want to involve you. I wanted to protect you. Especially when I found out that my KGB friend Eugene Zarkov had been killed, probably murdered. I knew it wasn't safe to be around me.'

'So you disappeared.'

'Jonny had seen intelligence that I was in danger. At one of Victoria's parties, just a few weeks before I met you, Zarkov told me about the Soviets' true nuclear capabilities. Through his work, he'd been in a unique position to find out how many missiles the Russians really had. He was worried that America could blow his country to smithereens and they wouldn't be able to retaliate. Despite Brezhnev's rhetoric, they didn't have the firepower.'

'How many people knew about this?'

'Hardly anyone. It made us vulnerable, a liability. It was information that put us at risk. Jonathon heard that Zarkov had been killed, and that there was going to be an attempt on my life. So I escaped through the jungle and ended up in Central America, where I stayed for twelve months, until Jonathon sorted me out with a new identity, a new life.'

'Miguel, Willem,' she said, thinking of the other men on the expedition. 'Did any of them know?'

Dominic shook his head.

'But I could have come with you,' she croaked. 'We could have disappeared together.'

'How could I ask you to give up your whole life for me, leave your friends, family, everything you knew and cared about, to spend the next, what? Forty, fifty years looking over your shoulder? It was too much to ask.'

'But at least you could have got in touch.'

He turned away and walked towards the edge of the garden, where a cliff overlooked the sea. He breathed in deeply, his eyes lost on a point on the horizon.

'Looking back, there are things I would have done differently.'

Ros looked around: a herd of sheep bleating in a neighbouring field, the sound of the waves crashing on the shore, the sight of nothing but glorious nature for miles around.

'It's a long way from Tavistock Square,' she smiled.

'It's a long way from you.'

Her eyelids fluttered shut with regret.

'But Dom, the Cold War ended over twenty years ago. We could have had all that time together.'

He paused before he continued, and Ros opened her eyes to look at him.

'I wanted to come back to you. Jonny discussed feigning my death in a more obvious way, leaving some sort of evidence in the jungle, but I always wanted to show up on your doorstep. I thought we could run away together, live in Cape Town, Bogotá, even here. But then Jonny told me that you'd got a job at the *Observer*, that you'd found a boyfriend and were happy . . .'

He looked away for a moment, lost in the memory.

'I came to see you in Dublin. A literary event. I wanted to let you know that I was alive, hoped I could convince you to come and live with me. But then I saw you . . . I was on the street, you were getting out of a taxi, and you kissed someone, and you just looked so happy, so alive, so absolutely where you should have been, a successful writer on top of the world, that I turned around and left.'

Ros felt her breath shudder. She remembered that night well, remembered the excitement she'd felt about attending an important literary evening, but she hadn't realised for a second that she was being watched by the man she had loved so much.

'You came for me?' she whispered.

'Came and left,' he said, his mouth a firm, unhappy line. 'I spoke to Jonathon a few weeks later. He said you were engaged and I knew that I had to leave you to live the life you'd created for yourself, a life you deserved.'

'I called it off, Dom. I got engaged a few days after Dublin, but I called it off.'

His face fell with a strange, sad regret.

'I've lived for over forty-five years in this spot,' he said slowly. 'It's not been the life I ever imagined for myself, but I had friends, a job. I tried to forget all about you, but that was an impossible task. I should have come and spoken to you . . .'

'And I shouldn't have stopped looking for you,' she said. She knew they were both picturing themselves in Dublin, at that one moment that changed the course of their lives for ever.

'Did you ever marry?' she dared to ask.

'No. Did you?'

Feeling her heartbeat slow with relief, she dipped her hand in her pocket and pulled out the ruby ring. It looked very old-fashioned after all this time, but in the palm of her hand, it glinted pink in the sun.

'This is the only ring I ever wanted.'

She thought she heard him sigh with happiness.

'I'm sorry for all those missing years. I'm so, so sorry for leaving you.'

She clenched her fist and held it towards her heart.

'You never left me, Dom.'

He opened his arms and folded them around her. He felt thinner than he used to, softer and less strong. But he still felt like the man she loved.

'I'd get down on one knee,' he whispered into her hair, 'but I fear I might never get up again.'

Laughing, they drew apart, holding hands and watching the horizon.

'I bet you have wonderful sunsets over here,' she said, squeezing his fingers.

He looked up at the sky, where the clouds were parting to reveal a clear expanse of cornflower blue.

'We can watch one later,' he said, settling his arm across her shoulders.

Ros nodded, her golden years suddenly feeling full of hope, love and promise.

Chapter Thirty-Seven

'The one up-side of my recent divorce is being able to sit next to this lovely lady at my son's wedding,' said Larry Donovan, reaching for the red wine as soon as he had got to the table.

'Larry. Larry Donovan,' he said, giving Abby a presumptuous kiss on the cheek before filling his goblet. 'And who might you be?'

'Abby Gordon,' she replied, smiling politely.

She felt a hand on her shoulder and turned to see Matt eyeing Larry suspiciously.

'I've told my father to be on his best behaviour, but if he doesn't keep his hands above the table, feel free to hit the button on his ejector seat.'

They all laughed as Matt went to sit next to his bride.

It had been a beautiful wedding.

Anna had always insisted that she wanted to keep it small and low-key, and perhaps, compared to William and Kate's celebrations, it was. But Abby had been impressed by every detail. The venue, Syon House, was on the western fringes of London, a grand old Robert Adam house with castellations and a long gravel drive set in acres of lush parkland.

Eighty people had assembled in the marble-lined Great Hall for a short civil service and the bride had looked exquisite, her long dress, a simple column of ivory satin, perfectly judged, her shoulder-length hair tied back and pinned behind her ears with tiny white flowers. A champagne reception had been served in the inner courtyard before the guests followed Matt and Anna along a wooded walkway to a stunning conservatory full of palm trees and exotic flowers, where dinner was to be served.

Abby had felt tears in her eyes when her friends had recited their marriage vows. Not out of sadness for her own situation, but from the hope in those words. *I give you my heart for as long as we both shall live.*

Matt particularly had every reason to be cynical. Not only was it his second marriage, but he was a divorce lawyer who spent his days dealing with the breakdown of commitments that had once meant something to his clients. And yet when he kissed Anna in front of the registrar, the only thing Abby could think about was that she still believed in love. Looking around, she knew that every person in that room did too.

'Abby Gordon, of course,' nodded Larry thoughtfully. 'We didn't meet the other day. That business with your husband got sorted out quicker than I thought it would have done. I was convinced they would press charges, but some things surprise even long-in-the-tooth old dogs like me. So how is he?' he asked, his bushy eyebrows rising to a more pronounced peak.

'He's fine. He had a lucky escape,' smiled Abby, taking a sip of her wine. She didn't want to dwell on the subject. Larry was sharp, knowing. She didn't need him asking difficult questions about Jonathon Soames that she wasn't at liberty to answer.

She smiled to herself, thinking about what she could say about Nick. That she was proud of him, that she would never forget the way he had supported her, even if his attempts at hacking into

Jonathon Soames's phone and email hadn't been entirely successful. He'd been quickly found out, and what he had done was criminal, but something about him had clearly impressed Jonathon, who had told Abby in Ireland that he had some work he wanted to talk to Nick about once things had settled down.

The wedding breakfast was served, a delicious but very unbreakfast-like three courses involving celeriac, beef and something sweet and creamy in tiny china pots. The speeches were short.

'No one wants to hear you bang on about love when they've heard it all before,' whispered Larry, telling Abby that he'd dispensed with speeches altogether by the time he got to his third marriage.

A jazz band started to play, just as the light was fading outside.

'I'm nicely warmed up,' said Larry, finishing off his wine. 'How about I take you for a spin on the dance floor?'

Abby smiled kindly. She had enjoyed the day, loved seeing one of her closest friends walk down the aisle, but now she desperately wanted to leave.

'Larry, there are thousands of women around London who would love to take you up on that offer, but right now . . .'

'Right now, you want to go home.' He nodded with some secret complicity. 'You know, we spared each other the delights of the singles table, but weddings are hard on your own,' he said, looking suddenly old and vulnerable.

Abby kissed him on the cheek and went to get her coat and phone for a taxi, which promised to be there in twenty minutes. She killed time putting some make-up on in the loos, and peered back in at the wedding. Anna and Matt were on the dance floor, foreheads touching, oblivious to the rest of the world. Everyone seemed drunk and happy. Abby just felt exhausted.

She slipped outside at a little after nine, not even saying

goodbye, not wanting to tell Matt and Anna that she was going. She didn't want to disturb them; besides, they would only make a fuss, pair her off with some colleague, or make her dance with Larry or Suze, none of which she felt like doing.

'Where to, love?' asked the driver.

She told him her address and settled back in the seat. Her mobile vibrated in her bag, the arrival of a text. She pulled it out and smiled when she saw it was from Rosamund.

Just watching a glorious Connemara sunset. I didn't think love could be better the second time around. But it can. Have fun at the wedding. Thank you for everything. Rosamund.

She wondered what Ros and Dominic had been up to in the two days since she and Jonathon had left Ireland. She imagined them going for leisurely walks along the coast, playing bridge in the garden, reading the newspapers together or perhaps doing the crossword.

She clicked on the internet icon on her phone and found herself googling the *Chronicle* story of *The Last Goodbye*. The screen was only small, but it was enough for her to see the magnificent black-and-white image that had started it all. The words from the wedding echoed in her head as she switched off her phone.

I give you my heart for as long as we both shall live.

'I'm going to go over Kingston Bridge if that's all right, love,' said the cabbie. 'Terrible traffic over the others.'

Abby nodded vaguely, realising that while she hadn't wanted to stay at Syon House, she didn't want to go home either.

The car wound its way through the streets of Isleworth and Twickenham, and suddenly Abby knew exactly where she wanted to be.

'Do you know what? You couldn't take me to Bushey Park, could you?'

When Nick had given her the tickets for the showing of *Casablanca* under the stars, she'd been thrilled for the two minutes it had taken her to realise it was on the same night as Anna's wedding.

The taxi driver looked surprised, but he dropped her off at the Hampton entrance to the park. Abby had worried that the path to the cinema might be dark and lonely, but it was well lit, and peppered with stray couples who were either late like her or were milling around.

Two girls were sitting behind a table, a makeshift booth for collecting tickets. Abby burrowed in her purse for a twenty-pound note.

'It's sold out. I'm sorry,' said one of the girls flatly.

'Please,' said Abby, suddenly desperate to go in.

'I'm sorry . . .'

She put the note on the table and placed her hand over it.

'It would mean a lot. I was supposed to come here with my husband . . .'

The girl's face softened.

'It's halfway through.'

'That doesn't matter.'

The girl smiled in sympathy and waved her through, directing her to the bar and the popcorn stand.

The park was beautiful at night. The trees looked as if they had been printed against the mottled purple sky. It was warm; the grass was dry, so Abby kicked off her shoes. It was the perfect summer night.

She looked up at the screen, the giant sepia images of Bogart and Bergman, suspended between two oak trees. She had seen the film so many times she could almost recite the dialogue word for word, but she never grew tired of it, even if she had never been able to understand why Rick let Ilsa get on the plane at the end. Nick had explained it every time they had watched it together. 'He knew she would have a better life without him.' But Abby didn't buy that story. She didn't think Rosamund Bailey and Dominic Blake would buy it either. How could you have a better life not being with the person you loved? It just didn't make sense.

If the past few weeks had taught Abby anything, it was that you had to be brave to love. It was a potent force, one that dispensed great highs and dreadful lows, but the magical moments made everything worthwhile. She pictured Rosamund and Dominic holding hands and watching a golden sunset together, remembering the countless times she had done the same thing with Nick on the beach in Cornwall, imagining them doing it every warm summer's evening if they lived in St Agnes.

She let her eyes trail across the grounds, looking for somewhere to sit.

There were bodies all over the grass. Couples lying under duvets, others propped up in beach chairs.

And then she saw him. Her heart started to beat faster and she had to peer through the darkness to check that she wasn't imagining it. A little voice in her head told her that she'd known he would be here. After all, she'd seen the tickets propped up on the mantelpiece when she'd gone round to his Kennington flat.

She hopped over legs and cool boxes to get to him. To get to her husband.

She next down next to him and bumped her shoulder against his arm.

'How could a girl miss *Casablanca* under the stars?' she said softly, watching his face crease with pleasure when he saw her.

'You came,' he said, looking at her as if she was the only girl in the world.

'I still don't like the way he lets her get on that plane, though,' she said, stretching out and touching his fingertips.

'I wouldn't let you go,' he said, putting his arm around her.

And as the moon cast its silvery light around the park and the music swelled in the distance, Abby smiled and knew that she believed him.

Acknowledgements

The inspiration for *The Last Kiss Goodbye* came from a trip to the treasure trove of wonder that is the photographic archives of the Royal Geographical Society – so hearty thanks go to Jamie Owen at the RGS who allowed me to come and visit and, in doing so, kick-started an idea.

Benedict Allen is a real-life Indiana Jones who helped me bring the character of Dominic Blake to life. He's actually been into the depths of the Amazon jungle and told me all sorts of fascinating detail – from jungle rituals to how to pack a mule for a trip to Peru.

To Nyree Belleville, Kay Burley, Belinda Jones, Polly Williams and Jacquie Lawrence – I do enjoy all our 'book' chat! Margaret Perry provided colour from London in 1961. Christopher M gave me insight on Cold War Russia.

Continued thanks to the fabulous team at Headline, especially Sherise Hobbs, Beth Eynon and Mari Evans, and my agent Eugenie Furniss. Thanks also to Liane-Louise Smith for all your help.

Thanks as ever go to my family; Mum, Dad, Digs, Far and Dan. My son Fin is a nine-year-old creative dynamo and is always right when I run titles and character names past him. And for John – as ever, for everything. If you ever got lost in the rainforest, you know I'd always come looking for you until I found you.